FORGED IN BLOOD

BROKEN BLOODLINES

FORGED IN BLOOD

BROKEN BLOODLINES

SADIE KINCAID

This book is a work of fiction. Names, characters, places, and incidents are the product of the author's imagination or are used fictitiously. Any resemblance to actual events, locales, or persons, living or dead, is coincidental.

Copyright © 2024 by Sadie Kincaid. All rights reserved, including the right to reproduce, distribute, or transmit in any form or by any means. For information regarding subsidiary rights, please contact the Publisher.

Entangled Publishing believes stories have the power to inspire, connect, and create lasting change. That's why we protect the rights of our authors and the integrity of their work. Copyright exists not to limit creativity, but to make it possible—to ensure writers can keep telling bold, original stories in their own voices. Thank you for choosing a legitimate copy of this book. By not copying, scanning, or distributing it without permission, you help authors continue to write and reach readers. This book may not be used to train artificial intelligence systems, including large language models or other machine learning tools, whether existing or still to come. These stories were written for human connection, not machine consumption.

Entangled Publishing, LLC
644 Shrewsbury Commons Ave., STE 181
Shrewsbury, PA 17361
rights@entangledpublishing.com

Amara is an imprint of Entangled Publishing, LLC.
Visit our website at www.entangledpublishing.com.

Edited by Baker Street Revisions
Cover design by LJ Anderson and Bree Archer
Edge design by Bree Archer
Cover images by Eclectic Anthology/Creative Market, D-Keine/GettyImages, CRC_Studio/GettyImages, and Tatiana54//GettyImages
Case design by LJ Anderson
Case images by lunokot/Shutterstock, and paprika/Shutterstock
Interior design by Britt Marczak

Hardcover ISBN 978-1-68281-644-8

Printed in Canada
First Edition July 2025

10 9 8 7 6 5 4 3 2 1

ALSO BY SADIE KINCAID

BROKEN BLOODLINES

Forged in Blood
Promised in Blood
Bound in Blood

MANHATTAN RUTHLESS

Broken
Promise Me Forever
Rebound

For anyone ever made to feel like you didn't belong, you're going to fit right in here at Montridge University. The Professor and his boys will take good care of you.

Love Sadie x

And to Jaime, who poured her blood sweat and tears into this book along with me. x

Forged in Blood is a dark and spicy paranormal "why choose" romance. And we mean extra spicy! Between the general stress of college life and a millennia-old prophecy unfolding, there are four irresistible and commanding vampires who will captivate your heart. However, the story includes elements that might not be suitable for all readers. Sexually explicit scenes with one or multiple consenting partners, themes of violence, bullying, attempted sexual harassment, blood play (well, they *are* vampires), and the questionable use of feminine hygiene products are all shown in the novel. Readers who may be sensitive to these elements, please take note.

THE LOST PROPHECIES

WHILE THE LIBRARY OF ALEXANDRIA BURNED, FOUR BRAVE KNIGHTS OF THE DEMONIC ORDER OF AZEZAL ENTERED THE FIERY RUINS AND RESCUED SIX SACRED SCROLLS. THESE SCROLLS WERE SAID TO CONTAIN THE PREDICTIONS OF THE ANCIENT PROPHETESS FIERE.

LATER CAPTURED BY CAESAR'S ARMY, THE KNIGHTS WERE MERCILESSLY TORTURED IN AN ATTEMPT TO LOCATE THE SACRED TEXTS. HOWEVER, THE KNIGHTS' FORTITUDE PROVED TOO UNYIELDING FOR EVEN THE FIERCEST ROMAN CENTURION TO OVERCOME. THE SCROLLS WERE NEVER RECOVERED, AND LEGEND HAS IT THAT THE ORDER OF AZEZAL FELL THIRTEEN DAYS AFTER THE GREAT LIBRARY ITSELF.

SOME SAY THAT THE VALIANT KNIGHTS FAILED IN THEIR RESCUE EFFORTS AND THE SCROLLS BURNED. BUT THOSE WHO SPEAK THE ANCIENT TONGUE KNOW THE TRUTH: THE KNIGHTS DID NOT FAIL AND THE ORDER OF AZEZAL DID NOT FALL. INSTEAD, THEY SCATTERED ACROSS SIX CONTINENTS, HIDING THE SCROLLS FROM THE WORLD OF MORTAL MEN FOR FEAR THEY WOULD BRING ABOUT THE RUIN OF ALL NONHUMANKIND. THE SACRED SCROLLS BECAME KNOWN AS THE LOST PROPHECIES OF FIERE, AND THE ORDER BECAME GUARDIANS OF THE SECRETS HELD WITHIN THEM.

PROLOGUE

NAZEEL DANRAATH
GRAND HEALER OF THE ORDER OF AZEZAL

Flames lick at my feet, and heat so intense it blisters my skin engulfs the three of us. Insignius releases a loud sigh and hitches his cloak up while Kameen bares his teeth, a growl rumbling from his throat. With a wave of his hand, Kameen douses the blood-orange fire consuming the trees and plunges us into darkness.

I chant a quick incantation that bathes the surrounding area in a soft glow borrowed from the light of the moon. Kameen and Insignius have no problem seeing in the dark, but although witch magic tends to be infinitely more powerful, it requires the intention of the user, unlike the inherent magic of demons and wolves.

Insignius rubs at a scorched patch of skin on his hand, and I send a wave of healing energy over us both and survey the scene we were summoned to. I count at least half a dozen charred corpses lying scattered in the nearby woods, not to mention the broken demon at our feet and his human mate dying slowly and quietly behind him, her belly swollen with child.

"You dare to summon me?" Kameen asks with a low growl.

Jadon pushes himself into a kneeling position, wincing and clutching the wooden spear lodged in his side. He pulls it free and allows the wood to fall from his hand. It rolls to Kameen's feet, covered in blood. The wound, fatal to most mortals, is not what will kill Jadon. Demons are notoriously quick healers. It is the deep cut on his neck, the one turning his blood to poison in front of our very eyes, which will be his end. The spidery veins around the laceration are already blackened, proof that he has only moments to live. It was an injury made by a blade of rare painite—the only weapon that can kill a demon.

"I had to, brother." Jadon glances at his pregnant mate. "She must live."

"You summoned *me* to save a human?" Kameen's voice vibrates through the trees, rumbling the ground beneath our feet.

Jadon shakes his head. "The child. She is…" His nostrils flare. "They came for us. For our daughter. They know she's special. She could be the—"

"Who burned them?" Kameen jerks his head at the nearest charred body, his eyes narrowed. "You cannot summon fire, and your human…" His lip curls in disgust. Jadon is a powerful water demon, and him taking a human as his mate is a source of great dishonor to his family. His choice caused his exile. Summoning his brother—the most powerful demon alive—was a huge risk. Jadon could have used his last shred of magic to put out the flames and used any remnants of healing energy to try to save his mate. And maybe he should have.

"*She* did," Jadon insists. "Our daughter burned them all."

A shiver of lightning ignites my veins. "The child caused the fire from her mother's womb?"

He nods, beseeching me with his eyes, likely trying to appeal to the feminine compassion I cannot help but feel for an unborn child. "You must protect her."

Insignius clears his throat. "You know we cannot intervene."

Jadon tries to stand, but his body is too weakened by the painite, and he stumbles back to the ground. He makes a grab for his older brother's cloak, his fingers slipping over the thick black material without finding a hold. "Please, Kameen. You know what the prophecies say. She could be the key."

Kameen snorts, but I feel his iron will softening under the pressure of his brother's dying plea.

"Jadon," the human calls, her voice weak like her body. Her eyes flicker closed, and Death takes her quickly, as though aware He is in the presence of a being so powerful they could bring her back to life with a snap of their fingers. But Kameen would never allow me to so blatantly disobey the ancient laws.

Jadon takes his dead mate's hand in his and looks at his brother once more, his black eyes glistening with an urgent plea.

Kameen glances at me, and I lick my lips, tasting the ash in the air. Something in this dark night brought us here—something stronger than Jadon's summons.

A wolf howls close by.

With another wave of his hand, Kameen turns the human woman into a flaming pyre.

Jadon howls his pain but continues to hold his mate's hand, allowing the flames to engulf his own body.

"What are you doing?" Insignius barks. "You're going to kill the child."

Kameen responds with a nonchalant shrug. "The child will die anyway now that its mother's heart has stopped beating. And we are not supposed to interfere."

Insignius rolls his eyes. "Then what do you call this?"

The corner of Kameen's eye twitches. "Call this curiosity."

The sound of a baby's cry pierces the air. The cry is not one of pain, but rather one of declaration. Goose bumps prickle along my forearms. Once again, Kameen douses the fire with a flick of his wrist, then crouches before the incinerated human corpse and the body of his brother.

"Thank you," Jadon croaks with his dying breath.

Kameen closes Jadon's eyes and bows his head in a rare display of sentiment. "Rest well, brother."

The child's cries continue to ring out through the night, and Kameen lifts the baby, covered in a thick film of blood and ash, from her mother's charred womb. Insignius removes his cloak and swaddles her tiny body before pressing her close to his chest.

Content now in the wolf's arms, she blinks up at me with eyes so radiantly blue that they appear otherworldly. I squeeze my lids shut and fumble in the darkness to connect with her new energy. Except it is not new at all. A force like a lightning bolt hits me in my chest, and I stagger back a step. *For the child borne of fire and blood...*

Pressing my lips together, I suppress the squeal of delight that wants to tumble free. "Her energy is old and powerful."

"Do you think she is the one?" Insignius asks.

"It matters naught. We cannot interfere," Kameen warns, his tone stern and commanding.

"We already have," I remind him.

He looks down at the baby too, his dark brow furrowed.

"She summoned fire from inside her mortal mother's womb, Kameen." Insignius's voice is full of awe, his focus locked on the baby's face. "And Nazeel sensed..." He looks up at me now, blinking. Pleading.

I shrug, aware of Kameen's eyes on me. It is too soon to allow my mind to run away with itself. How many times over the last millennia have I allowed myself to believe, only to have my hopes dashed? "I sense an old power in her, but she is a descendant of Azezal himself. Perhaps it is nothing more than the echoes of the ancient bloodline."

"She needs to be protected," Insignius insists. "We won't interfere in her life, but now that we know she exists—who she *could* be..."

Kameen snorts. "She could be nothing more than a powerful witch."

"The most powerful witch I have seen for centuries," I say, peering down at her as she gazes up at the three of us. "She sensed she was in danger and summoned fire to protect herself. Before she was even born." I trace a fingertip over her tiny nose and she blinks.

Insignius looks to our leader for guidance. "We have to take action. There is no telling what damage she might cause without her father to guide her."

Kameen trains his eyes on me. "Then bind her powers."

I open my mouth and close it again. Finding my backbone, I shake my head. "That's barbaric."

His face contorts in a deep scowl. "More barbaric than having her burn her entire kindergarten class alive when she throws a temper tantrum?"

I shake my head. "Kindergarten? You intend for her to be raised with humans?"

"If there is any chance that she is who you both think she is, this child is already in great danger. These creatures..." He glances around at the scorched remains of the attackers and sniffs the air, determining their origin. "These vampires already killed her parents because of her power. Regardless of who she is—or who she will be—she *is* a powerful being. Without her parents' protection, the safest place for her is with the mortals."

My heart breaks for the tiny babe. "But we could—"

Kameen's lips curl back, his teeth bared as he edges closer to me. The fire of his rage burns through my veins. Forever bonded to him, I cannot keep him out no matter how gifted a witch I am. "We could what, Nazeel? Raise her in the Order?"

I tip my chin in defiance. "Why not?"

He grabs my jaw in his strong hand, squeezing tightly enough to make me wince. "We. Do. Not. Interfere."

"Says who?" I bite back.

"Says I."

Even if she is not the child from the prophecy, she is your niece! You are so stubborn, you refuse to even consider change, even for—

Do not, Nazeel!

Insignius sighs, aware Kameen and I are speaking through our bond. It is impolite, but I would never challenge Kameen openly. His position could not allow it.

I wrench my jaw from his grip. "We could find a witch family to take her in. Teach her how to control her power."

"And put them in danger too? Could you live with that, my caring little witch?" he says, his eyes narrowed.

Stop mocking me!

Then stop pushing me, my sweet.

I despise you.

He laughs. *We shall see about that when I have you in my bed tonight.*

He conjures a memory that has heat burning my cheeks and between my thighs.

"She might not be a witch." Insignius cuts through my internal debate with Kameen, and I am thankful for the distraction.

Kameen turns his fierce glare on his most trusted general. "Humans cannot give birth to demons. Only witches."

The nearby wolf howls again, and Insignius cocks his head, his face a mask of concentration. "He is waiting for us to leave so he can feast on the carcasses."

I nudge my friend in the arm. "What kind of creature do you think she could be?"

He arches a thick eyebrow at me. "You already know, Nazeel."

My heart hammers against my ribcage. The implication is preposterous.

Kameen shakes his head. "Impossible."

Insignius puts his hand on Kameen's shoulder. "You, of all creatures, know that nothing is impossible, old friend."

Of course, Insignius speaks the truth. Each of us has lived long enough to witness the impossible before. But this child… She could be more than impossible.

She could be the one we have all been waiting for.

1

OPHELIA - 19 YEARS LATER

Rolling back my shoulders, I swallow down my apprehension and force myself to approach the table of girls closest to me. One of them steps forward, her plaid skirt bouncing against her thighs and her white tank complimenting her golden tan. A shy smile flickers across my face when I realize we're dressed almost identically. Maybe I will fit in here after all.

She doesn't smile back. Instead, she regards me with what seems like curiosity. "Do you play field hockey?"

"No." I shake my head, looking over her shoulder at the group of girls at the table behind her. "But I could try."

She wrinkles her nose and shakes her head. "I mean, you've got the build, but we're regional champs. We need players with experience. Sorry, Pink." She winks at me before brushing past and approaching a girl a few feet behind me.

I have the build? Was that her way of saying I'm chunky? No. This isn't high school, Ophelia. Even if a significant enough portion of people from my old high school also attend this college to ensure I will never forget my place, there are thousands of students on this campus.

I shake off my disappointment at not being able to try out for the field hockey team. It's entirely unfounded to feel such rejection over a sport I've never played before—one I've never had the slightest interest in. I've spent the past week on campus keeping to myself and gearing up for today's activity and club fair, and I am not going to leave until I find something I want to do.

With my head held high and a smile on my face, I carry on down one of the paths that splits Gaea's Green, affectionately known as the quad, into four sections. Today's the first day of the fall semester, and each path is lined with tables showcasing the various groups and societies at Montridge University. Unlike most colleges, Montridge doesn't have sororities or fraternities. Instead, it has twelve societies which, according to the brochure I was sent with my acceptance letter, have been around since the school was founded in 1672. Given that it's the second oldest college in the country, the exclusive societies are some of the most prestigious and elite groups in the country. And that's why I haven't bothered applying for any. Plenty of famous—and infamous—individuals have attended this school.

Wandering through the society stands, I notice that the four Vale societies, each named after a precious metal, seem the most welcoming, with their balloons and cupcakes and smiley members with glittery face paint.

"Hey, girl with the pink hair. C'mere," someone shouts. I'm the only person in the vicinity who fits that description. The girl who called for me reminds me so much of my high school bully that I almost lose the burrito I had for lunch. Impossibly beautiful, model tall, honey-blond hair pulled into a pristine ponytail. Perfect white teeth and button nose. Tanned skin. The list goes on.

"C'mere," she shouts again, this time waving me over to the Silver Vale table.

I glance around again, still hoping she's not talking to me, but she most definitely is. And now it's too late to pretend I don't see her. I mutter a curse and roll my shoulders back, prepared for whatever it is she's about to throw at me.

She's smiling when I reach her, but I can't tell if it's because my appearance amuses her for some reason or if she's being genuinely nice. Experience tells me it's the former, but the positive outlook I'm working to cultivate reminds me to reserve judgment. "Hi," I say, my voice annoyingly little more than a squeak.

She tosses her ponytail over her shoulder. "What are you doing here?"

"E-excuse me?"

She rolls her eyes. "What are you doing? Are you hoping for a pledge invitation? Join the soccer team? What?"

Rudeness or curiosity? Hard to tell. Her tone is friendly enough, but girls like her aren't usually friendly to me.

"Hey, Meg. Have you seen who's hanging out at the Ruby Dragon table?" Another girl, equally gorgeous but with dark curly hair, links her arm through Meg's.

Meg cranes her neck, peering over the crowd. A second later, she sinks her teeth into her lip and groans. I turn to see what she and her friend are looking at, but I'm too short to see over the crowd. I've heard whispers of the Ruby Dragon Society, and based on my research, that was the home of some of the most notorious Montridge graduates. They boast such alumni as the current director of the CIA, along with the biggest drug lord in Colombia.

"They are so fine," Meg says with a sultry sigh. "Such a shame, huh?"

I'm about to ask what she means when the crowd parts and I finally see the objects of their attention. My mouth drops open unbidden. Shirtless and tanned, basking in the heat of the afternoon sun, three demigods stand among a throng of mortals.

All rippling biceps, chiseled abs, and strong jawlines. "Who are they?" My voice comes out even quieter than before.

"The commanders of Ruby Dragon," Meg says. "They're hot, right?"

"I guess."

"Stay away from them, new girl," she warns, and when I drag my attention back to her, she's glaring at me.

I snort a laugh. Does she seriously think I'm any kind of competition?

Her eyes narrow. "I mean it."

I hold my hands up. "I'll stay away."

The girl with the curly hair looks me up and down. "Are you hoping to pledge?"

I blink at her. I never considered pledging one of the societies. I'm not a group activity kind of person. Not through personal choice… I just seem to have trouble fitting in. I'm only here today because I promised my advisor—and myself—I'd check out the clubs rather than sit alone in my dorm all day, reading. "I d-don't think so."

Meg scrunches up her nose and studies me like I'm an unknown specimen. "You're different."

Yeah, been made to feel that my whole damn life. Before the words can escape, I press my lips together, staying silent. Experience has also taught me not to provoke the popular girls. Don't want to make any enemies on my first day. Memories of my high school experience flash through my mind, and my stomach rolls. I press my hand to my damp forehead. I need to get away from here. Away from the scrutiny of these two popular mean girls who no doubt only called me over here for their own amusement.

"I h-have to go," I blurt. Not giving them the opportunity to respond, I turn and dart off through the crowd. Hurrying past the remaining tables, I head straight for the safety of my dorm room.

2

OPHELIA

Aside from the sound of the gravel crunching beneath my feet, the evening is eerily quiet. I haven't passed a single soul on my way back from the library despite it only being a little after nine. I guess most people went to the start of term bonfire at the Temple, which I realized on the second day of classes sounds way grander and more mysterious than what it is—a hill where most of the outdoor activities on campus take place. When I first heard people talking about it, I assumed it was some kind of religious thing, but thankfully I learned the truth before I could make a fool of myself by asking someone.

I did consider checking out the bonfire, but I haven't managed to speak to anyone yet…at least nothing more than a polite hi during class. But it's only the third day, and the unsurprising reality that I haven't made friends yet is way less important than the fact that I'm here. I'm free! For the first time in my entire life, I'm in control of every aspect of my life. My own freaking destiny. It sounds corny, but for someone who's always been at the mercy of a broken system, it is freaking monumentous.

I get to sleep all by myself in my own room, and I chose my own bedding. The softest fleece comforter I've ever felt in my life—which, by the way, is covered in unicorns. Going to classes that I choose to go to, without fear of someone tripping me up in the hallway, knocking my books out of my hand, or calling me by that god-awful nickname. Getting to go to the library at any time of the day or night and getting lost among rows upon rows of shelves, all bursting with data and hopes and dreams. A dreamy sigh escapes my lips at the mere thought.

So it isn't a big deal that I'm not doing all the regular college stuff right away. It will come with time, and I'll make some friends soon enough. This is nothing like high school. The other students seem way friendlier than my high school classmates. My advisor says I'm painfully shy, and I didn't bother explaining to her that I'm actually not. Rather I'm a product of my environment—twenty-six foster homes and half as many schools isn't exactly a recipe for making friends.

"Hey! What are you doing?" A feminine shriek pierces the chilled evening air. Every hair on the back of my neck stands on end. "Get off me!"

I break into a run and round the corner, coming face-to-face with a sight that makes my blood freeze in my veins. A girl with blond pigtails, who I vaguely recognize from my English class, is pinned to the wall by a large hand around her throat. Her dangling feet kick a few inches from the ground, and her attacker has his face buried against her neck. His two companions stand behind him, bouncing on their toes like they're waiting their turn. But for what?

It takes me a few beats to recognize the three guys, and I gasp when I do. Perhaps if I'd known it was *them* I was about to interrupt, I would've thought twice. Although that's not true. I have always run headfirst into reckless situations. Still, I swallow nervously.

After I saw them that day in the quad, I did a little digging into the Ruby Dragon commanders and found that they are every bit as feared as they are revered.

The girl's screams have been silenced, and the quiet feels very wrong. "Let her go, you dicks! Or I'll call campus security," I shout, my voice coming out way more confident than my trembling legs reveal I am.

Axl Thorne lifts his head, and a gasp erupts from my lips. Blood drips from his mouth...no, from his *fangs*. What in hell's name?

"Stop her," he commands, then returns to the girl's neck.

Malachi Young licks his lips while his bestie, Xavier Adams, flashes me a maniacal grin. I should run like hell, but my legs won't let me. I'm frozen to the spot, and it's not fear gripping me. "Let her go," I say, my hands balled into fists at my side.

The words have barely left my mouth when Xavier and Malachi are at my side. How is that even possible? They were at least thirty feet away. Both of them reach for me, and their large hands easily encircle my arms. I try to wrench myself from their grip, but they're freakishly strong.

"Get the hell off me," I snap. "Or I'll scream."

Xavier laughs darkly. Psycho! "Ain't nobody coming even if you do, Cupcake."

Cupcake? What the...

"Take her back to the house. I'll meet you there in five," Axl says, the blond girl cradled in his arms.

I shake my head. "No! What are you going to do to her?"

Xavier tightens his grip on my wrist and runs his nose over the back of my neck, inhaling deeply. "You should be more concerned about what we're going to do to you." I look over my shoulder, and he bares his teeth, revealing a gleaming set of white fangs that match Axl's.

I suck in a deep gulp of air. "What the hell are you?"

Xavier cocks his head to the side and grins. Meanwhile, Malachi curls the end of my ponytail between his fingertips. "Such pretty pink hair," he says, his voice way gentler than I expected it to be.

"Get the hell off me," I shriek.

Xavier sighs. "Let's get her out of here."

I don't have a chance to protest further before they start to run. Except it doesn't feel like running—more like floating really fast. They move so swiftly that the gentle breeze rushes through my hair like a tornado-strength gale. My feet don't touch the ground, but I see theirs skimming over it. My stomach rolls and my head spins, and the next thing I know, we're standing in front of a small house at the opening of a cul-de-sac. The house next door has a flag depicting a red dragon hanging from the eaves, so it must be the Ruby Dragon Society house—and the blue dragon on the house across the street tells me it's for Lapis Dragon Society. Why is this house smaller than the others? Why doesn't it have a flag? Why am I asking questions that don't matter?

"What in hell's name are you?" I ask instead, although I know the answer to that one. What creatures have fangs, drink blood, and have superhuman strength and speed? It all leads to one conclusion. Except for the fact that vampires don't exist.

"We're your worst nightmare, Cupcake." Xavier flicks his dark hair out of his eyes and flashes me a wicked grin.

I twist my upper body, and this time they release me. Xavier jogs up the steps of the wooden porch and opens the door, and Malachi gestures toward it. "After you, sweet girl."

I shake my head. "No way am I going in there."

"You can walk or I'll carry you," Xavier says, his lips twitching. "And if I have to chase you down and carry your ass in here, Cupcake, it will officially belong to me."

I blink at him. "What? Is that like some vampire rule or something?"

His grin widens and turns downright wicked at the same time. "Yeah."

A shiver runs down my spine, and my mouth goes dry. But Malachi's snort of laughter snaps me from the daze I was about to fall into looking into Xavier's intense dark blue eyes. I put my hands on my hips and turn my attention to Malachi. "He's fucking with me, isn't he?"

Xavier points to the open doorway and growls, all trace of his grin now vanished. "Try it and find out, Cupcake."

Given how quickly they traveled across campus, I stand zero chance of outrunning them. But perhaps I can outsmart them.

So just like that, I walk inside the house, putting myself at the mercy of the commanders of the Ruby Dragon Society. The three most popular and powerful—not to mention dangerous—guys at Montridge University.

3

Xavier

She sure shocked the hell out of me when she didn't run away. They always run, but not this little bundle of sass. Which is a shame given how much I enjoy the chase. I'd call it sport, except humans don't stand a chance against our kind. When she rolled back her shoulders and willingly walked through the open door, a flicker of excitement flared in my chest. I do like them feisty, and she smells sweet enough to devour whole.

I guide her toward the basement. This is the professor's private residence, and he and the three of us are the only ones who live here, so there's no risk of being caught by clueless pledges. Still, the basement is the best place for her—where nobody will hear her scream. And I do intend to make this one scream.

She stumbles down the dimly lit hallway, hands grasping at the walls.

"Ouch!" she yelps and sucks her finger into her mouth. A stray nail protruding from the bare brick glistens, and the scent of her blood immediately fills the hallway. She smells sweeter than cupcakes. My fangs protract painfully, aching to take her. But not yet.

Her heart races, echoing along the narrow corridor. Not unexpected for someone in her predicament. But despite her obvious nerves, she keeps her head high and her shoulders rolled back, like she has even a modicum of control here. I can't sense an overt level of fear from her. No trembling knees or sharp, raspy breathing. Aside from her elevated heart rate, she seems entirely unaffected. I admire her fire, and I'm itching to see how far I can push her before the icy fingers of terror start to claw at her. Because, afraid of us or not, this little pink-haired girl interrupted the wrong party. And for that, she will have to pay.

I prod her between her shoulder blades, just above her backpack, to hurry her along.

"Where the hell are you taking me?" she snaps.

I can't help but laugh at her sass. "You'll see soon enough, Cupcake."

"Will you stop calling me that?" she says with a dramatic huff.

I flick the ends of her hair between my thumb and forefinger, dislodging the scent of her candy-scented shampoo. Something unfamiliar and warm stirs in my chest, but I push it down. "Then don't color your hair this ridiculous shade of pink."

"Ugh!" She twists her head away from my touch and marches forward. It's funny how she thinks she has even a chance in hell of escaping me.

We reach the steel door at the end of the hallway, and she spins around, her blue eyes wide. "I'm not going in there."

I tilt my head. "I think you are, *Cupcake*."

Her nostrils flare. "Will you stop..." She presses her lips together, and I can't help but laugh again. She is fucking adorable. It's a shame we're not going to get to keep her as a pet. Or maybe...

She barrels into me, trying to push her way past, and I wrap my arms around her, holding her close. Her juicy tits are squashed against my chest, and I drop my eyes and lick my lips. I'm going to enjoy feeding from them and leaving my mark all over her creamy flesh.

"Let me out of here. I swear I won't tell anyone what I saw."

Malachi reaches around us and opens the door. The steel hinges groan in protest. "Oh, we know that."

Her heart hammers against my chest as I carry her inside the room and set her on her feet. The sound of her blood pumping through her veins stokes the beast inside me, and my fangs ache with the desire to taste her. She blows a strand of hair out of her eyes and glares at me. "What exactly are you planning to do?"

I arch an eyebrow and rake my gaze over her curves. From those perky tits being hugged way too tightly by her tank top to the tiny plaid miniskirt that barely covers her ass and exposes the creamy expanse of her thighs. They are going to look fucking beautiful with her blood dripping down them soon. She's a blank canvas, and I plan to paint. And then there are her black lace-up boots that stop mid-calf. She dresses like she's looking for attention, and she just found it.

She shuffles her feet against the dusty concrete. Oh, I'm going to fucking devour her. My eyes travel back to her face. "We're going to fuck with you, Cupcake." I flick my tongue over my fangs. "And if you're real good, we might just fuck you too."

Her pulse spikes. She opens her pretty pink mouth to protest, but no words come out. Still, I can't smell her fear—at least not the kind I'd expect her to be feeling. I sniff, scenting the air, and catch the faintest hint of her arousal. My dick stiffens, aching to be let out of my jeans. "Oh, I think our little prisoner likes the thought of being fucked by us, Kai."

Malachi grins and stands behind her, running his nose over her hair and inhaling her intoxicating scent. His eyes lock on mine, and his thoughts fill my mind. *She smells fucking incredible, right? Or is it just me?*

hand. He tips his head back and runs his tongue along the vein in Malachi's neck. My cock twitches in my jeans at the sight. They've always been so fucking hot together. "Let me bite you," Xavier growls.

"No." Malachi wrenches out of Xavier's grip, but his eyes are hooded with desire. "I'm too fucking hungry."

Xavier rolls his eyes and flops onto the sofa, obviously aware this is a battle he won't win. Malachi might submit to us when he chooses to, but he's always been able to kick both of our asses, and clearly Xavier isn't in the mood for that kind of fun right now. Besides, we have more important matters to discuss.

Malachi sits forward, hands clasped between his thighs. "So, the girl? Has he ever forbidden either of you like that before?"

Xavier casually runs a hand over Malachi's shaved head. "You know he hasn't, Kai."

Malachi shakes his head. "I know that hasn't happened in the last hundred and however many years. But you've both been around a lot longer than I have."

It's true that he's the youngest of us. We were on a trip to Ireland when the professor found him on the side of the road, sobbing over a dead horse. He'd been riding the animal when it stepped in a hole and broke its leg. A traumatized soldier just back from the First World War, Malachi used the bullet he'd been saving for himself to put the animal out of its misery.

Despite swearing he would never turn another human and being content with Xavier and me for over a century, Alexandros saw something in Malachi that he wanted. And, well, over a hundred years later, here we are.

Xavier shakes his head, dragging me back to the present. "He's never asked me. You?"

It was just the professor and me for twenty-seven years. He rescued me from a baying mob who chased me through the streets of London, having accused me of trying to fuck some rich prick's

No, she smells good, I reply without talking. No need for our new pet to know how much we want her. She might get the idea that our desire gives her power here. It doesn't.

"Let me go!" she demands. Her voice trembles, but not from fear. She wants us. Her body does anyway.

"Nuh-uh." I shake my head. "We're gonna have way too much fun with you to ever let you see another sunrise."

Her heart beats an erratic rhythm, and she lashes out, scratching my face while she shrieks for help that will never come. She catches my lip with her nail, and my tongue darts out to lick away the blood. I grin at her. "That was a bad move, Cupcake."

"Fuck you!" she spits.

"Grab the cuffs," I bark.

Malachi goes to the wall that holds an array of weapons and restraints, and she turns her head to see what he's doing, obviously realizing for the first time since we entered the room what this place is. It's a cell—and a torture chamber when the occasion calls for it.

"Please?" she begs, and that only makes my dick harder for her.

I shake my head and suck on my top lip, watching Malachi pull off her backpack and slap the cuffs on her before she can process what's happening.

"On your knees, Cupcake."

"No." She shakes her head. Still so fucking feisty.

I sigh and nod to Malachi. He nudges the backs of her knees, and she drops to the floor with a thud and a cry of pain.

"He was a lot gentler than I would have been." I stand in front of her, her lips almost level with my aching cock. "He's always been that way though. Ever since he was turned." I run the backs of my knuckles over Malachi's cheek, and he bites down on his lip. "Such a sensitive soul, aren't you, pup?"

"You're an asshole." Malachi barks out a laugh, and I return my attention to the girl on the floor. I caress her cheek and trail my fingertips along her jawline. She snaps at them, and dammit, it makes me even more feral for her.

Hurry the fuck up, Axl, or there will be nothing left for you.

Don't you fucking dare get started without me, comes his angry reply. *I'm on my way.*

"What's your real name, Cupcake?" I ask.

Her glare is fierce. "Why?"

I shrug. "I like to know who I'm eating."

Her lower lip quivers, and I ball my hands into fists so I don't grab her jaw and sink my teeth into it. I know that once I taste her, I won't stop. "Ophelia," she says, chin tipped up in defiance.

"Pretty name," Malachi says.

Her dark eyelashes flutter over her pale-pink cheeks.

"Let's get this party started." Axl's deep voice fills the room and steals her attention, making me irrationally pissed.

I grab her jaw and turn her face back to me. "Don't look at him. It's me who's about to bite you, Cupcake."

She tries to shake her head out of my grip, but I don't let go. "Is that girl okay?"

Axl steps closer. "Shouldn't you be worried about your own welfare right now?"

I snort a laugh. "That's exactly what I said."

"Are you vampires?" Her bottom lip is full on trembling now as a sliver of fear finally cracks through her armor of pink hair and sass. The scent of it thickens the air around us.

I flick my tongue over the end of one of my fangs. "What do you think, Cupcake?"

Her blue eyes narrow, and she shakes her head. "But vampires don't exist."

Malachi huffs another laugh while Axl spreads his arms wide. "You think you're dreaming us, then?" He crouches in front of her and tilts his head to the side, his eyes raking over her pretty face, down to the ripe tits straining the fabric of her tank top. She smells so good. I don't know how she isn't already pinned to the floor with the three of us feasting on her. Her busting us tonight is the best thing that's happened in weeks, because she is going to taste so much sweeter than the snarky wannabe cheerleader we had lined up earlier. Axl brushes his knuckles over her cheek. She flinches at his touch but doesn't pull back. So fucking feisty. "Are we what your fantasies are made of?"

"Yeah, I bet you dream about this kind of thing, hey Cupcake? On your knees for three guys." I grab my dick and squeeze. "Looks to me like you're thirsty for some cock."

Her cute little nose scrunches in disgust, and fuck me, it makes her look even cuter. "I do not and I am not!" she insists with a dramatic huff.

Fuck, I'm gonna nut in my pants if I don't have those juicy lips wrapped around my cock real soon. "Yeah, we'll see about that."

4

OPHELIA

Goose bumps cover every inch of my skin, and I shiver in the dank basement. My knees ache from the cold concrete floor. I want to go back to my dorm. I want these three assholes to stop messing with me. But despite their taunting, I'm not afraid. Not as afraid as I should be, anyway.

I mean, on some level I'm concerned about what they have planned for me, but I seem to lack the natural human instinct to feel true fear. I can sense when I should feel it—like when you're watching a horror movie and you scream at the TV for the silly virgin not to go look for the source of the sound she just heard—but I don't experience it the way other people do. Sadness. Loneliness. Despair. Hell yeah, I feel those all too acutely. But I'm rarely, if ever, afraid. And one of these days it's probably going to get me killed.

Or eaten by three vampires.

My skin burns where Xavier's hand clutches my jaw. He lets out a hoarse groan. "She's gonna look so fucking good with your cock buried in her pussy while I fuck her sweet mouth, Kai."

And now my face isn't the only place that burns. My core contracts, and a deep gnawing in my belly has moisture building between my thighs. I do not want this. I do not. I chant the words in my head. Because they're true. My body, however, appears to have missed the memo. Thighs trembling, I whimper when Xavier brushes the pad of his thumb over my lips.

There's no rhyme or reason to the way I'm feeling. Sure, I'm inexperienced, but I've liked guys. I've been turned on and given myself plenty of orgasms, but this feels completely different. So much *more*. And there are no words to explain the raft of emotions that are currently overwhelming me. Despite every part of my logical brain screaming no, my body will not stop quaking with the anticipation of pleasure. Nothing about what they're going to do will be pleasurable, so what the hell is wrong with me? Am I a masochist?

Baring his teeth, Axl rakes his eyes down my body, his hard length bulging against the zipper of his jeans. "Who says you two get to fuck her first?"

Before Xavier or Malachi can reply, the door bursts open like a tornado is tearing through the house. A tall silhouette fills the wide doorway, appearing like some kind of avenging knight. My foolish overactive brain immediately wants to call out Batman.

Batman steps into the room, a low growl vibrating through the air. So vicious in its warning, my three attackers take a wary step back.

"What the hell do you three think you are doing?" His dark, dangerous voice sends a chill racing down my spine. He steps into the light, and I recognize the face of Professor Drakos, dean of the history department. According to the girls who sat near me on the first day I had his class and spent the entire first lesson talking about everything from his star sign to his favorite color—black—Alexandros Drakos is also the faculty head of Ruby Dragon Society. I must admit, their level of research was impressive. As he stalks closer, my mind conjures all the irrelevant facts I learned about him. He's apparently a Leo and is also a ruthless grader, cold and unfeeling, which they seemed to see as a challenge...and a turn-on. He keeps the shortest office hours of any professor, and he—

"Just having a little fun, sir," Malachi answers, interrupting my random juggernaut of thoughts and reminding me of my imminent peril.

"Fun?" He snarls, taking a step closer. "Take those cuffs off her and get her the hell out of here."

Axl grabs my elbow in a bruising grip and angles his body so he's facing the professor. "But she interrupted us eating tonight's dinner. We brought her here to deal with her."

How exactly do they intend to *deal with me*? That's right, the eating me whole thing. My core contracts at the very thought. What the hell is wrong with me?

"And do you have a plan of how to do that without biting her?" Professor Drakos asks, his brow furrowed in a deep scowl. Feeling like I've stepped into some alternate reality, I shift my attention between him and the three guys. Is this some kind of hazing ritual? A weird act they put on to scare pledges? The lack of pledges in the vicinity makes that scenario unlikely.

"No. Do we need a plan where we don't bite her?" Axl asks, drawing my attention back to him. His dark features are pulled into a frown, but he keeps a firm grip on my elbow.

The professor's snarl reverberates through the room, making me shiver. "Yes, you need a plan. You bring this girl to *my* house, and you intend to do what with her?"

"We fuck with her and we bite her," Xavier replies with a puzzled shrug, like this is a common occurrence for them.

"The hell you will!" I tug my wrist in an attempt to free myself from Axl's grip despite being acutely aware of the futility of such an effort.

The professor shakes his head, his tongue darting out and moistening his bottom lip. "I forbid you from biting her." His tone is calm and even now. "Let her go."

Confusion ripples through the room, so tangible it's as though I could reach out and touch it. My own confusion peaks when Axl uncuffs me, and I rub at the reddened skin on my arm where his fingers bit into me.

"But why can't we bite her?" Malachi asks, his brow furrowed.

"Yeah, she's just some nobody," Axl adds.

"Hey!" I protest. Technically, that's true, but still.

Glaring at me, Professor Drakos jerks his head toward the open door. "Leave before I change my mind and let my boys tear you to pieces."

His *boys*? Now that's something I'd like to unpick. My eyes flit between him and my three tormentors. Is he being serious about letting me go? Why is the notoriously cold and ruthless Professor Drakos sparing me?

Axl huffs. "I told you, she saw us. What if she talks?"

Professor Drakos's eyes lock on mine, and a current of something runs through the air. He tilts his head to the side. "Who will believe the lonely little girl who couldn't even get a roommate to share a dorm room with her this semester?"

His words cut me deeply, piercing my heart like a scalpel. Tears burn behind my eyes. Cruel jackass. At least *his boys* are open about being callous jerks, but he's a whole other level of vicious. And how does he know I couldn't get a roommate? How does he know a single thing about me? I'm just a nobody, right?

I wipe the tears from my eyes with the backs of my hands. "Yeah. Nobody will believe me." The truth of that statement hurts more than anything else that's happened tonight. "You assholes are free to bite anyone on campus."

I snatch my backpack up from the floor and march away before any of them change their minds and stop me.

5

ALEXANDROS

The scent of her blood—of her—still fills my senses. My mouth waters, and I tell myself that it is nothing more than the shadow of a memory. It has nothing to do with the girl.

I scan the text on my computer screen before lingering on the headline: TEEN GIRL BURNS DOWN HIGH SCHOOL

The article reveals the cause of the fire was never confirmed, but an ambiguous title will not sell nearly as many newspapers. I make it a personal mission of mine to know about every student who attends this college, and the unfortunate fate that met Miss Hart's dorm mate a few weeks ago was bizarre enough to bring them both to my attention. At the time, as gruesome as that whole affair was, it seemed entirely unrelated to Ophelia. Thanks to the university's efforts to keep the incident under wraps, Melinda Navarro never existed as far as any of the students here are concerned. But perhaps I was remiss in not doing a more thorough background check on Miss Hart. There is more to her than meets the eye.

I pulled up her records as soon as she left the house. We have a mix of human and nonhuman students at Montridge, and the humans are usually selected from a curated list. Chosen because they are easy prey or ripe for recruitment, the students are then seduced to enroll. When I saw the pink-haired girl with incandescent-blue eyes who showed up without a friend in the world, I assumed Ophelia Hart was human, but on closer inspection, she appears to meet neither of the requirements.

There are no clues on her application as to what—or who—led her here. Perhaps the fire at her high school was enough to convince one of my colleagues that she possessed some kind of magical power.

Her story is not an entirely uninteresting one. An orphan raised in the foster care system. She was expelled after the fire during her junior year of high school, and she did some kind of self-paced program to graduate. But nothing in her records suggests that she is anything special. In fact, Ophelia Hart is an average student with moderately above-average grades. She has been on campus since the dorms opened a week and a half ago, but I failed to pay her much attention beyond noticing that she sits in the second row of one of my ancient Greek history classes.

Until tonight. When I walked through the door and caught the scent of her blood, hunger burned in my veins as strongly as if I had tasted her. And the memories of all the other times I have felt such hunger and power threatened to devour me whole.

Perhaps she has some latent power she is unaware of, because the alternative is unthinkable. Not just unthinkable—impossible. Fall is always a time of reflection. That is all this is. A familiar scent invoked powerful memories that have nothing to do with Ophelia Hart.

Axl walks through the open door of my study, his movements cautious. "So…you want to tell me what that was about?"

Although I am thankful for his company and the distraction

it brings me, I keep my eyes on the screen. "I gave you an order. I expect you to follow it without questioning me."

He takes a few steps closer, running a hand over his square jaw. "It's just... I can't recall you ever having given us an order like that before. Not to bite someone. Why now? And why her?"

I run my tongue over my lip and suppress a sigh.

"Alexandros?" he asks again, but there is a wariness in his tone, as there should be when questioning me.

"There are thousands of women on this campus. Bite any one of them, Axl, just not her."

He nods, his head dipped and his shoulders slumped in a show of compliance. "Then we won't, okay. But just tell me why."

My eyes drift back to the screen, and he wanders behind my desk. "That was her?" he asks, staring at the yearbook photo of the plump seventeen-year-old girl with dark braids and braces on her teeth. "Ophelia's the girl in the article?"

I nod.

"So why did she burn her high school down?"

"Nobody knows for sure that she did. But she was the only one in the room where the fire started, and she walked out of the blaze without a mark on her skin."

He whistles between his teeth. "Is she a demon? A witch? But if she can control fire, why didn't she use any of her magic on us tonight?"

I shake my head. Creatures who can channel fire magic are considered some of the most powerful beings. "I believe she is unaware that she possesses any magical abilities, if indeed she does. And as for what she is, that is complicated."

"How complicated?"

I ignore his question, partly because I am unwilling to confront the potential answer. But something about the girl has piqued my curiosity. Even without her heady scent scrambling my senses, it is clear that somebody invited her to this school, and I want to know why. "If she has any power at all, then it is worth keeping a closer eye on her. I want you and your brothers to monitor her. And no biting means I also expect you to make sure nobody else bites her."

He scowls. "So we have to be her fucking bodyguards?"

"No. Simply monitor her movements and warn others away from her. Discreetly. She's a loner by nature. Ensure that she stays that way. Feed into her insecurities. The fewer friends she makes, the easier it will be to exert control over her should we ever need to."

Axl's eyes light up, and I wonder if he is excited at the prospect of torturing the girl or because her scent calls to him and his brothers the same way it does to me.

I growl a reminder. "No biting."

He nods. "Noted."

My attention is drawn back to the screen, but my mind swims with images of her kneeling in our basement, my boys standing over her, salivating at the mere prospect of a taste.

The psych report summary attached to her application file says that she consistently denied any knowledge of what started the fire at her school. But she did disclose an incident with a group of bullies that left her feeling humiliated and upset. Emotions and power are inextricably linked, especially for—

No. I will not go there. Cannot.

My head spins with the wave of anger and grief that washes over me, and I force myself to focus on the facts I know rather than wild speculation. And the facts lead me to one conclusion regarding the little orphan who lived in the foster system her whole life—someone bound her magic when she was a child. And that someone must have been a powerful witch with an even more powerful reason to inflict such a cruel fate.

6

Axl

"But has he ever forbidden you from biting anybody before?" Malachi asks before stuffing an entire slice of pizza into his mouth.

He licks the grease from his lips and frowns. I'm as baffled by this whole no-biting-Ophelia deal as they are, but I'm stopped from answering by Xavier. "Why do you eat that shit?" he asks, his nose wrinkled in disgust.

Malachi pulls a face. "Because it fucking tastes good, numbnuts." At least I think that's what he mumbles with his mouth stuffed full.

Xavier makes a fake vomiting noise that has me suppressing a smirk. He's never taken to junk food despite its prevalence in today's culture. "It has like zero nutritional value. Even for humans."

"Well, we're not as bloodthirsty as you," Malachi snaps back. "Some of us enjoy actual food too."

Quick as a flash, Xavier has Malachi's throat grasped in his daughter. I mean, I did try to fuck her, but still.

I pleaded with him constantly for a companion or a brother, having lost my mortal brother, Frederik, when we were both children. Every day since, I have both regretted and thanked all the demons in heaven and hell for Xavier's presence in my life. He is my biggest ally and my immortal enemy. "No. Not me either."

Malachi grunts with frustration. "So why this girl? Why is she so special?"

I recount the conversation the professor and I just had in his office, leaving out no detail in the hopes they might find an answer in his words where I could not.

Xavier growls. "So, we're supposed to babysit her, but we can't fucking bite her?"

I grunt, my frustration mirroring his. "That's what he said."

"Well, this fucking sucks," he grumbles.

Malachi shrugs. "It might not be so bad. She was kind of interesting."

The pink-haired pyromaniac is exactly his type—curious to the point of rabid, not to mention fearless. I guess she's kind of like him. The last thing we need is for him to catch feelings. He's only just gotten over his last breakup, and that was sixty years ago. "You will not go making friends with her, Kai."

He rolls his eyes. "Never said I was."

"Doesn't mean we can't fuck with her though. I mean, when those cheeks get all pink with indignation and then she opens that pretty little mouth..." Xavier grunts. "Yeah, I'm gonna have a lot of fun."

"And he never said we couldn't fuck her, right?" Malachi adds, a wicked glint in his eye.

"No, he didn't," I agree. "And I have to agree with Xavier for once. Pissing her off made me hard as fuck. Such a bratty little mouth she had on her."

Xavier moans, and Malachi shakes his head like he disapproves. Pity he doesn't get to make the rules. No biting is our only boundary. Still plenty more fun we can have without breaking our oath.

Yeah, Ophelia Hart is going to regret the day she ever met us. I'll make damn sure of it.

7

OPHELIA

Everything looks exactly the same as it did yesterday. There are still groups of students studying on the lawn. The same black-haired senior, wearing artfully torn jeans, stands beneath the maple in the quad and recites his poetry to a crowd of awestruck bystanders. Everyone laughing and talking and walking to class the same way they did the past few days, like they have no idea that vampires exist. That all those TV shows and movies aren't fiction after all. And not only that, but they're here on campus. Pretending to be students while preying on their peers and feasting on our flesh.

Are all the Ruby Dragon Society members vampires? Unlike most college sororities and fraternities, students have to be invited to pledge the societies. Which will never happen to me. I'm simply a nobody who ended up here because of a weird clause in the trust that was set up before I was born. For the past several years, I dreamed of escaping Havenwood, and now I'm stuck here for four more years.

A shiver runs down my spine as the memory of the girl from last night burns fresh in my mind. I recall her name now too—Rachel. She sits in the back of my English class with the popular kids, but I recognized her pigtails. Shame burns my cheeks at the realization that I didn't think to check on her after I got back to my dorm last night. I was so relieved to be away from those bloodsucking creeps that I barricaded my door and crawled straight into bed. Not that I would have known where to find Rachel's dorm, but I could have asked around.

I search the mass of students hurrying to class, trying to catch a glimpse of her. This campus is huge, and we only have the one class together. Dammit. What if she's not okay? What if Axl hurt her or made her disappear? My stomach rolls, and I'm considering abandoning class to find Rachel with the pigtails when I see her up ahead.

Relief washes over me. At least she's alive. That's something, right? She's surrounded by a group of girls, and they're all talking animatedly. I wonder if she's telling them about what happened last night. Will they even believe her? I mean, she's popular and people tend to take note of the popular kids, but it's pretty far-fetched to be bitten by a vampire.

I jog over, clutching my books to my chest. "Hey, Rachel." I blow a strand of hair from my damp forehead.

She turns at her name, her brow pinched in confusion.

I take a deep breath. "I saw what happened last night."

She blinks at me.

"With Axl? I totally saw everything. I can be a witness if you need one."

Her top lip curls into a cruel sneer while the two girls on either side of her hold their hands to their mouths like they're trying to suppress their laughter. "Ew! Were you spying on us? You freak!"

"What? No. I just…" My eyes drop to her neck, looking for

evidence of Axl's bite. What the hell? Her skin is completely blemish free.

"Perverted little freak!" one of the other girls says.

"No. I saw him bite you. I..."

Rachel's cheeks turn pink. "Ugh. You were spying, you disgusting little pervert."

"I wasn't. I heard you scream, and I saw you behind Hermes Hall—"

"Ugh. Screaming behind the fine arts building," the other girl says with a snort. "Real classy, Rach."

Rachel's skin darkens to a mottled red. She marches forward a few steps and presses her pretty face up close to mine, her bubblegum-scented breath warm on my lips. "I don't know what you think you saw, freakazoid, but Axl and I had a perfect date. He walked me to my dorm and we kissed. End of story, you lying little bitch." She draws her arm back and slaps me across the face hard enough for tears to prick at my eyes.

I rub my stinging cheek while she and her friends strut away. They shoot me a final look of disgust over their shoulders before disappearing. Staring after them, I wrestle with my confusion and block out the people staring at me like I'm some kind of freakish circus act. I'm used to the insults they mutter as they pass me—or say outright if they're particularly mean.

Tears burn behind my eyes, and I scrub at my cheeks with the sleeve of my sweater. How stupid was I to think that Montridge was a new start? There are no new starts for people like me.

Keeping my head down, I hoist my backpack up and stumble toward my first class. A fat droplet of rain lands on my eyelash and rolls down my cheek as I focus on how lucky I am to be here at all. College is usually only a dream for a foster kid with slightly higher-than-average grades. And it was a dream I never imagined coming true until my social worker discovered a college trust fund that had been set up by my parents before they died. There's enough to pay my entire tuition to Montridge, as well as room and board. As soon as I have my degree, I can go somewhere completely new. Somewhere far away from Havenwood, where nobody knows or cares about 'Opeelia' Hart.

...

My college algebra class lets out, and I head for the library. Keeping my head down like I always do, I swear I feel his presence before I hear his voice.

"Hey there, sweet girl." His breath dusts over the skin on the back of my neck, making a not entirely unpleasant shiver run the length of my spine.

Still, I huff in annoyance at him invading my space. "What the hell do you want, Malachi?"

He falls into step beside me, the goofy smile on his face so at odds with his appearance. He runs a hand over his shaved head and rests it on the back of his neck, drawing my eyes to the dark swirling mass of tattoos that wind around the thick column of his throat. The same ink adorns his hands and forearms and, combined with his tongue piercing, serves to give him an overall menacing appearance.

He runs his tongue over his teeth. Perfectly straight teeth with no hint of the fangs I saw last night. Maybe they're retractable? Or maybe last night was merely a dream. I have so many questions, but I start with the one burning a hole in my frontal lobe. "How does he do it?"

Malachi frowns. "Who do what?"

"Axl. I saw him bite that girl last night. I saw it running down her neck. The blood." He hisses at the mention of blood, and when I steal a glance at him, his green eyes glisten back at me. My stomach clenches, but I force myself to continue. "But this morning, there was no mark on her neck. Not even a scratch."

"Vampire saliva contains healing properties," he says with a casual shrug, like we're discussing something as mundane as the weather.

My morbid inner geek shrieks with excitement. "It does? Like how? Can it heal any kind of wound? Like one from a knife?"

His laugh is so warm and unexpected that my breath catches in my throat. "No. Small puncture wounds and stuff. Our blood can heal much bigger wounds though."

"It can?"

He shoots me an amused look, and I'm aware that I'm grinning like a moron, but this is way too fascinating to even bother curbing my excitement for. "So, if someone were to say—" I chew on my lip. "Get shot, and they were dying... Could your blood save them?"

He nods. "Theoretically, yes." His eyes crinkle at the corners, and his lips twitch in a smile. Is he making fun of me, or is he actually being nice?

Don't be so ridiculous, Ophelia! He's a vampire. They are not nice. I ignore that fact and allow my curiosity to get the better of me once more. "You've never tried?"

A freshman I recognize from my history class almost barrels into me while catching a football, and Malachi grabs him by the shirt and pushes him halfway across the hall. "Watch it, asshole," he says with a vicious snarl.

The freshman stumbles, then opens his mouth like he's about to argue, but as soon as his eyes land on Malachi, his face goes pale. "Sorry, sir," he says in a low whisper.

Sir? Well, now I have even more questions, but before I can ask them, Malachi takes me by the elbow and maneuvers me through the bustling crowd. As soon as we're outside, I find my voice again. "Why did he call you sir?"

He tilts his head, hand still gripping my arm. "Do you always ask this many questions, sweet girl?"

I try to wrench my arm from his grip, but he holds firm. "Well, forgive me for being curious," I say with a roll of my eyes. "But it's not every day you get to meet a *vampire*."

He glances around like someone just called his name, although I didn't hear anything. Without looking at me, he sighs. "Pretty sure you've met plenty, Ophelia."

"I have? So there are more of you?" His nostrils flare, and he grinds his jaw. "Hey, it was you who came to me in the hallway," I snap, defensive. "I was minding my own business."

He directs all of his attention back to me, but a frown is marring his features. He's actually pretty handsome—pity he's a vampire. "What?" he barks.

"You seem kinda pissed, and I said—"

He mutters something unintelligible, cutting me off. Then he cocks his head, and when his eyes roam down to my tank top, I'm painfully aware of how my breasts strain the fabric. He licks his lips. "Where are you headed?"

"The library. Why?"

He glances around again. "Go straight there. Okay?"

This is the singular most confusing conversation I've ever had in my life. "Why?"

Our eyes lock, and his pupils grow wider, obscuring the vibrant green of his irises. "Just do it, Ophelia."

I shrug out of his grip, and this time he doesn't offer any resistance. "Well, I will. But only because I was headed there anyway. Not because you told me to."

He gives a single nod of his head, his brow furrowed. Clearly, he's still distracted by something.

"I guess I'll see you around, then? No doubt skulking around the shadows looking for some poor unsuspecting hot girl to feast on." I bite the inside of my cheek to stop myself from snickering at my own joke.

"Oh, you'll be seeing plenty of me, sweet girl. Promise." And with a wink, he's gone. Leaving me to stare at his retreating back and wonder what the hell just happened.

8

MALACHI

I said I'm on my way, jackass, I tell Axl as I leave Ophelia, tamping down the rage simmering beneath my skin.

You got a crush on the cupcake, Kai? Xavier teases me, and I shrug off his comment. Pair of goddamn assholes. A crush? What am I, twelve years old? All because I enjoy making conversation with her. Fuck! I wish I could have one goddamn moment without two fuckwits in my head. I've never been good at blocking them out. No matter how much time Alexandros spends teaching me how, I can't do it. And ninety-nine point nine percent of the time, I don't want to. But now, well, there's a girl with pink hair and radiant blue eyes who smells like fucking heaven that I'd love to get to know a little better without those jackasses acting like teenage boys about it.

Just get the hell over here, Axl orders.

Shaking off my frustration, I move quickly and a few minutes later, I reach the field behind the Opal and Ruby Dragon Society houses. Axl scowls at me. His eyes, usually the color of melted milk chocolate, are dark with annoyance. "You decided to grace us with your presence at last?"

"Since when do I have to explain myself to you? Just because you're the oldest doesn't make you the boss of us." I don't normally bother pushing back against his tendency to pull rank and order me around, but I was enjoying talking to Ophelia.

He shakes his head. "You know the first few weeks are the most intense. There'll be plenty of time to fuck around with our new toy once pledges are finalized."

Xavier wraps an arm around my neck. "Yeah, we got Trials to plan for." He flashes me a wicked grin, and I can't help but smirk back. I do love the Trials.

I shrug out of Xavier's grip. "How many pledges do we have this year?"

"Only thirty-two." Axl frowns at the house where all pledges eat and sleep for the first six weeks of term, until we've successfully weeded out the ones who aren't strong enough to be turned. Becoming a vampire isn't a gift that can be bestowed on just anyone. Only those with a strong mind and spirit can survive the agony of the transformation.

I grimace. "That's less than last semester."

Axl pinches the bridge of his nose. "So let's hope they're all fit to be here and we can keep most of them."

Xavier snorts. "Unlikely."

Axl punches him in the arm. "Stop being such a dick."

Xavier snarls and returns the favor by slamming his fist into Axl's jaw. A split second later, the two of them are rolling around on the lawn, punching the hell out of each other. I fold my arms and wait, accustomed to their constant bickering.

"Hey, are they okay?" A Ruby Dragon member with long black hair and a nose ring whose name currently escapes me stands beside me, her gray eyes alight with fascination and her lips curved in an appreciative half smile.

Xavier straddles Axl, holding him down by his wrists. Axl's huge biceps strain the seams of his T-shirt as he tries to buck his assailant off, but Xavier tips his head back and laughs triumphantly, showing his pristine white teeth and perfect fangs. Sweet motherfuck, he's going to bite him right here.

My cock jumps in my pants, and I adjust myself while the girl goes on watching my buddies. As hot as their whole pissing contest is to watch…

I clear my throat. "Don't we have shit to do?"

Xavier dips his head and licks the column of Axl's throat, letting out a low hum of satisfaction. Axl growls and throws Xavier off him, launching him a few feet across the grass.

"Those two are so fucking hot," the girl next to me says with a dreamy sigh.

I roll my eyes while Axl and Xavier wipe the grass off their clothes and join us, their fight already forgotten.

Xavier snarls at her. "Who are you?"

Her heart rate spikes. "I'm Jay. Professor Jackson said you could use some help with the Trials."

Axl's narrowed eyes roam over her body, drinking her in. "Professor Jackson is your sire?" Professor Jackson is Alexandros's cousin and the dean of the economics department. He always gets his pick of the Ruby pledges to turn at the end of the Trials, and he only chooses the best. In our seventy plus years at this college, we have met and lost far too many pledges to remember them all. But I recall Jay from the Trials two years earlier, particularly the Hunt. She covered herself in rotten duck eggs to win.

She flashes her fangs, flicking her tongue over the tips and batting her eyelashes at him. "Yeah."

Axl snorts, seemingly unimpressed by her obvious interest in him, which is very unlike him. Ordinarily he'll fuck anything with a pulse. "I thought he was sending me his best."

She rolls her shoulders back. "I *am* his best."

Xavier takes a step closer to her, and she visibly shivers. He curls a lock of her dark hair between his fingers. "Forgive Alastair here. He's something of a misogynist. Doesn't think women can be the best at anything. It's not his fault though, he's a product of his time."

Axl growls, training his glare on Xavier—not because he cares about what anyone thinks of him, but because he hates his birth name. Weary, I roll my eyes and step between the two of them. I really don't have time for any more of their competitive bullshit. There's a certain pink-haired girl I'd much rather be spending time with right now. "Let's do what the fuck we came here to do and get out of here, yeah?"

I tip my chin at Jay. "You too." I head into the house, and the three of them follow close behind.

"Pledges in the den. Now!" I shout as soon as we step into the entryway. There's a stampede of feet from every direction, and I appraise each pledge as they file past us. Some are here because they know what we are and have been persuaded by their older family members to follow in their footsteps. Others have been recruited by the criminal organizations all over the world that fund this college. Vampires have infiltrated all of them. From the Yakuza to the Cosa Nostra, they all have some of our numbers among their highest-ranking members. An immortal with the strength of ten humans is a much more effective soldier.

Xavier steps into the room first, and the vibrant buzz of chatter stops dead, like someone switched off the sound in the room. A wicked grin spreads across his face as he scans the collection of potential recruits. His reputation as a sadistic fuck who will tear out a pledge's throat if they so much as look at him funny is well established and entirely founded in historical fact. Although, the last occurrence was almost two decades ago now, when the supply of pledges was more plentiful, thus making them more dispensable.

We have four girls in this group, double the number from last year. They usually opt for one of the less challenging vampire societies, Lapis or Opal. Excitement ripples through the room like a current of warm air, even from the stony-faced pledges who think they're too tough or too cool to show any emotion.

I lean close to Axl while the recruits find places to sit. "How many did the other houses have?"

"Only seventeen for Lapis and fourteen for Opal."

Wow, so few. I ignore the seed of worry that wants to take root in my gut. "And Onyx?"

"Thirty-five." His voice is barely more than a growl.

I squeeze his shoulder, acutely aware of how offended he is by the fact that our biggest rivals have more new pledges than us. "Doesn't mean they'll win, okay?"

He turns to me, a snarl twisting his lips. "We barely beat them last year, and we had four more pledges than they did."

I resist rolling my eyes. The Trials are fun, and I enjoy them, but Axl takes the whole thing way too personally. I get that the honor of House Drakos and Ruby Dragon are at stake, but it's not like we've ever lost before. If he paid as much attention to our world as I do, he'd realize that the real concern is the dwindling number of pledges and turned vampires as a whole, not whether we have enough to win the Trials. "Doesn't matter how many pledges they have," Axl says. "They'll never beat us because we always have the best of the best, right?"

"Right." Xavier pats Axl on the back. Just like that, their earlier disagreement is nothing more than a memory. Always a united front when they need to be.

Axl cracks his neck, and the sound makes me wince. He fixes our potential recruits with a fierce glare. "The first of this year's Trials will be held two weeks from Saturday. That gives you just over two weeks to prepare."

An eager beaver shoots his hand up to ask a question, but Axl ignores him. "There are four trials. The first is Fight Fest. You will each be matched to an opponent of similar stature and strength. No weapons are permitted. This isn't about not getting knocked down or who hits the hardest, but who can keep getting up again. Fight Fest is designed to test your strength, but also your resilience and your courage. It's the only trial where you will compete alone, so it's your chance to demonstrate what you're capable of. But make no mistake—there is no honor in this fight. Your opponent will play dirty. They will use any means within their power to beat you. Be prepared."

The eager beaver puts his hand down. Axl indicates for Jay to step forward, and she stands beside him, hands on her hips and a stubborn tilt to her jaw. Axl keeps his eyes fixed on the group in front of us. "Jay here will teach you the basics of what you need to know."

"We're supposed to trust a woman with this?" a guy says, standing up in the back of the room. Before he can take another breath, Jay has him hauled up by his throat and pinned to the wall, all two hundred pounds of him.

"You wanna repeat that, dipshit?" she says, offering him a saccharine smile.

I stifle a snicker while the guy being manhandled by the woman half his size tries to shake his head. "N-no."

"No what?" she asks.

He glares at her. "No, ma'am."

Tilting her head, she laughs darkly. Then she licks a trail along his jawline and hums. "I'm going to enjoy playing with you."

She lets him go, and he rubs at his throat before taking his seat again. A soft murmur runs around the room, and Axl holds up his hand, silencing them all once more. "Lesson number one, pissants. Never underestimate your opponent."

Jay arches an eyebrow and smiles at him. My brothers rarely pass up an opportunity to get laid, so it looks like she'll be staying over at our place tonight. They try to stay away from our own house vampires when possible, given the potential to piss Alexandros off if they do something stupid. But Jay is a gift horse, and Axl will definitely not be looking at her mouth. I glance at Xavier and roll my eyes, but he grabs his dick and winks at me. Fucking fantastic. Looks like I'll be listening to them both fuck her.

I give Jay a once-over. She's pretty enough, but too cocky for my liking. I prefer them sweeter, less aggressive. With pink hair and creamy white thighs...

Xavier's voice interrupts my thoughts. *Stop dreaming about the cupcake and get your head in the game, dickface.*

I'm not thinking about her.

He smirks. *Even if I couldn't hear you thinking loudly, I can see it written all over your face, sap.*

I glare at him. *Fuck you!*

He licks his lips, and I look away, refocusing on Axl and his speech to the new pledges.

"We are the Ruby Dragons. The strongest society on this campus. We remain undefeated after seven decades. Do not let this be the year we fail." He points at them. "Do not be the weak fucking links. Because there is no fucking place for weakness here. If you feel even a little uneasy about what you're about to go through, there's the door." He points toward it, but they all stare at him in silence.

He gives a similar speech every year, but never once has anyone walked out. They all think they have what it takes while they're sitting here, but half of them won't be lucky enough to make it to the final Hunt, and only a quarter will prove themselves worthy of being turned.

After giving the recruits a few last instructions, we step outside into the sunshine. "So, you guys wanna"—Jay runs her tongue over her bottom lip—"hang out?"

I suppress a sigh and glance in the direction of the library, wondering if Ophelia is still there.

"Nah. I have shit to do," Axl replies coolly, making my head swivel in his direction. I've never known Axl Thorne to turn down a blowjob, because that's surely where their *hanging out* would be headed.

"Aw," she purrs, before turning her attention to Xavier. "You're free though, right?"

He smirks. "No can do." He throws an arm around my neck. "Kai and I have some stuff to take care of."

Well, I fucking do. And her name is Ophelia.

"Besides, you're going to be busy teaching the new recruits the fundamentals of the Trials," Axl reminds her.

Jay rolls her eyes and flashes me a smile. "You want to help me?" She's obviously open to fucking any one of us, which isn't unusual. If they're not mate bonded, most vampires will—and do—fuck anything that moves. But I'm not most vampires.

"I just told you he has plans with me," Xavier says, and warmth flares in my chest at the possessiveness in his tone. I love belonging to him and Axl.

"Fine. I guess I read the room wrong."

"I guess you did. Now, back into the house and deal with the fresh meat, little girl," Axl says, not even bothering to look at her. His gaze drifts toward the library also.

"Fine, I'm going. Just wanted to burn off a little energy first. I'll find someone else to scratch the itch. Catch you guys later." Jay heads back to the house, giving us a casual wave over her shoulder that belies the sexual frustration rolling from her in waves.

"You two feeling okay?" I ask with a smirk. Horny female vampires are ordinarily a weakness for both of them.

Axl scowls. "What the fuck are you talking about?"

I suppress a snicker and shake my head.

Xavier gives a disinterested shrug. "He thinks we're into the cupcake as much as he is."

"Into fucking with her as much as possible." Axl's scowl disappears, and wicked intent makes his eyes twinkle.

Xavier grunts his agreement, and I press my lips together and say nothing. There's no reason to refute their claims when I know their thoughts and feel their emotions. And I know that they think about our little pink-haired problem as much as I do.

9

OPHELIA

My stomach growls at the scent of my burrito drifting out of the brown paper bag I have clutched in my hands as I take the stairs up to my dorm room. It was my hunger that forced me out of the solace of the library.

Libraries have always been special places to me. Not only a portal to another world, but the library was the only place I felt like I could hide from the pitying stares and rumors. *There goes that loser, Ophelia. The girl with no friends who peed herself in front of the entire school when she was seventeen.* I didn't. I mean, I know it looked like I did, but I didn't. However, high schoolers aren't exactly renowned for getting their facts straight before spreading rumors. Nor did I burn the school down in a fit of rage after, but nobody seemed to care about the truth regarding that either.

I push open my door and toss my backpack onto the bed with a sigh. A burrito and a shower, and I'll call it a night.

"You're home late, pyromaniac."

I let out a shriek so loud that I almost burst my own eardrums and toss my burrito at his head. Axl ducks, and my dinner flies out of the window. I clutch my chest as though it might stop my heart from beating right out of it. "What the hell? How did you even... You almost gave me a heart attack."

He shrugs. "I didn't realize you were so twitchy."

"I'm not twitchy. You're sitting in my window dressed in all black, looking like some cheap Black Panther rip-off."

He places a hand on his chest and adopts a wounded expression. "Ouch. So vicious, Pyro."

My mouth suddenly feels drier than a three-week-old falafel. The hairs on the back of my neck stand on end. "Why are you calling me that?"

He arches an eyebrow. "You did burn down your school, didn't you?"

My cheeks go hot. "No I did not."

He tilts his head and licks his full lips. "That's not what all your classmates and the principal told the newspapers."

I place my hands on my hips and glare at him, wishing he would burst into flames. "Yeah, well, you shouldn't believe everything you read, Axl."

He swings his long legs inside and plants his feet on my desk, and I gasp. "I thought you couldn't come in unless I invited you?"

His laugh isn't warm like Malachi's. It's cold and cruel, and it makes the hairs on the back of my neck stand on end. "You shouldn't believe everything you read, Ophelia."

Jerkwad! "What the hell are you even doing here? I think we've proven your secret is safe with me." I look out the open window behind him, mourning the loss of my burrito now that my heart has stopped racing.

He jumps off the ledge, and I press my lips together to stifle a yelp. I've never been a person who scares easily, but something about Axl Thorne makes me jumpy. Maybe because he's a vampire, Ophelia. Duh!

"But that's not true, is it, Pyro?" he asks, his voice dropping to a low growl.

He steps closer, and I take a step back. "W-what?"

"I have ears all over this campus. I heard about your little show on the quad today. You made quite the fool of yourself, didn't you?"

Another step back has me flat against my door with my heart hammering to get out of my chest and my brain yelling for me to run. "I was just checking if she was okay."

"You offered to be a"—he cocks his head like he's searching for the right word—"*witness*?"

I swallow the ball of anxiety lodged in my throat. How the hell do I manage to get myself into situations like these? Tipping my chin up, I glare at him. Yeah, he might have a foot and a hundred pounds on me, not to mention a set of fangs that could tear out my throat, but I'm not afraid of him. I mean, my legs may be shaking a little, but I'm pretty sure that's not from fear… "I thought you'd hurt her. I thought nobody would believe her if she spoke out, and I know what it's like to not be believed." A swell of sadness and shame washes over me.

A crack of thunder is followed by a bright flash of lightning and the sound of hammering rain, and it seems to snap Axl from his murderous intent because he glances back at the open window. It was sunny a few moments ago, but the weather in this area is always unpredictable.

"And now my burrito is turning into a pile of mush," I say with a sigh. "Thanks for that."

He turns back to me. "I didn't ask you to throw it at my head."

I roll my eyes. "You still haven't told me what the hell you're doing here."

He takes another half step forward, and now he's only inches from me. His breath rustles the hairs on the top of my head, and the heat coming off his body warms my own. "I'm here to warn you, little Ophelia," he says in a low growl.

"W-warn me?"

"You were told to keep quiet about your little discovery last night, yet you blabbed the first chance you got." He dips his head, and his lips hover dangerously close to mine.

My blood thunders in my ears. "I told you why I did that. But it doesn't matter. Like the professor said, nobody would believe me anyway. I just made myself seem like even more of a freak than people already thought I was. So you won."

"I always win." His lips inch closer until they dust the corner of my mouth.

I shiver. "A-are you going to b-bite me?"

"No." He pulls his face back an inch and sneers. Then he takes a lock of my hair and curls it between his thumb and forefinger. "A vampire is driven by scent. I only eat things I desire. And you, little pyromaniac..." He runs his nose over my hair and inhales deeply, and my stomach does a full somersault. "You stink."

I blink back tears. What a jackass! With another cruel laugh, Axl drops my hair but keeps his lips close to my skin so his warm breath dances over my lips. "I'll be keeping a close eye on you, Ophelia." In the blink of an eye, he's gone.

I suck in a calming breath and sink to the floor, sure of one thing—Axl Thorne isn't just a vampire. He's a monster.

10

ALEXANDROS

"What brings you to my office so early in the morning, old friend?" Osiris Brackenwolf's voice is little more than an angry growl, and he continues standing in front of the arched window, his attention on the view of Gaea's Green. He twists his neck and grunts, his powerful shoulder muscles rippling beneath his thin cotton shirt.

"Heavy night hunting?" I drop into the seat opposite his desk, curious about his obvious ire but not bothered enough to ask.

He sighs, his anger abating almost instantaneously. He has never been able to stay mad at me for longer than a moment or two. "I forgot how exhausting the start of term can be. All the eagerness and excitement of those leaving their packs and experiencing that initial taste of freedom. It's like trying to herd a pack of dogs that have been let off their leashes for the first time."

Not for the first time, I find myself thankful that my boys deal with the bulk of responsibilities surrounding the new vampire pledges and the Trials. For wolves, it is an entirely different process. "The exuberance of youth."

That gets me a deep chuckle, and he finally spins around and faces me. "Something you would know very little about, Alexandros."

I suppress a smile. Whilst I am ancient compared to him, there are tiny flecks of gray in his black beard now, an affliction I am unlikely to face for at least a thousand more years. Although he looks much younger than his eighty-four years, he is still approaching middle age for a werewolf. "Well, not everyone can be blessed with immortality, Osiris."

He smirks, his dark eyes flashing with flecks of yellow the way they do when his wolf wants to play. The memory of his bite on my flesh has heat coiling at the base of my spine. He feels it too and licks his lips, another low growl rolling in his throat.

"I am looking for some information on a student."

He waves a hand dismissively. "You have access to all the students' applications. Do your own research."

I lean forward in my seat. "I have, but things are not adding up. And if I go digging into the origins of this student, I will draw attention to her, which is the last thing I want. But nobody would be suspicious if the dean of admissions were to do a little research."

He tips his head back and groans. "Oh, it feels so fucking good to be on the other side of this exchange for once."

A deep sigh rolls out of me. "Being an ass about it is entirely unnecessary. Are you going to help me or not?"

He drops his head, his eyes fixed on me once more, and I catch the way his nostrils flare as his gaze rakes over my neck and chest.

"Osiris! I am not here to scratch an itch." No matter how appealing that might be right now. "This is important. You know there are very few people I trust…"

He narrows his eyes and sinks back against his chair. "Okay. What is it?"

Aware that the walls have ears, even in a dean's office, he lets down the wall he has had up since I walked in here and allows me freely into his head. He knows I could force my way inside if I chose to, but he also knows I would never violate his trust in that way.

The student's name is Ophelia Hart. Her tuition was paid by a trust fund, but I cannot figure out who is responsible for it. It is recorded as her parents, but something is off. And why is she here? I would like to know who recruited her. Can you find out?

Wolves have strong minds, and while they can communicate with their packs, they cannot do so with other beings. They are much harder to read than vampires, and although he's dropped his guard, he's still preventing me from hearing his thoughts. "I should be able to. Give me a couple of weeks. These new recruits are hard work." He rolls his neck again until it cracks and lets out a loud groan of relief. Then he winks at me. "But so much fucking fun."

"Always so driven by your base desires, Osiris."

His deep laugh echoes off the walls of his office. "I seem to recall many nights when you were the same, old friend. I have the scar to prove it, and you know how hard it is to scar a wolf." His eyes sparkle, and I recall the night he is referring to. Although it was decades ago, when he was a young wolf, it still seems as fresh to me as yesterday. A curse of living so long is that time starts to lose any real meaning. "But you're so restrained these days. If you only allowed yourself a little more pleasure, you might actually enjoy life. You know, crack a smile."

"Whilst your concern about my welfare is touching, Osiris, it is entirely unnecessary."

He arches an eyebrow at me. "I disagree, but I know you too well to argue any further." He steeples his large hands beneath his chin. "So, who do you think this girl is?"

"I am as of yet unsure of who she is. Which is why I want you to look into her."

"It's so unlike you to show any kind of interest in anyone, Alexandros. Why this one?"

Osiris is one of the few men I trust in the world. The only wolf worthy of that status. But I will tell not even him that her scent stirred something in me that I thought was buried centuries ago or that her presence in my house felt so familiar that it made me yearn to take her to my bed and claim her. Nor do I tell him of the innate power I sensed in her. "She is an anomaly" is all I offer.

"I guess I'll find out more about this girl who has captivated the great Alexandros Drakos, then."

I growl. "I did not say she had captivated me."

Grinning, he lifts his eyebrows. "Not with your words, old friend."

I stand and straighten my jacket. "I suddenly remember why I have avoided speaking to you for six months."

He puts his feet up on his desk and crosses his ankles, locking his hands behind his head. "And you know how I hate being ghosted." That explains his anger when I first entered his office. "But I also recognize why you try to pretend I don't exist for months at a time. It's because I know you too well, Alexandros. And you fucking hate that, don't you?"

"Let me know if you find out anything useful." I hold his gaze for one short moment before turning and walking out of his office.

"You can let me know if you want to have some fun in the woods sometime," he shouts after me.

As I stride away from his office, instinct tells me that he and I will never be that to each other again, but I shake it off and bury all thoughts of why that might be true.

11

OPHELIA

Malachi lies on my bed with his hands locked behind his head, the result of which is his already tight T-shirt straining at the seams of his tattooed and incredibly muscular biceps. He sings softly to himself. It sounds like an Irish folk song, sad and soulful and entirely distracting. Just like him. I pick up the unicorn plushie that's fallen on the floor and throw it at his head.

He catches it and tucks that behind his head too, flashing me a grin. "Sorry, was I distracting you when you're trying to study?"

I wave my textbook in the air. "Um, yes."

"What are you studying with such ferocity on this fine evening, Ophelia?" There's a playfulness in his tone that makes me want to smile. But I don't, because he's not here out of the kindness of his heart.

"Psychology."

His eyes sparkle with curiosity. "Is that going to be your major?"

I glance at my textbook. I really do need to study. "Yes." I turn back to my desk and scan the pages of my book, but I'm unable to focus on the words.

"And what will a sweet girl like you do with a degree in psychology?"

I roll my eyes. Is he genuinely interested, or is he mocking me? I swear I can't tell with all that smooth vampire charm he has going on. "I'm going to be a social worker."

"A noble profession. Not going to make you rich though."

I snort a laugh. Rich! Not everyone is motivated by money. Maybe I just want to help little kids who have nobody to look out for them. Nobody to be there when they're alone and scared and... I choke back a sob and don't tell him any of that. "Have you considered that I don't want to be rich?"

"I guess I've seen a lot of greed in my long life, Ophelia Hart." The sorrow in his tone pulls at my heartstrings. But I can't let whatever this thing is get any more comfortable to me than it already is. It's dangerous. *He's* dangerous.

"What are you even doing here, Malachi?" The ease with which he lets himself into my dorm room and makes himself at home is astonishing. This is the third time this week I've come back from class to find him in my bed, reading my well-worn copy of *Wuthering Heights*. I don't even bother voicing my annoyance any longer. At least he isn't a douchebag like Axl and Xavier. He's actually kind of nice to talk to.

"Just keeping an eye on you, sweet girl."

I sigh. "Like I've already told you all, your secret is safe with me, okay? I'm not about to go drawing more attention to myself by telling people about the three vampires I met on campus."

"Four."

"Four?"

"You've met the professor."

My eyebrows shoot up, and I'm pretty sure they must reach my hairline. "The professor's a vampire too?"

The deep, throaty chuckle that rolls out of him makes goose bumps prickle along my forearms. If it's not bad enough that him calling me sweet girl turns my insides all warm and mushy, he has to hit me with that sexy-as-hell laugh too. "Yeah, he's a vampire. He sired me. Axl and Xavier too."

I spin my chair all the way around and give him my undivided attention. "What was that like? Being sired? How old were you? Did it hurt? Did you want to be a vampire?"

He sits up, frowning, and his green eyes appear darker than usual. "You ask a lot of questions, Ophelia Hart."

I suck on my top lip and resist rolling my eyes. "Well, this stuff is fascinating to me. I mean, you're a fricking *vampire*. I am sitting in my dorm room, chatting with a creature I only ever read about or saw on TV. One that I assumed was complete fantasy until a little over a week ago."

He remains silent but goes on staring at me. My stomach ties itself into a knot. "If the professor's a vampire, does that mean some of the other professors are too?"

He shrugs.

I'm taking that as a yes. "And are there any other kinds of creatures I should know about?"

He arches one eyebrow, a hint of a smirk back on his lips now, which causes his adorable dimples to make an appearance. "Such as?"

"I dunno. Werewolves? Witches? Unicorns?"

"Yes. Yes. And no."

Putting aside my disappointment about the unicorns, I shriek, "What?" Then clamp my hand over my mouth when he frowns. "Sorry," I whisper. "But…for real? Werewolves and witches are real?"

"As real as I am."

I lean forward, my heart rate increasing with each passing second. "Are they here at Montridge too?"

He scrutinizes my face with such intensity that my skin flames with heat.

"You can trust me, Malachi. I swear even if I thought someone would believe me, I wouldn't tell a soul."

"And why should I trust you, sweet girl?" The deep smoothness of his voice warms my insides.

"Because…" I swallow hard. His eyes burn into mine, and I can't lie. "You're the only person I talk to."

His expression softens, and he blows out a breath. "The societies at Montridge represent different factions of supernatural beings. Each faction has four societies; vampires have Ruby, Onyx, Lapis, and Opal Dragon. The witches have their own four, and so do the wolves."

"So, the societies named after four of Jupiter's moons have to be the wolves, and the witches must be the vales, then, right?"

"You know astronomy?"

He knows astronomy? Wow. Could he be any more perfect? Well, aside from the whole vampire thing. "I know about a lot of stuff. I read a lot." That's an understatement. I read way more than a lot.

The way he looks at me, like he's impressed by my hitherto useless knowledge of Jupiter's moons, has my cheeks heating. Before I can ask another question, Malachi tosses my unicorn plushie back to me. I catch it and hold it to my chest, immediately regretting it when his scent wafts into my nose. Malachi Young smells every bit as good as he looks. Fresh and citrusy with a hint of spice. The impulse to lick his skin has me wondering what on this earth is wrong with me.

"How old are you?" I ask.

"One hundred and twenty-eight."

"And not a single wrinkle. You should be in skincare commercials." I snort a laugh at my own joke.

He rolls his eyes. "You think you're funny, huh?"

Another unexpected laugh bubbles out of me. "I do, actually."

"Then you're the only one in this room who does, Ophelia," he says, but there's no malice in his tone. Not like the cruelness of Axl's and Xavier's taunts when they happen to bump into me, usually quite literally, which has become a daily occurrence. Malachi's teasing is friendly almost.

"How old were you when you became a vampire?"

He sighs. "Twenty-two." Then he swings his legs over the edge of the bed and fixes me with a glare that makes my core feel warm and tingly. "No more questions."

"Aw, just a few more? Please?"

He narrows his bright green eyes and a few seconds later says, "One more."

"Two?" I suggest hopefully.

"One."

"Fine." I press my lips together and try to think of the best one. But so many race through my head that I can't focus. Finally, I blurt, "Are you really repelled by garlic?"

The booming laugh that explodes out of his mouth makes me giggle. I put my hands over my eyes and shake my head. Of all the things I could have asked, I can't believe I opted for that.

His laughter subsides, and when I take my hands away from my face, he's standing right in front of me. He rubs the pad of his thumb over my cheek, and I swear his touch sets my skin ablaze. "No, not repelled by garlic, Ophelia. Not by crucifixes or holy water either." He winks, and if I wasn't sitting, I would crumple to the floor because my legs just turned to Jell-O.

"G-good to know."

His lips twitch, and his hypnotizing eyes lock on mine. I feel helpless. Like if he were to lean down and bite me right now, I would wrap my arms around his neck and pull him closer. Is this how they entrap their victims? Vampire voodoo?

"Be good, okay?" he says, his tone soft.

I nod meekly, which I know I'm going to be so annoyed with myself for later, but I'm literal putty in his hands at the moment. Without another word, he leaves my dorm room.

I should be relieved he's gone, shouldn't I? But instead, I feel lonely and…

And sad.

Which is ridiculous. I've spent my whole life alone and learned to find happiness in my solitude. This is my factory setting, so why does that emptiness inside me feel like it's grown into a swirling vortex? And why do I feel like it's going to swallow me whole?

12

OPHELIA

With a deep breath, I run my hands over the pleats of my skirt and check out my outfit in the mirror. Not that I need to, it's the same thing I always wear. Plaid miniskirt, check; white tank, check; black lace-up boots, check; hooded sweatshirt tied around my waist in the event it gets a little chilly, check. It's like my uniform. No, my armor. My *fuck you* to the world. There's comfort in the familiar, particularly when everything else around you is in a constant state of flux.

I give myself a reassuring smile and grab my backpack, ignoring the kaleidoscope of butterflies fluttering in my stomach. Partly from excitement, partly from nerves. Tonight I'm going to my first football game. Go Dragons…

I take my seat in the second to last row of the student section. I've watched enough football on TV to know that the rules of seating do not apply to sports the way they do in the classroom. Here, the back rows aren't for the cool kids.

The stands around me are mostly empty, probably because

the Montridge Dragons football team is notoriously terrible, despite their awesome name. Apparently they only scored two touchdowns all last season.

Whatever the reason, it suits me fine because there are at least half a dozen empty seats on either side of me and I'm sitting close enough to the end of the row that I can leave whenever I want without any fuss. Not that I mind people, but there's something about being surrounded by groups and couples that makes my solitude feel all the more acute.

The team takes the field, and cheers erupt from the meager crowd. I smile, glad that they're not being booed. It must take a lot of guts to put yourself out there every week the way that they do.

"Is this seat taken?"

I tear my eyes from the field and look up at the source of the deep voice. He's half-smiling. He looks almost…hopeful. I glance around. There are plenty of empty seats. Why does he want the one next to me?

"You're here on your own too, right?" he adds with a self-deprecating laugh. "I find it's always more fun to watch the game with someone. If you don't mind?" He indicates the seat beside me, his deep-brown eyes crinkling at the corners when his smile widens.

I nod. "Sure." Really? One word. One syllable. Is that all you have, Ophelia? I would face-palm myself if he wasn't staring at me.

Why is he staring at me?

He narrows his eyes. "I think I've seen you in the dining hall. You're in Vasilakis Hall, near the library, yeah?"

Why does he know what dorm I live in? Suspicion makes me edgy, but his vibe is so warm and friendly. He wipes his hands on his torn jeans, flicks his dark hair out of his eyes, and laughs again. "That must make me sound like a creep, huh?"

I don't answer.

His Adam's apple, covered by a thick coating of dark stubble, bobs. "I'm not a stalker, I swear. I'm in Galanis."

"Oh yeah, that's right next to my building."

He blows out a breath and blinks. "Yeah, see, not a stalker."

Am I making him nervous? "Or a creep," I add, before a smile spreads over my face.

"Glad we got that ironed out." He settles back in his seat and directs his attention to the field. "They have a new quarterback this year. Caleb Lambert. He's supposed to be good. Scored four touchdowns in the winning game against the Tigers last year."

I don't really know much about football, not high school or college, or even the NFL, but I hum like I'm impressed.

"Fuck knows why he agreed to come to Montridge and play for the Dragons," he adds.

"Yeah, I heard they're not very good," I admit.

He shoots me a sideways glance. "Not very good would be an understatement. And you are...?"

Before I can give my name, a familiar voice behind us growls, "Move it, dickface."

My heart jolts like I was hit with an electric current, and I spin around to find Xavier and Axl sitting directly behind us.

My companion turns around too. "I didn't know you were with them," he says, a hint of terror in his tone.

I shake my head. "I'm not."

Xavier punches the back of the guy's seat. "Did you not fucking hear me?"

The guy jumps up and scrambles away without so much as a "see you later, when you're not being tortured by two giant assholes." I scowl at my tormentors, but they don't look at me. Xavier leans backward, his feet resting on the back of the empty seat beside me. He rests his arm around the back of Axl's shoulders, and they both stare at the field like it's the most interesting thing in the world.

God, they're infuriating. "Why the hell did you do that?" I demand.

They ignore me. "You know that new quarterback is an Onyx pledge, right?" Axl says to Xavier.

Assholes! "Why are you sitting here? Go away!" I yell this time.

They go on ignoring me. With an indignant huff, I grab my backpack and stand. If they won't move, I guess I will. Xavier's foot darts out, his long leg stretched out to its full length, blocking my path. This is ridiculous. I can't catch a break. "What do you think you're doing?"

He finally looks at me, and I almost wish he hadn't because the danger in the depths of his dark blue eyes makes my knees wobble. "Sit down, Cupcake," he orders.

I sling my backpack over my shoulder. "The hell I will."

Axl twists his neck and glares at me too, flicking his tongue over his sharp fangs. "Sit the fuck down, Ophelia. Now."

Anger sizzles beneath my skin. A quick glance around informs me that people are already watching this little display of whatever this is. The last thing I want is to draw unnecessary attention to myself. With a huff, I plonk back into my seat and focus on the game. We watch in silence for a few minutes, and I'm actually starting to enjoy myself when the two jackass vampires ruin it once again by opening their fat mouths.

"You fucked that cheerleader, right?" Xavier says.

Axl laughs. "Which one?"

"The perky one with the blond hair and the juicy tits."

"Dude, half the girls on the fucking squad have blond hair and juicy tits, and they're all perky. You'll have to be more specific."

I roll my eyes and try to tune them out, but my eyes go to the all-girl cheerleading squad on the sidelines. Every one of them impossibly beautiful and toned, they bounce on their toes, pom poms clutched to their chests as they recite simple cheers for the crowd.

"The same one I fucked in the locker room at the end of last season."

"You fucked them all in the locker room," comes Axl's reply, followed by their combined howls of laughter.

They're even bigger assholes than I thought they were, and that's saying something.

Axl's laughter subsides while Xavier goes on snickering. "Do you mean Delilah? The one you, me, and Kai ran a train on?"

"You're both disgusting," I spit out the words, and while it's true that the callous way they speak about women is disgusting, there is something very not disgusting about the images flashing through my mind. Only they're not of them with Delilah, whoever she is. They're of the three wicked yet undeniably hot vampires. And me.

Warm breath tickles the nape of my neck, making me shiver. "So why is your heart racing, Pyro? Why is the skin right here..." Axl traces a fingertip down the side of my throat. "As pink as your hair?"

"Because you're both a pair of animals and I hate you," I blurt, before I can accidentally say anything remotely close to the truth.

I squeeze my eyes and my thighs closed and try to think of anything but the way Axl's touch has electricity sizzling under my skin. How Xavier's possessive growl earlier, while annoying as hell, also made me feel seen, if only for a fraction of a second. I don't want to see Axl's sandy-blond hair or Malachi's sparkling green eyes or Xavier's dimples. And I definitely do not want to think about their toned abs.

"Which peppy little cheerleader should we fuck tonight?" Xavier's voice slices through me, and it's enough to stop all the ridiculous fantasies racing through my mind.

Axl hums like he's deep in thought. "That one with the curls who keeps jumping up and down like the ground's on fire. I walked past her earlier. She smelled good."

Xavier grunts. "What did she smell like?"

"Like apple and cinnamon. Plus, did you see how easily she did a split? I mean, the wider they can spread their legs, buddy…"

They both laugh again, and I look down at the girl I assume they're talking about. She has a huge smile on her face as she plays to the crowd, trying to get them to cheer for the Dragons, who despite their new quarterback, still manage to put on a terrible performance according to the scoreboard. She doesn't deserve what Axl and Xavier have in mind. I'd warn her if I thought for a millisecond she'd listen to me.

"Almost halftime. You think we can grab a quick bite before the second half?" Xavier laughs at his own joke.

Why are they here taunting me when they'd so clearly rather be sinking their teeth into a cheerleader? I manage to stifle the sob crawling up my throat, but I'm unable to stop a solitary tear from running down my cheek. Thankful that the two monsters sitting behind me can't see it, I wipe it away.

13

OPHELIA

The usual hum of chatter in the Dionysus Commons dining hall seems to have gone up a hundred decibels. A group of about twenty students, some of whom I recognize from high school, are crowded in the corner, and I crane my neck to see what's causing all the fuss. Too many people block my view, so I give up and turn to study my options for lunch.

"Penelope!"

My feet and heart falter. Surely it's a coincidence that someone just called out that name. It isn't totally unique.

But when I turn around, the crowd parts enough for me to see that my misfortune is real. My worst nightmare comes alive before my eyes. Standing there, larger than life and surrounded by sycophants, is Penelope Nugent. The girl who made so much of my time in high school a misery. The same person responsible for the nickname that will haunt me forever—Opeelia.

The memory of that night in the school auditorium sears my brain and makes my knees wobble. I grab onto the back of the nearest chair to keep myself from dropping to the floor. Emotions wash over me like I'm back there—excitement at playing Lady Macbeth in our school production, then the humiliation and crushing despair. The sting of their taunts.

I suck in a deep breath and drag my eyes back to my tormentor. I heard she went to some fancy college in California, so what the hell is she doing here? Please tell me she's just visiting. There are a few people from our old class in the year above me, so that's entirely plausible. Please God, do not be this cruel to me.

"Everything okay there, sweet girl?" Malachi's concerned voice cuts through the fog in my brain.

"I'm fine," I grit out.

"You sure?"

"She said she was fine, Kai." Axl's voice carries its usual bored tone. "Let's go."

I tear my eyes away from Penelope and her crowd of admirers. Xavier is watching her with an amused look on his face, and Axl is scowling, seemingly at nobody in particular. Malachi stares at me, the look in his eyes mirroring the concern in his voice. "You two go ahead. I'll catch up," he says, not tearing his gaze from mine.

"Don't take too long." Axl shoots me a look filled with disgust before getting in the coffee line next to Xavier.

"Who is she?" Malachi asks.

"Who?" My voice comes out in barely a whisper.

"The girl you were gawking at like you'd seen a ghost."

I shake my head, trying to dampen the onslaught of painful memories brought to the surface at the sight of my high school bully. I guess Malachi knowing who she is doesn't matter. If she's here as a student, my life at Montridge just got one hundred times worse. And there's not a single thing I can do about it. Thanks to the stipulation attached to my trust fund, I'm required to attend Montridge University if I want to go to college.

"She…" I swallow down another knot of emotion. "She went to my high school."

He frowns. "I take it you weren't friends?"

"Definitely not," I croak.

"Seems like there's more to it than just going to the same school though." He probes further, his green eyes burning into mine.

I shrug. "She was kind of mean to me." That's the understatement of the century, but to tell him the full extent of her cruelty would take me at least a week and no doubt make me come off deranged. Nobody could put up with that level of torture without doing something about it. Except that I did. I was completely powerless to stop her.

"Kind of mean, huh?" He searches my face for more answers, but I refuse to give him any further information about my traumatic time in high school.

"Kai. You coming or what?" Xavier yells from the other side of the dining hall.

Malachi keeps his eyes locked on mine for a few beats longer, then blows out a breath. "Don't let her get to you, sweet girl," he says, before he heads off in the direction of his friends.

Yeah, right. If only it were that simple.

14

Axl

Ophelia tucks a lock of pink hair behind her ear, her brows pinched together as she peers down at the textbook on her lap. She sits cross-legged on the grass beneath the shade of a tree on the edge of Gaea's Green. Alone. Friendless. And if I have my way, that's exactly how she'll stay. Much easier to sneak into her dorm room and make her life a misery when she has no one else to look out for her.

After we met Ophelia, the professor told us about her intended roommate suffering a nasty case of getting her head trampled by one of the wild colts who roam the mountain ranges near here a few weeks before the semester started. What a way to go. I was trampled by a horse once. It was after I was turned, so I was fine, but it still hurt like a motherfucker. Whatever happened and whether it was an accident or not, it worked out better for us. It's easier to keep a close eye on a lonely little pyromaniac that nobody cares about.

My lips twitch as I saunter over to her. She keeps her head bent over her book, her painted fingernail running along the lines of text.

"You're such a fucking nerd, Pyro." I flop down beside her on the grass.

She glances up and rolls her eyes at me. "What the hell do you want, Axl?"

I look out over the quad in a display of disinterest. "I'm bored."

"So go be bored somewhere else." She huffs and refocuses on her book. At least she pretends to, but I don't miss the spike in her heart rate. And it isn't fear—Ophelia Hart isn't afraid of me. Not even a little. And that intrigues the fuck out of me.

"Why do that when I can annoy the hell out of you instead?"

Her pupils are blown wide when she looks up at me. "If you're not careful, people are going to start thinking you like me."

I narrow my eyes, allowing them to rake over every inch of her. Her perky-as-fuck tits. The curve of her hips and her thighs that I've imagined having wrapped around my neck more than once. "Me...like *you*?" I snort a laugh. "Nobody is gonna believe that for a second, nerd, and you know it."

She blinks away tears. Why does hurting her make my cock so hard?

Malachi comes up from behind me and sits beside Ophelia, nudging her shoulder with his. "So this is where you're hiding."

Her pulse spikes again, and a faint smile tugs at the corners of her lips when she looks at him. But her smile turns to a groan when Xavier walks up and stands over her with his hands on his hips, and I can't help but smirk.

"What the fuck are we doing?" Xavier asks.

"Leaving so I can get back to my book." She holds up her textbook, waving it for emphasis.

"Nah." I lie back on the grass with my hands behind my head. "I think I'm gonna stay right here. Such a nice spot."

I close my eyes and smile, aware of Xavier snickering as he lies down beside me.

"Well, I'm going to study." Ophelia huffs, feigning indignation, but she isn't fooling anyone. We can all sense the excitement sizzling through her veins. She pretends to hate us as much as we pretend to hate her.

"I'll just sit right here and watch," Malachi says, and I open one eye to see him leaning back against the tree beside her.

It really is a nice spot, and we're all silent for a few minutes before there's another unexpected spike in Ophelia's heart rate. I open one eye and check to see if Malachi's doing something to her, but he's simply sitting as he was before, his eyes focused ahead of him rather than on Ophelia.

"Why does that always happen when you see that girl?" he asks.

Ophelia startles. "What? Who?"

Malachi turns to face her, and I roll my eyes at the concerned expression on his face. "That girl from your high school. The one you said was mean to you."

The slender curve of her throat works as she swallows. "Why does what happen?"

"Your pulse spikes. You feel…" His nose wrinkles. "Not scared, but uneasy. Anxious?"

"H-how do you know that? Can you read my mind or something?" She clutches her book to her chest like that might stop him if he could.

Malachi laughs. "Not exactly, sweet girl."

"So how?"

He sighs. "We can read people. If they're in close proximity, anyway."

She puts her book down, angling her body so I can no longer see her face. I close my eyes and listen, not only to the sound of her voice, but her racing heart and that intoxicating life-giving blood pumping through her veins. "How?" she asks him.

"We can hear your heartbeat and feel the vibration of your pulse. And we can sense emotion. Not all emotion, but when someone has a strong reaction to something, it changes their scent. So we can literally smell fear. Anxiety. Excitement."

"So you can smell my emotions?"

He laughs again. "Kind of. It's a whole lot of small things added together."

"But only if I'm close by?"

"Yeah. Unless we bite you."

I stifle a groan as an image of sinking my fangs into her juicy flesh sears itself in my brain like the negative of a photograph. What I wouldn't give to bite our little pyro.

"And if you were to bite me?" Her breathing grows faster. "Could you read my mind then?"

"No. But if we bite someone, we can tune into their emotions, their feelings and intentions, wherever they are."

"Like forever? Like you're in their head? How many people have you bitten?" Her voice goes up at least two octaves.

"Not in their head exactly. And we have to actively tune into them. Most people we wouldn't bother with because we have no need, but we could if we wanted to."

Find out more about the chick from high school, I tell him through our bond.

"And every time you see that girl, Penelope, you have the same intense reaction."

"Oh," she murmurs.

"What did she do to you, sweet girl?" His tone is soft, and I can picture him smiling at her in that reassuring way he has about him.

She barks out a harsh laugh. "You don't want to know."

"Try me."

I figure she must glance at Xavier and me because Kai assures her we've probably fallen asleep and that we aren't listening. Whether she believes him or not, she answers. "She was kind of a bully. Scratch that, a lot of a bully."

"Just to you or to everyone?" Malachi probes.

She pauses, then drops her voice to little more than a whisper. "Mostly to me. I grew up in foster care, so I moved a lot. There were always established friend groups at whatever school I went to. It was hard to fit in, and because I didn't have cool stuff, I guess it was easier to single me out."

"Sounds tough."

"Yeah, but I usually made a friend or two, you know? Except at Caulfield High. It was… I dunno. Penelope took a dislike to me on my first day when I accidentally spilled a smoothie on her new white sneakers. She demanded that I pay for new ones, but my foster parents didn't have that kind of money. I offered to save up and pay her back, but she said that wasn't good enough." She's quiet for a long moment, but just before I tell Kai to get her to keep going, she continues. "After that, she made it her mission to make my life miserable. She was queen bee, so nobody dared to risk being my friend. And I guess I could have lived with all of that, but…"

She stops talking, and the scent of her despair fills the space around her.

I open my eyes and watch Malachi put a hand on her arm. She shivers at his touch. "But what, Ophelia?" he asks.

"Then I got the part of Lady Macbeth in our high school production, and she wanted it. I guess I didn't realize how badly until opening night, when she humiliated me in front of the entire school."

The wave of shame that washes over her is so palpable I can taste it. I glance at Xavier, and he frowns like he felt it too.

"And after that there was a fire and they accused me of starting it and I got expelled and had to go to therapy and live in a group home." She vomits the words like she can't wait to be done with it all.

Malachi lets out a low whistle. "No wonder you hate her."

Ophelia sniffs and swats a tear from her cheek. "I never said I hated her."

"Then I'll hate her for you," Malachi says with a wink.

I roll my eyes before closing them again. He is so fucking soft for her.

15

Xavier

"So, you wanna come hang out at my place?" Floss giggles, fluttering her fake eyelashes at me and pressing her perky tits against my arm.

I nicknamed her Floss because she smells like the sickly-sweet strands of cotton candy and has a voice to match. Plus I can never remember her actual name despite having fucked her and fed from her several times in the three years she's been at Montridge.

But I'm not in the mood for cotton candy. I could maybe go for a cupcake though. I lick my lips, and Floss giggles harder, probably thinking I'm imagining eating her instead of the freshman with pink hair and vibrant blue eyes. Who, for some reason, I'm not allowed to bite.

I shake my head. "Can't. Got too much to do."

Her lower lip juts out. "Are you hazing the new Ruby pledges? We could hang out after! I'm supposed to be studying, but I…"

Ronan King, one of the commanders in charge of pledges for Onyx, walks by, following a girl around the side of the library. I tune Floss out, but it isn't Ronan I'm interested in. The girl he's following is Penelope Nugent, Ophelia's school bully. What the fuck does she want with him?

I brush past Floss, and I'm vaguely aware of her yelling after me as I jog toward the other side of the quad to get a better view of Ronan and Penelope. When they come into view, I find a space behind a tree that's a safe distance away.

Penelope leans on the outer wall of the library, Ronan's hand planted beside her head. She's smiling, her head tilted to the side, and although I can't see his face, over two hundred years of studying body language tells me they aren't flirting.

If anything, I'd say they're conspiring. Are they talking about my cupcake? I strain to read Penelope's lips, but Ronan's stupid forearm is in the way. Her eyes crinkle at the sides and her nose wrinkles, like she's super fucking pleased with herself. What the fuck are these two up to?

...

Axl scowls as I fill him and Malachi in on what I saw between Ronan and Penelope.

"Do you think it's a coincidence? Or something we need to worry about? If Ophelia is on the professor's radar, maybe she's on Onyx's too. And you know he said we can't let anyone else bite her either," Malachi says.

Axl shakes his head, his scowl deepening. "She's not our concern. We're supposed to monitor her, make sure other people stay away, doesn't mean we have to worry about her. We warn Ronan off if we have to, but we just keep doing what we're doing. Make sure she goes nowhere but classes, the library, and then back to her dorm. It's not like she's going to go looking for trouble at Onyx."

"We are talking about the same girl who barely flinched when she stumbled upon three vampires feeding from one of her classmates," I remind him. "The same girl who willingly walked into this house and has more questions than Alex Trebek."

Malachi snorts a laugh.

"Fuck," Axl grumbles. "So not only are we babysitting the pyromaniac, we need to keep an eye on Ronan and this Penelope bitch. Like we don't have enough to do babysitting pledges."

"How about one of us bites her?" Malachi suggests. "Then at least we can keep track of her emotional state. If she's planning something, there'll be a spike of anxiety or excitement or whatever."

Axl shrugs. "She's hot, right?"

"You can't fuck her though. Ophelia would be really upset," Malachi warns him.

Axl's eyes glint, and I lick my lips with anticipation. What better way to mess with Cupcake than to fuck her nemesis? This could actually be a whole lot of fun.

16

Ophelia

"Shh! I told you it's a secret," the girl whispers, her cheeks red with indignation.

Penelope makes an exasperated sound and flicks her long blond hair over her shoulder. We're standing in line in the dining hall inside the Commons, the one place I can't seem to avoid her, not even when I come outside of regular mealtimes like I did today. Thankfully, we don't have any classes together, but she's in here every time I come. It almost seems like it's her personal mission to make me as uncomfortable as possible. As I do whenever I'm near her, I feel her disgust for me emanating from her pores, and my skin prickles with anxiety from the moment I see her until she's out of sight again.

From the corner of my eye, I see her glance my way, her lip curled in a sneer. "Don't worry about *her*, she's nobody."

I drop my head and stare at the floor, shuffling as far away as possible without moving past the cash register while I wait for the employee to finish getting my order together.

"So tell me more about these trial things. They're full of hot guys, right?"

"Penelope!" the other girl admonishes.

Penelope laughs her snooty little laugh. "Relax, Madison, there's nobody here to hear us."

Rude bitch. Still, I want to hear more about the Trials, so I keep my gaze averted, pretending my boots are the most fascinating thing in the world.

"Yeah, well, I told you I'm not supposed to tell anyone," Madison whispers. "I could get Caleb in a lot of trouble."

Penelope drops her voice to a whisper now too. "If there is some kind of secret society Olympics full of hot guys on this campus, wild dogs couldn't keep me away. If you don't tell me, I'll just sniff them out like a piggy looking for truffles."

I stifle a snigger at the image that metaphor conjures and strain to hear Madison's reply.

She sighs dramatically before she answers. "Just meet me outside Urania Hall Saturday night at ten."

The employee comes back and shoves a brown paper bag at me. I snatch up my lunch and pay before hurrying out of the dining hall, my mind buzzing with questions about Trials and secret societies. And I'm so lost in my thoughts that I don't see him until I literally walk into—and subsequently bounce off of—his solid chest. I stumble backward, but he stops me, circling his strong fingers around my wrist. Goose bumps break out over my arm.

"Watch it, Cupcake," Xavier says, his lip curled in a faint sneer.

"S-sorry," I stammer, trying to wrench free of his grip.

He licks his full lips, flashing me a hint of his fangs. An unexpected and frankly unwelcome shiver of excitement runs up my spine, and he laughs. It's mocking and cruel, and my cheeks flush pink. I yank harder, desperate to get away from him.

He rubs the pad of his thumb over the pulse point on my wrist, and I swear my veins fill with electricity. "I can feel your blood racing through your veins, Cupcake. I bet you'd come in your pretty little panties if I bit you right now."

I squawk a feeble protest that only makes him laugh harder. "Let me go!"

He releases my wrist but continues to loom over me, fixing me with a fierce glare. His eyes smolder and darken like coal from the pits of hell, and he steps closer. His solid form is mere inches away, and the heat from his body warms me all over, enveloping me. The flush on my face races down my neck and chest, and his eyes follow the path before landing on my boobs. I suck in a shaky breath.

"You're hot," I whisper, by way of explanation for the heat spreading across my skin.

He licks his lips, his eyes still on my chest. "Thanks, Cupcake."

I roll my eyes. "I didn't mean... I expected vampires to be cold."

His gaze travels back up to meet mine. "Nope. Hot-blooded. Hot-tempered. Hot-as-fuck in every way."

"Humble too, huh?"

That earns me another dark laugh. He dips his head, skimming his nose along my jawline, and I remember what Axl said about vampires being driven by scent. And how I stink. My aroused flush turns to shame, and I shrink back from him.

His growl is low and deadly. "Watch where the fuck you're going in the future, Cupcake."

I draw in a shaky breath but lift my chin. "I could say the same about you."

He hisses, and his warm breath dances over my neck, causing my heart rate to spike alarmingly. It feels like time has stopped and there's no one in this entire world but him and me. And now my legs are trembling too. The space between my thighs is growing hotter and wetter with each passing second, and he's going to know.

"Tell me about the Trials," I blurt.

He steps back, his face a mask of confusion, and I take the much-needed opportunity to regain some self-control. "What do you know about the Trials?"

I shrug. "I heard someone talking about them is all."

His eyes narrow. "Who?"

I hesitate for a second, but then I realize I have no reason to keep Madison's secret, so I tell him what I overheard her saying to Penelope.

It's his turn to shrug. "Never heard of a Madison or any Trials."

A strange swell of contentment encompasses me at the knowledge that he doesn't know Penelope well enough to know her friend, but I don't buy his ignorance of the Trials for a second. "So there isn't one happening Saturday night, then?"

He grinds his jaw until the thick vein in his neck throbs. "You stay away from anything to do with any Trials, Cupcake. They're not the place for little girls like you."

Well, now I only want to know more. "But you just said you didn't know—"

He grabs my jaw tight, cutting off my sentence. Tears leak from my eyes. "You will forget what you heard, or I will make you forget." His dark eyes bore into mine so deeply I feel like he's piercing my soul. "Do I make myself clear?"

Not a chance in hell, I think, but I nod meekly.

"Words, Ophelia," he growls.

My breath gets caught in my throat. I don't think he's ever used my actual name before. "Yes!"

He lets go of my jaw and taps the side of my face with his palm. "That's a good little cupcake."

Before I can say anything else, he strolls off, and I stare after him, rubbing the ache in my jaw.

17

XAVIER

"This is her, right?" Axl nods at the blond with the high ponytail and the skintight white jeans striding past the library like she owns the goddamn place. She has a nice rack though, I'll give her that. Her face is a little pinched for my usual tastes, but I don't need to look at her face while I'm fucking her. Axl can take the front, and I'll take the rear.

I nod. "That's the one."

Don't you dare fuck her, Malachi warns us.

Just watch the pledges and let us do our thing, dickface, I fire back.

Axl rocks his head from side to side. "Are we double-teaming her?"

I flash him a smirk. I do fucking love him. "She sure looks the type."

"Then let's do this."

We walk toward her, planning to head her off at the end of the path, but as she grows closer, I get an uneasy feeling in my gut.

Something's not right about her.

His eyes narrow, and he gives me a subtle nod of agreement.

She's gonna taste so fucking bad, Axl. I can already tell.

I know. But let's just get this over with. One of us bites her and then we're done.

Well, as you constantly like to remind us, you're the oldest. So I think you should take one for the team. I nudge his arm. *Because I might barf if I have to drink her blood. She smells like...*

Like she has a little troll in her, he offers, and I bite back a laugh because our target is a few feet in front of us and she's eyeing us both like we're finger food at a troll buffet.

He shoots me a warning look before stepping forward and flashing her his best panty-dropping smile. She stops in her tracks, her eyes raking over his face and down his muscular torso, the outline of which can be seen clearly through his fitted white T-shirt.

"Hey there," she says with a sultry purr.

Axl flicks his sandy-blond hair out of his eyes. He's such a handsome fuck, and she's practically drooling. "Hey. I saw you in the dining hall earlier, right?"

She flutters her eyelashes, glancing between the two of us now. "Yeah."

"You were with some of the Onyx pledges?"

She pulls her bottom lip through her teeth. It's like she's trying to look sexy, but she just looks like an idiot. Maybe she is stupid, and that's why she's so mean to the curious little cupcake. She twirls the end of her ponytail between her thumb and forefinger. "I was with my friend. She's dating one of them."

I step forward and flash her a wink, and when her heart rate doubles, I can't hide my smile. She thinks my grin is for her and smiles back at me, displaying her perfect white teeth. This is going to be way too easy. "You're not dating one of them though, are you? Because we don't like them."

"No," she purrs. "I'm a free agent."

Axl tips his chin. "You wanna grab a bite?"

Smooth! I suppress another snicker.

He gives me a sideways glance. *Let's just get this over with.*

I couldn't agree more. Penelope Nugent is rotten to the core, and even the prospect of making the cupcake incandescent with rage isn't enough to make me want to spend time with her.

18

OPHELIA

"Dammit!" The girl sitting a few seats away from me pushes her long auburn hair out of her face as she shakes her pen and curses again.

"You want to borrow one of mine?" I ask her.

I brace myself, waiting for the sneer or eye roll that usually follows me attempting to spark up a conversation with anyone. But she smiles, and it lights up her pretty, lightly freckled face that reminds me of the models in makeup commercials. "Do you mind?"

I rummage through my pencil case and pull out a pen for her. "Not at all. I have dozens of them."

She reaches along the table and takes it from me. Holding it aloft, she eyes the unicorn pattern, and I cringe. I just turned nineteen; it's probably time for me to stop buying shit with unicorns on it. "Cute," she says with another smile. "Thanks so much. You're a lifesaver."

I smile back. "You're welcome."

She reaches across the desk again, holding out her hand. "I'm Cadence."

I take her outstretched hand. "Ophelia."

"It's so nice to meet you, Ophelia." She giggles. "I love your hair, by the way."

I unconsciously curl a strand between my fingers. "Thanks. I love yours too."

She glances at my history textbook. "History, huh? Are you in Professor Drakos's class?"

His name makes my pulse race. Or maybe it's the image of him striding into class with his battered briefcase. How he takes off his jacket and folds it neatly over the back of his chair. Before he rolls his white shirt sleeves up over his powerful forearms. Every single time. Does the man not own a short-sleeved shirt?

Calm down, Ophelia. Just because he's a hot vampire doesn't mean you have to geek out at the mention of his name. "Uh, yeah."

She pops an eyebrow. "He's hot, right?"

My cheeks flush. Hotter than the fiery pits of hell. "I guess so."

She lets out a dreamy sigh. "I swear I spent my entire first semester last year just drooling over him. It's a wonder I took any notes at all." She giggles again. "But if you have the same problem, let me know." She nods at my textbook and taps the side of her nose. "I took that same class last year, so I have all the inside knowledge."

"Thanks, Cadence. I'll keep that in mind."

She winks at me and goes back to her studying.

I go back to my textbook, pressing my lips together to suppress my giddy smile. It was one conversation—a brief conversation, at that. Nothing to get excited about. But it was a connection. The most positive one I've had with a person for as long as I can remember—other than Malachi, who's technically not even a person. And she thinks unicorns are cute, so she must be both intelligent and fun.

Maybe it's a sign that things are looking up for me.

...

Tipping my face toward the fading sun on my way back to my dorm, I smile. Today has been a good day. A guy from my algebra class jogs by, his shirt emblazoned with the Ruby Dragon logo, and I idly wonder where the guys are and what they're doing. I want to kick myself for giving them even a second's thought, but despite their annoying presence in my life, they at least talk to me. Aside from the girl I met in the library this afternoon, they're the closest thing I have to friends. And sure, that's totally pathetic, but I'm not going to think about that right now.

I round the corner and come face-to-face with Xavier. He smirks at me, and my deluded heart skips a beat at the sight. Stop it, Ophelia!

"Out for an evening walk, Cupcake?"

I roll my eyes. "That's allowed, right?"

He rocks his head from side to side. "You recall what happened the last time you went walking alone at night."

My eyes dart to the shadows of the building behind him. The same place I first met them. "Is... Are Axl and Malachi with you? Are you keeping watch?"

He shrugs. "Malachi is indisposed."

I peer over his shoulder. "But Axl's back there?"

"Run along, little girl, before you get yourself into a whole mess of trouble. Again."

I shake my head. "You guys are going to get caught dining on students one of these days. You do know that?"

His grin widens, and he inches closer, his large frame towering over me. "But you already know what happens to the people who catch us, Cupcake." His voice is deep and dark, and it makes goose bumps break out along my forearms, which only makes him laugh. I hate that they have the ability to read my body's reactions, especially since it seems to have a mind of its own around them.

"One day someone important could catch you."

He cups my jaw, tilting my chin so he can stare into my eyes. My breath hitches when he dips his head. "Are you not important, Ophelia?"

"You know I'm not," I whisper. "Now take your hand off me and let me get home."

"I can hear your heart racing, Cupcake. I think you like my hand on you." His husky tone goes straight to my core.

"I do not," I say, but even I hear how weak it sounds.

He laughs darkly and releases me. "Run home, little girl."

I huff out a sigh and brush past him, his psychotic laugh ringing in my ears. As I pass the building, I steal a glance at the shadows, unable to resist seeing who Axl's latest victim is. Regret strikes immediately, my heart laid bare with surgical precision as I fight to catch my breath.

I stand, rooted to the spot as though my limbs have become part of the earth, and watch him suck on *her* neck. Penelope claws at his thick sandy-blond hair and moans, her head tipped back and one leg wrapped around his waist as she grinds against him. I suck in a loud, stuttered breath that catches his attention. His fangs still in her skin, he winks at me.

Bastard!

I have no idea why my heart just shattered into a billion fragments and fell into the pit of my stomach. We aren't friends, Axl and I. Not even acquaintances. He's made it clear how much he despises me. But fool that I am, I clung to some ridiculous notion that our daily interactions had grown into something more than his desire to make my life hell.

It's now abundantly clear how wrong I was.

Tearing my eyes away from him, I force my feet to move. I want to run, but I refuse to allow him or Xavier the satisfaction of knowing how much they've hurt me. So I steadily put one foot in front of the other, tears blurring my vision and my legs trembling with each shaky step.

Axl bit Penelope. And he only bites people that he likes—people who smell good. Not people like me. What the hell is wrong with me? Like I even want to get bitten by a vampire! I'm not insane. Or am I?

A heaving sob rattles through my chest. I swallow it down and wipe my cheeks with the backs of my hands, furious at myself for crying. Except my tears aren't alone. Rain streams down my face and hammers onto the sidewalk below my feet, soaking through my clothes and streaking down my cheeks. So I let myself cry, safe in the knowledge that even if someone could see me under the blackening sky, nobody would be able to distinguish my tears from the freezing rain. Nobody but me anyway. Because each one burns my skin with a fresh wave of anger, shame, and sorrow.

I imagine that it must be heartbreaking to get hurt by someone who cares for you. But realizing you never meant anything to a person to begin with—that has to be the worst kind of pain there is.

19

OPHELIA

I pull up the hood of my sweater and step behind a tree, my eyes fixed on Penelope and Madison and a third girl I don't recognize. They giggle and each take a swig from a bottle of clear liquid, which I assume is some kind of alcohol. After a few minutes, they head in the direction of the woods at the edge of campus, and I wait until they're a safe distance ahead before I follow after them.

After we've been walking for about ten minutes, the sound of cheering and shouting drifts through the trees. Penelope and her friends squeal delightedly and pick up their pace, and I hasten my own steps to keep up with them. As we draw closer to the noise, the sense of excitement and anticipation grows thicker in the air. What are these Trials, and why the hell was Xavier so secretive about them? Like he has any right to tell me what I can and cannot do. Jerkwad!

The sound of the crowd gets closer until we reach a clearing in the woods lit by floodlights and surrounded by a ring of people. I move around the periphery of the crowd. Everyone's too focused on whatever is happening in the center to pay any attention to me. Finally there's enough of a gap between bodies for me to see the two guys they're all cheering for. Both shirtless, they grapple and throw punches, one wearing black shorts and the other wearing red. Is this one of the Trials? A fight?

I crane my neck to see more, then duck when I spot Malachi. He's also shirtless, his tattooed abs glistening beneath the harsh LED lighting. Objectively, I have to admit he is incredibly hot.

A loud cheer pulls my attention back to the two guys fighting, and I wince as the guy in red slams the other guy to the ground and continues raining blows on him even after he's stopped moving. Quick as a flash, Malachi steps into the clearing and pulls Red from Black with ease, dragging him to his feet and lifting his hand in the air, declaring him the victor.

Another chorus of cheers celebrates Red's victory, and someone rushes to Black's side before lifting his limp body and carrying him away. I stand on my tiptoes, trying to see where he's being taken. Is he dead?

"What's a pretty little thing like you doing out here all alone?" Hot breath dusts over the back of my neck, and my skin crawls like it's been overtaken by a million scurrying ants.

Before I can spin around and see who the creepy voice belongs to, a meaty hand is wrapped around my throat, pulling me back against a sweaty chest. I can tell from his solid form that he's a lot bigger than me, and I open my mouth to scream, but he squeezes my windpipe, cutting off the sound.

He presses his wet lips to my ear, and although his hold is too strong to escape, I try to twist away from him. "Shush now, sugar. Nobody will come to your rescue here." He runs his nose up the side of my throat and inhales. "You smell real pretty too."

Oh god. Not another vampire? "Let me go," I croak.

His maniacal laugh rings in my ears, and he slips his free

hand beneath my skirt and sinks his fingertips roughly into the soft flesh of my inner thigh. Tears leak from the corners of my eyes. "I don't think so, pretty thing. You see, you're trespassing in these woods tonight. Only those invited are entitled to be here, and anyone else, well, they're..." He licks a path along my jawline, and I shudder, disgusted. "Fair game."

"I do have an invite. I'm here with Malachi."

His low growl vibrates against my back. "Malachi Young?"

I close my eyes and hope this isn't going to bite me in the ass. "Y-yes."

"That makes what I'm about to do to you all the sweeter, pretty thing." His fingers dig harder into my thigh, traveling higher. I elbow him in the ribs as hard as I can. He doesn't even seem to register it, but at least he releases my throat and uses that hand to pin my wrists behind my back.

"Try to scream and I will rip out your throat before you can make a sound."

Having witnessed how quickly vampires can move, I don't dare scream. Still, I wriggle in his grip, but he's too strong for me. I try to squeeze my thighs together, but he pushes them wider, using his knee to drive them apart.

"Get your hands off me," I yell, but for the first time in my life, I feel afraid. Because now I have something to lose. My life only just got interesting, and now I'm going to die in these woods and nobody will even notice that I'm gone.

He grunts, dragging his fingers over my panties. "Oh, you even beg pretty."

I close my eyes, bracing myself for what he's about to do. I'm about to be raped and bitten and probably killed, and maybe if I think hard enough, I can—

A vicious roar pierces the air around us, and I'm hauled backward. I stumble to the dirt, and his hands are gone. Blinking, I look up and gasp.

Xavier shakes my attacker like a ragdoll with one hand wrapped around his throat. "What the fuck do you think you're doing? No one gave you permission to touch her."

The guy snarls, but he doesn't try to fight back. "I don't need your permission."

"Oh yes you fucking do." Xavier snarls back. "You ever touch her again and I will take your head. You understand me?"

What's happening? Why is Xavier defending me? This is too confusing.

"Yes," comes the reluctant reply.

With a guttural growl, Xavier throws the guy across the clearing and turns his fiery glare on me. "I told you not to come here."

I swallow hard. "I know, but I—"

"But you wanted to get yourself killed? Because that's what was about to happen."

I shake my head. "No. Of course I didn't."

"I should have let him do whatever the fuck he wanted with you."

"So why didn't you?" I demand, needing the answer to that question more than my next breath.

His nostrils flare as he advances on me with eyes so dark and dangerous that they make me shiver, and I vaguely register that my fear has been replaced with excitement. I should want to run, but all I want is for him to touch me. His hands on my body, mouth on my skin. He edges ever closer until he's towering over me, the toes of his shoes touching mine. He breathes hard. My knees tremble, and I'm thankful I'm still on the ground.

"Oh my god, Opeelia, is that you?" Her sarcastic bitch laugh rings through the air like a damn fire alarm. My heart sinks.

Penelope stumbles through the clearing. Madison follows, accompanied by the loser of the fight I witnessed, his arm draped around her shoulders. And if their presence wasn't awful enough, Axl comes into view. Of course, Penelope is with him. Because my life is just one crushing disappointment after another.

"What the fuck is *she* doing here?" Axl barks.

What is it about me that offends people so much? All I ever did was get a part in a damn play. Had I known getting the part over Penelope would have caused me so much heartache, I never would have auditioned. But I did, and here we are.

Again.

Penelope and her friend stare at me with disgusted expressions on their faces while Axl and Xavier simply exude raw, unrestrained anger. At least the guy from the fight seems too dazed to do anything other than look at me blankly. I stand and brush the mud and dirt from my legs. In my mind, I'm back on that stage on opening night, an entire auditorium full of people laughing and pointing at me. The memory is forever burned into my brain like the negative of a photograph.

Xavier bares his teeth. "I dunno why the fuck she's here, but she's not welcome. Get lost, reject."

Reject? But he just... I'm thankful for the sudden downpour because at least the rain hides the tears running down my face.

"Yeah, bye, *reject*." Penelope flicks her wrist, shooing me like I'm a stray cat begging for scraps.

Rolling my shoulders back, I force my trembling legs to carry me out of these godforsaken woods. It was stupid to come here. Stupid to think that things would be any different at Montridge and that I might find my place here.

20

Xavier

Malachi pulls on his T-shirt, and the wet material sticks to every inch of damp, muddy skin. The silver in his tattoos shimmers in the moonlight, and I drink in the sight. By the time we were finished dealing with Ophelia and Ronan, Malachi was already shirtless and fighting a junior from Onyx. Every single fucking year, some hotheaded asshole challenges my boy at Fight Fest, and every single year, they have their asses handed to them. Malachi is undefeated. Strong as a demon five times his size and smarter than every other person on this campus, with the exception of Alexandros.

However, as much as I love watching him fight, what happened with Ophelia and that prick, Ronan, still has me all kinds of tense. Fucking Kai's ass might be the only thing to relieve that pressure. I stretch out my neck until it cracks.

"Ophelia was out here? In the woods with Ronan?" he asks, his eyebrows pinched together.

"Not with Ronan by choice," I say, and the possessive growl that follows takes me by surprise.

He runs a hand over his shaved head. "Fucking prick."

"We'll deal with him," Axl says, tossing Malachi his sweatshirt before directing his attention to me. "But what the fuck was Ophelia doing here? I thought you warned her?"

I shrug. "I did. I guess she didn't fucking listen."

Malachi shakes his head. "Doesn't surprise me. She's the most curious and fearless human I know. And that's a dangerous combo."

"She's a pain in my ass," Axl grumbles. "She's going to get herself or one of us killed."

"It would be so much easier if we could just bite her." I release a frustrated sigh. "Make her forget what she saw here. Because I can guarantee this isn't the last time she'll get herself into trouble trying to find answers to all her questions."

"We should let the professor know and see how he wants us to deal with Ronan," Malachi says.

I groan inwardly. He'll be pissed that Ophelia saw what she did. But if he won't let us bite her, maybe it will be enough to convince him we need to keep her chained in our basement. My dick jumps in my pants at the thought of keeping her prisoner. Using her for whatever pleasures I want, whenever I want them. Breaking her beautiful body and her strong spirit. My fangs throb in time with my cock.

We head through the woods toward the house, walking at a steady pace rather than running. None of us are in any hurry to face Alexandros's wrath.

Malachi breaks the heavy silence. "How did you say she found out about tonight?"

"That Penelope bitch. Ophelia overheard her and her friend talking about it. And she was with some of the Onyx pledges tonight." It's not unusual for a few humans to find out about the Trials and sneak their way in. Onyx recruits are the usual suspects. The asshole jock types they attract like to brag to their girls about what they're doing. At this stage of the Trials, it looks like run-of-the-mill secret hazing shit and nothing more sinister, so we let it slide. It's only once a pledge has earned their way to the final trial that they have to start keeping secrets.

"So Ronan tried to bite her after you saw him with Penelope the other day." Malachi frowns. "Seems too much of a coincidence that this wasn't some kind of trap."

"Seems like."

He scowls at me like this whole mess is my fault. "I think we need to warn Ophelia that Ronan and Penelope are up to something."

"We're not her fucking besties, Kai," Axl grumbles.

Malachi sighs. "I never fucking said we were. But we're supposed to be keeping an eye on her, right? It wouldn't hurt to clue her in so she can protect herself."

Axl smirks at me and rubs Malachi's shaved head. "Aw, I think our boy has it bad for the pyro."

Malachi shoves him back with a snarl. "Fuck you! Just because I don't act like a complete jerkwad to her like you two assholes doesn't mean I have it bad. So she's smart and funny, even when she doesn't mean to be. And yeah, I like her, but stop busting my fucking balls about it. And stop being assholes to her."

"But fucking with her is so much fun." Recalling the tears running down her face earlier and the mud streaking her pale thighs, I sink my teeth into my bottom lip and groan. How badly I wanted to pin her down in the dirt and get mud all over her. Right there in front of Ronan too. How dare he touch what's mine.

"Ronan is going to fucking pay for messing with our toy," Axl growls, reading my mind without needing to hear my thoughts.

• • •

Alexandros is staring out the window in the den when we arrive back at the house. My gut twists in a knot. I hate to disappoint him, even though I seem to be pretty fucking good at it. Axl is the first he turned of our unit and therefore the golden child. And Malachi is the one he chose because he saw something in him that he wanted. He chose both of them, but he only turned me because Axl begged him for a brother. I will never be as good as they are—at least not in his eyes.

He doesn't turn around when we walk into the room. He could climb into our heads and read our thoughts if he chose to, but he doesn't ever do that. As callous as he can be, trust is a big thing for him. However, our emotions and our intentions are things he feels whether he wants to or not. He can dampen them, but he can't not feel them, and I'm sure he sensed the surge of anger Axl and I felt earlier, not to mention my crushing guilt over the whole situation with Ophelia and Ronan. What if I hadn't gotten to her when I did? I let Alexandros down. I should have made sure she didn't show up there. I should have done more.

"What the hell happened?" Alexandros barks.

"We won," Axl says. "Fourteen wins. Onyx only got nine and—"

"Not with the Trials, with the girl." He spins around to face us, anger radiating from him in waves.

Axl rolls his shoulders back. "Ronan got to her. She was on her own in the woods, and he—"

"What the hell was she doing in the woods tonight? Did I not ask you all to ensure she stayed out of trouble?"

"We didn't know she'd be there, sir," Malachi offers. "We had no idea."

"I did," I admit with a sigh. Malachi shoots me a look of concern, but he knows as well as I do that there's no hiding anything from the professor. "She asked me about the Trials, and I told her to stay away, but I should have made sure."

His nostrils flare, and his dark eyes bore into mine with such ferocity it makes me wince. "Yes, you should have."

"I doubt it would have stopped her, sir," Malachi says, risking our sire's wrath by defending me. "She doesn't exactly stay out of trouble."

"No, she finds it like a goddamn heat-seeking missile," Axl adds.

Alexandros is still scowling at me, and I glare back, daring him to say the words that I know must be in his heart. How he wishes he'd never turned me. How I'm a constant disappointment to him. Instead, he directs his attention to Axl. "Where is the girl now?"

Axl answers. "Back at her dorm. We went by there before we came back here to check, and she was sitting in her window."

"And Ronan?"

"I warned him to stay away from her. He ran off with his tail between his legs," I say.

Alexandros hums. Thinking.

I was so goddamn stupid for believing she'd do as she was told. She's the most infuriating human I've ever met. I should have chained her in our fucking basement. We *should* chain her in our basement. It's the only way to keep her from getting herself killed. I recall Ronan's filthy hands on her. The jealous, possessive vortex of rage that swelled in my chest and threatened to swallow me whole. Ophelia Hart is mine.

The professor takes a few steps closer, his eyes searching mine. "Did he question your warning? Give any indication that he wouldn't heed it?"

"I think he got the message, but it's worth repeating." Plus, I want to know exactly what's going on between him and Penelope.

Axl grunts his agreement, and Alexandros gives a single nod of his head, effectively dismissing us while giving his approval.

"I'm sorry," I tell him, but he spins on his heel and walks away, not bothering to acknowledge my apology.

21

Axl

"You saw the way he looked at me, right? Like I'm a constant fucking disappointment to him?" Xavier grumbles.

I roll my eyes. Not this again. "It's all in your fucking head, Xavier. He looks at us all exactly the same."

We stop in the front yard of Onyx Dragon house. Ronan and his sidekick, Simeon, will be skulking around here somewhere, licking their wounds after we annihilated them in the fight. I have no idea how they seem surprised to lose to us every single year when it's such a regular occurrence.

"You're imagining it," Malachi adds. "He was disappointed in all of us."

"But I was the one who fucked up, as usual. I was the one who should have stopped Ophelia from going to look for fight night. I should've—"

"Yeah, this time it was you, fuck-knuckle." I punch him in the arm. "But you have such a fucking chip on your shoulder."

He cracks his neck and grumbles something unintelligible. From the moment I met Xavier Adams on the streets of New York, I was fascinated by him. His blue eyes and sharp cheekbones—not to mention the dimples when he cracks a smile—are fucking mesmerizing. He has an easy confidence about him that draws people to him like a magnet. Yet inside, he harbors deep insecurities that color his every interaction with the world.

The moment I saw him, I knew I wanted him. What I didn't realize was what a giant pain in my ass he'd become. It makes sense that never feeling good enough for his biological father, who threw him out of the house at eighteen and turned his back on him, left an indelible mark on his soul. But I wish to fuck he'd get over it.

"There they are," Malachi tips his chin in the direction of the bushes planted along the side of the house. Sure enough, Ronan and his fellow commander, Simeon, stroll toward the front porch, the latter fishing a stray twig out of his long hair.

I flash Xavier and Malachi a grin. "Let's go have a chat, shall we?"

We're on them before they make it to the porch. I wrap a hand around Ronan's throat, and Xavier takes Simeon in a headlock, twisting his arm behind his back. They both snarl, and Ronan tries to wrench from my grip, but I hold him fast. "What the fuck do you want with the pink-haired girl?"

He struggles, and I squeeze tighter, my clipped fingernails digging into his flesh. "I'd rather not rip out your throat, fuck-knuckle, but I will if you don't answer me. And I will make it fucking hurt."

Simeon grunts a loud protest beside me, and Xavier twists his arm higher, warning him to quit his whining.

Ronan's lip curls and his body shakes with impotent rage. "She was alone. She smelled good, and I wanted to fucking taste her. Since when was that a crime?"

"Since she fucking belongs to us, you stupid fuck!" Malachi barks.

Ronan's eyes narrow. "How the fuck was I supposed to know that? She doesn't have your scent on her."

We would love nothing more than to mark Ophelia Hart with our scent and warn her off any other vampire within a thousand-mile radius, but that isn't an option. Ronan doesn't need to know that though. "She might not have our scent. Yet. But make no mistake, she is ours. Sometimes we like to play with our food before we eat." I lick my lips. "Makes them taste all the sweeter."

Ronan scowls, and I'm not entirely sure he believes me, but he wouldn't dare voice that aloud. We might hold the same rank, but that in no way makes us equal. I'm older, faster, stronger, and smarter. "Why are you all so interested in her anyway?" he asks instead.

"Because she smells like fucking cupcakes," Xavier growls.

"And she's different from the usual giggling idiots who throw themselves at us every single semester." Not that Ronan would understand our dilemma. He was blessed with neither good looks nor charisma, and all he knows is the chase. "We like the chase. Don't we, boys?"

Malachi and Xavier voice their agreement, but I keep my eyes fixed on Ronan. "So what were you doing with that new girl? Penelope?"

His frown deepens. "What?"

I shake him and bare my teeth. "You heard what I fucking said."

He tries to shrug, but my grip on his neck makes him look like he's having a muscle spasm. "She told me she hated the chick. Offered to suck my dick if I scared the shit out of her."

I search his face for a hint that he's lying. He's not the smartest. However, like most vampires, he's good at masking his feelings, and I have no desire to bite Ronan King and discover any of his secrets that way. "Just scare her? Or more?"

"I got the impression she would have been happy with more, but she didn't explicitly say that."

So Penelope wants the little pyro dead? But why? This has to be more than some petty high school bullying. The memory of the taste of her blood makes me gag, and I dip my head to mask my reaction from Ronan. Xavier was right, she did have a hint of troll about her, but she was fully human. Human and rotten to the core. There was something definitely not right. I clear my throat and focus my glare on Ronan once more. "Did she know what you were?"

"I dunno. She just said she'd heard I was the kind of guy who liked to fuck people up and said the chick with the pink hair would be sneaking around the woods during Fight Fest. That she'd be on her own and nobody would miss her if she didn't make it back to her dorm after."

I release my grip on his throat, having no reason to suspect he's lying to me. "Did Penelope say why she wanted you to target that girl in particular?"

Ronan stretches his neck and rubs at the reddened skin on his throat. "Just said she was a freak and she hated her. I thought if I saw her and she was easy prey, then it wouldn't be a big deal for me to bite her." He shrugs. "Then when I found her, she smelled so fucking good..." His tongue darts out to the corner of his top lip, but he snaps it back into his mouth at the furious sound that rumbles from my throat.

Yes, I know how she smells, you sack of shit. Even the memory of her scent has my mouth watering, chasing away the foulness of Penelope Nugent. Jealous rage snakes its way through my veins. "Yeah, well, I don't care how fucking good she smells. You stay the fuck away from her from now on. Anyone goes anywhere near her and I'll tear out their hearts and fucking eat them while they're still beating. Do I make myself clear?"

He scowls but nods his agreement, and I turn my attention to Simeon, who's still being restrained by Xavier. "And you?"

He glowers at me but seems to think better of arguing and mutters, "Crystal."

22

MALACHI

Stifling a groan when her unique scent floods my senses, I fall into step beside Ophelia. I want to bite her so fucking badly. And if I can't do that, kissing her would be a pretty close second. And then kissing would inevitably lead to fucking, and the thought of that makes my dick stiffen.

She keeps her eyes fixed firmly ahead, her jaw set with determination as she quickens her pace. Thunder cracks loudly in the sky above us as dark clouds roll overhead.

Undeterred, I match her step for step. "Where are you headed?"

She ignores me and I frown.

What the hell did you pair of numbnuts do the other night? I ask Axl and Xavier.

Oh, yeah. Xavier laughs. *Probably should have told you… Cupcake will be pissed today.*

What did you do? I keep my eyes fixed on Ophelia, who is actively turning her head away from me now.

What needed to be done to get her the fuck out of there, Xavier says.

I suppress a sigh and shake my head. *Fucking assholes.*

We heard that, Axl growls.

You were fucking supposed to.

Blocking out those two clowns, I focus all my attention on Ophelia. "You okay, sweet girl?"

She stops and spins on her heel to face me, her beautiful face incandescent with rage. "Don't you *sweet girl* me!" She stomps her foot, and the action makes her delicious tits jiggle in her tight tank top. My cock twitches. Fuck, she's so cute when she's pissed. I bite back a smile and let her go on chewing me out. Her delicate hands ball into fists by her sides. "No, I am not okay, you jackass."

I hold up my hands in surrender. "Whatever Axl and Xavier did Saturday night was for—"

"Don't you dare defend those heartless douchebags to me." She stomps her foot again, and my eyes roam to her chest. Fuck, I wanna sink my fangs into them like a pair of ripe peaches.

"Malachi!"

I press my lips together and allow my eyes to travel back up her slender throat, over her fluttering pulse to her bright blue eyes, which spark with indignation. "Sorry, but you are kinda cute when you're angry."

She gasps, her mouth open in shock and her cheeks as pink as her hair. "I... You... Stop trying to distract me. Stop pretending to be nice to me. You're a jackass just like your friends, and I want you all to leave me the hell alone." She turns and marches off in the direction of her dorm, her fine ass swaying hypnotically in her plaid miniskirt.

I watch her stomp away for a few seconds before I chase after her, catching up in three strides. "Not gonna happen, sweet girl."

She huffs. "What's not?"

"Leaving you alone."

She stops again and turns to face me, her eyes swimming with tears. "Why?" The word comes out as little more than a whisper.

"Why what?"

"Why won't you leave me alone? Why can't you all just leave me alone? I never..." She sucks in a heaving sob, and the sound feels like a blade slicing into my heart. "I've never hurt any of you." Tears run down her cheeks, and she swats them away with the back of her hand. Rain pours from the sky, soaking us in seconds, but she doesn't seem to notice. "All I want is to be left in peace. Why can't any of you let me just...be?" She shivers, her thin tank top plastered to her body. "You can all have Penelope and bite all the hot girls you please. I'll never tell a soul. I swear on my life. But please, please leave me alone, Malachi."

The plea in her voice breaks me. How the fuck has life made this incredible girl feel so worthless? And how do I even begin to tell her that she's not? I don't know how to explain to her that as sure as I know the moon orbits the earth, I know that she is everything.

She doesn't give me a chance to speak anyway. Spinning on her heel, she offers a quick glance at the dark sky and takes off, hurrying to escape the quad like the rest of the people around us. Except I have no doubt she's rushing to escape me rather than the rain. I stand rooted to the spot, unable to do anything but watch her leave.

23

Alexandros

Nicholas Ashe was once a formidable man and a prominent member of House Chóma until he betrayed his roots and his family's honor to further his own ends. He remains alive only because he was calculated enough to not technically break any oaths made to his father. Now he is the faculty head of Onyx and the sire of many of their vampire pledges. He is disliked by our counterparts at Lapis and Opal as fervently as he is by me. A fact of which he is well aware.

He sits behind the black mahogany desk in his office in the west wing of Zeus Hall, as far away from my own office as possible. "Alexandros, to what do I owe the honor of a visit from such an esteemed colleague as yourself? Surely you are not taking an interest in the Trials this year." His attempt at sarcasm has no effect on me.

I take a seat without it being offered and glare at him. "I am simply here to deliver a warning, Nicholas."

He puffs out his chest, making a show of bravado, but anxiety rolls from him like the mist pours down Montridge Peak at the end of every fall. "A warning?"

My jaw tightens and anger bristles beneath my skin. "Did I stutter?"

He sits up straighter, his eyes narrowed in suspicion. "About?"

I am taking a risk bringing Ophelia to his attention, but the greater risk would be to allow one of House Chóma or their Onyx sireds to bite her. "This is not the first time that I have had to warn your offspring to keep their hands to themselves, and one day I will not be around to intervene and stop my boys from tearing off your commanders' heads."

His answering snarl is an instinct, but one I refuse to tolerate. Leaning forward, I bare my teeth and growl, and he presses his lips into a thin line, sufficiently chastised. "The girl with the pink hair—Ophelia Hart. She belongs to my boys, and they do not share. Especially not with Ronan."

Nicholas's rage simmers ever closer to the surface, but he knows better than to challenge me. "If they have claimed her, she would have their scent, and he—"

"They have not claimed her. But make no mistake, she belongs to them. To House Drakos."

He sits back in his chair, running his tongue over his teeth. He is well aware that by invoking the name of my family, I am making it clear that she belongs to me, and he is far too cunning to risk my wrath. Still, he chooses not to back down entirely, pushing me as far as he dares. "What's so special about this girl that they want her so badly, yet they haven't laid claim to her?"

"I do not claim to know the inner workings of adolescent vampire minds." Keeping my eyes locked on his face, I pause and straighten my cufflinks. "But if you wish for peace to remain between the societies, you will ensure that nobody from Onyx touches the girl. Understand?"

The hesitation in his nod speaks to his reluctance, but I do not require enthusiasm. Only obedience.

"Ensure that they all know it too, Nicholas. Every one of them. Make them swear an oath if you must."

His lip curls again. "I'm sure that won't be necessary."

"I shall leave it to you to ensure their compliance in whatever way you choose." I push back my chair and suppress a smile when he flinches. Before I leave his office, I give him one last parting reminder of who holds all the power here. "If you would prefer it, I could have your father make you swear an oath."

He bangs his fist on his desk. "Get out of my office."

"Do not make an enemy of me again, Nicholas. Or I will exact my just revenge."

On my way back to my office, I do everything I can to banish all thoughts of Ophelia Hart. But, as the day goes on, the worry of what she might be and what that would mean for all of us lingers like an uninvited guest in my mind.

24

OPHELIA

Sitting in my usual seat in the second row of the lecture hall, I absentmindedly flick through the pages of my textbook. The sound of laughter makes me look up, and I stifle a groan as three girls make their way along the row to sit near me. The front couple of rows are usually for people like me who sit alone or are a little *unusual*, for lack of a better word. Not for the popular girls, which these three clearly are. Being an outcast all my life, I can tell.

One of them sits beside me and smiles. "Hi."

"Hey." I offer a faint smile in return.

Her friends sit too. Each of them gives me a quick wave and a smile, and I offer an awkward wave in return. They chatter among themselves, and I tune them out, taking out my battered copy of *Wuthering Heights* and getting lost in the words of Emily Brontë. After a few minutes, the girl next to me nudges my arm. "Hey, you know her, right?"

I look up from my book and shake my head. "Know who?"

She tuts. "Penelope Nugent. I heard you went to the same high school."

"Yeah." I shrug, feigning disinterest. "We weren't friends though."

Her nose wrinkles. "No? Well, I heard she's a bitch."

That's putting it mildly, but I don't say that. Instead, I give another shrug and go back to my book, but the girl beside me is undeterred. "So was she?"

I glance up again. "Was she what?"

She rolls her eyes. "A stone-cold bitch? Because she's still giving off those vibes, you know what I mean?"

Not sure what to say, I nod.

"So you know, right?"

"I guess, yeah," I admit, even as uneasiness builds in my gut.

The second girl peers over her friend's shoulder. "Yeah, a bitch, right?"

If only so they will stop talking to me about Penelope Nugent and let me get back to Cathy and her tortured soulmate, I agree with a nod and a polite smile.

The three of them laugh but don't say anything more to me. Grateful to be done with the conversation, I return to my book and barely suppress a groan when the girl next to me nudges my arm again. "Of course, I also heard that she was actually kinda cool and it was really this freak who made everyone think she was a bitch when she wasn't."

Icy fingers of dread curl around my heart, and when I look up again, the friendly smile has disappeared and she's glaring at me like I'm her mortal enemy.

"This freak peed herself on stage in front of the entire school, and then she tried to say that poor Penelope threw the pee on her. Can you imagine that, freak?"

Shame and anger wash over me, threatening to take me under with the force of their fury, and I fight back the urge to release all my pent-up rage and punch her in the mouth. I glance at the door, ready to bolt, but as I go to gather my things, Professor Drakos walks in.

I close my eyes and remind myself that I can't afford to keep skipping this class. I've already missed over a week because I couldn't bear to face him and be reminded of anything to do with those three Ruby jackasses. Sure, I have a trust fund paying my tuition, but Montridge still has GPA requirements. If I flunk out of here, I have no future. When I reopen my eyes, his dark gaze is locked on my face. A spark of warmth flares in my chest.

A sudden boldness infuses me and sweeps away my insecurities. These girls have nothing better to do with their time, and they want to make me feel like a loser? I roll back my shoulders and turn to the girl beside me. "Well, I guess it's a good thing that I don't give a single sliver of a fuck what your little group of gutter rats thinks of me."

Without waiting for her to respond with whatever vitriol she intends to spew next, I turn back to the front of the class and watch the professor roll up his shirt sleeves. Taking several deep breaths, I tell myself that I'm okay. As long as he's here, I'm okay.

I have no idea why I believe that and zero evidence to base it on, but somewhere inside the deepest part of me, I know without a doubt that it's true.

...

After my last class of the day, I head straight for my dorm, unable to stand the thought of being around people for a moment longer. When my phone dings, I consider leaving it for tomorrow but remember that I'm expecting an email about the psychology paper due next week.

But the message in my inbox is from Dr. Underwood, my geology professor, and my heart sinks. I didn't even know field trips were a thing in college. I scan the body of the message for the details. Apparently, we're visiting the crystal caves a few miles down the river from campus tomorrow evening, and it's mandatory. The only bright spot of the whole email is the bus route information he provided, so at least I won't have to throw myself at any of my classmates' mercy.

Who plans a field trip on a Thursday night? Maybe I could tell the professor I already have plans that I can't cancel. I'm pretty sure sitting in my dorm alone eating Cheetos and watching superhero movies is vital to my college education. With a loud groan, I flip over and bury my face in my pillow.

25

ALEXANDROS

As soon as I step foot inside the house, the sound of the boys arguing in the den rings in my ears. I close my eyes and draw in a deep breath, trying to ease the tension that feels like it is solidifying my muscles. Their noise may not be responsible for said tension, but it has not helped.

No, this started earlier while I was teaching class. The class during which I felt Ophelia Hart's eyes on me the entire time, and even now my skin prickles at the mere memory of the heat of her gaze. The girls sitting next to her looked at her with such disdain, and it took all my resolve not to tear all three of them to pieces after feeling the anguish radiating from Ophelia when I stepped into the lecture hall. She drew my attention immediately, as she always does. And then, as keenly as I felt her hurt, I experienced her calm when her eyes locked with mine.

I swallow down my unease and step into the chaos of my three deviant offspring bickering about the Trials. Sensing my presence, they fall quiet.

Axl releases Xavier from a headlock and sits down on the sofa while the latter brushes his thick dark hair back from his face. He's just as captivating as he was the day we found him stealing from a bakery, practically starved. As skinny as he was, his high cheekbones and turbulent blue eyes stopped me in my tracks.

"Hey, Professor," Malachi says with his usual smile.

I only nod in greeting. "How are the pledges faring in the Trials?"

"Last night went well. We won."

I shrug off my jacket and remove my cufflinks. "Unsurprising. We always win the Maze. How many fell?"

Malachi leans forward. Hands clasped between his thighs. "Two of ours. Four from Onyx, and another three across Lapis and Opal."

I slip my cufflinks into my pocket before rolling up my shirt sleeves. We have so few pledges across all four societies, we cannot afford to lose so many. Whilst the honor of House Drakos and the Ruby Dragon Society is paramount, it does not fare well for all of vampirekind when so many from the other societies fall. I pinch the spot between my brows. "So how many pledges do we have left?"

"Twenty-six," Xavier answers.

"And how many do you expect to make it to the end of the Hunt and be suitable for recruitment?"

Axl tucks a cushion behind his head and leans back against the arm of the sofa. "I'm guessing about nine."

I frown. That is a higher percentage than normal, which is at least some good news. "More than a quarter?"

Xavier nods. "We had fewer pledges this year, but the standard was up."

"Do any of them stand out?"

Axl's throat works as he swallows. "Why? Are you going to turn one yourself this year?"

Unease rolls off the three of them, and I have no need to read their minds to know what they are thinking. For decades, pressure has been applied from House Drakos for me to turn some of our pledges for my own, but I have no desire to have any more beings dependent on me than the three men sitting in this room. I leave the turning of new vampires to my cousins, and very occasionally, if one pledge shows exceptional promise, my brother. And on the rare occurrence they show the kind of unparalleled cruelty that runs in the veins of House Drakos, my father. Many of my kind turn as many as possible, desiring an army of sireds to protect their own immortality. But the truth of it is, I would be happy to die tomorrow. Only these boys stop me from breaking an oath that would bring about that end. And when they are gone, so shall I be.

I shake my head. "You three give me more than enough trouble without adding more to our unit."

Relief washes over them, and I am grateful that they, too, are content with the status quo. Perhaps I have been cruel in not allowing them a bigger family unit, but I barely have room in my head for these boys, and far too little in my heart. There was once a time... I bring a wall of granite crashing down on those memories, ones that lurk far too close to the surface these days for my liking.

I clear my throat. "Are you still keeping a close eye on the girl?"

Malachi answers first, his delight palpable. "Yeah. We're still watching her."

Her effect on them is not unnoticed, and I wish there was more I could do to prevent it, but the risk of them getting too close to her is far outweighed by the risk of another discovering what or who she might be. "And Ronan is keeping his distance?"

Xavier nods, but Axl speaks. "This Penelope chick is trouble though."

I am aware there were issues between the two of them in high school, but I would not have expected that to have followed them here. Rarely do students, even those who blossomed under the glory days of homecoming and prom, carry such trivial matters with them to college. I motion for him to continue.

"She hates Ophelia. Like really hates her. And she's up to something. I can feel the rage inside her."

Mere high school rivalry, or is it something more? My mind races with possibilities. "You bit her?"

Axl nods. "So I could keep closer tabs on her. Something's definitely off with her."

I arch an eyebrow. "Then perhaps you need to do more than bite her."

Xavier holds up his cell phone. "We're tracking her phone too. If she goes to Ophelia's dorm, the Onyx House, or anywhere suspicious, we'll know."

"If she becomes more of a problem, you know how to deal with her." I catch the way their eyes light up at the prospect. "*Only* if she becomes a problem that cannot be dealt with another way." The last thing I need to be dealing with is smoothing over a human death or drawing attention to Montridge for any negative reasons. The university frowns upon the killing of their kind, and with good reason. Whilst they are often chosen because they are considered easy prey, the university ensures that they graduate alive and without any lasting damage. Thereby ensuring a healthy and constant supply of fresh food for the vampire food chain.

"How long do we have to keep doing this?" Xavier asks. "Babysitting this girl and not being able to bite her? Because if we could just—"

"You will not be biting her," I snap. "Ever."

He slumps back in his seat with a frustrated grunt.

"You will continue to monitor her for as long as I tell you to." The truth is, I have no idea what my next step is or how long I can expect them to keep this girl out of trouble when she is so intent on finding it for herself. Nor why I am so desperate to.

Except that—in my heart—I know exactly what she is.

I close my eyes and concentrate, searching for the one man I can talk this through with. It takes me only five seconds to find him.

I need to talk to you.

His reply comes swiftly. *Of course, brother. I shall be there as soon as I can.*

...

This place has changed not a bit. Still smells of ink and parchment. Giorgios's voice resounds in my head, and I look up to see him weaving his way through the shelves of the old library, the one deep in the bowels of Zeus Hall.

"Why would an ancient library need to change, brother?" I give him a brief hug before pulling out a chair for him.

He glances around and takes a seat. "It need not change. It was not a complaint. I find it nice to have some familiarity in a world intent on changing."

"Well, it is nice of you to visit. How long has it been?" I tilt my head as I take a seat across from him. "Seventeen years?"

He arches an eyebrow. "Sixteen, and you know it."

"Close enough."

"Is it my fault that you choose to hide out in these old university buildings rather than face the real world?"

Annoyance prickles at my skin. "Not hiding out. Securing the future of our species, Giorgios."

"And that would be admirable, brother, if you ever permitted yourself to leave these grounds. If you experienced any of what life has to offer."

I run a hand over my beard and sigh. "I am over two thousand years old. I figure I have experienced enough of this thing called life to last me an eternity."

His laugh brings back too many bittersweet memories. Even without our bond, he must sense my sorrow because he changes the subject. "So, tell me why you asked me here. I cannot recall the last time you needed my help. Or at least *admitted* that you needed my help."

I glance around the almost-empty library. Built into the bedrock of the mountain, it is reserved for faculty and is rarely used. The library is protected by demon magic and is impenetrable. Even a bond cannot be felt in here. The secrets of millennia have been shared and kept within these walls, and I trust nobody else in the world with what I am about to discuss with my brother.

"I need you to tell me that I am not crazy."

His blue eyes narrow. "You are the least crazy man I know, Alexandros."

I scrub a hand through my hair and rest my forehead on the table for a few seconds before looking into his reassuring face. "So tell me why I am having such ludicrous notions."

He edges closer, his forearms resting on the table between us, hands clasped tightly. "What kind of notions?"

"There is a girl. No, a woman." I shake my head, recalling her sitting in the front row of my class today. How drawn I always am to her. How her essence calls to my soul like no other ever has before.

"Alexandros, are you falling in love?" He grins at me.

I roll my eyes. "Please, brother. Refrain from such absurdity."

He looks visibly surprised by my refutal, like he actually thought I dragged him halfway across the world to tell him that I am in love. "But I thought I felt a little…" He clears his throat. "Passion?"

I have been thinking about *her* a lot. The only woman I have ever chosen to bond with, and therefore the only one I will ever be capable of loving. Perhaps that is what he felt. But passion would not be a word that I would associate with what I felt for her. Our love was tamer than that. Gentler. "This is about something else."

"The girl?"

"Yes. The girl. She..." I run my tongue over my teeth. Saying this aloud makes my ridiculous notion somehow more likely to be real, and I am unsure that I feel ready for that. But I would be surprised if I ever felt ready, and he is the one man I can share this with. He is also brutally honest. Our father taught us well. "My boys brought her home one night. Her scent—" The memory of that first encounter is as fresh in my mind as the day it happened. "She smelled familiar. She smelled like...like one of them, Giorgios."

He frowns.

"It rains when she feels sad."

His Adam's apple bobs. He opens his mouth, but I continue before he can speak.

"She started a fire that burned down an entire building. No trace of accelerants was found, and she walked out without a mark on her skin."

"Alexandros." He drops his voice to a whisper and leans as close as he can with the table between us. "Are you really saying that you think she is one of them?"

"No." I shake my head, adamant. "No, that is impossible. Their entire line was erased from existence."

Giorgios pinches the spot between his brows. "If an elementai had been born, then we would know. Our father would know. There would be no hiding that kind of power. Not from him."

I take a breath before I tell him my other suspicion. "I think someone bound her powers."

He recoils. "What? That practice died out so long ago, and with good reason. Why would you think that?"

"Because whatever or whoever she is, she has power, Giorgios. I can sense it. I can smell it like lightning in a storm cloud. But she has no idea."

He shakes his head, his jaw slack as he digests the insanity of what I am suggesting. "But there are so few capable of binding powers. Nobody but the Danraath witches, and they are healers."

"I know, brother. It makes no sense." The Danraath all but died out with the elementai. Those who remained retreated to Europe, and their line has lived in near solitude since.

Giorgios leans back in his chair, his blue eyes twinkling with unsuppressed excitement while he works through what I just told him in his usual methodical way. I might be the one hiding myself away within the walls of this ancient university, but my brother is the scholar. He looks so much like our mother, who with mastery over air and water, was one of the most powerful elementai who ever lived. Still, even she was not strong enough to withstand the armies of witches, warlocks, and wolves that came for her. The elementai never stood a chance. Grief threatens to drown me, but I hold it back, closing the dam in my mind before it can take hold. Now is not the time for sentiment or emotion.

"You were right to summon me here, Alexandros," he finally says. "This girl of yours is most definitely worth keeping a closer eye on."

"Do you think she could be a demon? She is no witch, and she's certainly not a wolf. It is unusual for a demon's powers to be suppressed in such a way but possible, no?"

His brow furrows. "Why would you think she is a demon? Does she smell like a demon?"

Because I am grasping for any other explanation. Because even as the thought of her being one of them lights a fire in my veins that I assumed had long been extinguished, I want nothing more than for it to be impossible. "No," I admit. "But perhaps there is some witch in her blood somewhere and that is what's behind her unique scent. The fire magic would be more consistent with demons." Still grasping. Some of the most powerful elementai have possessed fire magic, but I am not ready to face that truth. Not yet.

"I do not think she's a demon, Alexandros. I think you know exactly what she is or you would not be seeking my counsel.

But I also understand why you are unwilling to face your true suspicions." His blue eyes soften. "So I am willing to let you live under the illusion that she is not what you fear she is for a while longer. But she must be protected at all costs. If you bond with her—"

I slam my fist onto the table. "I have no intention of bonding with her, or with anyone, Giorgios." I snarl, my fangs bared.

He continues without flinching or any visible reaction whatsoever. "Our father must never learn of her existence."

On that, we are in absolute agreement. Whatever her power, she is something different. Unique. And even if I will not allow myself to believe in the impossible, it has brought me a measure of comfort to have shared the burden of Ophelia Hart. The enigma who has burrowed her way under my skin like a splinter.

26

OPHELIA

I glance around the empty parking lot, certain this is where Dr. Underwood said for us to meet. A feeling of unease settles over me, but I breathe a sigh of relief when a lime-green Dodge Charger turns in and is followed by a second car. I shield my eyes from the glare of the headlights but still can't make out the features of the person who climbs out of the passenger seat of the Charger until they get closer.

My stomach lurches. God, how could I have been so stupid?

"Hi, Opeelia." Penelope says my name in her annoying singsong voice, and it's like nails clawing down a chalkboard. I wince and take a step back, noting the guy standing beside her, preening in his football jersey and backward hat. Must be the driver of the flashy car and, if I had to guess, her latest boy toy.

"What do you want, Penelope?"

"I heard you were talking shit about me, Pee-pee. Telling people what a horrible bully I was to you back in high school." She tilts her head and juts out her bottom lip, looking like one of those creepy sad clowns playing it up for an audience.

Dammit. I should have known this was a setup. "I just told people the truth."

She lets out a shrieking laugh. "That you're a freak and a loser who burned down our whole school?" The people from the other car come to stand beside her. I recognize Madison and her boyfriend—the quarterback who lost the fight in the woods—but not the other guy.

All five of them advance toward me, and I have nowhere to go but back toward the steep edge of the riverbank.

"What does it matter to you? Like you said, I'm a freak and a loser. Nobody ever listens to me anyway."

She steps closer, her upper lip curled. "You fucking disgust me."

"Why do you hate me?" I shout, my hands balled into fists. "What the hell did I ever do to you?"

"You came to *my* school and took *my* role. And besides that, I just don't like you, Opeelia. You're weird and you're a freak. A *reject*."

It hurts me more to remember Xavier's words than it does to hear hers now. "You're such a bitch, you know that?"

She snort laughs, her tiny nose scrunched up like she smells something rancid.

"What the hell did you bring me here for?"

"To finally do the world a favor and get rid of you for good, Pee-pee." She sings the insult that's haunted me for the last two years.

"It was a part in a goddamn play." I glance at the steep ravine behind me. "You're going to kill me over a part in a stupid play?"

She continues to advance, her cheap, cloying perfume invading my nostrils. "You know my dad blamed me for what happened at school. He took away my credit card for a whole year and stopped me from going to parties. I missed out on junior prom with Pete Hill." She stomps her foot. "Goddamn junior prom!"

"Yeah, well, I didn't get to go to junior prom either. You know, on account of me being expelled from school after you made it look like I set an entire building on fire!"

Her lips twist in disgust. "My daddy always felt sorry for you. I wanted that part to make him proud, and *you* took it! He never looked at me the same again after that. Because you had to go and act like a spoiled little bitch."

I shake my head. Penelope's dad was a teacher at our high school, and he was always nice to me, but not in a way that would justify the level of vitriol she has directed at me since the day I met her.

I scan the parking lot for an escape, but there isn't one. My heart beats so fast I can barely hear anything except for rushing water from the river below. The screech of tires from a third car racing into the parking lot reaches me, but I don't bother to look. More of Penelope's friends wanting to see her greatest achievement, I'm sure. But her face twists in confusion, and she looks behind her, saying something to her boyfriend who holds out his hands like he has no idea what's going on.

The engine of the new car cuts off, and the headlights dim. The sound of breaking glass follows, and the headlights of the other two cars go black, leaving us with only the fading light of the sun. Taking the group's distraction as an opportunity, I look around again for a way to escape. Fast-moving shadows blur toward me, freezing me in place. A scream is cut off abruptly by the sound of tearing flesh and breaking bones.

I need to run. Now. But before I can take a step, a pair of strong arms bands around my shoulders, a unique but familiar scent washing over me.

Sighing with relief, I find myself melting into Malachi's solid warmth. My eyes are adjusting to the dim light, and I can make out Axl and Xavier. They're holding Penelope and her jock boyfriend in the air by their throats.

Axl slams the guy's head back against the hood of the Charger, and I wince at the sound it makes. Axl's fangs glint in the light of the dying sun as he leaps on top of the jock like a hungry lion making a meal of a zebra. My heart stutters when he dips his head and shakes it like a rabid dog, ripping out the other guy's throat.

My hand flies to my mouth as bile burns my esophagus. I want to yell at them to stop, but my mouth can't seem to form any words.

Malachi presses his lips to my ear, and as though he's reading my mind, he says, "They were going to kill you, sweet girl."

I shiver in his arms, and he holds me tighter. In my heart, I know he's right, but it doesn't make this any easier to watch. Penelope's crying snaps me out of my fog. Xavier has dragged her close enough that I can see her face etched with fear and horror, his giant hand still wrapped around her throat.

He shakes her like a rag doll. "Apologize to her," he growls.

"I-I'm s-sorry," she rasps.

Axl roars and jumps off the bloody corpse of Penelope's boyfriend. He goes to his car and switches on the headlights, bathing the whole scene in a stark white light. My stomach lurches. The parking lot is strewn with the remains of four mutilated bodies.

Malachi presses a hand over my heart. "Just breathe, Ophelia. You're okay."

His voice feels like a warm blanket. Penelope's cries grow louder. Fat tears stream down her pink cheeks. Xavier laughs and presses his face close to hers, taunting her. "I see you've had yourself a little accident, Penelo*pee*." I follow his gaze to the yellow stain on the crotch of her white jeans.

"What did you want with Ronan King?" Xavier barks.

"W-what?" Penelope blinks rapidly.

"Who is Ronan King?" I whisper.

Malachi presses his lips to my ear and shushes me, so I suppress my curiosity and listen.

Xavier shakes her again. "Why were you talking to Ronan?"

"H-he's just... Someone slipped a note into my dorm room telling me he could..." She sucks in a shaky breath. "He'd help get to... That he could deal with Ophelia."

"So you wanted Ophelia to overhear you talking about the Trials? Was the plan for Ronan to bite her and kill her so you wouldn't have to?"

Tears race faster down her cheeks. "Y-yes," she snivels.

"Who the hell is Ronan?" I ask again, unable to keep my thoughts to myself any longer.

Malachi sighs, his warm breath dusting over my skin. I guess he knows better than to shush me again, given that I appear to be incapable of doing so. "He's one of the leaders of Onyx Society. Basically their version of us."

I press my lips together and don't ask anything more, leaving the interrogation to Xavier and Axl, who don't take their eyes off Penelope.

"And did he have any part in this?" Axl asks with a vicious snarl.

"N-no. He r-refused."

"But why do you want me dead?" I demand. It makes no sense. "You're right. I'm nobody. Even if you hate me, this is..." I look around the parking lot that looks like a scene from a slasher flick. "I don't understand."

"People like you will never understand," she spits, sneering at me.

Anger prickles beneath my skin. "People like me? Rejects?"

Xavier's knuckles turn white as he tightens his grip on her neck, and he presses his face close to hers, his fangs on full display. "Who left the message under your door?"

"I d-don't know." She's back to trembling with fear. "It was there when I came back from class."

A rumbling growl rolls out of Xavier's throat. "I think you do know."

"I swear I don't. Puh-please, let me go," she whines.

FORGED IN BLOOD

Xavier glances at me. "What do you think, Cupcake? Should we let her go?"

I take in the tears running down her face. The raw fear in her eyes as they bore into mine, silently pleading with me to spare her. And a part of me can't help but think she deserves every second of this. This girl has made my life a living hell, and she wants me dead. I suspect it will only be a matter of time before she pulls something else, but I still can't let him do this. Not for me. I nod. "Let her go."

"You see how merciful she is, Penelo*pee*? Such a kind soul, our little Ophelia." He hoists her into the air, and her feet dangle a foot above the ground. She claws at his arms, but her struggle is futile. "Isn't that right, boys?"

Malachi and Axl hum their agreement.

Xavier grins wickedly. "Too bad we're not." With a single flick of his wrist, he tears her throat out and lets her lifeless body drop to the ground.

I freeze. My feet take root in the ground, and my mouth falls open on a silent scream. My limbs tremble. My stomach rolls. I'm going to be sick. Placing my hand over my mouth, I swallow it back down. "Oh my god." The words are a mere whisper, but they seem loud in the quiet of the night.

Xavier crouches down and wipes his hands on Penelope's blouse. "No god here to save you, Cupcake."

"You just..." My eyes dart around the parking lot. More bile burns the back of my throat. "You killed them all."

"They were about to do the same to you," Xavier says with a shrug. "Not with quite the same flair as we pulled off, but they had no intention of letting you walk away from here tonight."

"You can't know that." I insist.

"*You* know that, Ophelia. Come on, sweet girl." Malachi tucks my hair behind my ear. "What the hell do you think they had planned?"

"M-maybe they just wanted to scare me?"

Axl wipes the blood from his shoe on Penelope's jeans. "You're not afraid of anything, Pyro. Pretty sure they knew that too."

"I'm afraid of what you just did," I admit, my knees still trembling.

Xavier grins. "Well, you should be afraid of that."

I swallow down the horror and guilt that burn in my throat. Despite everything that just happened, I am grateful that they saved my life. "Thank you," I murmur, although thanking Axl and Xavier, two men who have tormented me since the moment I met them, feels completely unnatural.

Axl dismisses my gratitude with a shrug. "We were in the right place at the right time."

"We knew she was up to something nasty," Malachi says, his breath warm against my neck.

"Wait. What?" How could they possibly know that?

Axl shoots Malachi a stern look. The kind that makes Xavier let out a psychotic laugh and Malachi mutter something unintelligible.

I step out of Malachi's embrace and turn so I can see all three of them. "How did you know she was up to something nasty?"

Axl shakes his head. "Let's get the fuck out of here." He turns to leave, but I refuse to follow until I have answers.

"No. How did you know she was planning something?" And then I remember what Malachi told me about vampires being able to tune into the emotions of the people they've bitten if they choose to. Axl must have been monitoring Penelope. Which means he likes her enough to tune into her thoughts.

My heart sinks, and I'm filled with shame for believing for even one second they were being kind to me because they like me. But if he likes her, why did he just…

My head swims with confusion. I need to get away from them and sort through the jumble of thoughts and emotions clouding my senses. I shrug out of Malachi's arms and walk away from them. It's not fully dark yet. I'll take the bus back.

"Where the hell are you going?" Axl calls after me.

I ignore him and carry on walking, but a second later he and Malachi fall into step beside me. "Where are you headed, sweet girl?" Malachi asks. "Our car is the other way."

Tears burn my eyes, but I blink them away. "I can get the bus."

Axl grabs my forearm, stopping me in my tracks. "Get in the fucking car, Ophelia."

I tip my chin up and glare at him. "Why her? Of all the girls who fawn all over you, why did you have to like her?"

Axl blinks at me, but it's Xavier's sadistic laugh that rings in my ears, and I realize he's standing with us now too.

"What the hell is so funny?" I bark at him.

He holds onto his side, still laughing like the psycho he is. "You think Axl liked that stuck-up bitch?"

Malachi's face wrinkles like he smells something foul. "He took one for the team biting her."

I'm so bewildered. I stare at Axl, hoping his expression might give me some clue as to what's going on here, but he simply glares at me. "You don't like her?" Well, of course he doesn't, he just allowed Xavier to claw out her throat. But I still don't understand what's happening.

Xavier presses his lips close to my ear. "He said she tasted even worse than she smelled," he says, his hot breath making me shiver.

I blink, my mind swimming with questions and my brain fogged with confusion. But Axl's expression only grows angrier. His jaw tics as he glares at me. "So why did you bite her?" I demand.

"Let's get the fuck out of here," he growls.

I shake my head. "Not until you tell me what's going on. You hate me, but you showed up here tonight and stopped whatever Penelope was about to do. Why? And why did you bite her?"

Xavier snickers. "He only wishes he hated you, Cupcake." He flicks his tongue over his fangs, which are still on display, and eyes me like a prime rib, giving me an idea to make Axl talk. Or squirm. Either is fine by me.

I arch an eyebrow. "Do I smell bad too?"

Xavier grins. "You smell sweeter than cupcakes, baby. I'd bite you in a heartbeat if it wouldn't get me in a whole heap of trouble."

Malachi groans. "So fucking tempting."

Well, now I have even more questions, but first, Axl. "But he said that I stink." I jerk my thumb at the wall of vampire muscle towering over me, vibrating with anger.

Xavier grins at Axl. "You told her that?"

Malachi scoffs. "Such a fucking liar."

Axl snarls and stalks toward their car, calling out over his shoulder, "Go get the fucking bus if that's what you want to do."

"Why did he bite Penelope?" I ask the two remaining vampires.

Xavier curls a lock of my hair between his fingers, that wild-ass smile still on his lips. "I think you must know the answer, Cupcake."

I shake my head. "I don't."

Xavier rolls his eyes, but Malachi answers. "So he could know if she had any shady shit planned for you."

"But why?"

Xavier tilts his head, his eyes raking over my body and making heat bloom between my thighs. "You're *ours* to fuck with, Cupcake. Only ours. That means nobody else gets to even look at you funny."

Malachi stands behind me, and Xavier presses up against my front. Their warmth and proximity make me shiver. "And anyone who tries," Malachi says with a throaty growl.

"Will regret the day they were born," Xavier finishes, then he sinks his teeth into his bottom lip. A possessive growl vibrates through his body and into mine.

Oh, hell balls. My brain short-circuits. This can't be happening right now. They're playing with me. They have to be. Guys like this aren't attracted to girls like me, no matter how much they're looking at me like I might be their next snack.

"In the car. Now!" Axl shouts across the parking lot.

Xavier grins. "I guess we'd better go before he busts a blood vessel."

27

OPHELIA

For some reason, both Malachi and Xavier climbed into the back seat with me, so the three of us are squashed together in the back of the red Mustang.

I wedge my hands between my thighs to stop myself from fidgeting. I can't get the image of the mess they left in the parking lot out of my head. What the hell is going to happen when someone finds those bodies?

Xavier lets out a low frustrated growl. I look down at my chunky thighs, and heat flushes over my cheeks. "I'm sorry. Am I taking up too much room? I guess you're used to smaller girls than me sharing the back seat."

"Fuck, Cupcake," Xavier groans, then he yanks me into his lap, making me squeal in surprise. "You have no fucking idea, do you?" He brushes my hair back from my face and rests his free hand on my bare thigh.

"No idea about what?" I whisper.

"How much the three of us want to fuck you."

Wow! Heat from my cheeks races down my neck and chest.

"I mean, I have no fucking clue how you don't know. I'm sure you wear these cute little skirts just to fuck with us." He fingers the hem of my skirt, lifting it enough that Malachi must get a flash of my pink panties.

I yank my skirt back down, trying to push his hand away at the same time, but he simply laughs at my effort. "If that were true, why are you and Axl so mean to me?"

He looks at me like I'm an idiot. "Didn't the boys who liked you ever pull your hair in grade school?"

I roll my eyes. "No, because that's bullshit, and besides…" I shake my head, annoyed with myself for buying into whatever cruel game he's trying to play with me.

He trails his fingertips over my knee and along the inside of my thigh, raising goose bumps over my flesh along the way. "Besides?"

"Boys don't like me that way. So you can stop whatever game you're playing because I don't buy it for a second."

Xavier scowls. "You don't buy it, huh?" I shake my head, and he takes my hand and places it over his dick. His incredibly large and very hard dick. "How about now?"

"Stop teasing me, Xavier."

He grins, revealing the tips of his fangs, and slides his hand farther up my thigh until he reaches the apex. One finger brushes my panties, and he curls a fingertip around the edge of the fabric and tugs it aside before dragging his pointer finger through my sensitive center.

"The teasing hasn't even started yet, Ophelia." He presses his lips close to my ear. "But this teasing we do tonight will be the best kind, I promise."

"Stop," I whimper, my eyes fluttering closed.

"Why would I stop when we all know how much you want this?" He releases a wicked laugh. "You think we can't all smell you dripping for us?"

My cheeks burn with shame. "You can't."

Xavier growls. "You're soaked, Cupcake, and I didn't have to touch you to know that."

Malachi's staring between my thighs at Xavier's hand. He licks his lips and inhales through his nose. "You smell so fucking sweet, Ophelia. I can't wait to find out how good you're gonna taste."

"But you're forbidden from biting me," I argue, recalling their earlier conversation.

Xavier runs his nose over my neck. "So naive, Cupcake. He's talking about eating your pussy. And I'm going to enjoy having these beautiful thighs clamped around my head too."

I close my eyes, willing this all to be a dream. At least then it won't hurt when the inevitable happens and they reveal this has all been some kind of sick joke.

"Your heart is beating faster than a racehorse," Xavier goes on. "And when I do this…" He skates a fingertip over my clit, and my stomach contracts with pulsing need. Xavier chuckles.

"Yeah, she likes that," Malachi says with a groan. The fact that they're so easily able to tell what's going on in my body makes me feel way too vulnerable.

I steal a look at Axl. His knuckles are white on the steering wheel, his jaw clenched tight. "Oh, he wants you too," Xavier taunts me. "All three of us are going to take you."

His words pull me from whatever stupor his teasing fingers put me in. "What? Three of you?"

"You have three holes, Cupcake. And we'll use all of them."

I swallow, not wanting to admit that I've never done this before. Never had sex. Never even used any kind of toy, although I've thought about it often. But before I can offer any protest at all, Xavier applies a little more pressure to my clit, and my back arches, a keening moan pouring out of my throat. Why does that feel so good? So good that I'm willing to forget that this must be a cruel prank. I rock against his fingers, seeking relief for the throbbing ache in my core.

I fist my hands in his T-shirt, unable to stop the soft whimpers coming from my mouth. I glance down at his thick-veined forearm, his muscles flexing as he works his fingers over my sensitive bundle of nerves.

Malachi pushes himself up to his knees, and my eyes are drawn to him, notably the outline of his thick cock straining against the zipper of his jeans.

Maybe they do want me. He unfurls my fingers from Xavier's T-shirt and places my hand over his dick. I squeeze gently, and the deep growl it elicits from him makes me bolder. I rock my hips against Xavier's skilled fingers, chasing more friction, but he refuses to give it to me, continuing to gently tease me while he licks a path along my throat.

"Please?" I beg, against all my better judgment.

Xavier groans. "Begging will only get you fucked harder, Ophelia." He tips his head back and sinks his teeth into his bottom lip. "Get us the hell home, Axl, or I'm gonna fuck her right here in the car."

Axl grunts. "We'll be there in five minutes."

A violent wave of euphoria has wetness slicking my inner thighs. Malachi leans forward, one hand still holding mine against his hard length, and licks the bow of my lips. I part them on a gasp, allowing him to slide his tongue inside my mouth and take me in a bruising kiss. With Xavier's lips on my neck, his fingers toying with me, and Malachi's heady kiss stealing the breath from my lungs, I feel a familiar stirring in my abdomen. Except it feels so much more intense than anything I've experienced alone. I'm going to scream. Shatter into a thousand pieces. And in front of these men, two of whom—at best—have bullied me for the past month and a half for their own sick amusement. At worst, they actually hate me and are only doing this to torture me further.

I want to stop it. I want to not be so vulnerable and exposed, not in front of them, but I'm powerless. My back bows in half and my fingers claw at Xavier as my body ignites like it's been struck by lightning. Pleasure snakes through my limbs before exploding in my core. My head spins. My heart races. I pant for breath.

The car skids abruptly, tires screeching on the asphalt.

"Shit! You feel that?" Axl asks.

I blink. Feel what? Did they feel my orgasm like they can hear my heartbeat?

"Just an earthquake," Malachi says to Axl, although he keeps his eyes fixed on me. "Not even a big one."

Xavier slides his hand from beneath my skirt. "All I felt was Ophelia coming hard for me." He places his fingers in his mouth and sucks. His eyes roll back in his head, and I can't help but smirk at his unguarded reaction. "I was wrong about you. You don't taste like cupcakes at all." He licks his lips and flashes me a wink. "You taste way better."

28

AXL

Listening to her soft moans when Xavier made her come in the back seat of my car was exquisite torture. The scent of her arousal flooding the air around us had my cock aching like never before. As soon as we pulled to a stop outside the house, I dragged her off his lap and carried her inside, then threw her onto my bed.

She pants for breath, her pert tits rising and falling, the shape of them clear even in the loose hoodie she's wearing. Her plaid skirt is bunched up, offering me a view of her panties and the unmistakable wet patch. I growl, desperate to taste her.

Xavier flops down on the bed beside her, hands behind his head as he waits for Malachi and me to take our turn. We've shared plenty of women before, but none that we were forbidden from biting, and none nearly as irresistible as this one.

Malachi crawls onto the bed on the other side of her and runs a hand over her stomach, pulling up her sweater and her tank top and revealing an expanse of creamy white skin. She tries to push her clothes back down, but that only makes him yank them higher.

"Don't ever stop me, sweet girl," he warns with a growl. "You're fucking beautiful, and we all want to see you."

She presses her lips together, like she's desperate to disagree but won't disobey him, and fuck me, but I love that this feisty, fearless little pyromaniac is unexpectedly submissive with her body.

I peel her pink panties down her legs and toss them onto the floor, then run my hands up the inside of her calves to her thighs. I follow their path with my mouth, inhaling her intoxicating scent. She's always smelled so tantalizingly delicious to me, but now, with her arousal thick in the air around us, I'm crazed with the desire to taste her. I want to bite her, to suck her blood and let that rich coppery goodness overwhelm me, but my oath to Alexandros prevents me from acting on that particular impulse. So instead, I focus my attention on her wet pussy.

Spreading her thighs wider open, I allow my gaze to linger on her center, which glistens with the evidence of how much she wants us. I drag my pointer finger through her folds, causing her to whimper into Malachi's mouth. "You're soaked for us, Pyro."

Her thighs tremble, and white-hot anticipation shudders up my spine. I'm so eager to taste her. Fuck her. Make her scream my goddamn name. From the moment she caught us in that alley, she has belonged to me. To us. Our little pet to toy with as we please. And toying with her like this…it's the best kind of torture. I inch the tip of my finger into her tight cunt, and her hips buck while she cries out. The sound is swallowed by Malachi, who keeps his lips sealed over hers while he squeezes her breasts and rolls her hard nipples between his finger and thumb. Trailing my lips up her inner thigh, I growl, aware that I'm going to devour her whole once I get a taste of her. I'm going to make her come on my tongue and then fuck her hard.

I edge my finger deeper inside her, groaning at the way her tight heat squeezes around me. She wrenches her lips from Malachi's, and her cry is full of pain and pleasure. Exactly what I love to hear. I swirl my tongue over her pulsing clit and sink my finger deeper, and she goes on moaning until Malachi captures her mouth in another forceful kiss. Working my finger in and out of her tight channel, I feel her juices run down into my palm while I suck on her clit. Closing my eyes, I savor the taste of her, my tongue dancing over her flesh until it joins my fingers at her dripping entrance.

Her arousal coats my tongue, and pleasure surges through my veins. She's sweeter than nectar. Like nothing I've ever tasted before in my life.

Fire burns through me. Fire and power. Unsurpassable, transcendent, life-affirming power. Feeling invincible, I bask in the incomparable rush and wish I could live in this singular moment forever. Her juices flow down my throat. My fangs pulse painfully, and my tongue is coated in more than just the flavor of her cum.

"Alastair!" Alexandros's voice slices through me, and the fiery grip of his rage curls like a vise around my heart. My head snaps up, and I lick her blood from my lips. How did… I know for fucking sure I didn't bite her.

Ophelia gasps, scrabbling for the covers to hide herself from him, but I already know without looking that Alexandros's eyes are firmly on me. I tasted her blood. And it was like nothing I've ever experienced in my life.

I spin around. "I swear I didn't bite her."

He bares his teeth, but he must know I didn't bite her. If I'd disobeyed him, he would have already torn my head from my body. I glance down at my fingers and notice a faint line of red streaked over my knuckles. Holy shit. Ophelia being a virgin was a plot twist I didn't see coming. But all I can think about is her blood thundering in my veins and how the slightest hint of her taste has lit my insides up with pure euphoria.

Alexandros scowls at me from across his study, his face darkening with rage. "You disobeyed me, Axl."

"I did not! You ordered me not to bite her, and I didn't. But you didn't say *anything* about fucking her. I swear I had no idea she was a virgin. I didn't know she'd bleed. If I had..." I run my tongue over my lip, and the mere memory of her taste has my own blood coursing through my veins like lightning-laced wildfire.

He scrubs a hand through his hair and sinks into the worn leather chair behind his desk. "I warned you, Axl. I warned you not to... You should not have tasted her." He shakes his head, a thick vein pulsing in his neck. He's livid, but fortunately for me, he seems distracted by something else.

I'm unable to shake the uneasy feeling that whatever happened here tonight has fundamentally changed something, even if I have no idea what or why. I inhale a shaky breath.

He pinches the spot between his brows and sighs. "And before you brought her here? What happened at the river? I felt your rage. All of you."

Fuck. With the whole Ophelia thing, I'd forgotten about that added complication. I crack my neck and take a deep breath. "You remember you said we weren't supposed to let anyone else fuck with her or taste her?"

He plants his elbows on his desk and leans forward, his dark eyes narrowed to slits. "Yes."

"Well, that girl, Penelope—" I pull at the collar of my T-shirt and twist my neck. The faculty doesn't take kindly to us killing the humans. Not unless it's necessary. This was necessary. All I can do is hope he sees it the same way. I roll back my shoulders and look him in the eye. "She lured Ophelia to the river tonight. The bitch was planning to kill her, sir. My best guess, she was gonna make it look like a suicide."

That sure gets his attention. "She was planning to kill Ophelia?" His voice vibrates with unsuppressed rage, and the unguarded reaction fills me with relief. Maybe he won't punish us for the lives we took tonight.

"They went to high school together, did they not? Did she have anything to do with the incident before the fire?"

"Yeah. She humiliated her in front of the whole school at the school play or some shit." I still can't fucking believe how juvenile it was. Who gets that angry over something so trivial? I'm a fucking vampire with anger issues, and I don't even get it. "The fire started after that. Funny thing is she transferred here two weeks after school started. And she was the one there the night of the fight too."

He gives me a single nod. "I recall. So where is this girl now?"

Here goes nothing. "In pieces in the parking lot out by the crystal caves. We're gonna go back and clean up. Make it look like two car wrecks."

He hums, giving nothing away yet. "How many people were there?"

"Five." Pausing, I swallow. He might not tear me a new one because of the humans, but this could be the thing that tips him over the edge. "Two of them were Onyx pledges."

As I expected, this is a more problematic turn of events. His outward demeanor remains calm, but his rage grows palpable in the small room. I close my eyes and take another breath to tamp down my own frustration before I look at him again. "What were we supposed to do? Let them kill her?"

He inhales a deep breath, his nostrils flaring like he's trying to keep himself from ripping off my head. Or at least tearing out my throat. Fortunately, he does neither. "I will speak to the faculty heads about the humans. And Professor Ashe about the pledges." His voice drips with the fury he's suppressing, but he knows we did the right thing.

He also knows there is something special about Ophelia, and I suspect he knows what that something is. For some reason, he's withholding that information from us, and after over two hundred years with him, I have zero doubt that he's doing what he feels is best for everyone—especially Malachi, Xavier, and me.

But I'm starting to chafe at the secrets he's keeping from us. From me. "What the hell is she, Professor?"

He runs his tongue over his lip, avoiding my gaze now. And my question.

I persist, undeterred. "She's not human. I've never felt a rush like it."

His eyes return to my face, and they pierce my soul. There's something behind them, something deeper than rage. Curiosity, perhaps. "What did she taste like?" he asks.

I take a step closer to him. "You felt her. That's why you came to my room. Tell me what she is."

He growls, revealing a glimpse of his fangs. Experience tells me I should back down, but I can't. I need to know the answer more than I need air.

He hisses out a breath, and it's enough to make the hairs on the back of my neck stand to attention. "Tell me how she tasted," he commands once more.

I lick my lips, desperate to taste her again. But she's already gone, and the memory of her is not nearly enough to satisfy the building craving that's already snapping its teeth at me. I haven't experienced bloodlust since I was turned, and it's not an experience I wish to repeat. But that's the closest sensation I can compare this to. "It's hard to explain. Sweet as fuck. Addictive. But it was more than that. It was the way she made me feel. Like there was literal fire running through my veins. Fire and immense power. What is she?"

His jaw tics. "A witch, maybe. A powerful one."

I shake my head again. He's lying. "I've tasted witches before. That wasn't it. What the fuck is she, Alexandros?"

He rubs a hand over his thick beard and sucks on his bottom lip. "I do not know."

"*You* don't know?" I scoff. He's thousands of years old. There is no creature on this earth he hasn't tasted.

He glares at me, that low growl simmering in his throat.

"So taste her for yourself. Taste her and tell me."

He's out of his seat in a flash, and he wraps one strong hand around my throat, pinning me against the wall, his fangs exposed. The swiftness of his reaction takes my breath away. "No! And you are forbidden from tasting her again. Do you understand me?"

The beast inside me responds on my behalf. A growl rips from my chest, and my upper lip curls back, baring my own teeth. *He wants to taste her again, even if that means my certain death.*

Alexandros slams me against the wall. "I said, do you understand me?"

My throat works beneath his palm, and I grit out, "Yes."

He releases me, and I rub at my raw skin, twisting my head from side to side.

He returns to his position behind the desk and slumps back into his chair. "I know you are thirsty." Through our link, he can easily feel the need for her coursing through my veins. "But tasting her again is not going to slake that thirst, Axl."

How about I don't give a fuck if it slakes my thirst. I need to taste her again, even if I die trying. But I don't say that, and I suspect I don't have to. He knows what this feels like. "You speak like you know from experience."

The vein in his temple throbs. *I have lived for over two millennia. There is very little I have not experienced.* The anger in his tone comes through even more keenly with him speaking into my mind.

Yeah, he knows. Of course he does. "So tell me what she is."

He shakes his head. "As I said, I do not know for sure."

So taste her! That beast inside me taunts him, and I growl at him to shut the fuck up.

Alexandros snarls. "Keep your bloodlust under control, Axl, or I will be forced to do it for you."

Closing my eyes, I twist my head from side to side and try to drown out the ravenous hunger pervading every cell of my body.

His hands are on me again, this time on either side of my face, and his voice is gentler. "You are stronger than the beast inside you. I taught you better than this."

I gnash my teeth. *I know.*

I reopen my eyes, and he gives me a single nod before turning back to his desk. *Go clean up your mess.*

29

Xavier

Despite her hooded sweatshirt, Ophelia shivers and tries to curl into a ball on the porch bench. I resist the urge to wrap my arms around her and share my body heat. I know how this night will end, and there's no sense making it any more painful for her than it's already going to be. Not even I am that cruel. At least not to her. Not anymore.

"You want my sweater, sweet girl?" Malachi asks.

I shoot him a warning look over the top of her head. *Don't be acting like a fucking sap.*

Fuck off, he fires back.

If she didn't wear those tiny little skirts, she wouldn't be cold.

I love her tiny skirts.

Ophelia shakes her head and pulls at the sleeve of her own sweater, completely unaware of our alternate conversation. "No thanks. I'm okay."

I glance down at her bare legs, and my cock twitches. Yeah, I love her tiny skirts too.

"Why did he get so mad?" she asks, her lip quivering.

I stuff my hands into my pockets because her scent is still on my fingers and it's driving me wild with the desire to touch her again. Not just touch. Taste too. But Alexandros's rage was enough to convince my libido to let my brain take over for a bit. The only reason we haven't taken her back to her dorm is because Malachi and I agreed that it wasn't worth the risk of doing anything else to incur his wrath.

"He forbade us from biting you," Malachi says. "And when Axl tasted your blood, we all felt it. The professor too. I guess he thought Axl disobeyed him."

I snort a laugh. "If he thought that, Axl would have no head."

"What?" Ophelia blinks at us.

Malachi takes her hand and squeezes it. "Decapitation is the only way to kill a vampire."

I punch him on the arm. Like she needs to know how to kill us. "Way to go, jackass."

Malachi scowls at me. "What? It's not like she could do it. Have you ever tried to deprive a vampire of his head?"

"Have you?" Ophelia asks.

He shrugs. "No. But it would be tough." He rolls his neck. "We have very strong spinal cords. It's an evolutionary thing."

Ophelia scrunches her tiny nose. "The professor would never hurt any of you though. You're like his...sons."

Fuck, she's so damn naive and sweet. My yearning to corrupt her makes every part of me ache.

"He wouldn't have much choice if one of us broke an oath to him," Malachi explains. "He'd be bound by vampire law."

Her eyes go wide, the expanse of her pupils shadowing the electric blue of her irises. "So you have to obey everything he says or you get your head chopped off?"

I roll my eyes. She makes it sound like puppets. "It's not like that. He doesn't go around making us take oaths for the hell of it.

We have very few rules we're not allowed to break." Which makes me wonder even more why we're forbidden from biting Ophelia. I felt only an echo of the power and the euphoria Axl felt when he tasted her virgin blood, and it was one of the most intense experiences of my life. It has to be something to do with that. And Alexandros knows what she is, so why the fuck won't he let us in on the secret?

Malachi interrupts my train of thought. "It doesn't make sense for bloodborne vampires to go around tearing off the heads of the vamps they sire."

She chews on her lip. "But why?"

I scrub my face with my hands. "Why do you have so many fucking questions?"

"Excuse me for being curious about the world of supernatural beings that I didn't know existed until a few weeks ago," she snaps.

Malachi shoots me a smug smile. "Yeah. It's natural to be curious."

She tilts her head and bats her eyelashes at him—he's such a dick—before returning her attention to me. "So why can't they go around tearing heads off?"

We're stuck until the professor tells us what to do with her, so I might as well humor her. "Because sired vampires can't survive if their master is dead, which means turned vampires protect their sires at all costs. Survival instinct 101."

Her expression takes on that excited quality she gets when she's learning something new, and I struggle to keep myself from getting caught up in her enchanting web of enthusiasm. "So what happens? If he dies, you'd just drop dead too?"

Malachi takes this one. "Not immediately. We'd grow weaker over time. Older, more powerful turned vampires can survive for up to two years without their master. With younger vampires, it can be a matter of days."

"So it's like the master vampires like Alexandros have their own personal armies?"

Malachi grins at her, and I roll my eyes at his eagerness to please her. "Exactly. And so the oldest and most powerful vampires have generations at their disposal. Back then, each of the turned vampires would turn their own armies. All those vampires are bound to their own sire, who in turn is still bound to the bloodline vampire. To survive, they all must protect that single bloodborne sire."

"Wow! So vampires can be turned or born. And you can turn vampires of your own?"

Malachi nods. "Physically we are capable, but it's been forbidden for hundreds of years. Any vampire who breaks that law would be executed."

"Who forbids it? Is there like some sort of vampire police?"

Vampire history has never interested me. I know my life before I was turned—a miserable pit of despair—and I know my life after. Whatever his reason for doing so, Alexandros rescued me from hell when he turned me, and that was all I ever cared about.

Until now. For once I'm paying attention because now our sire is keeping secrets. I suspect at least some of those secrets have something to do with Ophelia Hart, and perhaps there's something to be gleaned about who she is from our history.

"All vampire lines can be traced back to four houses—Drakos, Chóma, Elira, and Thalassa," Malachi says, the register of his voice lowering into his teaching tone. Of all of us, he's the most likely to follow in Alexandros's professor footsteps, and I'm not entirely sure why he hasn't already. "Each of those houses has a corresponding society, and each is bound by ancient laws and is responsible for their own governance. To not enforce the ancient laws could result in the destruction of the entire bloodline."

"By who?"

Malachi shrugs. "There are higher powers that most of us younger generations know nothing about. And despite my best efforts, it's a question I haven't been able to get to the bottom of."

She's unusually silent for a moment, like she's digesting everything he said. "It all sounds very elitist to me."

I snort a laugh. "Then it's no different to humans, is it?"

She gives me a wry smile. "I guess not." She's quiet again for all of two seconds before she's back with more questions. "Okay, so how are vampires born? Can you all have kids?"

"I don't know how they're born." Malachi frowns, and I stifle a snicker. The smart fucker isn't used to not having all the answers, and he hates it. "But turned vampires can't have kids, and a bloodline vampire hasn't been born in over half a millennium."

She gasps again. "Really?"

"Yeah."

"Wow, this is all so fascinating, can you tell me how…"

The rest of her question is drowned out by Alexandros's voice in my head. *Escort her to her dorm and break off whatever this thing is that you've started with her.*

Yes sir, I answer.

Malachi protests, but the professor cuts him off. *She is not to set foot in this house again. You are not to see her again.*

Malachi tries again. *But—*

She is not to come seeking you out either. She's already too fixated on all three of you. So make it brutal. Make her hate you.

Malachi's pain washes over me, and the professor sighs. *Let Xavier handle it.*

I give him my assurance that I will take care of it, and Malachi offers no further resistance. He knows better than to argue a lost cause.

Ophelia chatters the whole way to her dorm, and I notice how Malachi slows his pace so he can spend more time with her before we break her heart, but I allow it. I think I'm going to miss our little pink-haired question monster too, although I'm not nearly as attached as he is.

We get to her building, and Malachi looks at the ground instead of at her face.

She glances between us, nervous energy radiating from her. Tonight probably meant something to her, even though we didn't fuck her.

Pity.

"So..." She wrings her hands.

"So what, Cupcake? We had our fun, and now it's time for you to go back to your sad, lonely life."

She blinks. "W-what?"

"You heard me. It's over. We wanted to fuck you, and well..." I shrug. "Virgins are too much bother for us. Too messy."

She looks to Malachi, but he continues to avoid her gaze. "Malachi?" she asks, her voice shaking.

He finally looks up at her, his eyes empty like he's completely shut down. "Like he said. Too messy."

That's my boy, I tell him.

His heart breaks. He's such a fucking sap.

Tears fill her eyes. "But I thought..."

"You thought what, Cupcake? That the three of us could be interested in a nobody like you? Come on." I toss my head back and laugh, but Malachi's anguish is making me feel guilty. Or perhaps this isn't as easy as I thought it would be. Because I want to taste her again. I want her to ask me a thousand ridiculous questions just so I can roll my eyes at her.

Her lip wobbles, and I hear Alexandros's voice ringing in my head. *Eviscerate her and get back here.*

"It was all just a joke, Ophelia. We were fucking with you."

Tears run freely down her cheeks, and it starts to rain. She scrubs at her face. "You're a pair of assholes anyway."

After she runs into the building, Malachi doubles over, hands resting on his knees as he blows out a breath. "That was fucking brutal," he rasps. Standing, he looks at me with tears in his eyes.

I wrap an arm around his neck. "It had to be done, little brother."

He swallows. "I know, but it doesn't make it hurt any less. Why do you think he's so against us tasting her blood?"

"Did you feel what it did to Axl? That was some heavy shit. And he had what, a few drops?"

Malachi glances back at her building. "There's something really fucking different about her, isn't there? Like special different?"

I can't disagree. As much as I'd like it to not be true, I know better. Ophelia Hart is fucking special.

30

MALACHI

I fall onto my bed and bury my head in my pillow. Recalling the look on Ophelia's face hurts so much. I try to block it out because even thinking about it makes nausea roll in the pit of my stomach.

Footsteps pad into the room, and I groan. "Go away!"

Ignoring me, he sits on the bed. A rough hand skates over my back and palms the nape of my neck. "I said go away, Xavier."

He lies on top of me, running his tongue along the side of my throat. "But I don't wanna."

I want to wallow in my own misery, but my body betrays me. I push my ass into him and grind against his hard length.

He works his hands under the band of my sweatpants. "Oh, my little pup wants to be fucked?"

"I want to forget what we just did, numbnuts."

He makes a tutting sound and sinks his fangs into my neck. The sharp pain that lances through my body makes me groan. He always knows what I need, and this is what I deserve after hurting

Ophelia the way we did. Not that I'm usually concerned about the fickle emotions of humans. Despite what Axl and Xavier say about my soft nature, I'm perfectly capable of cruelty. Sometimes I even revel in it. But compared to those vicious fucks, I guess I do come across as the sensitive one.

Ordinarily, causing someone to cry wouldn't register on my radar, let alone cause me a second of discomfort, but Ophelia is… I drag in a breath as Xavier goes on sucking my blood. I recall her scent. The taste of her lips. How she moaned into my mouth when Axl was eating her pussy.

She's so kind and sweet and good. So fucking good. Despite all the shitty things that have happened to her, she sees the best in people. Sees the best in me. And since the day I was turned, I haven't cared one iota about anyone seeing me for anything other than the monster I am.

So what is it about Ophelia Hart that calls to the last shreds of humanity in my blackened soul?

Xavier works my pants down farther, tugging them over my ass cheeks and letting them rest on the tops of my thighs, his fangs still embedded in my neck. *Stop thinking about Cupcake when I'm about to fuck you, pup.*

I growl. *I'll think about whoever the fuck I want.*

He fumbles with his jeans, and a few seconds later, the head of his thick cock is nudging at my ass. He's going to make this hurt, and that's precisely what I need. His hand slides up my back, fingers rough on my skin until they reach my throat. He pulls my head back sharply and sucks harder as he drives his thick cock inside me.

"Fuck, Xavier!"

He rips his teeth from my throat and tears out a chunk of flesh. "Not thinking about her now, huh?" He pulls out and slams back inside.

I grunt harshly, pushing myself back and taking as much of him as I can get while he laps at the blood pouring from the wound in my neck until it slows to a trickle and finally heals.

His lips return to my throat, this time kissing and nipping gently as he slows his pace. "I love fucking your tight ass, Kai," he groans. "You are such a good boy for me."

I press my face into the pillow. I don't want to be his good boy, but my body is too weak to resist him. I'm too weak. Driven by the pleasure that his unique brand of pain brings me so that I can forget about the agony lingering at the edges of my consciousness. That other pain waits patiently, sentient and confident in its knowledge that the moment will come when I'm not overwhelmed by the delicious torture being delivered by Xavier's mouth and cock. It lurks, big and bold, ready to tear at my soul.

With a growl of frustration, Xavier tears my T-shirt in half and trails hungry kisses over my skin while he fucks me. I arch my back, giving into the exquisite pleasure that his body brings mine.

He burrows his hand between me and the mattress and wraps his fingers around the base of my shaft, squeezing so hard that my eyes roll back in my head.

He laughs darkly, his lips not leaving my hot skin. "That's it, pup. Let me fuck it all better."

Oh fuck! Heat slides up the base of my spine, spreading out to my limbs. He jerks me off to the same rhythm that he fucks me, and my cock aches with the need for release. "You can let go, Kai. I've got you." He follows it up with an evil chuckle before sinking his fangs into my shoulder blade, and I lose all sense of space and time.

My climax erupts out of me, soaking Xavier's knuckles, and he moves his hand to my mouth. "Suck them clean."

I flick my tongue over his cum-streaked fingers, and he groans, rocking into me a few more times before he roars his release.

When he's finished, he collapses on top of me, pinning me to the mattress with his forehead resting between my shoulder blades.

"I think we both needed that, pup," he says quietly.

I sure as hell did.

"You two done?" Axl climbs into the bed and lies facing us, propping himself up on one elbow. An emotion I don't think I've felt from him before seems to pour out of him. Desolation. Am I projecting?

Grunting, Xavier rolls off me and onto his side, sandwiching me between the two of them. I flip onto my back, and they each rest a hand on my stomach, their fingertips touching.

The air is thick with unspoken tension. "How pissed was he?" I ask.

Axl sighs and rubs the spot between his brows. "Super fucking pissed. Even more than that time we destroyed the main house."

"Damn," I mumble.

"Fuck," Xavier mutters.

"Yeah. But he was more than pissed. He was…" Axl pauses for a moment before continuing. "Curious, you know? I mean, did you feel it? What happened when I tasted her?"

Hell yeah, we fucking felt it. Whatever *it* was, I've never felt anything more intense or spectacular, and I'm practically green with envy knowing that I won't get to feel it for myself.

"It was fucking incredible. I swear I have never felt a fucking rush like it." Axl blows out a breath.

Nor have I, and I only felt it secondhand. Who or what the hell is Ophelia Hart, and why are we forbidden from biting her? "Did he say what she is?" I turn my head and study his face. "Give any more information about why we're not supposed to bite her? Why he made us tear out her fucking heart?"

Axl frowns. "He wouldn't tell me. Suggested maybe she's some kind of witch, but I didn't buy it. He was trying to placate me."

I stare back up at the ceiling and wonder why the fuck the man we trust more than anyone else is keeping so many secrets from us. While Alexandros Drakos can be cruel and ruthless, he has never given us any reason to think he doesn't trust us. Nor has he given us reason to doubt him. Yet there is clearly something about my sweet pink-haired girl he's refusing to tell us about.

Xavier snorts and pulls my attention back to the conversation. "It figures you'd be the one to break the rules and get away with it, golden boy."

Axl reaches over me and hits him in the chest. "I didn't break the rules, fuck-knuckle. But I bet you would've loved if I had though, right? See him tear my head off?"

Xavier narrows his eyes. "Don't be so fucking dramatic. All I'm saying is you got to taste her, and we never will. It's unfair."

Axl rolls over onto his back and puts his hands behind his head. "Yeah, well, I'm kind of sorry I did because all I can fucking think about is tasting her again. It's like being given the one thing you've always wanted and only getting to have it for a second. Then having to go the rest of your life knowing you'll never feel that good again."

I've been feeling sorry for myself, but now I realize how much worse he has it. Xavier must be thinking the same thing because he reaches over me and rests his hand on Axl's chest. "Fuck," Axl groans. "We have to go clean up the mess we left in the parking lot."

Xavier and I grunt our agreement, but none of us move. I suspect we're all trying to process what the hell happened tonight.

More importantly, who—and what—the hell is Ophelia Hart?

31

ALEXANDROS

Rain pounds against the roof of the history building like it is trying to get to me. Perhaps it is. I close my eyes and try not to think of the reason for the twelve inches of rain that have fallen since last night, but she is never far from my thoughts.

It has been that way since the moment I met her. But now, after last night, I have been consumed with questions that I lack the desire to know the answers to. Yet I cannot stop asking them.

What is she? Why does her soul call to mine like it does? Who is responsible for Ophelia Hart's attendance at this institution? And given what happened with Ronan two weeks ago and the girl from her high school last night, who else knows what she is and wants her dead?

I looked into Penelope Nugent, and yes, she had a cruel streak. Not unlike most humans, in my experience. But murdering Ophelia seems a step too…unhinged. The only thing that makes sense is that someone was pulling her strings.

The door to the classroom opens, and I snarl at the man who steps inside. I was expecting his visit, but that makes him no less unwelcome. Nicholas Ashe marches toward me, his hands balled into fists. "Tell me that your feral offspring didn't have anything to do with two of my pledges being in a car accident last night."

I slip my papers into my briefcase and shrug. "I could tell you that, but I would be lying."

He slams his fist down onto my podium. "That is against the rules of fair play and you know it, Alexandros."

The rage inside me has been relentless in its pursuit to be let loose lately. I stretch my neck and will it to subside. Experience reminds me that it can only be held at bay for so long before something has to give. I need some form of release. Something more than feeding from a willing but bland, faceless victim and making them forget after. "Your pledges stepped out of line, and they suffered the consequences."

"Out of line?" he says with a snarl. "Your vile hell spawn—"

Not giving him a chance to finish that sentence, I cut off his airway with a firm grip on his throat. "You utter one more word about my boys and I will tear out your throat with such meticulous precision that it will take your body months to heal."

I push him backward, and he growls, rubbing at his reddened skin. "We are two pledges down, and you have the audacity to come at me? What the hell! Are you so afraid of losing that you would stoop to evening out our numbers this way? I had no idea that you'd be so threatened by Onyx having more pledges than you."

"You could have five hundred pledges and Ruby Dragon would still win. It is the way it has always been." I take some small pleasure in his increased heart rate and the rage he feels at his own impotency. As head of the Onyx Dragon Society, he has a lot of power within these walls, but not where I am concerned. The knowledge that I choose not to tear off his head, despite having every right to do so given his past indiscretions, is always enough to keep him firmly in his place.

"I demand to know what happened. Why is it that your sons broke the rules that are there for the protection of all?"

I shake my head. "There is no rule that says pledges are not to be dealt with when they misbehave, Nicholas. It is only once they are turned that they are offered such protections. While they are human, they are fair game."

"Fair game, you say?" He runs his tongue over his top lip. "Does that go for your pledges too?"

"You could try, but the Ruby pledges are neither misguided enough to get in anyone's way nor are they stupid enough to fuck up so spectacularly as to come to the attention of three powerful vampires the way that two of yours did last night. You have my word that their punishment fit their crime."

"And just what was their alleged crime, Alexandros?"

I inch closer, a warning growl rumbling in my throat. "They tried to take something that did not belong to them. I warned you to tell your offspring about the pitfalls of playing with my boys' new pet."

He blinks. "This is about the girl with the pink hair?"

The girl who continues to draw more and more attention to herself without even trying. "Yes."

"But I did warn them. The pledges were… I didn't know they weren't supposed to…" He trails off because he knows this is a fruitless argument. He fucked up.

I scrutinize his face for telltale signs of deception but find none. If indeed someone is using the members of Onyx to bring about Ophelia's downfall, I doubt that Nicholas is aware of it. He lacks the power and capability to hide such intentions from me. Perhaps it goes deeper than the society and involves House Chóma itself.

"That you failed to warn all of those in your care is no concern of mine, Nicholas." I pick up my briefcase and brush past him, not wishing to be drawn into any kind of discussion about Ophelia. About the girl who felt like lightning in my own veins when Axl tasted her. About the girl who I already know will bring about my ruin. "Turn the lights off when you leave."

32

OPHELIA

After pulling up the hood of my raincoat, I slip out of my dorm building and make my way toward the library. Raindrops bounce at my feet, and my boots splash through the puddles as I pick up my pace. I usually enjoy walking in the rain, but this downpour is torrential. Even the quad is empty, but that's no surprise, given that it's Saturday and there isn't much of a reason for people to be out and about if they don't have to be. I suspect most students are cozy in their dorm rooms, hanging out with friends or snuggled up in their beds with a warm body to keep them company.

Sucking in a stuttering breath, I choke back the sob that threatens to escape. I've done enough crying over those jerkwads. They don't deserve a single tear. So why do I feel like my heart has been torn out of my chest and trampled by a herd of rhinos, leaving a black hole in its place? A black hole of despair that threatens to pull me in and consume me every time I picture their faces. Every time I recall Xavier's unhinged laugh, Axl's scowl, or how Malachi's green eyes twinkle when he smiles.

Sharp pain stabs my chest, and I press my hand over my heart. It's still there. Still beating even though it wants to stop. Even though I want nothing more than to sink to the ground and curl into a ball until the rain washes me away. And it could. Nobody would notice I was gone. Anger and despair crash into me again, and I tip my face to the sky as I slow my pace, letting the rainwater cleanse some of it, some of me, away.

But as angry as I am with those assholes, I'm beyond livid with myself for believing them. For allowing them to make me feel like that seventeen-year-old girl again, sobbing in the dressing room while flames swirled around me. Because I made myself a promise that day—that if I got out of that room alive, I would never allow anyone to have that kind of power over me again. Never again let anyone make me feel worthless. Because despite every shitty thing that's happened in my life—being left on the steps of that church, getting passed from foster home to foster home, Penelope and her crew of mean girls making my life hell in high school, and the year I spent in the group home after the best foster parents I ever had kicked me out because nobody would believe that I didn't start that fire—I am somebody. I am worthy. And one day, I will find my people.

I hasten my steps, eager to reach the library and its warmth. Solace has always greeted me when I opened a book. For a person who has spent their entire life alone, I relish the magic that can be found and the experiences I've had thanks to what's written on those pages. Making a new friend. Traveling to faraway lands and being swept away by the kind of heroes and heroines who have made entire generations fall in love.

Perhaps today I can find the comfort in words that eludes me in life.

...

"Hey, girl. I didn't think anyone would be in here today. That storm's wild, huh?"

I rest my book on my lap and watch Cadence shrug off her coat and shake droplets of rain from her bangs.

"It is, yeah."

"I had to get out of my room. My roomie's boyfriend came over, and we were gonna chill and watch a movie, but then they started getting all hot and heavy, and I did not want to be there for that." She giggles. "And then there was a ruckus in the common room because somebody's earrings went missing, so I thought why not try the library. I really need to do some studying anyway. Drakos's class is kicking my ass this year."

The mention of his name is enough to have that swirling vortex of sadness, shame, and anger raging in my chest once more. A loud crack of thunder makes us both jump.

She shivers. "Wow. We might have to hole up in here all day." She glances at the empty chair beside me. "You mind?"

"Not at all."

"Great. I know libraries are supposed to be quiet and all, but I like having another person around. You know what I mean?"

Unexpected tears fill my eyes, and I blink to clear them.

She puts her cold hand on my arm and squeezes. "Hey, Ophelia."

She remembers my name!

"Is something wrong?"

I swat away the tear running down my cheek. "I'm just being stupid."

"No way. I know I don't know you that well, but I know you aren't stupid." She leans forward and waits for me to meet her gaze, and when I do, she offers a gentle smile. "Now, in my experience, there's very little that a good chat and a pack of Tate's chocolate chip cookies won't fix." She reaches into her backpack and pulls out the familiar green bag before tearing it open. "What do you think?"

I blink at her when she opens the smaller packet inside and holds it out to me. "Take four. One is never enough."

I take two. "These are my favorite," I murmur. "Thank you."

"Mine too." She bites into one and hums with satisfaction. After she's done savoring her first bite, she licks the crumbs from her lips and eyes me with concern. "So, tell me what has you in here all alone on a Saturday afternoon."

I shrug. The last people I opened up to turned out to be heartless douchebags with the emotional intelligence of dung beetles, so I'm not exactly eager to repeat that experience.

She arches an eyebrow. "A guy, right?"

"Yeah." More like three.

"Ugh!" She takes another bite of her cookie. "They're such jerks." Crumbs fly out of her mouth, and we both bust out laughing.

"They sure are," I say, once I've caught my breath.

"I'm swearing off boys this semester. My grades weren't great last year, so I promised my parents I'd study more." She holds up her history book and pulls a face.

Cadence ends up getting zero studying done over the next few hours, but she does make me laugh with stories of all the disastrous dates she had last year. And for a few short but wonderful hours, I almost forget about the three vampires who broke my heart.

...

"Hey, we're having a party at my house tonight. You want to come?" Cadence asks as we step out of the library. Thankfully, there's a break in the clouds and the rain has stopped.

"Thanks, but I'm gonna grab some dinner and head back to my dorm. I'm not really a party kind of person."

She rolls her eyes. "Me neither, but I have to go to some events for the society and all that."

"You're in a society?" I have no idea why that surprises me so much.

"Yeah. Silver Vale." She flashes me a grin. "It's cool, but sometimes I prefer doing my own thing, you know?"

I walk beside her toward Dionysus Commons. "Why did you join a society? If you don't mind me asking."

"Not at all. It's a family tradition. Generations of my family have attended Montridge, and they all joined Silver Vale."

I recall Malachi telling me Silver Vale was a witch society. If generations of Cadence's family were members, does that mean she's a witch too?

"You should come check us out. We don't make pledges go through the stupid hazing some of the other societies do. You either fit or you don't."

I frown. "That seems a little elitist."

She shakes her head and laughs. "I get that, but it's not. Some people are right for it, and some aren't. It's nothing to do with popularity or grades or who dated the hottest guy in high school. It's purely based on"—she chews on her lip and looks at me as though she's wondering how to finish the sentence—"ability."

"I don't have any special abilities," I tell her.

We reach the Commons and come to a stop. She places a hand on my arm and offers me a smile that makes her hazel eyes twinkle. "You'll never know unless you give us a try, Ophelia."

I open my mouth to tell her she's mistaken, but we're interrupted by a guy running toward us and almost knocking Cadence over. "Jake!" she admonishes him.

"Sorry, C," he replies with a sheepish grin. "But have you heard what happened?"

She rolls her eyes. "This is my friend Ophelia, by the way. Neanderthal."

Her friend? Did she actually just call me her friend? A surge of happiness warms the cavernous black hole around my heart.

Jake gives me a quick once-over. "Hey, Ophelia." I squint back at him as the sun peeks from behind the clouds, glaring directly in my face.

"There was a crash down by the river Thursday night." He huddles closer to both of us and drops his voice, making me feel for the first time in my life that I belong in a secret conversation. "Two cars were involved, both of them burned-out wrecks. Five students were killed."

My stomach drops through my knees, and I force my mouth to remain closed. This isn't the kind of gossip I hoped for.

"Oh my word," Cadence says. "Who?"

"Madison Cummings from our history class. Some new girl, Penny whatsherface and her boyfriend." He snaps his fingers. "The football player. Aiden? Hayden?"

Cadence shakes her head. "I don't know them."

Her admission floods me with relief. She isn't Penelope's friend. And more importantly, maybe she won't hate me if she ever finds out I had anything to do with their deaths.

"Well, they were in one car, but the other one had two new pledges from Onyx Society."

I swallow. That means Madison's boyfriend and the guy I didn't recognize were vampire pledges.

Cadence's eyes widen. "Oh, interesting."

If Cadence is a witch, she must know about vampires. I want to ask her, but I wouldn't dare. Especially not with Jake here. "And th-they all died in the car accident?" My words stick in my throat as I recall the bloody mess of bodies left behind in that parking lot.

Jake nods. "That's the official report. From the horse's mouth."

"Jake's dad is the chief of police," Cadence explains.

My stomach churns. The chief of police. I'm going to jail. My arrest, trial, and ensuing life sentence flash by in a montage of horrible images. It doesn't matter that I didn't kill those people, just like it didn't matter that I didn't burn down my high school. I was there. Axl, Xavier, or Malachi can't be trusted to tell the truth about my part. And it's not like I can tell anyone that vampires were responsible.

"You sure you don't want to come to this party tonight?" Cadence asks me, and I force the blur of images that could be my potential future from my mind.

"It's gonna be a rager." Jake pumps his fist in the air.

Cadence swats his chest. "You're such a caveman."

He blows her a kiss, and she makes a retching sound like she's disgusted by him, even though it's clear she's not.

I force a smile. "Thank you for the invite, really, but I'm gonna pass."

"Then you should definitely stop by next week sometime. Just ask for me, and I'll show you around." She takes me by surprise when she pulls me in for a hug, and I awkwardly return it before Jake is pulling her away, demanding she help him get a keg. He says a quick goodbye to me, and I watch the two of them head off in the direction of the Silver Vale house.

There's still a smile on my face, but that bone-crushing sorrow is already snaking its way back into me, filling me up from my toes until it reaches the top of my head. Droplets of water splash on my face, and I tilt my head back to see dark clouds rolling overhead once more. At least the weather matches my mood.

33

Alexandros

Malachi's anxiety and concern for his brother hits me before he even steps foot inside Zeus Hall. I am typically able to block him and his brothers out whenever I choose, but for the most part, I simply dull my connection to them. I prefer a little solace in my own head. It is a skill all vampires possess, but one not all can master.

However, such is the strength of Malachi's worry today, it permeates my thoughts as strongly as if it were my own. Perhaps it is because I know why he has come here and I share his concern. I also know how to fix the problem he is bringing to my door. And that unsettles me even more.

His brow is etched with tension when he walks into my office. "It's Axl," he says, his voice pained.

I close my laptop and rest my hands on my chin. "I know."

"He's getting worse. He won't feed. Can't." He shakes his head. "He's burning up. I've never seen him like this. We don't get sick. It doesn't make sense. What's wrong with him?"

The time has come to accept reality and fix this. I grab my jacket and shrug it on. Axl has been growing sicker with each passing day. We have all felt it, and I have wished more than anything that it would get better for him. The sickness took hold much more quickly than is usual, and a part of me hoped that it meant it was different, that *she* was different. That perhaps it would burn through him and I would be spared from having to do what must be done. His teeth never penetrated her flesh. It was such a small taste.

I stride past Malachi and gesture for him to follow me. "Let's go."

I cup Axl's jaw in my hand. His bloodshot eyes are heavy, and his waxy skin is so pale he almost looks translucent. His fangs are bared, and he scents the air with a feral sniff.

Malachi's distress is palpable. "What the hell is wrong with him, Professor?"

I snarl, frustrated and angry. If I had any doubt as to the kind of creature Ophelia Hart is, Axl's reaction to her blood has removed every shred of it. Stupid, stupid boy! "He needs her blood."

Xavier runs a hand through his hair. "But why? I know she smelled good, and he said something happened when he tasted her, but why the fuck is he like this? Has she made him sick? Is this some kind of spell?"

I shake my head. It is easy to forget that my boys know so little of the old magic, having never experienced it. Perhaps I have been remiss in not schooling them in the ancient ways. "Not a spell. But magic, nonetheless."

Malachi gapes at me, wide-eyed. "So she is a witch? Has she cursed him?"

Axl snaps his teeth, and I release my grasp on his jaw, letting him fall back to the bed. Despite his rabid state, he is as weak as a kitten. "Not a curse. Well, not exactly."

Xavier's eyes meet mine in a silent plea before he speaks. "So, what the hell is it? Stop talking in riddles and tell us what's wrong with him. Please."

I run my tongue over my teeth. "It is an ancient magic. The blood of the elementai is toxic to vampires on the first bite."

Malachi's emerald-green eyes narrow. "Elementai? She's a fucking elementai? I thought they were a myth. Like dragons."

Malachi has always been the most curious of my boys regarding our species' past, but now is not the time for a history lesson. "Not a myth. Neither elementai nor dragons."

Xavier stops pacing and scowls at me. "What the fuck is an elementai?"

"A powerful creature. More powerful than vampires, demons, witches, and wolves."

He blinks at me. "And she's one of them? Ophelia? The girl with pink hair, who has no friends and blushes when anyone so much looks at her… *She* is more powerful than us?"

I glance at Axl again, and the answer to that question literally stares me in the face. "I believe so."

Malachi's mouth is still hanging open, but he finally speaks. "Dragons are real too?"

Xavier nudges him in the ribs. "Not the time, dickface."

Seeming to shake himself out of a stupor, Malachi casts a worried look at Axl. "But her blood is toxic? Like a poison?"

"If poison gave you an insatiable thirst for more, then yes. But it is merely an evolutionary tactic to ensure the survival of the species. Once the elementai's blood has been tasted by a vampire, a bond forms. Only the second bite, or in this case, taste, can cure the sickness, which ensures the vampire will return and cement the bond."

"So if he bites her, he won't be like this, right? She won't be toxic to him anymore?" Xavier asks, his eyes turbulent with concern.

"Yes and no. He will not suffer from this kind of thirst, but…" I shake my head. Anger surges through my veins. I told them to stay away from her. I warned them not to taste her.

Xavier paces the room, grumbling to himself.

"But?" Malachi says.

"They will be forever bonded. His thirst for her will be controllable, but her blood will be no less desirable to him. Vampires can learn to live without their bonded elementai. It is agonizing, but it can be done."

Xavier stops pacing and shakes his head. "So he's stuck with this chick forever? *We're* stuck with her forever?"

Axl curls into a ball, shivering and gnashing his teeth.

"I can teach him how to resist the bond."

Xavier scowls. "But what if she wants the bond? These elementai things need vampires to survive, right?"

I shake my head. So ignorant, and I have only myself to blame. "Not at all."

"But you said it was an evolutionary thing," he says, confusion marring his features. "To ensure the survival of the species."

"Not their species, Xavier. Ours."

34

MALACHI

I sit on the edge of the bed and watch Axl, completely helpless in the face of his pain. All of our pain, because Xavier and I feel the same bone-deep, soul-aching despair that he's feeling right now. I rub a hand over his hip, and he shivers, his blank eyes staring through me.

"What the fuck's an elementai, Kai?" Xavier growls. "You've heard of these things before?"

When we first came to Montridge and I met other vampires, I was obsessed with the ancient magic. Then I met Osiris, a young wolf who was in Alexandros's class and shared my love of the subject. He and I would pore over old texts the professor would borrow from the faculty library. But then Osiris graduated and left me behind. The pain overshadowed my interest, and then I found other things to dedicate my time to. "Yeah, but like I said, I thought they were a myth."

Xavier paces from one end of the room to the other, his hands stuffed in the pockets of his sweatpants. "But now you know they're not. So what the fuck are they? Why are they so powerful?"

"From what I recall, they don't channel magic, they create it from nothing." Xavier stares at me blankly. "You know how witches and demons channel magic from the elements?"

His brows pinch together like he's deep in thought, which is a rare occurrence. "Yeah, like fire and water and shit?"

I arch one eyebrow. "Not shit, no. That would be fucking gross."

He snarls. "You know what I fucking mean, Kai."

A smirk tugs at the corner of my mouth. "Yeah, like fire and water and shit. Well, an elementai doesn't need any of those things. They can make magic from nothing. An elementai with mastery over fire could be in a vacuum and still summon fire."

His frown deepens. "So how does that make them so powerful? We don't live in a fucking vacuum."

I shake my head. "I know that, numbnuts, I was just trying to explain."

He flops onto the sofa and tosses a cushion at my head. "Explain better."

"It's not only fire, it's the magic that comes with fire. They can access magic anywhere. Without spells or incantations. It's hard to explain, and I can't recall everything I read."

He pulls a face. "Still don't get it. So she can make fire or air or water or whatever. Still doesn't mean she's this all-powerful being."

"Yeah, well, I guess it's complicated. But legend has it that they were so feared by all other magical creatures, including vampires, that they were wiped out hundreds of years ago. Before you and I were even born."

Xavier snorts. "If these beings were so powerful, how the fuck did they manage to get themselves killed? Why didn't they just wipe everyone else out?"

I swallow, thinking of the sweet girl with the pink hair we didn't know until less than two months ago. "Because elementai are inherently good. They don't use their powers for war or vengeance. It was a calculated strike, and by the time the genocide was underway, there were too few elementai left to make a stand. They were all wiped out. Every last one of them."

"And now Ophelia is here, and she's one of them?"

It's unbelievable, yet it explains everything. "According to the professor, and when have you ever known him to be wrong about anything?"

"But he said elementai were vital for the survival of our species. Why would the vampires help wipe them out if that were true?"

I shake my head and shrug. "I dunno."

"I guess we'll wait and see if Ophelia is one of these things and hope she can cure our boy." He nods toward Axl.

I take in the sight of him once more, unwilling to consider what it would mean if we lost him. I swallow down the lump of despair that sticks in my throat. "Yeah. Let's hope so."

Resting my hand on Axl's leg, I tell him that help is coming and he's going to be okay, but he goes on staring through me, teeth chattering, and mutters something I don't quite catch. Something about fire and blood. His mind is closed off to me, so I can't tell what delusions are running through his brain. But I continue to feel his anguish and his desperate need for Ophelia.

35

OPHELIA

I lean against the wall, watching droplets of rain sluice down the windowpane before funneling off the sill and dripping onto the rose bushes below. Despite the space heater blowing full blast beside me, I shiver against the cold. According to the thermostat, the room is balmy, but I'm still freezing.

It's been five days since that night at the house, and I've replayed every moment of it on repeat in my mind. The carnage in the parking lot by the river haunts my sleep, but the story about the car wreck seems to have been accepted by everyone, so my nightmares about spending the rest of my life in prison have abated.

But mostly I can't stop thinking about how the guys rescued me and how good they made me feel after. How my body lit up at their touch. The way it felt like they actually wanted me and weren't simply pretending. Then I recall the professor and how mad he was. Malachi and Xavier breaking my heart when they walked me home. How despite them being a constant pain in my ass for the past six weeks, I haven't seen any of them since. And how much that hurts.

"Does it always rain when you are sad, Ophelia?" The deep, smooth timbre of his voice startles and soothes me at the same time. For the first time in almost a week, I feel a spark of warmth inside me.

I spin on my heel and stare into the face of Professor Drakos. He's standing inside my dorm room, and I didn't even hear him come in. He watches me intently, waiting for my reply. "Maybe I'm sad because it's raining," I offer.

He looks out the window behind me. "It has rained almost nonstop for five days now. Unusual weather for Havenwood, even in October."

I shrug. "I've lived in this area all my life. The weather's always been unpredictable."

He doesn't reply, but his black eyes fix on mine. Something warm and familiar coils in my gut. I feel pinned in place by his gaze. Is this more of that vampire voodoo? Desperate to break the spell he seems to have me under, I focus on a spot above his head. "Did you come here to discuss the weather, Professor?"

He takes a seat on my bed uninvited, and I should be mad at his intrusion into my life, but all I can think about is how the sinfully delicious Professor Drakos is sitting on my unicorn comforter. My mind fills with the dirtiest images of him sinking his fangs into the most intimate parts of me.

His eyes, darker than the depths of hell, narrow. "But we are not simply talking about the weather, Ophelia."

"We're not?"

He doesn't reply. Instead, he inhales deeply, and a shiver of excitement laced with something unfamiliar shudders up my spine. It takes me a second to recognize that it's fear. He frightens me, and I don't understand why. Despite his ruthless exterior and rumored cruel streak, his actions have only ever protected me.

My legs tremble, and I croak, "So why are you here?"

"Axl is sick."

Well, that was anticlimactic. "I hope he feels better soon," I say in a dry tone, not really caring one way or the other.

Professor Drakos licks his lips. "Oh, he will."

That sliver of fear snakes its way into my lungs, making it difficult to breathe. I lean against my desk and grip the edge tightly. "Why are you telling me this?"

Before I can blink, he's standing in front of me. "Because you are what he needs to cure his sickness, Ophelia."

I bark out a laugh at the absurdity, and he frowns, no amusement in his eyes at all. "You are...*special*."

I snort. "I think we both know I'm not."

"Your blood is special, Ophelia. He had a taste, and now he needs more. You are the only thing that will cure his sickness." He looms over me, his eyes burning into mine, and a jolt of something dark and wickedly dangerous ripples through my entire body.

He needs my blood? Oh, the irony of him needing me tastes like poetic justice. Well, pity for him, I don't give a donkey's butt crack about him being sick. "So you expect me to let him bite me?"

"Yes," he says coolly, like it's nothing to have some evil bloodsucker feasting on me.

I scoff. "No way. I'm not letting any of you freaks drink my blood. I hate you all."

His tongue darts along his full bottom lip, and another image of his mouth on the inside of my thigh sears itself into my brain like the negative of a photograph. It's like déjà vu. He leans closer, dipping his head a little so that his warm breath dusts over my forehead. "You let him drink it from your virgin pussy." The low growl in his voice rumbles straight to my very core.

"That was different," I mumble, my cheeks burning.

"Why? Because you enjoyed it? I can assure you a vampire's bite is quite pleasurable."

I shake my head. "No, not because I enjoyed it. I didn't agree to let him drink my blood. It was a..." I swallow hard.

"But you knew you were a virgin and must have known there was a good chance you would bleed. You are not *that* naive, Ophelia."

My face grows hot with shame. "I didn't think about it."

"Well, your lack of thinking put Axl in danger. If he does not drink your blood, he will die."

"Wait, what? He'll die?"

He gives a short nod, and I suck in a shaky breath. This is all way too confusing. "I thought—they told me vampires could only be killed by having their heads chopped off."

He inches closer. "That is the quickest and surest death, but unfortunately not the only one."

"Are you messing with me? Is this some kind of trick to get me to—"

His hand goes around my throat, and he pushes me back against the desk and steps between my thighs. In spite of every rational cell in my body shouting that this is bad, a helpless, hungry whimper tumbles from my mouth as his body presses flush against mine. He rests his lips against the shell of my ear. "Do not underestimate me, Ophelia. This is not a request. I will not allow Axl to perish when you are so easily capable of saving him. Now, you will come with me, and you will give him what he needs. Do you understand me?"

I feel the power radiating from him, aware that he could easily snap my neck with a mere twitch of his fingers. What the hell have I gotten myself into? "Y-yes," I rasp.

He releases me, but his eyes stay fixed on mine while I rub at my tender skin. "Let us go."

He turns, and having no choice but to obey, I grab my raincoat from the peg on the door and follow him out of the building into the fresh air. Heavy clouds darken the sky, but the rain seems to be held at bay for now.

"What does this mean?" I ask, practically jogging to keep up with his pace. "Why is my blood so special? Can all people make vampires sick? Will he get sick again? Will he always need my blood?"

He shoots me an annoyed look over his shoulder, then frowns. "Do you always ask so many questions?"

"When I'm about to have my soul feasted on by a creature of the night, yes!"

His frustration is palpable and makes the damp air even heavier. I should try to dial it down a little, but my innate curiosity won't let me. There's so much to know, and he's infuriatingly uncommunicative. "Can you at least tell me if I'm going to be his snack bag for the rest of my life? Because that would put a big dent in my life plans."

He turns and gives me his full attention once more, and I almost wish he hadn't because the fiery look he gives me makes my knees wobble. Why do I feel as though he'd like me to be his snack too? But that's ridiculous. A vampire as powerful as Alexandros Drakos would take whatever he wanted from me. Still, I can't help but notice the electricity that always seems to crackle between us. "He will not get sick again. And you will not need to be his *snack bag* unless you choose to be."

"Well, that's good, then. Axl gets better and I can go on living my life. Better yet, I never have to see any of you assholes again." I shove my hands into the pockets of my raincoat. "That's all good."

His sideways glance tells me he doesn't believe me, and I don't blame him. I'm not sure I believe myself.

I'm not in any way prepared for the sight that greets me when I walk into Axl's room. He lies curled up in the middle of his bed, his dry, cracked lips trembling over chattering teeth. The pallor of his skin makes him unrecognizable. As I draw nearer, I can see his usually sparkling chocolate-brown eyes are matte black. Bloodshot and drawn, they stare right through me, dominating his pale features.

Malachi puts a hand on my arm. "Careful, Ophelia. He's not himself." I shrug him off. He doesn't get to pretend to care after what he did.

"He poses no danger to her." The professor's calm tone carries across the room.

I take a step closer, feeling no fear because I sense that he's right, although I have no evidence to base that assumption on. I'm so driven by my feelings around them all, especially Professor Drakos. I seem to operate with my senses rather than any logical thought processes, which is probably a good thing given that they're, you know, vampires.

Axl's nose wrinkles. He sniffs the air and croaks, "Ophelia?"

I glance behind me at the professor, looking for guidance, and he simply nods at me to go on. I sit on the bed beside Axl. "I'm here."

His teeth snap together, and he snarls but makes no attempt to bite me.

Xavier and Malachi stare at the two of us, then shoot a worried glance at the professor. "Fuck, Alexandros. Give him permission," Xavier pleads.

I blink. "Permission?"

Alexandros steps farther into the room, rubbing a hand over his jaw and staring at Axl with such pain on his face that it makes my heart ache. I'm so out of my depth here, thrust into a world where I have no idea of the rules.

"Alexandros!" Xavier snaps. "He would never disobey you. You know that. Let him feed."

I swallow hard, my pulse spiking. Feed? That sounds so brutal. Once the professor gives permission, what then? Do I only feel safe because of the power he still wields over Axl, even in this near-rabid state?

I don't have any more time to worry because the professor's commanding voice fills the room. "You may bite her, Axl."

As soon as the words leave the professor's lips, Axl's hand is on the back of my head. I yelp with surprise when he sinks his sharp fangs into my skin and begins to suck, so gently that I don't feel any pain. Instead, warm waves of pleasure roll over me. To my mortification, I moan. Loudly.

With a grunt, Axl flips me onto my back and pins me to his bed while he drinks from my neck. It shouldn't feel this good, but pleasure engulfs me like the warmth from a fire on a winter day. Instinctively, I wrap my arms around him, holding him close as euphoria snakes through my veins, warming my limbs and setting my core aflame. It feels so good that I wrap my legs around his waist and shamelessly grind against him despite our audience. My brain screams at me that this is wrong, but I'm unable to stop my body from responding to his.

He lifts his head and licks my blood from his lips, his brown eyes sparkling once more. "Holy fuck, Pyro," he says with a grin.

"Are you okay now?" I whisper.

He laughs wickedly and runs his nose up the column of my throat. "I have a feeling I'm never gonna be okay ever again."

"Give them the room," the professor barks, and I don't understand why he's angry. This is what he wanted, isn't it?

Xavier growls. "What? No. Why the fu—"

"I said leave them!"

"Fuck's sake," Xavier mutters, but he obediently files out of the room behind Professor Drakos.

Malachi shuffles after them, but before he closes the door, he gives me a longing look and mouths *sorry*. I return my attention to Axl and find his eyes fixed on me, the weight of his body pressing me into the mattress and his warm breath dusting over my face.

Regret, shame, and humiliation ball in my throat, but I swallow them down. I need to get out of here and far away from him. He's taken what he wanted, and now it's time for me to leave.

So why don't I move?

36

Axl

In all my two hundred and forty-seven years on this earth, I have never felt even a sliver of what I feel right now. A heady mix of power, euphoria, and contentment courses through my veins, combined with an animal lust that's oddly contained around her. When she walked into my room earlier, the beast inside me wanted to rip out her throat and feast on her until there was nothing left. But at the same time, her presence soothed him, turning him into little more than a purring kitten.

"Why did he ask them to leave?" she asks, her dark lashes fluttering.

I press a kiss to the corner of her mouth and rest my lips lightly against her skin. "Because you don't need an audience for your first time."

"My first time? What makes you think I want to do anything with you?" she snaps, but she makes no attempt to move from beneath me. Not that I would let her.

"The way your heart's racing." I trail my fingertips between her breasts where it pounds against her ribcage. "Your heavy breathing." I kiss across the seam of her lips. "The way you were grinding against me while I was feeding." I rock my hips, finding a little relief for my aching cock against her pussy. "And you're soaked, Pyro."

A blush colors her cheeks. "That doesn't mean I want you. Those are purely physiological reactions."

Trailing kisses along her jawline, I growl as her scent floods my senses once more. My fangs protract and my cock throbs at the thought of being inside her. "You do want me, Ophelia. And make no mistake—I am going to fuck you the next time I feed on you."

Her tits shudder against me as she takes a deep breath, but she still doesn't try to move away. "But this was all about you getting what you needed. A guy like you would never be interested in a girl like me, right?"

The ache in her heart feels like a hot knife slicing through my chest. It's incomprehensible to me now that I could ever want to hurt her, and the memory of how cruel I was to her has guilt eating away at my insides. "I know I pushed you away. Partly because I enjoyed seeing you in pain, but also because it was easier to keep my oath if I pretended you were nothing."

"You made me feel like less than nothing." There's a tremor in her voice, and she inhales another shaky breath. "And you enjoyed that?"

Her eyes are so full of pain, and I want to look away from her, but I can't. "I'm a fucked-up guy, Ophelia. But you already knew that." I run my nose over her jawline. "You know that, yet you want me anyway."

She shakes her head. "No. You were… All of you…"

"I know what Xavier and Malachi told you, princess, but you have to know they didn't mean that either. They were just following orders."

She blinks back tears. "I don't know that at all. What they said was cruel and..." A sob catches in her throat. "I'm not here for your amusement, Axl. Now let me go and we can all get on with our separate lives."

That knife slices deeper. "There is no me without you, Ophelia. There is no separate. Not anymore."

She shakes her head. "You only want me because my blood is vampire catnip."

"No, princess. I wanted you before I ever tasted you. I will still want you if I never get to taste you again. I'm going to show you how much." I grind myself against her and smile when she whimpers. "Let me fuck you, Ophelia."

"N-no."

I arch an eyebrow at her. "No?"

She presses her lips together and shakes her head.

We'll see about that. I drag my lips down her throat and over her collarbone, working my way down her body until I'm kneeling between her legs. Pushing up her plaid skirt, I expose her pink panties and the cute-as-fuck strawberry-shaped wet spot at the apex of her thighs. I run my nose over it. "So motherfucking sweet, Ophelia."

"Axl!" she says, half warning and half encouragement.

"How about we get these off you, princess?" I hook my fingers into her panties and pull them off before she can protest. Caught by the incredible sight of her bare pussy, I stare at her glistening arousal and slip one finger inside her. Her back bows off the bed.

"Oh, you like that, don't you, Pyro?"

She presses her head back against the pillow, her pretty lips parted, but she refuses to give me an answer, so I pull out and slide back in. "Oh, hellfire," she whimpers.

"I fucking love that I am the only man who's ever been inside you, Ophelia." I drop to my forearms and suck her swollen clit into my mouth, sucking and licking while I finger-fuck her. And when her legs are shaking and juices are dripping down into my palm, I add a second digit, stretching her wider until she mewls like a kitten and her back bows off the bed.

I lap at her sweet release, letting it flood my senses the same way her blood did, knowing that the power of coming inside her while I'm feeding on her is going to be overwhelming and extraordinary and the wildest ride I have ever known. Feeding from her might not happen now, but it will happen again. As sure as night follows day.

"Come for me, princess," I growl against her wet flesh, twisting my fingers inside her to prepare her for my cock. I can't recall the last time I fucked a virgin, and the thought of being the first to fuck this magnificent woman is only adding to the painful need to take her.

"Oh, crap. I'm gonna..." She tosses her head back and cries out my name. Her entire body pulses with the strength of her climax. My own head spins, and I slip my fingers out of her, fall onto my forearms, and line my cock up with her slick entrance.

Her eyes focus on mine, and for a split second, the whole world stops turning. This isn't right though. The first time I take her, I want to feel nothing but her skin on mine. "I want you naked, princess."

She offers no resistance when I pull off her clothes. Once she's naked, I pull off my sweatpants and boxers and settle back between her thighs.

"Do you have any protection?" she asks, her eyes wide and innocent.

"Vampires don't need any. We don't carry any diseases, and I can't get you pregnant."

"Oh." She chews on her lip. "You're sure?"

I take her hand and place it over my heart. "Yes, I'm sure, and I would never ever put you at risk, princess." I grin down at her.

"One of the perks of being a vampire is not needing condoms, so I can fill your tight pussy with my cum and watch it drip out of you afterward."

The blue of her eyes intensifies with desire, and I place the crown of my cock at her entrance and edge inside, drawing a harsh gasp from her. Falling forward onto my elbows, I dust my lips over her cheek. "It will hurt a little, princess, but I promise I'll make it feel good, okay?"

"I know," she pants.

I sink deeper, pressing my face into her neck. "Dammit, Ophelia, you feel so good. So goddamn tight."

Pain and pleasure burn through her, and she sinks her fingernails into my shoulder blades and whimpers. I slowly pull out and push back in, her wet heat slicking my cock. "You're doing so good, princess."

She blinks up at me, her eyes damp with unshed tears. "I am?"

I drive in a little harder, stretching her tight channel wider with each stroke. "You're taking my cock so fucking well."

Her emotions are so connected to mine that the rush of pride and happiness she feels at my praise washes over me too. She rocks her hips, taking more of me. I press my lips to her ear and growl. "That's my good girl."

"Oh, hellfire." She wraps her legs around my hips and groans, "More."

Growling, I graze my fangs over her fluttering pulse. "More?"

"Please. I want all of you." She arches her neck into my mouth, and I sink my teeth into her skin at the same time I bottom out inside her.

She screams my name, the perfect combination of pleasure and pain searing through her body and into mine. And I take my fill, feasting on her blood and claiming her innocence, and I have never felt more alive or more sure of anything in my life as I am of the two of us and this moment right here. I drive into her harder, letting her blood fill my mouth as I fill her with my cum, and I'm certain I've discovered a new high that I will never be able to top.

Ophelia was meant for me. Meant to be mine. And the bliss of that discovery is dampened by the knowledge that my brothers will want her too. They'll feel her connection with me through our bond, and if they experience only a fraction of what I'm feeling right now, I have no hope in hell of keeping her for myself.

EXCLUSIVE BONUS CHAPTER

OPHELIA

My heart is racing so fast I'm seriously worried I'm about to have some kind of cardiac event. I'm quite possibly about to meet my untimely end trapped beneath a vampire—a vampire who seems to have regained all of his strength and who's looking at me like I'm the tastiest snack he's ever eaten. I guess that's all down to my *special* blood, though, and nothing to do with me. I'm so confused about what's going on here, but one thing I do know is that I need to get the hell away from Axl Thorne.

But first, I need to know something, because the professor's deep growling is still ringing in my ears. "Why did he ask them to leave?"

Axl kisses the corner of my mouth and then leaves his lips resting against my skin. It's almost…tender. Except that it's him, and I'm sure he doesn't know the meaning of the word. "Because you don't need an audience for your first time."

My what now? That's what he thinks is about to happen here? That's what the professor, Xavier, and Malachi think is about to happen, too? My cheeks burn with anger and shame. "My first time? What makes you think I want to do anything with you?" My tone might be full of indignation and fire, but still I make no effort to move from beneath him. While he's a lot stronger than I am and no doubt my efforts would be futile, I should at least try, right?

"The way your heart's racing." His warm breath dusts over my face as he skates his fingers down my collarbone and between my breasts, letting them linger over my pounding heart. "Your heavy breathing." He peppers three soft kisses across my lips. "The way you were grinding against me while I was feeding." Oh, hell balls! He felt that? He grinds his hips, letting me feel every hard inch of him. And as much as I shouldn't want this, I do. My body wants exactly what he's offering, even though my head should be screaming no. "And you're soaked, Pyro."

My cheeks blaze hotter. I hate that my body is betraying me so easily. I hate that he knows these things about me. Arrogant vampire jackass. "That doesn't mean I want you. Those are purely physiological reactions," I snap, trying to inject as much anger into my tone as possible, because then maybe it will be enough to convince my body we need to get the hell out of here.

His lips coast over my jawline, and he plants sweet kisses on my skin. Then he inhales deeply, and an animalistic growl rumbles in his chest. "You do want me, Ophelia. And make no mistake—I am going to fuck you the next time I feed on you."

Oh, hellfire. Why do those words have me practically melting into a puddle? The thought of him doing both of those things, and at the same time, has wetness seeping from me, soaking my panties, which I suspect are already embarrassingly damp. Why do I want this so damn much?

I take a deep breath, reminding myself that none of *this* is real. It's simply him fulfilling some twisted need. "But this was all about you getting what you needed. A guy like you would never be interested in a girl like me, right?"

His brown eyes grow darker, and his face clouds with... Well, if I didn't know better, I'd say it was sadness. But it can't be... because I mean nothing to him. He told me so in no uncertain terms.

"I know I pushed you away," he murmurs. "Partly because I enjoyed seeing you in pain, but also because it was easier to keep my oath if I pretended you were nothing."

Well, mission accomplished on that front, jackass! "You made me feel like less than nothing." My voice trembles when I speak, and I hate appearing so weak in front of him, but he's scrambling my senses. My body is on fire, flooded with need and desire. I can barely think straight between my racing mind and my pussy throbbing with its own heartbeat—an intense staccato rhythm that seems like it's trying to drown out every logical thought in my head. I take another shaky breath. "And you enjoyed that?"

He stares at me, his jaw working as tears burn behind my eyes. "I'm a fucked-up guy, Ophelia. But you already knew that." He runs his nose over my jaw and growls again. "You know that, yet you want me anyway."

I shake my head. I don't want him. I shouldn't. I shouldn't want any of them. Their betrayal still hurts, still stings like a scalpel piercing my heart whenever I think of the things they said to me. How cruel they were. "No. You were... All of you..."

"I know what Xavier and Malachi told you, princess, but you have to know they didn't mean that, either. They were just following orders."

Following Alexandros's orders? But why? Is he just using that as an excuse for their awful behavior? I blink back tears, refusing to let them fall. "I don't know that at all. What they said was cruel and..." I almost let out a sob but swallow it down. "I'm not here for your amusement, Axl. Now let me go and we can all get on with our separate lives."

"There is no me without you, Ophelia. There is no separate. Not anymore."

I shake my head. I don't believe him. Can't believe him. Because what he's saying sounds far too much like exactly what I've been waiting to hear all my life. And therefore it can't be true. This is all fake. "You only want me because my blood is vampire catnip."

"No, princess. I wanted you before I ever tasted you. I will still want you if I never get to taste you again. I'm going to show you how much." He grinds his thick cock against me, and I involuntarily whimper in response, which causes the smug jackass to smile. "Let me fuck you, Ophelia."

Both my sanity and my common sense are hanging by a thread. One that's about to snap. "N-no."

He arches a thick, dark brow. "No?"

I press my lips together to stop myself from screaming *yes please* instead. The only refusal I can muster is another shake of my head.

Undeterred, Axl trails his wickedly sinful lips along my throat before moving down my body until he's kneeling between my spread legs. My limbs are trembling. Heart pounding. Pussy aching for him to touch me there. He pushes my skirt up to my waist, exposing my panties before running his nose over the damp fabric. "So motherfucking sweet, Ophelia."

I'm too turned on to offer much of a protest. All I manage to utter is his name, which sounds more like a groan of encouragement than a warning.

"How about we get these off you, princess?" He slides my panties off before I can even think of a reason why he shouldn't. My body screams that there's no reason on earth good enough to warrant stopping him from doing whatever he's doing.

He stares at my bare pussy, seeming captivated by the sight, before sliding one thick, delicious finger inside me. Holy hellfire. Warmth ignites in my core, and I arch my back in pleasure.

"Oh, you like that, don't you, Pyro?"

I press my head back against the pillow, trying to remember how to breathe, while refusing to give him the satisfaction of answering. He slips his finger out of me before sinking it back in—deeper. It feels so good. Even better than the last time. Different. More. Pleasure coils deep in my core, and it's not just my own euphoria that snakes its way through my limbs—I'm sure it's his, too. His longing for me radiates from him and into me, and somehow it feels like we're connected by an invisible thread.

I'm hyperaware of the fast, steady beating of his heart. Is this something to do with him biting me? Tasting my blood? I have no idea, and maybe I don't need to know right now. Because he's still working his thick finger in and out of me, and it feels so good I can barely remember why this is such a bad idea. So I focus on the pleasure, letting it wash over me in wave after wave. "Oh, hellfire."

"I fucking love that I am the only man who's ever been inside you, Ophelia."

Just when I think this can't get any more intimate, he dips his head and his mouth lands between my thighs—warm and soft yet insistent. He sucks my hypersensitive clit into his mouth, and I'm sure all of my remaining logical brain cells have fled. My needy pussy is now fully in control and willing to allow Axl Thorne to do whatever the hell he wants to me.

He sucks and licks my sensitive flesh while he continues driving his finger in and out, matching the rhythm of his skilled tongue. My legs are shaking, and my breathing is growing faster and shallower with every passing second. And when I'm sure I can't take any more and I'm convinced I'm going to shatter into a million fragments, he pushes a second finger inside me, stretching me wide and sending shock waves of pleasure rippling through me.

"Come for me, princess," he growls while he twists his fingers inside me. My back arches off the bed and I cry out his name as the most intense orgasm of my life tears through my body. And he licks me through it, tender yet fierce. Growling with unrestrained hunger while his tongue laps up my release.

When my eyes can focus, I find him staring at me, a wicked glint in his eyes. He smiles. "I want you naked, princess."

He removes all of my clothes with ease before discarding his own. And what a sight he is. I've seen his bare chest plenty before, but seeing all of him... It's otherworldly. He's a work of art. His muscles ripple with every movement, toned and taut. My gaze rakes over his body, over his defined pecs and his toned abs, and that *V*... I bite down on my lip as my eyes land on his dick. It's long and thick and glistening, and I have no idea how it's going to fit inside me. He gives his shaft one quick tug, and suddenly my mouth is watering.

He crawls between my thighs, animal-like hunger burning in his eyes. This is really happening. "Do you have any protection?" I ask, aware of the enormity of what we're about to do.

"Vampires don't need any. We don't carry any diseases, and I can't get you pregnant."

Of course—that makes sense. "Oh." I chew on my lip. But what if...? "You're sure?"

He grabs hold of my hand and places it on his chest. His heart beats against my palm. "Yes, I'm sure, and I would never, ever put you at risk, princess." His lips curve into a grin. "One of the perks of being a vampire is not needing condoms, so I can fill your tight pussy with my cum and watch it drip out of you afterward."

Oh, my. Why is that image so damn hot? The image his words conjure has me blushing again. But I don't have much time to dwell on it before he nudges his cock at my entrance and inches inside. I gasp at the intrusion. As much as he prepared me with his fingers, this feels so different. He's barely inside, and already I'm stretched wider than I've ever been.

Axl falls forward, landing on his elbows with his forearms on either side of my head. He brushes his nose over my cheek. "It will hurt a little, princess, but I promise I'll make it feel good, okay?"

For some reason I can't fathom, I believe him. And more than that, I trust him. "I know."

He presses his face into my neck as he pushes himself farther inside me. "Dammit, Ophelia, you feel so good. So goddamn tight."

I'm overwhelmed with both pain and pleasure. Made up entirely of need. I grab onto his shoulders, my fingernails sinking into his skin. Given the feral way he's growling in my ear, not to mention everything else I know about Axl Thorne, I expect him to fuck me hard. I brace myself for the moment he loses control, but it doesn't come. Instead, he's slow and gentle. Sliding himself in and out of me so carefully that the pleasure is almost unbearable. I'm wet and in need of more, but I feel so out of my depth.

"You're doing so good, princess."

I blink at him. "I am?"

He drives into me with a little more force, every stroke a little deeper and harder than the last. "You're taking my cock so fucking well."

A rush of arousal seeps out of me as I'm overwhelmed with both pride and ecstasy. Emboldened by his praise, I rock my hips up into him, allowing him to sink all the way inside me.

His warm mouth is pressed against my ear. "That's my good girl."

"Oh, hellfire." Those words. The way he's moving inside me. The way every cell in my body is made of nothing but aching desire. It's everything. I wrap my legs around his waist and try to pull him even closer. "More."

He growls, his fangs trailing over the skin of my throat. "More?"

I don't just want more—I want everything. I'm on fire with the urge to feel him claiming every part of me. Desperate for the hit of euphoria that I know will come from him feeding from me, too. "Please. I want all of you." I press my neck into his open mouth so there can be no mistaking exactly what I'm seeking.

He rewards me by sinking his fangs into my throat and his cock into my pussy at the same time. Blinding white ecstasy washes over me like a tsunami, everything heightened and even more intense than before. I scream his name as my orgasm threatens to take me under its swell. But he brings me back to him, sucking harder, driving deeper, keeping me here in the throes of ecstasy while he chases his own release. And I'm still right there with him when he does—still riding the high of my own climax as he empties himself inside me.

When his hips still and my body stops shuddering, he rests his forehead against mine, our breaths mingling in the space between us, our hearts beating erratically.

And when I think I couldn't possibly feel any happier than I do at this moment in time, he proves me wrong. "You were right about being special, Ophelia Hart." He kisses the tip of my nose. "You are incredible. You are delicious in every single way there is. And you are mine."

37

ALEXANDROS

Students scurry across the quad like ants swarming on candy as I stare out the window of my office. It is the second straight day of clear skies after a week of rain, and the sun is shining brightly. It would be like any other summer day, except that it is the middle of autumn. The students are taking full advantage. After each class lets out, the quad fills up anew in case the rain starts again at any second. Which could happen—such is the unpredictability of the weather lately.

Except the rain will not start again any time soon, because Ophelia Hart is deliriously happy. I know this because not only is her bond with Axl so strong that I feel her in his head, I have also had to endure listening to her have orgasm after orgasm over the past two days. The ground tremors that seem to accompany her every climax have become less pronounced, but the frequency of the seismic activity will end up swallowing this whole goddamn campus if she does not find a way to get a handle on her powers soon.

And therein lies my dilemma. If it truly is raining when she is sad, if her orgasms literally move the earth, and if she did start that fire in her high school...

That means she has mastery of fire, water, and earth. And that makes Ophelia Hart impossible. The most powerful beings in the world have mastery over only two elements. In my two thousand years of existence, I have only ever known of one creature with power over all four, and that was the great Azezal himself.

Ophelia clearly has no idea about her powers, and I have zero desire to be the one to tell her who and what she is. Because then she will look at me with those shining blue eyes full of trust and mistake me for her knight in shining armor. Which will force me to prove how wrong she is by sinking my fangs into her soft flesh.

I possess neither the inclination nor the strength to endure that particular torture. There is also no escaping the fact that the less I know about her, the safer she is.

I continue watching the scurrying ants through the window, most of them with no idea of the true power that exists in this world, only a few hundred feet away from them at any given time.

Vampires, witches, and werewolves are all becoming less powerful, less potent in their abilities every year, and so few are prepared to accept the truth, because then it would mean admitting that they were instruments in their own downfall. The inescapable truth is that without the elementai, magic itself is dying, albeit so slowly that few would notice.

Only those unfortunate enough to have lived such long lives can see it happening before our eyes. And those who were taught to understand the ancient scrolls would have been warned of this fate. An entire species cannot simply be eradicated without dire consequences. It was the new blood and their armies who led the charge, too young and ignorant to know better.

Xavier's anger floods out of his pores, arriving in my office before he does and alerting me to his presence before he opens his mouth. "Why does he get to bite her and not me?"

"Get out of my office and return when you have something worth saying." Keeping my tone and expression neutral, I turn and give him my full attention, noting his hands balled into fists at his sides.

"*This!* This is worth saying, Alexandros. Why him? Why it is always him you favor over me?"

"You are almost two hundred years old, yet you still behave like an adolescent," I say, my tone weary. "I favor none of you."

"So why can't I—"

I snarl, unable—or unwilling—to contain my own rage any longer. "You do not want to bite her, Xavier!"

His face contorts with anger and confusion. "Yes, I fucking do."

I cross the room in a single stride, and I am close enough to see the indigo flecks in his blue eyes. Why does he refuse to reason? Does he believe me to be so cruel that I would deny him this out of spite? "No, you do not. You have no idea of the agony of being bound to someone like her for eternity. No idea of how much it will cost you."

He scowls. "You have no fucking right to tell me what I can and cannot have. I feel her bond with Axl. I know what it involves, and I—"

"No!" I roar, causing the walls to rattle. Xavier takes a step back. "You do not know anything of what it would mean to bite her. You feel only the euphoria and the power of her. You have no idea of the pain that will come when you lose her. Because you will lose her, Xavier." My head spins, my vision blurring with the memories clawing their way to the surface.

As soon as the world finds out what she is, there will be no protecting her from them, I say through our bond. *They will come for her, and they will take her from you, and you will die a thousand agonizing deaths every single day after she is gone.* Despair crushes my lungs, and I struggle to draw a full breath.

"I'll take my chances." Oblivious to my anguish, he sneers with all the arrogance of youth and a heart that has never been broken. "Since when have you ever cared about my well-being, Alexandros? Since the moment you turned me, I've been nothing but a burden to you."

His heart rate spikes in response to the growl that rumbles in my throat, and I hear his blood whooshing through his veins as keenly as if it were my own. "You will be tied to her forever."

"I already am. We're all tied to her through Axl, and you know it. At least let us take some fucking pleasure from it."

"And you will get so lost in the pleasure that when the pain comes..." The mere shadow of a memory steals the rest of the words from my mouth. He has no comprehension of the wretched desolation he is opening himself up to.

"I can fucking handle it."

But can I? I crack my neck, but it does nothing to relieve the frustration of this conversation or the knowledge that I cannot protect them from the cruelest fate to ever befall a vampire. Giorgios would say it was destiny that brought the only living elementai in over five hundred years to them—to me. "Your brother will not want to share her."

Xavier's lips twitch. "Like he'll have a choice. It's about time your firstborn was taught to share, just like Malachi and I had to."

Malachi. The youngest and most sensitive soul I have ever turned. I close my eyes and search for him. *Do you know what your brother is asking me? Do you want this too?*

Yes, comes his swift reply.

I never used to be this way. Cruel and unyielding. I was a good father once. But that was a long time ago. I am not even sure now whether it is cruelty or sentiment that makes me say "You're free to bite her."

Malachi's intense relief clouds my thoughts for a few seconds before I tune him out and refocus on Xavier. He frowns as though he had no expectation that I would relent. Then he flicks the tip of his tongue over his fangs, and animallike need for Ophelia runs through his veins along with his blood.

I dismiss him with a nod toward the door, and he rushes from the room. If I were a better man, I might feel an ounce of sympathy for Ophelia and what she is about to endure. But the truth is that my worries should be reserved for my boys. She is the one who holds all the power, even if she has no idea of that yet.

38

XAVIER

Axl sits upright in bed, glaring at the doorway like he was expecting me. Ophelia sleeps soundly beside him, and he growls but keeps his voice low. "You can't fucking have her, Xavier."

I step into his room and close the door behind me, clicking my tongue against the roof of my mouth. "You think you're going to stop me?"

"I'll rip out your fucking throat if you touch her."

"I'm sure it will be worth it." Offering him a casual shrug, I step closer and pull off my T-shirt. I frequently recall the taste of her pussy on my fingers, but her blood… My fangs and my cock throb with hunger to take all of her and make her my own. I have felt the high it gives him, and even secondhand, it's a rush.

He gets out of bed and comes to stand toe to toe with me, his bare chest pressed against mine, his vicious snarl vibrating through us both. "She's mine."

I tilt my head and glare at him. "Yeah, well, she's about to be mine."

He wraps a hand around my throat. "Do. Not. Fucking. Touch. Her." He squeezes, and I wrench out of his grip, but he doesn't budge when I shove him with both hands.

"I'll do whatever the fuck I want, Axl."

He bares his fangs and growls like a feral lion guarding its dinner. "Don't make me hurt you, Xavier."

I bark out a laugh. "Seriously? You think you're capable of that, old man?" I push him again, and he lunges for my throat, but I dodge out of his way. He roars with frustration before coming at me again. This time he barrels into me, taking me down to the floor, and my head smacks against the carpet, making me bite my lip and draw blood.

"Axl!" Ophelia calls out, distracting him long enough that I manage to pin him on his back. I drive my knee into his groin and bask in his pained groan.

"Xavier! What the hell are you doing?"

Glancing over my shoulder, I flash her a grin. "Just coming for my prize, Cupcake."

She blinks. "Your prize?"

Before she can take another breath, I pounce on her and wrap my hand around her slender throat. "Yes, my prize."

"She's not yours, asshole." Axl pushes himself to his feet.

"Pretty sure she's about to be." I squeeze Ophelia's throat harder. Her eyes widen with horror, and my pulse quickens. I'm going to bite her and fuck her, and there's not a single thing she or Axl can do to stop me. I tip her head back, exposing an expanse of creamy pale skin.

"Xavier!" Axl's hands are on me, but he knows my grip on her neck is too tight to risk trying to pull me off her.

"Xavier," she says softly, her jugular vein pulsing beneath my palm.

Her scent invades every cell in my body, and there's every chance I could rip her throat out with my fangs with the force of the hunger coursing through me. I have never needed or wanted anything more. She's always smelled sweet, but something's changed. Maybe when Alexandros rescinded his order not to bite her, my senses became more heightened in her presence.

Holding my gaze, she flutters her eyelashes, her blue eyes sparkling, and I'm done for. I'm vaguely aware of Axl cursing at me as I sink my teeth into her soft skin, but the second I taste her, everything else falls away. Her delicious taste floods my mouth, making my head spin with a heady mix of adrenaline and rapture. Her blood rushes through my veins, becoming a part of me. She becomes a part of me. And damn it all to hell and back, Axl could cut off my head right now and this would still be worth it.

We fall back on the bed, her on her back and me settling my body over hers as I continue to suckle at her vein. Despite my ravenous hunger, I feed way more gently than I ever have before. And although it surprises the fuck out of me, I have no desire to unpack what it means. Especially not when she moans, wrapping her legs around my waist and arching her back as I settle into a more comfortable position between her thighs. The perfect angle to rub my aching cock against her bare pussy.

And although I haven't taken anywhere near my fill of her, I stop sucking as soon as I feel her blood flow slowing a little. Humans can stand to lose a couple of pints without any long-lasting effects, but she'll begin to feel lightheaded if I drink much more. And the fact that I care about that, that I put her own needs above my own, also surprises the hell out of me.

I lick the trail of blood trickling down her neck before swirling my tongue over my bite marks to heal them. Next time I do this, I'm going to fuck her while I feed from her. The mere thought has my cock throbbing.

"Xavier." She breathes out my name and threads her fingers through my hair, her eyelids fluttering while she rides the remnants of the high I gave her.

"You're mine now too, Cupcake." I press a kiss at the base of her throat, then unzip my jeans and free my hard length, nudging my crown at her slick entrance. A vampire's bite is the best kind of foreplay, and this girl here is already dripping for me. "That means every part of you."

She arches her back, taking the tip of me inside her tight pussy. "Yes."

I can feel Axl's rage simmering, but he doesn't stop me, and I suspect he knows that he couldn't. Not only because I'd kill him—or die trying—but also because she wants this as much as I do, and he's incapable of denying her anything she wants. So I give her exactly what she deserves and sink my cock deep into her wet heat until her back bows and she cries out my name.

I pull out and drive back inside. "You feel so fucking good squeezing me like that, Cupcake."

She whines like a needy little slut when I pull out of her again. "Damn, you love my cock, Ophelia. Did Axl not fuck you properly earlier?"

She gasps, and Axl grabs me by the hair, yanking my head back. "Don't fucking push it," he warns, but I ignore him, wrenching away and focusing on Ophelia's face. Her cheeks are flushed the prettiest shade of pink and her eyes shimmer with tears, and for some reason I get an unfamiliar ache in my chest. Fuck me. I feel her fucking shame like it's my own.

"I didn't mean to embarrass you, Cupcake." I press a kiss on her forehead and gather her in my arms. "I love the way you whimper when I pull out of you. It makes it all the sweeter"—I slide out of her again—"when I do this." I sink balls-deep inside her, and my head fucking spins.

"Oh god," she moans, her lips pressed to my neck.

"You must know he doesn't exist," I tell her with a wicked chuckle. "But I'll be your god if you insist on calling out for him."

I roll my hips and hit her G-spot. Her walls ripple around me, and she groans out my name instead.

I trail kisses over her throat, and my fangs ache to bite her again, but I hold back and listen to the sounds we make. "You're so fucking wet for me, Ophelia. You hear how much your pussy wants me?"

"Yeah," she whimpers.

Axl lies on the bed beside us, watching me pull out of her again and smiling at the frustrated groan she lets out when I don't immediately push back inside. Instead, I flip her onto her stomach and spread her legs wide with my knees before I take her again. I pull back her hair and press her body into the mattress, resting my lips at her ear while I rut into her and draw out a series of needy whimpers and moans.

"Oh, you're so fucking tight like this, Cupcake. I'm gonna fuck you every way and everywhere I can. You're gonna be full of my cock every fucking day."

Her body trembles at my words, and I glance at Axl. His earlier rage at me has already dissipated. It's clear to us both that her being with me doesn't weaken his bond with her. In fact, it's only gotten stronger. I feel his connection with her, and I feel him more than I ever have before.

I grin at him. "You want to make her come with me?"

He turns onto his side and slides his hand between her and the mattress. He must start playing with her clit because she gasps before sinking her teeth into the pillow, her walls fluttering around me. I swirl my tongue over the shell of her ear. "That's my filthy little slut. Wait until we fuck you together, Cupcake."

There's no shame from her this time. She lifts her head and cries out, sinking her teeth into her juicy bottom lip. I'm desperate to do the same. I close my eyes and grunt with the effort of not giving in to that particular desire.

"You won't hurt her if you bite her," Axl assures me. "You can't."

I swallow. I can't explain why or how, but I know that to be true. As sure as I know my heart is beating, I know that I am incapable of harming her.

"And feeding on her while you come..." He finishes his sentence with a guttural moan.

Growling, I thrust deeper inside her. "Can I bite you again, Cupcake?"

"Please," she whines.

I lift her head and lick the pulse fluttering in her throat. Her pussy spasms around me, and I can smell how close she is to the edge. The monster inside me demands to take over and fuck her into oblivion, but I can't let him. Not yet. One day, after I've taught her how to take my cock in all her holes like a good slut, I'll let him loose. But not today.

My cock aches with the need for release, mirroring the throbbing in my fangs as they graze her soft skin. Her flesh yields to their sharpness with a satisfying pop before her delicious, soul-soothing blood coats my tongue. She cries out, her muscles squeezing my shaft tighter as her orgasm takes hold, and the pleasure running through her veins makes her taste all the sweeter.

My balls are heavy with the need to come, and I drive deeper and harder into her tight, wet center, suckling her neck until I'm completely engulfed by her. Blinding light steals my vision. Fire and ecstasy burn through me, lighting up every cell in my body. I swear the very earth beneath us trembles. And I lose myself in her, giving her every single fucking thing that I am.

I may have walked into this room intending to claim her, but I ended up handing myself over at the same time. Every atom that makes up my existence belongs wholly and irrevocably to Ophelia Hart.

39

OPHELIA

The past two days have been a whirlwind, and I need to take some time to process everything that's happened. I was determined to hate Xavier and Axl after everything they did and said, but now...

I feel things for them that are illogical and terrifying. They've already seen me naked, but they got dressed before they grabbed snacks from the kitchen, and the vulnerability of being the only one without clothes has me tugging the covers up over my naked torso. "I really need to get some of my things."

Xavier takes a noisy bite from his apple and nods at two duffel bags in the corner of the room. "Already got them, Cupcake."

"What? When?"

"While you were sleeping."

I jump out of bed, no longer concerned about my nudity, and unzip the larger of the two bags. My panties sit in a surprisingly neat pile on top of what looks to be half my wardrobe, and a little digging reveals my well-worn copy of *Wuthering Heights*.

The sight of my favorite book nearly melts me into a puddle, and I silently admonish myself for being so weak where they're concerned. I've become a slave to my hormones. "You went through my things?"

Xavier shrugs nonchalantly. "Kinda had to."

"But that's...you had no right to do that. What about my privacy?"

He comes to stand beside me and peers into the bag, then flashes me a wicked grin. "I've been inside you, Cupcake. You don't get more private than that. I didn't bring your little buzzy friend though. You won't be needing that anymore."

A blush races down my neck. I hadn't yet found the courage to try out the tiny bullet vibrator I ordered online, but after what happened in this room over the past couple days, I was looking forward to seeing how it would feel. I put my hands on my hips and lift one eyebrow. "You're really that threatened by a toy?"

He grabs the hair at the nape of my neck and pulls me toward him, squishing my boobs against his hard chest. "No, Cupcake, I am not threatened by anything. But we are the *only* place where you will find your pleasure from here on out." He licks a path along my jawbone, making me shiver. "Do I make myself clear?"

He tosses the apple core into the trash and trails his free hand down my ribs, grazing my hipbone along the way to the tops of my trembling thighs. "Y-yes."

"Good little Cupcake."

"There's my sweet girl."

I look past Xavier to see Malachi kicking the door closed and pulling his T-shirt over his head. The sight of his toned abs is enough to make me drool, but every muscle in my body is already aching, and I think my lady parts might close up shop if anyone else tries to gain entry right now. Not to mention I'm still mad as hell at him. Of all of them, he hurt me the most. He made me believe I meant something to him, and then he broke my heart. And I know now it was all because he was following the professor's orders, but that doesn't make it hurt any less.

Malachi pushes Xavier off me. "Out of my way, numbnuts."

With no protest and only a chuckle, Xavier goes to join Axl on the bed, and they both lie with their arms behind their head.

I make a halfhearted attempt to cover myself with my hands, but Malachi is too swift for me. He circles my wrists and pins them behind my back, and his voice is a commanding growl. "Let me get a good look at you."

"Stop!" I whisper, trying to wrench out of his grip, but he holds me tight.

His eyes grow dark as they roam over my body. "Even more beautiful than I dreamed, sweet girl."

"I'm not your sweet girl. I'm too messy, right?" Dammit, I hate the distinct crack in my voice.

"You'll always be my sweet girl, Ophelia. And I'm sorry, baby. I would never hurt you—"

"But you did hurt me, Malachi," I remind him.

He presses his lips together and nods before drawing a deep breath. "Then let me show you how sorry I am, baby. Please." Inhaling deeply, he runs his nose down my throat to my collarbone. When he reaches my breasts, he flicks my nipple with his tongue, catching it with his piercing. I whimper shamelessly and arch toward him.

"I h-have to go to class today. I already missed yesterday."

I wait for one of them to remind me that nobody will miss me, but the only sound in the room is Malachi's heavy breathing. "You smell *so* damn good, sweet girl. And I know you're going to taste even better."

He runs a hand over my ass and squeezes before he slips it between my thighs, lightly dusting his knuckles over my aching flesh. "Are you a little sore this morning?"

The stinging between my thighs has me nodding my agreement, and I'm overcome with embarrassment at him knowing exactly what I've been doing with his brothers.

He winks. "I can fix that."

I press my lips together and suck in a breath through my nose. "But I really need to go to class. And I have a meeting with my advisor."

Malachi's reply is to seal his mouth over mine. He flicks his tongue over my lips until I part them on a moan, allowing him entry. His free hand glides up my neck to palm the back of my head. He holds me in place, my wrists still pinned in one of his large hands. And then he kisses me so hard that my trembling legs almost give way. I would crumple to the floor if he wasn't holding me up. My body melts into his like I'm made of hot wax. His expert tongue dances against mine, drawing out a series of moans and whimpers. Unable to help myself, I grind on him, painfully aware of how hard he is. Am I really the kind of girl who melts for a boy just because he's a good kisser? I shouldn't even be contemplating letting him do this, but I keep picturing him throwing me onto the bed and taking me while Axl and Xavier watch.

Wetness pools between my thighs, but Malachi pulls back all too soon, leaving me gasping and needy. "You really should get to class, Ophelia. Because I haven't slept for two nights, and I'm feeling a little..." He rolls his neck. "Unrestrained."

I swallow the unexpected bubble of disappointment that jumps into my throat.

He tucks my hair behind my ear and smiles. "What time do your classes finish, baby?"

"Um." I'm distracted by his hard length still pressed against my stomach and his hand on my ass. "Four-thirty."

"I'll come meet you after. Okay?"

I nod.

He releases my wrists and taps me on the ass. "Go get showered and dressed before I change my mind."

I glance at his brothers and find their eyes still locked on me, but they don't protest me going to class either. I'm grateful because I really do need to go, and I suspect any one of them could convince me to stay.

...

I'm leaving the Commons after grabbing a cup of coffee when Cadence links her arm through mine. "Hey, girl. You want to grab some lunch together today?"

Lunch with Cadence sounds amazing, but I shake my head, disappointed. "Can't, sorry. I have a meeting with my personal advisor during my break between classes."

She pulls a face like she's disappointed too. "Maybe some other day, then?"

I nod eagerly, a smile stretching across my face. "I'd love that."

She keeps her arm linked with mine, and I continue walking alongside her. We may not be able to have lunch, but I have a bit of time. "You missed a fun party Saturday. It was a shame you didn't come. Better than sitting in your room on your own crying over some douchebag."

I clear my throat and avoid eye contact as I'm struck by the vivid memory of how a few nights earlier I spent the night losing my virginity to said douchebag, well, one of them at least, and letting him drink my blood. "Maybe the next one?" I say, trying to stop the thoughts of Axl and Xavier and their sinfully delicious mouths, not to mention their huge—

"You feeling a little better, though?" Cadence interrupts my thoughts and spares me from blushing. "You seem brighter today."

"Yeah. Much better. Thank you."

She squeezes my shoulder. "That's my girl."

An unexpected sob wells in my throat, and I swallow it back down. Surely none of this is real, right? I'm going to wake up from a coma any moment now and find out the past few days have been a dream.

Happiness like this cannot possibly be real. I, Ophelia Ilyria Hart—orphan with no money who has never had a friend in her life—am actually in college. I love all of my classes, and despite missing a couple days, I'm holding my own in every subject.

My dream of becoming a social worker and helping kids who have no one else to look out for them isn't the unattainable dream I considered it for so long. One day, I *will* change lives. And not just any lives. The lives of kids who are like me.

On top of all that, I have three absurdly hot guys interested in me. Even if it's only because my blood is special, I can live with that.

But some part of me always knew there would be a guy—definitely not *three* guys, but still. After everything that's happened, I never imagined true friendship, so Cadence wanting to be my friend is probably the best part of my unbelievable new life. She's friendly, funny, and so much cooler than all the other girls who've treated me like shit since I got here.

Cadence comes to a stop as we reach the building that houses all the natural science classes and labs. "This is me," she says, pulling me into a quick hug. "Don't forget what I said about coming by Silver Vale, okay? I'm at study group tonight, but I'll be home the rest of the week."

"Yeah, okay, sure. I'll drop by sometime."

"Cool. See you around, Ophelia."

She spins on her heel and goes inside Urania Hall, and I tip my face toward the sun and smile. Today is going to be a great day.

40

MALACHI

The doors open and students pour out of the building onto the pavement, laughing and talking. My girl will be one of the last people out. Alone, but no doubt with a contented look on her face. I admire her for not needing anyone else to complete her, but there's a dull ache in my chest when I think about her sitting in her classes by herself, with nobody to laugh with or copy notes from if she zones out. I hate that for her, but I hate more that she believes she's friendless because she's the kind of person people don't want to be around when that's not remotely close to the truth.

I knew from the moment we met her that she was special. Xavier and Axl picked up on her unique scent, but her soul called to mine. The undeniable attraction went deeper than her being sexy and curious. And now I know why. Because she is inherently different from the rest of the world around her. An elementai. Unique. Powerful.

And humans, while they lack the knowledge to even begin to comprehend her kind of power, there is something in their baser selves that senses it. An old survival instinct. And that's why they shun her—they're afraid of her, and they don't even know it. And she has been so used to that treatment all her life that she doesn't notice when the type of creatures who are inherently drawn to her try to befriend her.

She walks out of the building, and as I expected, she has a smile on her face. She shields her eyes from the sun, and I take a moment to study the sinful curve of her hips and the toned muscles in her thighs in those tiny skirts she insists on wearing.

The second her eyes find mine, that soft smile of hers spreads wider, lighting up her whole goddamn face. And fuck, it burns me up from the inside knowing that she smiles like that for me. I adjust my rapidly hardening cock, my mouth watering at the promise of tasting her and fucking her as soon as I get her alone.

I jog toward her, and her grin grows stronger with each step I take. "Hey, Malachi," a nasally voice says as I pass, but I pay no attention.

My girl does though. That incredible smile falters as she glances away from me, and I want to rip out the tongue of whoever dared speak my name like that in front of my girl.

I reach Ophelia and shield her body with mine, grabbing her jaw and directing her attention squarely back to me. "Right here is the only place you need to be looking, sweet girl."

Her cheeks turn the same color as her hair. "Hi," she whispers, sounding nervous even when she has no need to be.

"Hi, baby." I take her backpack from her and shrug it onto my right arm, slinging my left one over her shoulder. "Did you have a good day?"

"I did actually. Did you get some sleep?"

"A solid seven hours. So I'm good to go all night."

Her breath catches in her throat, making me laugh. I run my nose over her jawline. Fuck me, she smells so good that I'm tempted to bite her right now in front of all these people. Bite her, then throw her up against the nearest tree and sink my dick inside her. "I'll take it easy on you, sweet girl," I assure her.

Her blue eyes widen. "Do you want to bite me too?"

I lick my lips. "Since the second I first smelled you."

Her brow furrows. "But I'm just one person. And if you all bite me… I kind of need my blood to, you know, live."

I run my knuckles over her cheek, and the way she looks at me, so full of longing and a trust that I haven't earned yet, makes warmth spread in my chest. "We can't take too much blood. It's impossible."

Her frown deepens, and that cute spot between her eyebrows pinches together. "Why impossible?"

I lean closer and she shivers. "It's evolution, baby. Once we bite you, we're incapable of harming you, and that includes taking too much blood."

She blinks. "But you bite people all the time." Her voice is little more than a whisper as we make our way across the quad.

"But you're different, sweet girl. I thought you already knew that."

"I don't understand, Malachi. Last week, you told me that I meant nothing, and now all three of you…" Tears steal the rest of her sentence. I stop and cup her face in my hands, kissing the salty water from her face. Even her tears taste incredible.

"That was cruel, baby, and I'm so sorry. It fucking breaks me to think of how much we hurt you. But we weren't allowed to taste you. We were ordered to push you away. A vampire's oath to his sire is unbreakable." I press my forehead against hers. "Tell me you understand?"

She sniffs. "I guess I do."

I sigh and hug her to my chest.

"Was I forbidden because of my blood? Because the professor knew you'd get sick after one taste and need more?"

I nod. That and so much more, but now isn't the time to tell her everything. And not only because I'm thinking with my dick and my primary goal is to get her somewhere where I can have her alone, although that's the main reason. It will take me at least another ten minutes to get her to the house, but we just passed the library. I pick her up and wrap her legs around my waist.

"Malachi, what are you doing?" She giggles. "People are watching."

I nip her neck. "Let them watch. I heard you've been neglecting your studies, fucking around with my brothers instead of having your head buried in those books. So I'm taking you to do some studying, naughty girl."

She bands her arms around my neck. "We're going to study?"

"Well, I'm taking you to the library, but what we'll be studying won't require books, baby."

Her eyes sparkle. "What are we studying?"

I arch an eyebrow. "Anatomy."

She shakes her head, trying to wriggle out of my grip, but she has zero chance of doing that. "No. Not in the library. Take me home."

"That's gonna take ten minutes, and I can't go that long without fucking you, Ophelia."

Her chest heaves as she sucks in a heavy breath. "So do the special run," she whispers.

I press my lips together to stop myself from laughing. "The special run?"

She rolls her eyes. "The one where you move super fast. Like on the night I first met you."

I shake my head. "Can't, baby. Too many people around. Can't go drawing the attention of the humans."

"But you can fuck me in the library? You think that's not going to draw attention?"

I shrug. "Not the kind of attention that will get me in trouble with the professor. Besides, people fuck in the library all the time."

"They do not!"

I can't help but smirk at the look of indignation on her face. "So maybe we'll be the first."

She glances around and chews on her bottom lip. "People are already staring at us."

"Because my hands are on your sexy little ass and you're so fucking hot."

Sorrow clouds her features now. "Don't tease me."

I stifle a growl and place her on her feet. Taking her hand instead, I pull her along with me, making her run to keep up with my long strides. My girl doesn't think she's hot? I'll show her exactly how wrong she is.

As soon as we're inside the library, I head for the art history section at the back. Nobody who comes to Montridge to study art history actually studies, at least not in the library. When we reach the end of the narrow passageway, I drop her backpack and herd her back against the shelves.

"Malachi," she whispers, her eyes darting in every direction but the place I want them.

I grab her chin and squeeze, forcing her to look at me. "Eyes right here, sweet girl. Nobody comes back here. Nobody will hear us. Well, so long as you don't scream too loud." I wink, but she's clearly still nervous. I guess I'll have to do something about that.

I slip my hand beneath her miniskirt and find her panties, tugging them out of my way before she can utter a word of protest. She gasps when I sink a finger into her tight channel.

"Goddamn... Fuck, Ophelia." I push all the way in. "You're so snug and wet, baby."

"M-Malachi," she whimpers.

I take her hand and place it over my throbbing dick. "You think you're not hot, sweet girl? You've had me hard like this for weeks with just the thought of being inside you." I tip my head back and groan as her tight pussy squeezes around my finger. "And I'm probably going to nut in my fucking jeans if I bite you right now."

She pulls down my zipper, slips her delicate hand inside my boxers, and wraps her fingers around my shaft, and I bite on my lip with the effort of not roaring her name.

"Take out my cock, baby. I'm going to fuck you."

"Right here?" she pants, her breath hot against my neck.

"Right here. Right now. So take out my cock." I slip another finger inside her tight pussy, and her back bows as a keening moan rolls out of her lips. I press my lips to her neck. "Do it, Ophelia."

My submissive little powerhouse does as she's told, and as soon as my aching cock is free, I slip my fingers out of her and wrap her legs around my waist once more, pressing her back against the bookshelves.

"Malachi, I need you," she groans.

"I know, baby. I'm going to give us what we both need." I shove her panties aside and nudge the crown of my dick at her slick entrance. My fangs protract, throbbing to pierce her sweet flesh. The scent of her wet pussy is almost as strong and alluring as the smell of the blood shuttling through her veins. My cock aches to be inside her, my veins burning with the need to make her mine and feel that same euphoria that my brothers feel each time they take her. I want to be tied to her forever. Want her to be mine.

"Ophelia!" I grunt as I ease inside her tight heat.

She claws at my neck, and I bottom out. Her head tips back and her mouth opens on a silent scream as she accepts every inch of me. I dust my teeth over her neck, and the animal inside me taunts me to bite her and drink her dry. I feel like I could tear out her throat with the need coursing through me, except that I already know that I won't. I couldn't even if I wanted to.

"M-Malachi," she moans again, her snug cunt squeezing me tighter as I drive into her over and over again, nailing her to the bookshelves with each thrust of my hips.

"I can't get deep enough, Ophelia," I growl, my lips still on her neck. "I want to fucking climb inside you and stay there forever."

"Then do it," she gasps.

My blood is racing around my body so fast that my head is spinning. A desperate whimper falls from her lips, and that's my undoing. I sink my fangs into her soft flesh, and my mouth is flooded with her. Her power. Her soul. Her very being. Her blood is coppery and sweet and fucking addictive. It ignites inside me like my veins are made of gasoline and she is the spark.

But it sates the animal inside me, and I slow my pace, enjoying the slow burn of torture when I pull my cock out of her before sinking back in. I slice open a cut on my tongue and let my blood flow into her vein while I feed, soothing the burning pain between her thighs so I can go on fucking her.

"Oh!" She pulls on the collar of my T-shirt, wrapping her legs tighter around me. "Malachi, I can't stop… I'm going to…"

I place my hand over her mouth and muffle her cries, continuing to suckle at her neck and grind into her, chasing the euphoria of my release that's only a breath away. And when it comes, it almost knocks me off my feet, crashing over me with the force of a tsunami.

My legs are shaking when I pull out of her, and I flick my tongue over the puncture wounds until they heal over. Lowering her legs to the ground, I press my forehead against hers.

"I can't believe we just did that in the library," she says, giggling. Her cheeks are bright pink as she looks around.

"I told you I wasn't going to be able to wait." I kiss the tip of her nose. "I would have fucked you this morning, only I knew how sore you'd be."

She fists her hands in my T-shirt. "Thank you for waiting."

"I would wait ten thousand lifetimes for you, sweet girl."

Malachi. Where the fuck are you two? Axl asks.

I roll my eyes and tell him to go fuck himself. "We should get back to the house, baby."

She rolls her shoulders. "Maybe I should go back to my dorm tonight?"

I know she's not in any pain because I don't feel it, and the blood I gave her will have her feeling like she's invincible for at least the next twelve to twenty-four hours. So it's not like she needs to take a break, although we would give her one if she did. I shake my head. "Not happening, baby. You live with us now."

She throws her head back and laughs. "I do not. Don't be ridiculous."

I wrap my arms around her waist. "Yes, you do. And if you're worried about needing a little downtime, I'm going to run you a nice warm bath when we get home. After you're squeaky clean, we'll order some takeout and watch scary movies. How does that sound?"

She smiles. "Great, except for the scary movies. I prefer superheroes."

After fixing our clothes and grabbing her backpack, I thread my fingers through hers and kiss her knuckles. "Fine, you choose the movie."

On our way to the house, I steal glances at her every ten seconds. She looks exactly the same, but she's different. I'm different. I just willingly tied myself to her for eternity. And while I understand the professor's concerns about her not being immortal, we can prolong her life as long as she has our blood. And I know as sure as I've ever known anything that I would die a thousand deaths before I let anyone hurt her. She's mine for the rest of my life, and that's all that matters.

She flashes me a sweet smile, and my chest aches with the promise of the life we'll have together. She came here to me—to us—for a reason. Ophelia Hart is my reason for being.

41

OPHELIA

I spin around, sure I heard Axl's voice, but the bathroom is empty.

Yeah, let's go to the diner down by the highway that does the waffles Kai likes. I think Ophelia is gonna need a good breakfast after last night, Xavier says.

I shake my head. The acoustics in this house are so weird. I can hear them as clearly as if they were standing right next to me, but Xavier's in the kitchen, and I guess Axl must have joined him there.

You did make sure she had plenty to drink, right? We took a lot of her blood.

I smile at Malachi's concern for me. But… What the hell? Malachi went to check on the pledges. This is impossible. Their voices are in my goddamn head.

Malachi goes on talking to Axl and Xavier, and I shove my fingers in my ears, hoping it will drown out their chatter. But their voices remain as loud as if they were in the room with me. *What the hell?*

Ophelia? The three of them say at once.

Why are you all in my head? And why can you talk to each other in there?

Why are you in ours, Cupcake?

What in hellfire? How would I know? It's not like I want to be. What the hell have you done to me? How long have you been able to speak to each other like this?

Always, princess, Axl says. *It's part of our bond.*

Your bond? And you didn't think to warn me of this particular development? Get out of my damn head! I internally shriek the last few words, my hands gripping the basin so that my wobbly knees don't betray me by letting me fall flat on my ass.

What the fuck's going on? Malachi says, sounding as confused as I am.

Stop talking, Axl orders, and they go silent.

What? Wait! No. Don't stop talking. Tell me what's happening. Why are you in my head? Will this go away? Is this some kind of post-orgasm thing?

Silence.

Axl! Xavier!

Silence.

Malachi!

More silence.

I stomp my bare foot on the tile floor and curse at my stupidity when my heel throbs. *I know you can all hear me, dammit.*

They don't answer.

I stare at myself in the mirror. I still look exactly the same, but now I have three vampires in my head. At least I had them in my head. *It must have just been a glitch. Some freaky post–vampire bite thing. Now all is right with the world again.*

It wasn't a glitch, baby.

Malachi! Xavier and Axl shout in unison, making my head spin.

This is ridiculous. Why am I here arguing when I can go talk to them the old-fashioned way—in person with our mouths. I march down to the kitchen to find Axl and Xavier huddled together in front of the fridge, like coconspirators in an epic prank.

"You want to tell me why I can hear you in my head?"

Xavier tilts his head and grins at me. "Can you though?"

I shake my head. "Well, not right now. But I could. What was that? I thought it was only a one-way thing, like you could read me, but not the other way around. And it was only supposed to be emotions and intentions and stuff, not full-on telepathy. What is happening to me?"

The look Axl and Xavier share has the hairs on the back of my neck standing on end, then Xavier nudges Axl in the ribs, which only serves to ignite my temper further. "Will one of you tell me what the hell is going on?"

"Must you be so infernally loud, Ophelia?" the professor says from behind me

I spin around. "I'll be quiet if they tell me why I can hear them in my head."

He glares at me, his jaw ticking. Then he directs his attention to Axl and Xavier. "Is this true?"

Axl and Xavier nod sheepishly.

"Malachi too?" His dark brow furrows in a scowl.

"Yes." Axl glances at me. "This has never happened to us before either, Ophelia. Usually we can only talk to each other." He directs his attention back to the professor. "Have you ever known of this happening before?"

Alexandros sinks into the chair at the head of the kitchen table and eyes me suspiciously. "I have, but it ordinarily takes a bond built over many years. Even with the strongest beings, it usually takes months."

I open and close my mouth like a fish out of water. I have three million questions, and they're all begging to be asked first. Focus, Ophelia!

"Why has it happened to me? I'm just a human. I don't have any power."

Alexandros tilts his head to the side, glowering at me so fiercely that I can feel the heat of his eyes on my skin. I rub my hands over my arms and return his glare. It's not like I asked for this. "You do have some powers, Ophelia."

I snort a laugh. "I do not."

"How else do you explain the fact that you can hear people's voices in your thoughts? Is that not a power?"

I don't know how to explain it, but I do know it's all kinds of freaky. "Isn't that because they're vampires though? That's about them, not me."

Alexandros shakes his head. "Humans cannot communicate through a blood-sharing bond, no matter how powerful the vampire who bites them. It cannot be done."

This is all absurd, but I guess I'll play along. "So now you're telling me I'm not human?"

He sighs. "Must you be so dramatic?"

"Must you be so casual? Let's for one second pretend that I believe you. If I'm not human, then what am I?"

His Adam's apple bobs, and a thick snake of trepidation coils around my heart. Why is he looking at me like that? Axl and Xavier remain unusually quiet, and the tension in the room grows more cloying and uncomfortable with each passing second. "I think you're some kind of...witch."

"What?"

He doesn't repeat himself. Instead, he simply goes on staring at me.

I pace the small width of the kitchen, shaking my head. "I'm a witch? Me? I don't think so."

Cupping my chin in his hand, Xavier stops me in my tracks. He tips my head back. "You already know you're different, Cupcake. Don't you?"

His deep blue eyes hold me captive, and I must lose all sense of logic and reason because I find myself nodding. I do know. On some level, I must have always known. "But how...what does that even mean? Why don't I have powers? Other than being able to hear the thoughts of the vampires that bite me. What the hell use is that?"

Alexandros growls, his frustration growing more evident. "Do not underestimate the power of accessing another's mind, Ophelia."

How can I underestimate something I don't understand? "Well, I don't want it. So tell me, how do I stop it?"

He shakes his head. "You don't."

What in hellfire? This can't be happening to me. Just when I was starting to feel like a normal human being with a normal, happy life—aside from having three vampires infatuated with my blood, obviously—the universe, in all her wisdom, hits me with this. "That can't be true."

He glares at me. "It is."

I place my hands on my hips and glare right back. "So I'm just supposed to go around with these three in my head all the damn time?"

He sighs. "The fact that you can even hear them is an anomaly. Another marker of your unique blood. It's a problem, but you can learn to block them out."

Oh, well, this could be good. I like this development. "Like you all did with me earlier?" I direct my question to Axl and Xavier.

Axl nods.

I nod eagerly. Yes, this is good. "So how soon can you teach me?"

The professor flashes me a look of pure disdain. "It doesn't work like that. It takes time. Your bond is already incredibly strong. It can take some centuries to tune into the thoughts of those they share a bond with. You have done so in a matter of hours."

I snort. "Like I have centuries to practice."

Cue more awkward looks between Axl and Xavier. I don't like that look. What else can they be keeping from me?

The professor's lip curls in a cruel sneer. "Do you want to tell sweet Ophelia what she got herself into when she allowed you to taste her blood, Axl?"

I glare at Axl, my blood thundering in my veins. My head spins, and I feel faint.

"Sit down, Cupcake." Xavier pulls out a chair in a rare display of compassion.

I gladly take a seat and retrain the fiercest glare I can muster on Axl. "So?"

"Your bond. Our bond. It's unbreakable, Ophelia. That's why you couldn't stay mad at us after we bit you. Even though you had every right to after what we did. It would be impossible for one of us to live without the other."

"Agonizingly painful," the professor says. "But not impossible."

My head spins faster. "What does that even mean?"

"When a vampire bonds with—" Axl licks his lips and looks like he's searching for the right words. "Someone like you, it is forever. It's not something that can be undone."

"But I'm human. And you're immortal. So in about sixty years or so, you're all going to be screwed."

"Sharing our blood will keep you immortal too, Cupcake," Xavier says softly.

What now? I shake my head. "I'm not drinking your blood."

"You don't have to. We can transfer blood when we bite. A little is all you need."

I screw my eyes closed. Sometime soon, someone is going to wake me up with a bucket of cold water to the face and tell me this is all a nightmare. I open one eye, but they're still there, staring at me. "What if I refuse? What if I don't want to be immortal? I don't want to be bonded to you forever. I'm only nineteen!"

The professor blows out a heavy sigh and shakes his head. "It's already done."

"What do you mean, it's done. So undo it. I'm undoing it." I stand but immediately feel woozy, so I sit back down and close my eyes.

"It cannot be undone, Ophelia," he says. "You made your choice. Now you must live with the consequences."

Tears stream down my face unbidden. "But I didn't make a choice—I didn't know what I was agreeing to."

Axl drops to his knees at my feet and takes my hands in his. "We didn't know either, princess."

I look at the professor. "You did though."

He pushes back his chair and stands, unaffected by my accusation. "I warned them not to taste you."

Fury ignites inside my chest. How dare he treat this situation—treat *me* as inconsequential. White-hot rage clogs my throat, and I barely manage to choke out, "But you didn't warn me. You lied to me."

His jaw clenches tight and his eyes bore into mine. "You are not my concern."

Propelled by my rage, I launch myself out of the chair and stand in front of him, so close I can feel the anger vibrating from him too. The heat from his body warms me through the thin T-shirt I threw on earlier. How can someone so cold radiate such heat? I suck in a rasping breath that makes every cell in my body tremble. My words are stuck once more, but I tip up my chin and stare into his dark eyes, trying to direct everything I'm feeling into my glare. But there are too many emotions to feel, and I can barely focus a single thought. And between the pounding of my heart and the ache between my thighs, I can barely breathe.

It's as though my body has woken from a long sleep and is finally experiencing what it's like to be alive. His eyes are so hypnotic. If I stare into them too long, I will fall into their dark abyss, but I can't stop myself. What is this? More vampire magic?

I hold my breath, and the world stops turning. My head spins. I'm falling.

The professor's tight grip on my arm snaps me back to reality. "Ophelia!" he gasps.

I suck in a deep, soothing breath, allowing the cool air to fill my burning lungs. No longer held in place by the intensity of his gaze, I look down at where his hands are wrapped around my arms in a bruising grip. Heat radiates from the place where his body touches mine, blooming beneath my skin. My knees tremble.

His tongue darts out over his lips, and I get a glimpse of his fangs. Unconsciously, I tilt my head back, exposing the skin of my throat, and I only realize it when his eyes drop to where my pulse flutters like butterfly wings. A growl reverberates in his chest, and I gasp.

He dips his head, bending enough that his lips graze my ear and his warm breath dances over my skin. "*You* are not *my* concern," he repeats.

I blink back the tears that sting my eyeballs.

He releases my arms, and with a final snarl, he stalks out of the room. I stumble backward, dropping into the chair again, unable to stop the tears racing down my cheeks.

Axl presses my knuckles to his lips. Xavier crouches beside me and tucks my hair behind my ear. "Don't cry, Cupcake. You're killing me. Don't you want to stay with us? We sure as fuck want to keep you."

I shake my head. At this moment in time, I cannot imagine my life without them in it, but that's beside the point. "You took away my choice."

Axl brushes the tears from my cheeks. "We're sorry, princess."

I sniff. "Why are you both being so nice to me?"

Xavier chuckles, and Axl gives him a withering look. Redirecting his attention to me, Axl winces but answers my question. "Another side effect of the bond."

More side effects? Just how much of my life is going to change because of this bond?

"We're incapable of harming you, Cupcake. And when you hurt, we hurt."

Well, that's an unexpected development. Malachi mentioned being incapable of hurting me, but I assumed he only meant physical pain. "So you can't hurt me?"

Xavier grins. "Well, it depends, I guess."

My brain is fit to burst with the onslaught of new information and all my unanswered questions. "On?"

"On how you feel about it."

I shake my head. "Stop being so confusing. What does that even mean?"

Axl sits down beside me and pulls me onto his lap. "It means, princess, that we can hurt you if you want us to."

"Why would I want that?" I whisper.

"You don't ever fantasize about having your feisty ass spanked?" Xavier flexes his palm. "Because I think about it all the damn time."

Pleasure coils in my core, and heat sears between my thighs. They both laugh, and Axl presses his lips to my ear. "Yeah, she does."

A flush creeps over my cheeks. "Okay, I get it now."

"Yeah, you're gonna," Xavier mutters.

I wipe the tears from my cheeks and melt against Axl's chest. "It also means we'll always protect you from harm. You're ours, princess, just as much as we are yours."

"You are?" I've never fit in anywhere before, and despite my difficulty processing my new reality, I can't deny that this feeling of belonging, though unfamiliar, is something I've always dreamed about. It's like being wrapped in a warm blanket after spending hours in the cold.

Having never had a family of my own, I always consoled myself with not being able to miss what I never had. But I did miss it. There was always a part of my soul that yearned for connection and acceptance, not just because of the human condition, but because it knew a part of me was missing. A hole that could never be filled.

But now I know, without a doubt, this is what family feels like. This is what home feels like. And these boys are home to me. Perhaps that is simply the magic of the bond speaking, but for now I'm going to bask in the happiness and blissful contentment it offers me.

42

ALEXANDROS

"Why is your office so much bigger than mine?" Osiris Brackenwolf runs his fingertip along a shelf lined with books that I lack the time to read these days. He plucks one from the row and blows off a layer of dust. Then he holds it up and sinks his sharp teeth into his lip. "I remember this book well, Professor."

I scan the title. *Gods And Monsters: The Origins Of Ancient Greek Mythology*. "You were a good student."

He crosses the room in two strides, his large frame making my spacious office seem much smaller than it is, and places the book on my desk. "Oh, I was a *very* good student. Wouldn't you say?"

I take the book and run my hand over the soft leather. "If your mind resided someplace other than the gutter, you would know that I meant academically. You were particularly gifted, especially when it came to ancient Greece."

He perches on the edge of my desk. "Perhaps because I was trying to impress my ancient Greek professor."

Despite myself, my lips twitch. "Well, it was your mind that impressed me," I tell him truthfully. It was why I chose to mentor him and teach him some of the ancient texts.

He narrows his eyes and tilts his head. "You sure it wasn't my abs? I was pretty hot back then." He lifts his shirt, revealing he still has a perfect set of abs nestled beneath his golden skin.

I shake my head. "Did you have something for me? Or are you here to reminisce about your society days?"

"I have something interesting for you."

I lean forward in my seat. Now that I know what Ophelia is, I am even more interested in *who* she is and how she found herself here at Montridge. "Tell me."

"You were right about the trust fund. All of the official paperwork makes it look like it was set up by her parents, and I'll be damned if I can find any evidence to the contrary, but it's not possible."

"Why?"

"Because they died nineteen years ago, and they were broke. How could they have put away over a hundred and twenty k, which would have been worth what, double what it's worth now?"

I shake my head. "That is still speculation."

"Okay, but this trust also miraculously appeared when your girl was eighteen." *Your girl.* I know it is only a phrase, but his use of those words to describe her leaves me breathless. If he notices my discomfort, he neglects to acknowledge it. "Why didn't anyone know about it before then?"

I frown. "You tell me."

"Her social worker said it was an oversight, that these things happen," Osiris says. "She was just relieved to have found out about it before Ophelia was due to go to college."

"But how did the social worker find out about it?"

"The bank contacted her out of the blue. And when she checked, the trust had always been there. One hundred and twenty thousand dollars just sitting there for seventeen years and it doesn't earn a single cent of interest? What kind of jackass puts that kind of money into an account that doesn't earn interest? That seems a whole fuckload of strange to me."

I rub my temples. "That still does not explain how Ophelia ended up here at Montridge. With that kind of money, she could have chosen another college."

"Well, this part you're gonna love." His brown eyes twinkle. "The trust was very specific about her attending Montridge. It was here or nowhere. Now, why the fuck would someone do that to their kid before they were even born? And this girl has no powers, right?"

"Right." I lie with ease.

"So why the fuck? Someone wanted her here, but I'd bet my 550 Spyder that it wasn't her parents."

Knowing how much he loves that car, and also what I know about her powers being bound as a child, I completely agree. "So who else? Did you find anything more?"

"No. But that trust definitely looks legit, which tells me that someone with a lot of power set it up to look that way."

Someone powerful enough to bind an elementai's powers.

He runs a hand over his thick beard. "Looks like you were right to show an interest in this one, Alexandros. There is definitely something not quite right going on."

I hum my agreement, my mind racing with more questions than answers.

"Also made me think of that prophecy you told me about," he says with a casual shrug, like speaking of ancient prophecies is merely an afterthought and not something that could get us both in a whole lot of trouble.

"Prophecies are for fools, Osiris. You know that." I keep my tone light but shoot daggers at him with my eyes. Whilst I no longer believe in the folly of such fairytales, it is still prudent to exert caution when discussing them. The Lost Prophecies of Fiere are openly discussed as mythology, but most people know only the headlines, not the true secrets contained within them. In ancient times, to link an actual living being to a prophecy was to ensure them a swift and certain death, and only those of us old enough to remember are still conditioned to treat such open talk with extreme caution.

Tread carefully, friend. I warn him through our bond. *Walls have ears, remember.*

He nods his understanding, then barks out a laugh. "Yeah, bullshit, right."

Which prophecy and why? Find a way to tell me without implicating the girl.

He tips his face to the ceiling and bites down on his bottom lip. "God, I miss being a student." He chuckles. "You remember that night I got so drunk that I puked all over half the cheerleading squad?"

A smile tugs at my lips. "I do. It was the talk of the semester. Quite the feat for a werewolf to get so drunk."

His dark eyes burn into mine. "I was late to class the next day. You had me stay back and recite those fucking poems as punishment."

That is not what happened at all. I punished him in a much more memorable and pleasurable way, and afterward we lay in bed, listening to the storm roll in. I close my eyes and dread settles in the pit of my stomach. That was also the day I told him the first of Fiere's prophecies. The one that all bloodline vampires are taught. And even if it is little more than the ramblings of an ancient being, it is a prophecy that many fear.

The child borne of fire and blood?

He gives me a single nod. "Yeah, you were a mean motherfucker."

"I was merely securing your education."

"Yeah, and it was quite the education, Professor." He winks.

I grunt aloud but go on speaking to him through our bond. *Why did she make you think of that?*

He stands and picks up the book he was looking at earlier. "Okay if I borrow this?"

"Of course, although I would not have thought you had much interest in Greek mythology these days."

"Me?" He snorts. "I love a good origin story, don't you?"

With a final pointed look, he leaves the room. Origin story? He must be talking about Ophelia's origin story. Where the hell do I find that?

I can still feel him walking down the hall. *Do not mention this to anyone, Osiris. For your safety and Ophelia's.* I can't hear his response, but I know I can trust him.

After pulling her file up on my computer, I go through her application again, hoping it will give me some clue as to what Osiris alluded to. If he has been looking into Ophelia, he may have already attracted some attention, and I do not wish to draw further scrutiny by meeting with him again so soon. Her submission essay finishes loading, and I skim the first few paragraphs as I did when I first looked into her. It starts with references to the classic literature she loves and the impact of books on her life. Nothing different from the millions of other high school graduates who apply for college all over the country. That is why I failed to read until the end last time, but now I continue scanning until I reach the final paragraph. And there, in Ophelia's own words, is her undoing and the end of my world as I know it.

> I'm resilient and resourceful. From the little I know about my birth, my entrance into this world was a dramatic one. I was left on the steps of a church with nothing but the scorched cloak I was wrapped in, my skin covered in blood and ash. I never knew my parents or who placed me on those steps, but I've never let not knowing who I am stop me from becoming the person I'm supposed to be…

I have no need to read the rest. Those four sentences are enough to tell me that the impossible is reality. Closing my eyes, I focus hard on my brother. Our bond is strong enough to cross continents, and it takes but a few seconds to reach him.

I need to speak with you.

His reply comes swiftly and without question. *I shall meet you in the library at midnight.*

Thank you, brother.

・・・

The library is empty except for Professor Yakon. The werewolf has his head bent low over a stack of books, and I slip past him, seemingly unnoticed. After taking a seat at one of the two-seater oak tables, I switch on the small green desk lamp. I am lost in thoughts of demons and scrolls and my mother's fables when I hear footsteps approaching, and a second later, Giorgios sits in the chair beside mine.

"Thank you for coming, brother."

He places a hand on my arm, his brow furrowed like he knows the enormity of what I am about to reveal. "You know that wherever I am, I would come to you at a moment's notice."

"Yet it took you six hours to get here," I quip, needing to lighten the mood before I blow his world apart. I am lucky that a flight was not necessary to get him here because that would have taken three times longer. I envy him his power of teleportation, an ancient magic so few were blessed with.

He shrugs. "I had some business to take care of first."

I glance around again, checking to ensure nobody new has entered the library and that the biochemistry professor is still bent over his books. Satisfied that we cannot be overheard, I begin. "The girl. Ophelia. She is an elementai."

He nods like this does not surprise him.

"She's bonded with my boys. All three of them."

"But not you?" He regards me with suspicion. "I felt no shift in your emotions, although you have always been able to mask them so well."

"No, not with me," I grit out. "I already told you that will not be happening."

He presses his lips together and remains silent.

"You do not believe me?"

He places a hand on my arm. "I know that you believe you, and that is enough."

"Do not treat me like a fucking child, Giorgios!" Memories of our childhood and his cruel taunts echo in my mind. Born only five years apart, we were pitted against each other by our father from the moment I was born. Not until we were centuries old did we realize the futility of our sibling rivalry. It was our father who deserved our animosity, not each other. Still, those wounds run deep, and it is not difficult for them to rip open when one is already feeling decidedly on edge.

He shakes his head and sighs. "I am not. But to pretend that you are not drawn to her, Alexandros—to suggest that it is not fate that has brought the only elementai born in over half a millennium to you, of all people…it is foolhardy."

"I am *not* going to bite her," I insist. "Even discounting the fact that I do not wish to be bonded to an elementai ever again, I would never put her in that kind of danger. If our father found out what she is…"

He squeezes my arm tighter. "I know, brother. I know. You would never be so reckless as to endanger the only elementai in existence."

The overwhelming instinct to protect Ophelia still takes me by surprise. "I will never allow him to feel her."

"Your ability to close yourself off to others is unparalleled. Perhaps there is a way—"

"She is too powerful, Giorgios. Too powerful to contain. He would sense her. I know he would." But oh, how I wish there was a way. The desire to sink my fangs into her sweet flesh and drink her intoxicating lifeblood consumes almost every waking thought.

"Why do you think this? Even if she is an elementai…"

I swallow the knot of trepidation in my throat. "I have reason to believe she has mastery over three of the elements. Perhaps even all four."

His mouth falls open and he works to speak, but no sound escapes his lips.

"She started the fire at her school. It rains when she feels sad. When she…" I take a deep breath and will my cock not to ache with the mere thought of what I am about to say. "When she has an orgasm, the ground shakes."

He raises one eyebrow, and our bond is not necessary for me to be able to hear what he is thinking.

I sigh. "I told you she is bonded to my boys. I feel her through them."

"And air?" he asks.

"When she found out about the bonding, how she was going to be a part of the boys' lives for eternity, she lost her mind. She held her breath, and I swear that she stole all the air from the room."

His chest heaves with the deep breaths he takes. His anxiety is palpable, but so is his excitement and fear. "But you said her powers were bound?"

"Yes, and by who? Who else knows about her? Who sent her to this school? Who put her in my path? She is too dangerous, and she has not a single clue."

He looks down at the table and traces the wood grain with his index finger. "But without a powerful witch to break the spell, she is safe. I do not know of any who can do such a thing. Do you?"

"Only one." I lick my lips. "But she would never. She is constrained by greater laws than you and I."

"Of course." He looks back up and gives me a knowing nod. "Nazeel Danraath."

I wince at the mention of her name. Like so many other witches I know, she is tied to my most painful memories, the ones I keep barricaded behind a wall of granite. "But her powers are growing, Giorgios. She can communicate with my boys. Talk to them in their heads as clearly as I can. I feel her. As her emotions grow stronger, so does her magic. What if she breaks the spell all on her own?"

His frown deepens. "You must start teaching her how to control her powers, Alexandros. Prepare her in case that day does come."

My heart cracks wide open. "I cannot."

He takes my hand in his. "You must. And you are the best teacher I know. There is a reason she was sent to you, even if you refuse to accept it." His eyes scan my face. "Is there something else bothering you?"

"No." I shake my head. The ease with which I lie to my own brother surprises even me. But to tell him of the prophecy, now, on top of everything else... It is too much for one day. Too much for me to wrap my own head around. And besides, I am mistaken. Prophecies are but childish fairytales that have no basis in reality.

Osiris always loved the story of the knights and the Order, how they risked their lives to save the sacred scrolls before the Library of Alexandria burned. Maybe it is his curiosity that is feeding my ridiculous notions about Ophelia. And perhaps, as my father always told us, prophecies and legends are simply stories created to frighten children.

Giorgios leaves as swiftly as he arrived, and I walk quickly back to the house, unable to stop myself from recounting the segment of the prophecy that was revealed to me a very long time ago.

But there is one who can save the fates of all.
For the child borne of fire and blood,
Shall be our ruin or our redemption.
Bringing balance to the new world order,
Be it through peace or total annihilation.

"Alexandros," Malachi says cheerfully as he falls into step beside me, his face lit with a wide smile. "Did you not hear me shouting your name?"

I shake my head. "I was deep in thought."

He lets out a contented sigh and looks up at the stars.

"You are very pleased with yourself."

He laughs. "Pleased with life, I guess."

I resist the temptation to tell him to enjoy it while it lasts. Because despite the inevitable pain that comes from falling in love with someone like Ophelia Hart, every single second of soul-wrenching, agonizing torture is worth it for the simplest moments with her.

But I am not sentimental. Whatever goodness I had in my heart died with *them*. So I say nothing.

43

MALACHI

"Look at her." I nudge Xavier in the ribs and jerk my head in Ophelia's direction. I could—and often do—spend hours watching her read or study. I pay close attention to her features. The way her nose scrunches when she's thinking. The way she chews on the end of her unicorn pen when she's puzzled. The way she smiles to herself when she gets to a good part of her book or her eyes fill with tears at the sad parts. My heart beats double time in my chest just from looking at her. "She's so fucking cute."

He grunts, but he looks up from his cell phone, and the corners of his mouth curve. "Yeah."

I jump onto the sofa next to her, causing her to yelp in surprise. She closes her book and places it on her lap, resting her hands on the cover as she fixes me with a sweet smile. "I thought you were all too busy with trial business tonight to entertain me. That's why I brought a friend."

I take the book from her hands and examine the cover. "I

hope this isn't research, sweet girl, because our world is nothing like what happens in this book."

"And how would you know? You read a lot of vampire fiction?" She rolls her eyes and snatches the book back.

"I did read that series actually. And just so you know, I'm firmly team Edward." I wink at her, and a smile spreads across her beautiful face.

"Aren't you a little old for *Twilight*, Cupcake?" Xavier asks.

She huffs with indignation. "Nobody is ever too old for *Twilight*, Xavier."

He sits on her other side, squashing her between us on the couch. "I saw you reading Brontë last week. I assumed your literary tastes were a little more"—he narrows his eyes and taps his chin—"refined."

"*Twilight* is a modern classic. And my reading tastes are varied. I must have read close to five thousand books in my lifetime."

Xavier lets out a low whistle and sits back, draping an arm around her shoulder. "That's impressive, Cupcake. Did you not sleep as a kid?"

The slender curve of her throat thickens as she swallows, and her sadness permeates us. There's so little we know about the orphan girl who was left on the steps of a church. I want to unpack every memory she has, but I get that it hurts for her to talk about those times in her life. Fuck, I was so messed up as a human that I was about to put a bullet in my own head. If it weren't for my horse stepping in a hole and breaking her leg, leading me to use that bullet to spare her suffering, I would have killed myself before the professor found me sobbing over Moira's corpse. No doubt about it.

I cup Ophelia's jaw and turn her head so I can look into her bright blue eyes. As I expected, they're shimmering with unshed tears. All we really know about her childhood is that she was a foster kid and she was bullied in school. "What is it, baby?"

She blinks and tries to shake her head, but I hold her in place. "Nothing."

Xavier tucks her hair behind her ear and trails his fingertips down her neck, making her shiver. "Why did you read so much, Cupcake?"

I stare into her eyes, wishing I could truly read her mind. "Tell us, sweet girl."

She closes her eyes, causing a solitary tear to roll down her cheek. Xavier catches it with his thumb and licks it off, then wraps his arm around her shoulder. I allow her to lean back against him and study her face. Another emotion clouds her sadness—shame.

"We're your family now, Ophelia," I say, my heart splintering. "There's nothing we don't want to know about you. Nothing you can tell us that will make us love you any less than we do."

Her eyes snap open and she blinks rapidly. "You love me?"

Xavier snorts a laugh. "Understatement," he mutters.

Does she really not know that? Can she not feel it every day? We've never said it, but vampires are so driven by emotion and base instinct that we often let our actions speak for themselves. Clearly we failed her by not realizing she needed the words. "We're bonded for life, sweet girl. I don't even think love is enough to describe this." I wave a hand between the three of us.

Her lips curve ever so slightly. "I guess not."

Xavier rests his lips on her temple and murmurs, "Back to you reading five thousand books. How? Why?"

She licks her pink lips and glances between the two of us. Then she holds up her copy of *Twilight*. "I wasn't kidding when I said I brought a friend. For as long as I can remember, I've never stayed anywhere long enough to connect with people. I had twenty-six foster placements in total and half as many schools. It was hard to make friends, so I read a lot. Stories became my escape. I figured I didn't need actual friends when I could be best friends with a hobbit. It didn't matter where I lived when I could curl up in my bed in Hogwarts or visit Victorian England. Books have always been my only constant."

Oh fuck me, my heart just cracked in two. I link her fingers through mine and press a kiss to her knuckles. "Until now, baby."

That earns me the sweetest fucking smile that makes me want to kiss her, but I hold back. If I press my lips to hers, I'll want to bite her, and then, well, we won't be talking about books. Or talking at all.

Xavier pulls her onto his lap, and she offers a faint squeal of protest, but he wraps her in his arms. She melts into his chest, her fingers still entwined with mine. "You had twenty-six foster placements?"

"Yeah, I never stayed anywhere longer than a few months until I was in high school. That was the longest one I had, and I probably would have stayed until I graduated, except…" She winces, and I give her hand a reassuring squeeze.

"Fiona and Alan were a real nice couple. I can't really blame them for not wanting me to stay after the fire and everything…" She pastes on a big smile that breaks my heart, but before I can tell her she doesn't have to pretend for us, she continues. "Anyway. Alan was a mechanic, and he taught me a little bit about cars. How to change the oil, swap out a tire, that kind of thing. And Fiona loved to read too, so we would spend hours talking about books." Her face lights up. "We used to go out to dinner every Friday night, and I loved it because I'd never been to a restaurant before."

"Hold up," I say. "You never went out to eat until you were in high school?"

She looks down at her hands and shrugs. "Kids would always talk about going to grab a burger or pizza after school." She whispers, "I was so jealous," then clears her throat and continues in a ragged tone. "I would have loved to have been invited. Just once. I even got an allowance from Fiona and Alan, so I could have gone, but I guess…" She shakes her head and brushes away a tear. "Anyway, I think that's why they started taking me out to eat. So that I didn't feel like I was missing out."

Goddamn, my heart fucking aches for this girl. "So I guess you've never been on a date either?"

Her forehead wrinkles, and she slowly shakes her head.

How has this beauty, who has the kindest fucking heart of any creature I have ever known—not to mention the cutest goddamn laugh and the kind of curiosity that can make watching paint dry together interesting—never been on a date? That is practically criminal. I leap up from the couch and pull her with me. "Then let's change that right fucking now, baby."

She squeals with laughter. "But the Trials… You said—"

I silence her with a kiss. "Fuck the Trials. You're way more important."

Her smile makes lightning race through my veins. Xavier stands behind her and wraps his arms around her waist, resting his chin on her shoulder. "Where do you want to go, Cupcake?"

She bites on her lip, her eyes shining with excitement. "I d-don't know."

I cup her face and rub the pad of my thumb over her cheek. "To get food? The movies? Dancing?"

Xavier grunts. "Ugh. No dancing."

"We will take our girl dancing if that's what she wants to do, numbnuts."

Xavier rolls his eyes, and Ophelia laughs. "I don't even know if I like dancing. How about food?"

Xavier hums. "We could go to Henley's. I guess I could force down a burger."

"No." Ophelia gasps and shakes her head. "That's like where *everyone* hangs out. If we go there, everyone will know about us."

I shoot Xavier a puzzled look. It sounds like she doesn't want to be seen with us. No, that's not right. If I know my girl, and I definitely know my girl, she thinks we don't want to be seen with her. And that kind of bullshit is not gonna fly. "All the more reason we should."

"Fuck yeah." Xavier trails kisses over the side of her neck. "I wanna show off my girl."

Axl stomps into the den and greets us with a frustrated groan. "Can you two not keep your hands off Pyro for thirty minutes? I thought you were prepping for Saturday night."

"We were, but now we're taking Ophelia on a date instead," I tell him.

He stands beside us, hands on his hips, trying to look annoyed, but his eyes are raking up and down Ophelia's hot body, and I feel the desire for her coursing through his veins. Like he's any less distracted by her than we are.

"It's okay. You can work," she says. "I know the Trials are important."

I grab her jaw again and narrow my eyes. "What did I just tell you?"

She giggles, and dammit, the sound has my cock twitching so much I'm almost regretting this date idea. Our bed is calling me. Or the sofa. Anywhere I can lay her down and sink deep inside her. I'd also take standing up. Against a wall. The door…

Ophelia has never been on a date before, Xavier says through our bond, actively tuning her out of our conversation and snapping me out of my filthy thoughts.

Yeah, and given that we were complete jerkwads to her these past few weeks, I figure this is the least we owe her, I add.

Ophelia starts to fidget, probably aware that we're having a silent conversation and wondering what we're saying.

Not to mention, I want to claim her in front of every person at this school, Xavier growls.

Axl cracks his neck, directing Ophelia's gaze toward him. "I think we could all use a break from the Trials."

She sinks her teeth into her lip and flutters her dark eyelashes. "So you're coming too?"

He tilts his head to the side and licks his lips. "Not a chance in hell I'm missing our first date, princess."

. . .

As it usually is every night of the week, Henley's is so full that students spill out into the street. Axl opens the door, and I guide Ophelia inside, one hand on the small of her back.

"Everyone is staring," she whispers, her cheeks as pink as her hair.

"That's because you're so fucking hot, Cupcake." Xavier presses his lips close to her ear. "And you're here with us."

Her heart rate kicks up, and she glances around the crowded restaurant. Sure enough, almost every pair of eyes is on us. I take her hand in mine, and Axl heads to a booth at the back. We don't frequent this place very often, but when we do, we always take the same table. The six people sitting at our usual table include two Ruby Dragon pledges, and they all move without being asked.

Ophelia presses her lips together and looks at the floor. Axl places his index finger under her chin and tips her head back up. "Hey. No more fading into the background. You're one of us now, and that means you get treated like a princess by everyone. Not only us."

She rolls her eyes. "Not entirely sure you can equate how you guys treat me to royalty."

A low growl rolls out of him, making me wonder if he's going to punish her for sassing him in public. Instead, he leans down and seals his lips over hers while squeezing her ass in one hand and sliding the other to the back of her neck. I let go of her hand and allow him to have her to himself for a moment. When he breaks their kiss, she stares up at him, her lips parted and her tits heaving. He tugs her bottom lip down with the pad of his thumb. "That was before. This is now, princess."

Xavier hums and shakes his head. "Except she's not a princess." He drags her from Axl's arms and picks her up, holding her bridal style to his chest. "She's a fucking queen."

Her cheeks turn a deeper shade of pink, and she smiles that fucking smile that makes my knees feel weak. I can't help myself from tangling my fingers in her hair and planting a kiss on those sweet lips of hers. And now everyone in this whole damn place knows that Ophelia Hart belongs to us.

44

Axl

Watching Ophelia's face light up with excitement and surprise when the server brings her ice cream sundae has me feeling all kinds of things I'm not used to. She was just as excited by her burger and fries earlier too. Malachi told me about their conversation at the house. Learning that she never got to enjoy simple pleasures like going out for a burger made me want to go back in time, find that awkward teenage girl, and take her on a date every night of the fucking week.

"You want some?" She holds a spoonful of ice cream across the table, and I shake my head. I've never been into sugary shit, although there weren't a lot of options back when I was a human.

"You?" She turns to Malachi sitting beside her.

He smiles. "No. It's all for you, sweet girl."

"But it's bigger than my head. Surely you'll have some, Xavier?" She bats her eyelashes at him.

He scoops some of the ice cream from the spoon onto his index finger. "You know I'm only interested in one kind of dessert,

Cupcake." His blue eyes go dark as he stares at her and licks his lips. Then he holds his fingertip to her lips, and she parts them, allowing him to feed her the dessert.

She swallows, and the pulse at her throat flutters, silently begging me to sink my teeth into her neck. "And what type of dessert is that?" she asks in a breathy whisper.

Xavier leans across the table and cups her jaw in his hand, pulling her closer until their faces are inches apart. "You know what I want to eat right now, Cupcake. And if you don't stop fluttering your pretty eyes at me, I'll lift you onto this table and eat it right here."

Her pupils blow wide. "Eat w-what?"

Sweet motherfuck, how is she still so damn innocent when she's constantly surrounded by the three of us? It's so fucking adorable, and it makes me want to corrupt her right here while everyone in this restaurant watches us.

Malachi chuckles.

Xavier dusts his lips over hers and whispers, "Your cunt."

Ophelia's face instantly reddens, making Xavier laugh darkly. "Y-you wouldn't," she protests.

"I would do it in a fucking heartbeat, Ophelia. You want to push me on it and find out?"

She shakes her head as I silently urge her to push him. Then I won't be the jackass who ruins our first date.

"So eat your dessert like a good girl and I might wait until we get home before I eat mine." He releases her chin and sits back against the leather bench.

I lean across the table, my eyes raking over her face, down her neck to her pert tits. I flick my tongue over the tip of my fangs. The only thing I want to eat in this entire place is her. "I might not make it all the way home."

She presses her lips together and holds my gaze, almost like she's daring me to do something. And fuck me, I want to pin her down on this table and fuck her until she screams my name all over this restaurant.

Malachi slips an arm around her shoulder. "They're not playing, baby. You better eat your dessert real quick."

With her eyes darting between Xavier's and mine, she licks the ice cream from her spoon, deliberately and seductively swirling her tongue over the cold dessert like a wicked temptress begging to be fucked. Like my cock isn't hard enough already.

"I will have you ride my face at this table, Cupcake," Xavier warns her with a growl.

"I second that, princess."

"I'm not doing anything," she protests, taking another lick. "Well, except for enjoying our date, which has been incredible, by the way." She smiles sweetly. "Thank you, boys."

Malachi brushes his lips over her neck. "You deserve all the dates and all the ice cream you want, sweet girl."

Her smile grows wider, her eyes full of hope and excitement. "Does that mean we can do this again?"

I can barely stand this any longer. How is she this goddamn sweet? And how is it that making her miserable used to be my greatest pleasure in life? This lifelong bond shit is turning me into someone I barely recognize. Even when I was a human I wasn't a nice guy. A blackhearted cad, my mother called me. But Ophelia Hart has me wrapped around her pinkie finger. I plant one elbow on the table and curl my index finger, summoning her. "C'mere, princess."

She sinks her teeth into her juicy bottom lip and leans across the table once more. "What is it?"

I slide my hand to the back of her neck and pull her closer. "I think I will take a little of that dessert, after all." I lick the seam of her lips, tasting the sickly-sweet residual ice cream before she allows me entry to her delicious warm mouth. I slide my tongue inside, flicking it against hers until a whimper rolls out of her.

How do you feel about being fucked here at this table, princess? I ask through our bond so I don't have to pull my lips from hers.

She moans into my mouth even as her protests echo in my head.

Malachi laughs and joins our internal conversation. *At the table or on the table?*

On! Xavier answers for me. *Fuck, I want to spread you open and show this entire school who owns your hot pussy, Cupcake.*

That would be so fucking hot to watch. And then it would be my turn. I devour her mouth, stealing the breath from her lungs and wishing my head was buried between her thighs.

You can't, she says.

Pretty sure we can, I retort.

She tries to pull back and break our kiss, but I don't let her. I hold her in place and pierce the inside of her lip with my fangs. The faintest hint of her blood on my tongue has my own blood racing through my body like wildfire.

I'd rather we just enjoy our date though, she says, her voice breathless even in my head.

Dammit, she's right. This date is supposed to be about her, not us. Reluctantly, I drag my mouth from hers, already missing the sweet taste of her on my tongue. "You are getting fucked hard as soon as we get home, princess."

She gasps, her heart racing faster and her pupils blown so wide that her blue eyes look black.

Malachi grunts. "I second that."

"Not before I eat." Xavier takes the spoon and scoops up a glob of cherry sundae before holding it out to Ophelia. "But first our girl is gonna enjoy every second of our date, and that includes eating this ice cream sundae that's as big as her head."

She rolls her eyes, and I flex my palm on the table, resisting the urge to spank her, kiss her again, or do anything that involves having my hands all over her in any way. Because I am hanging by a thread. Then she parts her lips and accepts the spoon from Xavier's outstretched hand. I swear, the way she purrs like a kitten when she tastes the ice cream is intended to fire us up.

It's sure fucking working.

Ophelia rests her chin on her hand. "So, do you guys do stuff like this often? Date stuff?"

"Can't remember the last time I took anyone out on a date," Xavier says.

I shake my head. "Me neither."

"Last date I had was about six years ago," Malachi answers.

Her pretty face scrunches in confusion. "So you don't date? Like ever?"

Female attention has never been a problem for any of us. We could bite and fuck our way through about ninety percent of the female population at Montridge if we chose to—probably a quarter of the guys too. But I don't tell Ophelia that. Instead, I give her a casual shrug. "Never really had to, princess."

"Never really wanted to." Xavier grunts.

"But…" She opens and closes her mouth. "You were always surrounded by girls."

Xavier takes her hand in his and presses a kiss on her knuckles. "Whatever we've done with those girls is completely different from dating, Cupcake."

She swallows hard. "And this…between us all? What exactly are we doing?" Her voice is little more than a whisper.

I tilt my head, basking in her nervous anxiety while she waits for our reply. I guess a part of me can still feel a thrill of excitement from her pain, perhaps because I know her anxiety is baseless and that I'm gonna feel that warm rush of happiness in a few seconds when she realizes what she means to us.

Malachi tucks a lock of hair behind her ear. "We already told you we love you, sweet girl."

I narrow my eyes, watching every micro expression on her face and feeling the sparks of hope and happiness igniting in her heart. "This isn't close to dating or fucking or anything we've ever done before."

Xavier rubs the pad of his thumb over the back of her hand. "We're bonded for life, Cupcake. Do you have any idea what that actually means?"

She frowns. "A little, I guess. It's like you *have* to be with me and love me, right? Not necessarily that you choose to?"

Wow. That she actually thinks that our bond works like that hurts me more than I thought it would. I shake my head. "You have it all fucking wrong, Ophelia. A life bond isn't some chance occurrence. They happen for a reason. Only souls who were meant to be together form a life bond as strong as ours with you."

"But you bonded to me because of my blood, right? Wouldn't any vampire who bites me feel the same way?"

Xavier's animalistic growl takes even me by surprise. "No one else is biting you, Cupcake. Ever. Do I make myself clear?"

"I never said I wanted that," she says with a sigh. "I was just making a point."

How do I even begin to explain? "Technically it's true that any vampire who bites you would be bonded to you, yes. But this is… different."

She blinks. "How?"

Malachi kisses her temple. "We knew what biting you would mean, sweet girl, and Xavier and I bit you with full knowledge that it would bond us all for life. We chose you."

"But you didn't, Axl." Her eyes are fixed on mine. "You didn't know what would happen. You tasted my blood by accident."

I run a hand over my face and close my eyes, unable to find the words to tell her how I feel. That's why I climb over the table and wedge myself in the booth between her and the wall. I need to show her. Once I have her on my lap, I claim her lips in a bruising kiss, not giving her a chance to protest. Into this one kiss, I pour all my longing, my desire to protect her, the way my heart beats faster every time I see her, and the constant aching need to be near her. And she melts into me, letting me take everything she has as I try to give her all that I am.

I pull back, leaving us both wanting more, and stare into her bright blue eyes. "I wanted you from the moment you walked into that alley, Pyro. I might have been unaware of what tasting your blood would do to me, but I know my own mind. I would do it again in every single lifetime I have just to be with you. You are it for us, princess. There will never be anyone else besides you. Now tell me you believe that."

She nods, her bottom lip clamped between her teeth, but I already know she believes me. I feel it in her.

Malachi brushes his fingertips over her cheek. "And would you choose us if you had the chance again, sweet girl?"

She smiles. "Every second of every day."

I bury my face in her neck and inhale her intoxicating scent. "Get the check, Xavier. We're leaving."

45

OPHELIA

I sit up, pulling the quilt up over myself, which I realize is futile as soon as I do it because Xavier simply tugs it down again. "What have I told you about covering up this beautiful body, Cupcake," he says with a warning growl.

But it's not beautiful, I answer in my head, wincing as I do.

He arches an eyebrow at me. *You're about to be spanked for that.*

Before I can protest, he flips me over and smacks my ass. "Ouch," I cry, even as warmth spreads across my skin and a familiar ache pulses between my thighs.

Malachi jumps onto the bed, landing beside me, his skin damp from his shower. He cups my chin in his hand. "Naughty girl," he says with a grin.

"I didn't do anything," I whisper.

He makes a tutting sound. "I just fucking heard you."

Xavier spanks me again, and I bite down on my lip to stifle a groan. "I thought you couldn't hurt me."

"Am I hurting you, Cupcake?" He brings the palm of his hand cracking down on my ass once more.

I groan out loud this time.

"Thought not," he says with a wicked laugh and gives me one more sharp slap. Then he flips me back over and climbs between my thighs.

"So this reading minds thing? Are you guys going to be in my head all the time?"

Malachi props himself up on one elbow. "Are you in ours all the time?"

I scrunch my eyes closed and concentrate. I can't hear them. "I don't know."

Xavier trails kisses over my neck and collarbone, distracting me. "It isn't really mind reading. More like talking without talking."

"Talking without talking?"

Malachi nods as Xavier trails his sinful lips lower. "Yeah, like if we want to talk to you or each other, then we can hear what the other is saying, but we can't just read your mind. The professor can read minds, but that's like some ancient freaky vampire shit that only he can do. As far as we know, anyway."

I'm going to need to know so much more about that. It's a pity the professor is such a closed book.

Xavier trails his teeth down my abdomen, nipping at my flesh as he moves south. *Tell him to shut the fuck up. I'm about to eat here.*

Malachi laughs. "You see, I heard that." He bends his head and sucks one of my hard nipples into his mouth, then bites down gently, making me moan louder.

Xavier swirls his tongue over my clit. *You taste so sweet, Cupcake.*

Malachi hums. *Delicious.*

You see how helpful it can be? Xavier asks as he dips his tongue inside me. *I can still talk to you with my mouth full of your pussy.*

I press my lips together and close my eyes. *You have a dirty mouth.*

Are you being fucked again, princess? Axl joins our mental conversation.

Not yet, but she's about to be, Malachi answers.

Sitting in the woods babysitting these pledges while they practice for the Hunt is boring as fuck, so if you could make our girl come real hard for me, I'd really appreciate it.

We always make her come hard, don't we, Cupcake? He flicks his expert tongue over my flesh, and Malachi's hand slides down to join Xavier's mouth before he starts gently massaging my clit.

Y-yes.

You're such a good girl, princess. I'll be home in a few hours, and I want you waiting in that bed, naked and fucking dripping for me, Axl commands.

I c-can't. I have class.

No classes today, baby. Malachi sucks on my neck. *I'm gonna need you to stay right here all day.*

And all night, Xavier adds, pressing my thighs flat to the mattress and spreading me wider so he can get better access. My body ignites with pleasure.

I do have to go to class though. My protest sounds weak, even to me. *Please, I can't fall behind.*

Aw, are you begging, Cupcake? Xavier slides one thick finger inside me, and all the muscles in my body quiver.

You know how feral it makes us to hear you beg. Malachi sinks his fangs into my skin, and my orgasm tears through my body like a wildfire. The three of them talk me through it, telling me how good I taste, how sweet I sound when I lose control for them, how I belong to them. And I close my eyes and bask in their adoration, knowing that every single bad thing that happened before now must have been for a reason, because right here with them is the place where I was always meant to be.

...

Despite Axl's warning that I'm going to be severely punished for disobeying them, I did go to classes today. I had to. If those boys had their way, I would never leave the house—or more specifically, one of the many beds in the house. And while what we do in there is a whole lot of fun, I need some space too. It's been three weeks since Axl bit me and we had sex, and I've only been back to my dorm once for half an hour to grab a few of my things since. It's all gotten very intense, very quickly. So fast that it makes my head spin simply thinking about it.

"Hey, girl. Why are you just standing there?" Cadence's now-familiar voice shakes me from musing about my personal life, and I realize I've been staring into space in front of the Silver Vale Society house for a solid minute.

"Nervous about meeting everyone, I guess," I say, surprised at my ability to lie so easily. I mean, I am nervous, but that's not why I was standing here like an idiot.

"I'm so glad you came." She links her arm through mine, and we walk up the porch steps together.

I hope you're ready for a spanking, princess, Axl growls in my head, causing my legs to tremble and wet heat to pool in my core.

Stop. I'm with Cadence at the Silver Vale house.

You'd better be home in a few hours or I'm coming to get you, he warns.

I'll be home by eight, okay?

I'll be waiting.

"Hey, Meg, this is Ophelia," Cadence says to the familiar-looking blond girl who opens the door to us.

Meg bounds forward and grabs my hand in a firm shake. "Hey, Ophelia. I think we met at the activity fair before the semester started. At our table?"

Memories of that day come racing back to me, and I immediately feel ashamed of the way I judged her. I don't know what it is, but I can see things more clearly now, and the way she's looking at me is genuine and friendly, not bitchy the way I thought when we met.

Meg smiles. "Cadence has told us so much about you."

How many people have I pushed away because of my assumption that they were going to treat me the same way Penelope did? I swallow down the thick knot of regret and promise myself that it all changes today. "All good, I hope," I say awkwardly, and both Cadence and Meg laugh.

An elegantly dressed woman with silver-blond hair and sparkling gray eyes comes to stand beside Meg, and Cadence introduces her as Professor Green, the faculty head of Silver Vale.

"Call me Enora, dear," she says, taking my hand in hers and curling her warm fingers around my palm as she stares into my eyes like she's trying to see deep inside my soul. Does she sense any latent powers, like the kind Alexandros talked about?

With a final narrowing of her eyes, she lets me go and smiles again, directing us into the house. I walk inside and am immediately struck by how different Silver Vale is from Ruby Dragon. It smells of freshly baked cookies and flowers instead of cologne, pizza, and coffee, not to mention the paperbacks, textbooks, and leather-bound books that are stacked and arranged on every surface. The only books at Ruby Dragon are in Malachi's bedroom—and I suspect the professor's study, but I haven't dared enter that room.

But it's more than the smells and the books. It feels warm and homey and…happy. I bet it's amazing to live here. Two girls with dark hair walk hand in hand down the stairs, smiling at me as they pass. "How many pledges do you have this year?" I ask Cadence.

"Thirty-one so far."

"So far? I thought pledges had to commit during the first two weeks of the semester?"

Cadence leads me down a hallway decorated with flowery wallpaper and ornate gilded mirrors. "That's for the Dragon and Moon societies. Their pledges are usually signed up before school even begins. But the Vales sometimes find pledges weeks after school starts. Some students might not know they belong here until they've been at Montridge a while." She wrinkles her button nose. "I guess it's hard to explain."

What she's saying makes sense. Wolves already know they're wolves. Vampire pledges have already been recruited or identified by organizations who want them for some reason, so they'd come here with plans to pledge one of the vamp societies. But witches, well, I really don't know much about witches at all.

Cadence gives me a nudge. "Maybe you'll pledge. You know, if you like it here?"

I do like it. And I am a witch—so the professor says, anyway. She leads me into a huge room that smells of incense and candles and contains yet more books and several oversized armchairs. Professor Green is already sitting in a plush purple one next to the roaring fire. Weird.

Hey, can witches do that super-fast running thing too? I ask in my head, hoping one of the boys will hear me and respond.

Not like we do, but they can do all kinds of magic, Malachi replies. *Some can teleport, and a few can even time travel.*

"No way!" The matching expression on Enora's and Cadence's faces make it obvious that I accidentally spoke aloud. By way of explaining my outburst, I smile and say, "This place is incredible."

Enora smiles and indicates for me to take a seat across from her.

Don't let those witches try any mumbo jumbo on you, Cupcake, Xavier says.

Don't be ridiculous, I reply. Enora is looking at me strangely again, and I squirm in my seat.

"I don't mean to make you uncomfortable, Ophelia." Her laugh is lovely, musical almost. "But there is something very intriguing about you."

I shrug. "Nothing exciting about me. I'm as boring as they come."

"You have been spending a lot of time with the commanders of the Ruby Dragon Society lately. Perhaps they sense a similar…" She purses her lips and pauses for a moment. "Something."

My cheeks flush with heat, and I flounder for something to say but come up empty.

She laughs again. "There's no need to be embarrassed, sweet child. We are all of us physical creatures. And their kind is very alluring."

I frown. "Th-their kind?"

Enora dismisses the question with a wave of her hand and calls one of the other girls in to bring us some tea and refreshments.

...

By the time I leave almost three hours later, I'm filled with the impression that Silver Vale Society is a lovely, refined place where the members and pledges regularly partake in English breakfast tea and delicious homemade cookies. All while sharing pleasant conversation. No mumbo jumbo at all.

If Axl weren't growling in my head, threatening to throw me over his shoulder if I didn't leave of my own accord, I probably would have stayed longer.

You're incredibly possessive for someone who's known me for a matter of months, Axl Thorne, I snap as I step onto the sidewalk outside the Silver Vale house.

You haven't seen possessive, princess. You are mine, and you will get your sexy ass home before I walk in there and spank it in front of all your new witch friends.

I roll my eyes. *I'm already on my way.*

In that case...

Frowning, I wait for him to finish that thought. Not even ten seconds later, he's standing a hundred yards ahead of me, leaning against one of the trees surrounding the Temple and looking so ludicrously hot that my knees turn to Jell-O just staring at him.

"Are you stalking me?"

He flashes me a wicked grin. "Yes."

I shake my head and feign indignation, but when I reach him, he slings his arm around my shoulder, and I can't even fake being annoyed at him.

He presses his lips against my ear. "Did I or did I not warn you to stay in bed all day and wait for me, princess?"

I shiver. "Yes, but I had to go to class. And I'm here now."

His eyes rake unashamedly up and down my body, and he growls, making me giggle. Without any further warning, he hoists me over his shoulder and carries me the rest of the way home, with me giggling and making halfhearted protests that he should put me down the whole time.

We reach his bedroom and he tosses me onto the bed, then stands over me with a mischievous look in his eyes.

"Are you really going to punish me?" I ask, my voice raspy.

His eyes narrow and he unbuckles his belt. I swallow. "Naw." Relief runs through me, but then he adds, "We all are."

Oh, sweet hellfire. Nervous energy sizzles through my body. "All of you?"

"Such a naughty fucking cupcake." Xavier's sinful voice fills the room, and he steps up beside Axl, licking his lips, and nudges him in the ribs. "She not naked yet?"

Axl bites on his lip. "She's about to be."

Malachi walks into the room next and closes the door behind him. "I can help with that." He stands beside his brothers with his hands on his hips and a grin on his face.

My pulse races, but only from excitement now. My breathing comes faster and heavier.

Xavier arches an eyebrow. "I can already see a wet spot on your adorable unicorn panties, Cupcake."

I slam my thighs together. "You can...not," I protest, although I'm aware that's entirely possible because being around these three always has me feeling a certain kind of way.

Xavier chuckles, but Axl hands his belt to Malachi and nods toward the head of the bed.

My eyes widen. *What are you doing?*

Malachi climbs onto the bed and wraps the belt around my wrists before securing it to the metal bed frame. "Making sure you can't go anywhere, sweet girl."

"W-why would I want to go anywhere?"

Xavier produces a switchblade from his pocket and runs his tongue the length of the blade. Blood pours from his mouth, and Axl grabs him by the hair and tips his head back. Then he devours him, growling hungrily as he takes Xavier's mouth in a dominant, bruising kiss. It's so hot I almost combust. Half of me expects Xavier to plunge that knife into Axl's neck given how the two of them bicker sometimes, but he only moans and fists his free hand in Axl's hair.

"They're so fucking hot together," Malachi murmurs.

I pant my agreement. "Uh-huh."

When they pull away from each other, Axl licks his blood-smeared lips clean. Xavier's cut has already healed, and he crawls onto the bed holding the knife.

"What are you doing?" I ask, warm waves of pleasure already rolling through my body.

He flashes me a grin. "Getting you naked, Cupcake." He methodically slices off all my clothes, and I don't have the desire to argue that he could have simply taken them off and not ruined them. Xavier with a knife is all kinds of sexy, which I did not expect at all.

When he's done, he sits back on his heels and groans. "So much fucking better."

Within moments, there are three naked and absurdly hot demigod-esque vampires looking down at where I lie tied to their bed like I'm their favorite snack. Which I guess I am.

"Don't forget I need my blood to live," I remind them with a giggle.

"Did our naughty cupcake just fucking sass us while she's tied up?" Xavier asks.

Malachi tilts his head and stares at me. "I think she did."

Axl grunts. "So fucking feisty."

"About to be so fucking fucked." Xavier winks at me.

I press my lips together and squirm under the heat of their gazes. My skin feels like it's sizzling with kinetic energy, and they haven't even touched me yet.

"You smell so fucking good, Cupcake."

Malachi tips his face to the ceiling and groans. "She's soaked."

"And she's all mine first," Axl growls. "You two had plenty of fun this morning while I was working."

Xavier rolls his eyes. "Like we don't work just as hard, golden boy."

"We sure worked hard this morning, huh, sweet girl?" Malachi says.

My cheeks get so hot I'm surprised my face isn't on fire.

"My turn, princess." Axl crawls between my thighs, nudging them wider apart with his knees. Dipping his head, he inhales, and the most animalistic growl I have ever heard in my life rolls out of him. "Sweet mother of fuck, Ophelia."

Please tell me that sound he made wasn't because of what I think it is. I do some quick math in my head. "W-what is it?"

He ignores me and glances back at his buddies. "How long have we been fucking our sweet Ophelia?"

Xavier frowns. "Three weeks. Why?"

Oh no! I whimper inside my head.

"Oh fucking yes, princess," Axl growls.

Xavier grunts. "Has she? Is she bleeding?"

Axl licks his lips, his pupils so wide that I can barely see the brown of his irises. He growls again, his fangs bared.

I don't feel like I got my period, but I guess a vampire's sense of smell wouldn't be wrong about this kind of thing. "Please let me go to the bathroom. I must be a day or two early." Mortification burns through me.

Axl responds by burying his tongue inside me. His teeth graze my sensitive flesh, and I moan, my hips bucking off the bed so hard that he has to hold me down. And then Malachi and Xavier are beside me, wicked grins on their faces as their hands roam my body.

Xavier cups my face in his hand. "How many days, Cupcake?"

"What?"

He runs his nose along my cheekbone. "How many days does your period usually last?"

"Four," I croak. Oh my god.

Xavier chuckles. "This is like Christmas every month for us."

I shake my head. "It's…" I can't think of the word, but disgusting comes pretty close.

"It's blood, sweet girl. Whether we drink it from your veins or your pussy, it's the same thing."

Axl lifts his head. "It tastes a hundred percent better from her pussy."

If my hands weren't tied, I would put them over my face and quietly die of shame. I can see my tombstone. Here lies Ophelia Hart. Died of mortification.

Groaning, Xavier burrows his face into my neck and sucks on my skin. Malachi does the same to my other side while their rough hands explore every inch of my body that they can reach. Axl's tongue works inside me, licking and sucking until wet heat runs down my thighs and my head spins with the euphoria racing around my body. Right when I'm ready to fall over the edge, he strums my clit with his thumb, and my climax rips through me with the force of a hurricane.

As I'm catching my breath, I look down at his smiling face, his lips smeared with the faintest hint of blood. "Fuck, that was incredible, princess."

He scoots up on the bed and trades places with Xavier, who settles between my thighs. I have no desire to kiss Axl right now, but thankfully Malachi does. He grabs his jaw, and their lips crash together. Their groans mingle with my own as Xavier feasts on my pussy like a starving man. Axl and Malachi kiss each other, then me.

After I come for a second time, Malachi's hungry mouth is on me before I can even catch my breath. They talk me through another orgasm, their mouths and hands everywhere. I have no idea where one of them ends and the other begins, and I swear I lose all sense of time and space and reason. Their filthy words of how delicious I taste, how I belong to them, and how they're going to fuck me until sunrise are all that anchor me to reality.

46

Axl

I did intend to punish my little pyromaniac. Spank her pretty little ass until she begged me to stop and then maybe edge her for a few hours, but that all went to hell the moment I caught the aroma of her menstrual blood. I have never tasted anything so goddamn sweet and addictive in my entire life. And we have four whole fucking days of it, during which she'll be lucky if she gets to leave this bed at all.

I tell Malachi to untie her trembling limbs. He rubs her wrists, and I spread her thighs with mine, staring at her pussy glistening with pink juices. My fangs ache, but not as much as my cock, which is so hard I'm going to pass out if I don't sink inside her soon.

"Axl," she moans, her eyelids fluttering.

"I know, princess." I drive inside her with one hard thrust, and she cries out my name again. Her pussy ripples around me, pulling me in farther. I fall forward, bracketing her hips with my hands, and pull out slowly, savoring every frustrated whimper I wring from her. And when I sink into her once more, she grabs at my neck, nails clawing at my skin. Her back arches off the bed as she takes all of me. I rest my lips on the fluttering pulse at the base of her throat. "Such a good girl the way you take my cock."

"So good the way you take all of us, baby," Malachi says.

"Oh, god," she moans. Searing hot need ripples down my spine. Her walls grip my cock, milking me as she reaches the edge again, and I want to sink my fangs into her neck and fill her with my load, but Xavier yanks my head back, his eyes narrowed.

He shakes his head. "Don't come inside Ophelia."

Is he fucking serious? "Why the fuck not?"

He licks his lips. "Because I want to taste her on you."

I grunt with frustration but slide out of her, leaving her wet and needy and on the edge. "I told you I was going to punish you, princess." I flash her a wink and press a soft kiss on her forehead. "But Malachi will take care of you."

His deep growl fills the room, and he pulls Ophelia up to straddle him. Lying next to Malachi, I watch Xavier drool over my blood-smeared cock and run my fingers through his dark hair. This is such an unusual but welcome occurrence. "Do it."

He drops his head and takes me all the way into his hot mouth, deep throating me with such skill that my eyes roll back in my head. His grunts and groans are muffled by my cock filling his mouth, and I keep one hand on his head, holding him in place, and squeeze one of Ophelia's perfect tits with the other. My eyes drift between Xavier's sinful lips swallowing my dick and Malachi stretching our girl's pussy wide as he repeatedly lifts and impales her.

Xavier fucks his own hand, driven feral with the taste of Ophelia's blood and my precum sliding down his throat. I feel them reaching the edge along with me, each of us drawing ever closer to the sweet relief of oblivion. We're connected so deeply that it feels like four times the pleasure, and when Ophelia comes with a throaty cry, she drags the rest of us over the edge with her. I drown in the ecstasy of all four climaxes in one long, seemingly never-ending wave.

...

After we all got cleaned up and Ophelia insisted on at least wearing panties, we curled up in my bed to watch a movie.

Xavier nuzzles our girl's neck. "Do you wear tampons, Cupcake?"

Her already pink cheeks turn red. "Yes. Why?"

He licks his lips. "I'm gonna need them when you're done."

Her nose wrinkles in disgust. "Eww. No."

I suppress a dark laugh when he nods. "Yeah. I'm gonna freeze them and suck on 'em like popsicles."

Malachi snorts a laugh, but Ophelia gasps in horror. "What. No, you cannot freeze my tampons and…" She shakes her head, but Xavier simply pulls her into his arms and bands them so tightly around her she can't move. "If you don't hand them over of your own free will, I will simply remove them myself."

I shoot her a sympathetic look. "He will."

"No way. You are not putting my tampons in the freezer, Xavier. No."

He rests his lips on the top of her head. "We'll see, Cupcake."

"We will not."

Malachi cups her chin in his hand. "Stop arguing, sweet girl." He silences her with his lips, and while she's distracted, Xavier mimes sucking a popsicle. I can't hold back my laugh. The fucker is crazy enough to do it. Although, maybe crazy isn't the right word… I lick my lips at the thought of his genius idea, and he tips his head back and laughs too.

47

ALEXANDROS

Turning down the path, I head deeper into the trees that border the campus. The branches grow thicker here, the air is filled with the scent of pine, but it is not enough to mask the witch's scent.

"Why are you following me, Professor Drakos?" Her voice carries from the left of me, and I watch the figure ahead vanish into thin air.

I stop and face the direction of the sound. "You were always a very gifted witch, Enora."

She snorts. "A simple parlor trick."

"Why are you hiding in the shadows? You have nothing to fear from me."

Her musical laugh rings through the air between us. "All witches fear you, Alexandros."

I roll my neck, trying to stave off the centuries-old hurt that still rises to the surface whenever I recall the extent of their treachery. Sufficiently calmer, I speak. "As they should."

She hums softly, and I sense her drawing closer. "The sting of their betrayal has not lessened through the ages, no?"

"Not for some of us. There are others who were far too quick to forgive."

She steps into view, the moonlight highlighting her silver hair and delicate features. "Was I supposed to disown my entire species because of the actions of—"

"Of thousands, Enora," I growl the reminder.

"Most of whom are no longer with us."

True, and it is little solace to me. "But their legacy remains. Their teachings. Do you think I do not hear what the young witches are taught within these walls?"

She purses her lips, her gray eyes narrowed. "Why were you following me?"

"Why are you interested in the girl?"

Her eyelids flicker, but she hides her surprise quickly and folds her arms across her chest. "I take an interest in many girls in this school."

I resist the urge to wrap my hand around her throat. "You know who I am talking about. Why is she being summoned to Silver Vale? She has no magic."

Enora rolls her eyes. "She was not *summoned* to Silver Vale. One of my talented witches has taken a liking to her and simply invited her over."

I glare at her. "Do not insult my intelligence. Invitations to Silver Vale are not simply given out to just anyone."

She tilts her head, eyeing me curiously. "Why are you so interested in this girl, Alexandros?"

"It is no secret that my boys find her company..." I rake my fingertips through my beard to buy myself time as I search for the most appropriate word. "Enchanting. I am simply curious as to why the most powerful witch in Montridge is enamored with her too."

She flutters her eyelashes. "You do flatter me so, *filous mou*."

My friend. I scoff. Does she really think me so obtuse that I would fail to see through her avoidance tactics? She is skirting the question, and that alone tells me that she knows something about Ophelia. "Why, Enora? Does she possess magic?"

Her slender throat convulses. "Not that I am aware of."

I inhale deeply, trying to tune into her emotions and determine if she is lying, but as powerful a witch as Enora is, she can easily mask them from me. "So? Your interest in her is what?"

Her gray eyes turn stormy, and I feel the wall she is erecting between us. "A favor for an old friend."

My hackles rise. "What favor and for whom?"

"Merely to take the girl under our wing. Teach her the ways of our kind and determine if she has any latent power that we can bring to the surface."

I narrow my eyes and scan her face, but she has all her defenses heightened against me. "And does she?"

"Like I told you a moment ago, none that I am aware of."

She is hiding something else. "Who is this old friend?"

"There are secrets I must keep, even from you, Alexandros."

Frustration rages inside me. "I could bite you and discover your truths."

She shakes her head, her lips curved ever so slightly. "It would take you a century to break down my walls."

I flick my tongue over my fangs. She has forgotten who I am. Closer to a few years, but still…"Time is something I have plenty of," I say, bluffing.

Smiling fully now, she runs her nimble fingers over the lapel of my suit jacket. "But sweet Ophelia does not."

Dammit! My rage burns for a different reason, tinged with possession and fear. "Do you intend her any harm?"

Her beautiful face twists with her own rage, causing her facade to slip for a second and reveal the old woman beneath the youthful mask she invests so much power in upholding. "How dare you suggest such a thing. It is more than likely your offspring would cause her harm than I."

As much as that burns, if Ophelia were not what she is, that would be true, so I refrain from refuting her assertion. "If any harm comes to her, Enora…"

She tips her chin up. "If harm befalls Ophelia, it will not be at the hands of anyone from Silver Vale."

All my instincts scream that her sincerity is real. But someone is undoubtedly pulling the strings of Ophelia's destiny. Someone powerful enough to bind her powers and secure her attendance here with a minimum of suspicion. Is it the same *old friend* that Enora speaks of? Are the witches the key? And if so, I cannot believe that they are doing this for Ophelia's protection, not given their history with the elementai. So why? Do they intend to use her power for their own ends? Manipulate her somehow?

I rub my temples, plagued once more by too many questions and not enough answers.

48

OPHELIA

I'm stretching to return a book to its appropriate place on the shelf when an overwhelming current of desire strikes me. I clamp my thighs together and stifle a whimper. What the hell was that?

You make me so fucking hard, Kai, Xavier growls.

Malachi moans. *So shut up and fuck me.*

I glance nervously around the library despite knowing nobody else can hear what's going on in my head. Well, except for the guys already having sex in there. *What the hell are you two doing?*

Xavier comes back with a wicked laugh. *Fucking.*

Do you have to do it in my head, though? Can't you speak out loud to each other? I'm in the library.

We know, baby. Malachi laughs now too. *But even if you couldn't hear us, you'd still feel this.*

I have no idea what they do, but I'm hit with another rush of desire that has wetness slicking between my thighs.

Xavier speaks again. *Such a good fucking boy for me, pup.*
Malachi grunts.

A third wave of euphoria washes over me, and I hold onto the shelf before my legs betray me. This is so damn hot I can barely think straight.

Oh, hellfire! I pant in my head.

You enjoying this, Cupcake? You feel how good Kai's tight ass feels?

My head is filled with Malachi's moans and Xavier's grunts.

Heat races down my neck and chest, and I squeeze my thighs tighter to stop the ache in my core, but nothing helps. I'm dripping wet and aching for relief, and nobody is even touching me.

Touch yourself, Cupcake. Let me see if I can get you and Kai off at the same time.

I glance around the quiet library again. *I c-can't.*

Yeah you can, baby. Go to that quiet spot at the back where I first fucked you, Malachi says, before letting out another desperate moan.

I chew on my lip, unable to believe I'm considering their suggestion, but I swear I'm as edgy as Malachi. My core throbs, eager for relief. I make my way to the quietest part of the library, my head bent low in the hope that nobody will notice that I'm on the verge of an earth-shattering orgasm. My legs shake more with each step I take toward that high.

Thankfully, there's nobody in the art history section, and I head to the far end of the row and drop my backpack onto the floor.

Motherfucker! Malachi growls. Pleasure coils deep inside me, and I gasp for breath.

Good. Fucking. Boy, Xavier grunts.

Oh my god, I'm going to burst into flames.

Are your hands in your panties yet, Cupcake?

N-no.

What are you waiting for? We can feel you too. Slip your fingers inside your tight cunt and come with us, Xavier demands.

Unable to stand the torment any longer, I press myself into a corner, looking around me to make sure I'm alone, and slip my hand into my panties. As soon as my fingers graze my swollen clit, I whimper out loud with relief.

Good girl, Xavier groans.

I close my eyes, giving in to the overwhelming sensations taking over my body.

"I'd say she's more of a naughty fucking girl. Hand in her panties getting herself off in the library." Axl's voice raises goose bumps over my body, and it takes me a few beats to realize that he's not in my head.

I open my eyes and have to bite back a scream when I see him walking toward me, filling the space between the shelves with his large frame. My cheeks burn with shame.

Xavier laughs darkly.

My hand stills as I stare into Axl's brown eyes. He licks his lips, and my heart rate increases with each deliberate step he takes toward me. "Don't stop, dirty girl."

I sink my teeth into my bottom lip and wince. *I'm sorry. I couldn't help it.*

He steps directly in front of me, and I shiver. Axl takes hold of my wrist and slowly, deliberately, pulls my hand out from between my thighs. The promise of my impending orgasm ebbs away, and I whine.

He holds my fingers in front of my face, forcing me to look at my arousal coating the tips. "Naughty Ophelia." He tuts and places my fingers in his mouth, humming as he sucks them clean. At the same time, he slides his hand beneath my skirt and pulls my panties aside. "This pussy is mine, princess. If you want to come in the middle of the library, you ask my permission first."

Xavier's and Malachi's groans of pleasure seem to be dulled with Axl's presence here, but they go on in the background, like a movie with the volume turned down.

"Okay," I whisper, rocking against his hand.

He chuckles. "You want to come, princess?"

"P-please."

He makes a fake sad face, his eyes twinkling with wicked intent as he slowly shakes his head. "No."

I want to cry from frustration. "Why?"

He pulls his hand from between my thighs. "Naughty girls don't deserve to come, Ophelia. And judging by how soaked you are, you've been very naughty."

"I was just..." I blow a strand of hair from my eyes. He's messing with me, and I'm playing right into his hands. "That's okay. You kind of ruined the mood anyway."

His eyes flash with something dark and dangerous. "I did what now?"

I put a hand on my hip. "You heard me. I'm not in the mood now."

He sniffs the air and growls. "Sure seems like you are, princess."

I know I'm going to regret this, but I can't help it. "Well, that was all for Xavier and Malachi. Not for you."

His eyes narrow, and he snakes one arm around my waist, crushing me against his chest. A warning growl rumbles out of him. "Is that so?"

My knees threaten to buckle, but I force myself to stay upright and stare into his handsome face. "It is," I croak.

He brushes his fingertips over my cheekbone, and I'm vaguely aware of Xavier laughing and warning me that I'm about to be fucked into my next life, but I tune him out and focus on Axl.

"Knees, princess. Now."

Without hesitation, I drop to my knees, my mouth watering with anticipation. I've never done this before, and I so want to. Axl unbuckles his belt, and a rush of arousal soaks my panties.

He takes his cock out, stroking his hand up and down his thick, beautiful shaft. Precum beads on the slit of his crown, and I move to lick it off, but he grabs my hair and yanks me back. "Nuh-uh, princess. Not me." He laughs darkly.

I blink up at him, confused, but realization dawns a few seconds later when Malachi appears behind him.

"Wh-what? I thought you were with Xavier."

He arches an eyebrow. "I was. And now I'm here for you, baby."

I look between him and Axl. "But I thought you…"

"Oh, I'll be fucking you, princess, but"—he dips his head and brushes his lips over my ear—"I was the first to take your virgin pussy, so Kai here staked his claim on being the first to take your mouth."

I bite on my lip. "And what about Xavier?" I know there's no way he hasn't tried to stake his claims somehow.

Malachi chuckles. "Oh, I think you know what he's taking first, baby."

Oh god. That means… I swallow down a knot of trepidation at the realization of what Xavier wants to do, and despite my reservation, the thought of him taking me there causes another rush of heat to slick between my thighs. Axl steps aside, and Malachi takes his place, freeing his thick cock from his sweatpants. It bobs an inch from my lips, and I sweep my tongue over the tip, tasting him. Grunting, he fists his hand in my hair.

"Oh, sweet fucking Ophelia," he groans, rocking his hips and sliding into my waiting mouth. I flick my tongue over his shaft, taking my cues from his appreciative noises and hoping I'm doing it right.

"You're doing so fucking good, baby. So good," he groans, and his words flood me with pride.

I'm so focused on Malachi that I don't feel Axl kneeling behind me until my panties are halfway down my thighs.

What are you doing? I ask.

Fucking you, princess.

Here in the library?

Well, I would have taken you to bed and eaten your pussy first, but you were such a sassy little brat, I think you deserve to be fucked on your knees with Malachi's cock in your mouth. Like the naughty little slut that you are. He grabs my hip with one hand and holds me in place while he sinks his huge cock inside me, filling me so completely that I moan around Malachi's length.

"She's fucking soaked, Kai," he says, then he places his mouth against my ear. "None of it's for me though, right? Isn't that what you said?"

He drives harder, and I see stars. *I d-didn't mean it.*

He pulls out and thrusts back in even harder, forcing me to take more of Malachi's length down my throat. Tears leak from the corners of my eyes. *No?* he taunts.

No! I promise.

I think sucking my cock is what's got her so wet, buddy, Malachi says. *She's doing a hell of a job of it.*

Whose cock is making this tight little cunt such a mess, princess? Mine or Malachi's?

Pleasure seizes my every thought, preventing me from replying.

Because you're dripping down your legs, Ophelia. You hear that pussy crying for me?

My cheeks heat as I focus on the sound of him fucking me. It's so damn loud in the quiet library, but I don't care. I'd be willing to have an audience right now for the promise of the release he can give me.

Please, Axl?

He grunts. "Make us both come and I might take pity on you, princess."

I suck on Malachi's length, swirling my tongue over the tip, still hoping what I'm doing is right. His guttural noises spur me on and prove that he's enjoying himself. His hands fist in my hair. Axl holds onto my hips with a bruising grip, hammering into me from behind, and I squeeze my inner muscles around him, making him groan my name.

Malachi grunts his warning and gives me a chance to stop before flooding my mouth with his taste. He showers me with praise as he slides out of my mouth, wiping away the spit and cum that dribbles onto my chin. Axl squeezes my breasts in his huge hands and ruts into me. My eyelids flicker closed and white-hot euphoria shuttles through me.

"Who's about to make this greedy little cunt come, princess?"

"Y-you are," I pant, my orgasm crashing over me in a huge rolling wave.

"Don't ever fucking forget it." His hips still as he empties himself inside me. He bands his arms around me and holds me close, our hearts beating an erratic rhythm in our chests.

Fuck, that was hot, Xavier says, making me laugh. *You are a naughty girl, Cupcake.*

Axl hums, his lips against my skin. "Naughty and good in all the best ways."

I lean back against him, a smile on my face and his cum dripping down my thighs.

49

OPHELIA

"Are we all set?" Axl asks Xavier, who's sitting at the breakfast table making notes on a map.

Without looking up, Xavier nods once and places the pen between his teeth.

I take a sip of my coffee and stand beside him, looking at the map of the woods that border Montridge. Xavier has adorned it with various symbols and arrows. "Is this for the final trial?"

Malachi slips his arms around my waist and sits down, pulling me onto his lap. "Yeah, the Hunt. Our favorite."

"The Hunt?" A shiver runs down my spine, and Malachi laughs. "What happens? Do you hunt people?"

"Only the pledges, baby, and they all know what they're getting themselves into."

I wrinkle my nose, watching Xavier make more marks on the map. "What is he doing?" I whisper to Malachi.

"He's marking the quickest way through the obstacles. They're different every year."

"What exactly happens at these hunts?"

Axl tips my chin up with his forefinger. "Always so many questions, princess." Then he offers me a smile and presses a tender kiss on my forehead before declaring that he's going to shower.

As soon as he's gone, I lean forward and examine the map. "Why is there a picture of a bear?"

Xavier flashes me a wicked grin. "That's where the bear traps are."

I wrinkle my nose. "There are bear traps?"

Malachi presses his lips against my neck and hums. "There will be much worse things than bear traps in those woods tonight, baby."

I study the map again.

"No, you cannot come," Xavier says, without looking up. "Absolutely not."

I gasp. "I never asked. Not even in my head. Did I?"

Malachi chuckles. "No, baby. But we already know what you're thinking."

They aren't wrong. I would love to go to the Hunt and see how it all plays out. "Then please let me come. I'll be good. I'll do whatever you tell me to do. I promise."

Malachi cups my jaw in his hand and turns my face so I'm looking into his bright green eyes. "We'll be hunting, sweet girl. The witches cast a spell that prevents us from communicating through our bond during the Hunt because it gives us an unfair advantage. We won't be able to focus on the Hunt and protect you."

I pout, my arms folded across my chest. "I can look after myself."

"Yeah?" Xavier growls. "Like the last time you went wandering around the woods alone and almost got yourself eaten?"

Shame courses through me at the memory. Not only of Ronan but of how cruel Xavier was afterward. As though he feels that pain in me, he takes my hand and threads his fingers through mine before dusting his lips over my knuckles. "We're not risking your safety, Ophelia. You'll stay away from the Hunt. Do I make myself clear?"

I squirm on Malachi's lap, and he wraps his arms tightly around my waist. "Ophelia?" he says with a warning growl.

As unfair as this seems, I know they're doing it for my own protection. And that's kind of awesome. "Fine, I'll stay away. But you at least have to tell me what happens if I'm not going to be able to watch it for myself."

Xavier rolls his eyes and goes back to his map, so I look at Malachi.

"The pledges from each vamp society are split into groups of three or four. They get a two-hour head start, and they can choose to help or hinder each other, but their ultimate aim is to ensure they make it from one end of the woods to the other without getting caught, either by a hunter or one of the traps. Those who make it out on the other side are turned."

That seems so final and unfair. "So that's it? If you don't make it, you don't get turned? After all their hard work?"

Malachi nods. "We can only turn the best."

"So who are the hunters? All of you?"

"Each society chooses four hunters. For Ruby Dragon it will be Axl, Xavier, me, and one of our juniors."

"And if you catch someone, you get to bite them, right?"

He nods. "Bite them and help them forget anything they might have seen that they shouldn't have."

A wave of jealousy washes over me, and Malachi obviously senses it because he nuzzles my neck. "We have to eat, baby."

"I know. It's just that your bites are so…" I'm not being unreasonable. One of their bites is enough to set off an orgasm.

"They're so what, sweet girl?" His hand slips beneath my skirt and along the inside of my thigh.

"Pleasurable," I whisper.

Xavier snorts a laugh, but he keeps his eyes on the map. "Not always, Cupcake."

"They're not?"

Malachi shakes his head, his fingers skimming over my panties at the apex of my thighs. "Our bite isn't unpleasant. And it isn't supposed to hurt because we don't need people screaming while we bite them. But we only make it *pleasurable* for people we like, baby."

I run my fingers across the nape of his neck, and his eyes twinkle as he smiles at me.

"Is our little cupcake jealous?" Xavier asks.

"No," I insist, even though it's a lie. The thought of them doing to any other girl what they do to me makes my stomach roll and my heart ache a little. "I'd just rather you didn't go around making random women feel…"

Xavier looks up, his dark eyes burning into mine now. "Feel what?"

"The way you make me feel," I whisper. I'm being foolish. They're vampires, and that's what vampires do.

"Sweet girl," Malachi says, peppering kisses over my throat before he tugs my panties aside and begins to tease me. "What we do with you is very different. And you know it is." He slides a finger inside me, and my back bows. "Don't you?"

"Y-yes," I whimper, wrapping an arm around his neck and holding onto him. Then he sinks his teeth into my throat and reminds me exactly how good he can make me feel.

· · ·

I settle into the armchair and flick through my novel, but I can't focus. My mind keeps going to the boys out at the Hunt and how exciting it all sounds. Despite them warning me how dangerous it is, I'm fascinated. And it's not like those who are hunted are ever in any danger. They get bitten if they're caught, but then they get a happy memory inserted instead of the bite and they're fine. Not that I want anyone other than Axl, Xavier, or Malachi to bite me, but surely if I mentioned I was with them, whoever caught me would let me go.

I glance at the window. The sun has set, and the Hunt will begin soon.

Can you guys still hear me? I don't get an answer. Looks like the witch magic is already in place. A few weeks ago, I would've sworn I'd be happy to have their voices out of my head, but it's been less than an hour and I miss them.

I put my book down and go to the window, peering out into the fading light. And that's when I feel it, like a punch to the solar plexus. They're hurt. Or in danger.

Or both.

I have no idea where the sudden overwhelming dread is coming from, but the sensation is so acute that I can taste it, like a bitter residue in the back of my throat. I need to get to them and warn them.

Something is very, very wrong.

50

Xavier

Axl's dark laughter fades into the distance as he takes off in the opposite direction. I stretch my neck, enjoying each satisfying crack. The Hunt is my favorite night of the year. All that adrenaline and fear. The thrill of tracking prey before we devour it is a rush all its own. I've already earmarked three Onyx pledges who look particularly tasty, and I'd be more than happy to prevent them from becoming immortal members of House Chóma.

The pledges have a two-hour head start, and they're allowed to bring weapons, maps, or anything they think might assist them in making it to the final checkpoint. The smartest ones know that the key is to mask their scent, and to do that most effectively they need to get creative. Skunk spray is particularly effective, as is anything with sulfur. Surprisingly, ash, particularly from pine trees, is one of the stronger substances for masking scent.

A few years ago, the Ruby Dragon pledges set fire to half a dozen trees in their attempt to cover their scent, and a water demon had to be summoned to put it out before it caused a forest fire. In hindsight, the whole situation was hilarious, but burning entire trees has been—understandably—forbidden ever since.

I make my way through the thick woods, dodging the sharp branches and scanning my surroundings for signs of movement before I make my way to the river where the low-hanging fruit usually go in the mistaken belief that water is enough to cover their smell. Spoiler alert—it's not.

The acrid scent of sulfur reaches my nostrils, but it's laced with something. Something strong and familiar that makes my fangs throb. Despite the horrendous smell, my mouth waters, and I know what's causing my reaction.

Fucking Ophelia.

Willing my senses to be deceiving me, I taste the air and follow the scent, heading down the steep riverbank. I keep my ears tuned to the sounds of the night, trying to hear something more than the hammering of my own heart. With every step, I become more certain of one thing. My cupcake is in these woods.

Anger and fear rage inside my chest, each battling for dominance so much that I have no idea which one to focus on.

I am going to spank your ass, Cupcake! But she can't hear me. Nor can Malachi and Axl. Nobody within these woods can communicate through their bond tonight.

Except one person—one man whose powers far outweigh any witch's spell. But he will only hear me if he wants to. If it were Axl or Malachi, I'm sure he'd respond. Hopefully…

I close my eyes and focus on him. *Alexandros. I need you.*

What is it, Xavier? he responds immediately.

Thank fuck. I let out a relieved sigh. *I think Ophelia is in the woods.*

She what? With only two words, he manages to communicate a world of disappointment. I'm used to getting that reaction from him, and I usually get pissed, but this is too important to let my emotions get in the way.

We warned her to stay away. She promised she would, but... Dammit, I was so sure she would keep her word. I can't fucking believe she put herself in so much danger.

What makes you so sure she is there?

Well, my heart literally stopped beating in my chest a second ago. *I caught her scent, and it was laced with fear.*

And you are certain that you are not mistaken? His tone is clipped, impatient.

How I wish that I was. *You know her scent as well as I do. You honestly think you could mistake her for another?*

No. But the Hunt is on, and we know our enemies will employ any tactics at their disposal. Perhaps someone is trying to trick you.

I know that's a possibility, but I also know my cupcake's scent. I am absolutely certain she is in these woods. Equally certain that she will be on a fucking leash when I get my hands on her. I struggle to ignore the niggling fear that I might not ever get my hands on her again, and I'm grateful when Alexandros cuts off my spiraling thoughts. *I am headed to the house now. I will see if she is there.*

Thank you.

Focus on the Hunt. We cannot afford to lose too many pledges.

He falls silent, and I scan the woods around me. How am I supposed to focus on the Hunt when Ophelia could be out here? I wish I could speak to Axl or Malachi. I strain to hear any sound of movement but hear only the soft rustling of leaves and the distant sound of a hooting owl.

She is not here, Xavier. Alexandros's words slice me in two.

Then I was right. She's here somewhere.

I will find her, he assures me. *Focus on the Hunt.*

I can't focus on the goddamn Hunt. This is...there are no rules tonight, Alexandros. No fucking rules. I've never directed this level of anger at him before, but I've never been this afraid before either. We cannot lose her. Many pledges don't make it out of these woods alive, and while our scent *may* protect her from other vampires, it won't protect her from any wild animals out in the woods or from the other pledges, some of which would gladly slit someone's throat to ensure their own survival. Their ruthlessness is exactly why they were chosen.

I will find her, Xavier, he repeats.

I can't do anything but think about her. Can't you force the witches to break the spell? Just until we find her?

His weary sigh rolls through my head. *We cannot put the entire Hunt at risk for the sake of one girl.*

But—

No matter how much we might want to, Xavier. Nobody can know what she is. What she means to you all.

My head is spinning. Why the fuck couldn't she do as she was told?

We will find her. I will ensure that she is safe, and then you will get back to the Hunt. Understand? His commanding tone brooks no arguments.

As soon as I know she's safe, I'm one hundred percent focused on the Trials. I swear.

Where did you first detect her scent?

At the fork in the river. I tracked it east for a few hundred yards before it vanished.

Then I will start at the river.

With a heavy ache in my chest that I haven't felt since I was human, I head back in the direction I came from and hope we find her quickly.

51

OPHELIA

I scramble through the trees, the sensation of impending doom growing heavier with each step I take, but every second I'm even more convinced that the boys are in some kind of trouble and that I need to help them.

I stumble over a broken branch and fall to my knees. "Ouch!" I hiss as a sharp piece of bark tears open my skin.

Hushed voices and footsteps draw near, and I hold my breath, willing my heart to stop racing. Vampires will be able to hear me from hundreds of yards away no matter what I do, but perhaps they are my vampires.

The noises grow ever closer, and I push myself to my feet, squinting to see any figures dipping between the trees, but there's so little light. I take a deep breath and make a run for it, repeatedly chanting Axl's and Xavier's and Malachi's names in my head in the hopes that they'll hear me if I'm close enough, despite the magic they told me about.

But the noises grow closer, and I instinctively know that

the source isn't friendly. They seem to circle me, taunting me. I run faster, using my hands to guide me through the thick trees. The sound of flowing water reaches me, and I recall something I read once about animals using water to mask their scents. With my heart thumping loudly in my ears and adrenaline thundering through my veins, I run as fast as I can toward the river.

But I'm not fast enough. A bulky body collides with mine, bringing me crashing to the ground. He breathes heavily, and I retch as his stench overpowers me. One of the foster kids I shared a home with was once sprayed by a skunk, and it's the exact same foul smell.

"Hey, Malone! I got her," he says to his accomplice.

A sinister laugh rings through the trees beside me.

"Is she a pledge?"

He flips me over onto my back and straddles me, and that's when I see he's wearing night vision goggles. "Don't think so. I don't recognize her."

Malone steps closer. "She anyone important?"

He grabs my face and squeezes my cheeks together. I buck my hips and shove at his torso, trying to throw him off, but he's too strong. He pins my wrists in one of his huge hands. "Nah. She ain't nothing special."

"What do we do with her, Jensen?" Malone asks. "We could have a little fun, but we don't have time."

"Hmm." Jensen squeezes my cheeks tighter. "I think we use her as bait. What do you think?"

What the hell?

"Bait?" Malone says.

"Yeah. Smear her blood over the trees. Cut off her fingers." He trails his hand over my jaw, down my collarbone, and roughly squeezes and twists my breast. I yelp. "Maybe a few internal organs. Keep those fuckers distracted. Scent is a big deal, right? That's what all the prep has led us to believe. You know we all had to hand over our T-shirts and change into clean ones. They must use dogs to track our scent or something."

"You seriously think you can just cut me up and nobody will notice?" I scoff.

Jensen picks me up and hoists me over his shoulder. "We can do anything during the Hunt, darlin'. There are no rules tonight."

I punch at his back and kick my legs, but he only laughs. And he only laughs harder when I let out a blood-curdling scream. "Nobody will hear your screams 'round here, darlin'."

"Get the hell off me. I'm—" A piece of stale cloth is forced into my mouth, and I gag as the taste of gasoline coats my tongue.

"Still fucking annoying though," Malone says. "Where shall we take her?"

"I'm thinking the steepest part of the ravine. We get a good vantage point and see where we need to go. Then once we figure out our route, we smear ourselves with her blood, chop off whatever pieces of her we need, and stuff 'em in our packs and go. They won't be chasing her scent, so we're home free."

Malone grunts his agreement while my stomach threatens to relieve me of its contents. I swallow down the bile in my throat as tears leak from my eyes. My heart is going to explode with how hard it's racing now. Adrenaline and fear race through my veins, sending surges of strength to my limbs, but no matter how hard I struggle, Jensen overpowers me. Why am I so afraid when I never have been before? Is it because I see no way out of this? Maybe it's because for the first time in my life, I know that someone will miss me if I were to die. I recall Axl's pain and anguish when he needed my blood. Will that happen to all of them? Will they die without me? A strangled sob escapes my throat. What the hell have I done? And where the hell are my boys?

I don't know how long we walk, but my stomach aches from being carried over Jensen's shoulder. After my third attempt to get away and him threatening to tie me up, I stop struggling, figuring

I'll have better odds of making my escape once we get where we're going. If I'm tied up, that will be a hundred times more difficult.

We finally come to a halt, and I'm dropped to the ground with a thud. I force myself to a standing position and glare at the two men. Both are wearing night vision goggles, and both of them are at least six feet tall and three feet wide.

I glance around for an escape route. Throwing myself down the steep ravine would be preferable to what these two have in mind.

Jensen produces a knife from a side pocket of his cargo pants and holds it aloft. The metal glints in the moonlight.

I go to run, but he's way too fast, and he catches me by my wrist. "Shall we carve you up while you're still alive, darlin'? Or slit your throat and let you bleed out onto the ground first?" His rancid breath makes me shudder.

I try to pull away, but he holds firm. "A feisty little thing, aren't you?" His lips are twisted in a cruel smirk.

He trails the tip of the knife over my cheekbone, and I flinch. Oh god, I'm going to die out here in these woods all alone. And just when my life was getting interesting.

My legs are quaking so hard I'm sure my bones are shaking, and my stomach protests at holding its contents in once more. This is really it. There's no hope of my rescue. I can't reach the boys. Nobody knows that I'm here. My heart and lungs are unresponsive, frozen. Closing my eyes, I wait for the sting of his blade.

"Get your disgusting fucking hands off her. Now!" The vicious growl reverberates in the space around us.

I'm pushed to the ground, and my knees scrape on the jagged rocks, causing burning pain to lance through me. My chest heaves, and I chance lifting my head, hoping and praying that I didn't hallucinate the voice. Despite the dim light offered by the moon, I see him. My heart swells to double its usual size, and relief rushes through my veins. He's real. He's here.

He's here for me.

"Alexandros." His name falls from my lips like a prayer.

He moves so quickly and it's so dark that all I see are shadows, but I hear it all. Tearing flesh, screams, bones breaking, choking. Death. Within moments, the bodies of the two men who grabbed me lie on the ground around me. Except the scattered pieces littering the dirt can no longer be described as bodies. Bile surges in my throat, and I clamp my hand over my mouth. Then I see his feet planted directly in front of my knees. I follow the lines of his body up to his face. A deep, dark scowl mars his handsome features, and his eyes are narrowed to thin slits. The sight makes my mouth run dry and my throat feel like it's closing over.

He licks a single drop of blood from the corner of his mouth. "What in all the demons of hell are you doing here?" His low growl vibrates through my body like he's tuned into the frequency of my soul.

My heart beats so fast I'm worried I'm going to use my entire lifetime's worth of heartbeats in this single moment. What I'm about to say isn't nearly enough, and the words are going to sound weak, but I have nothing else. "I'm sorry."

52

ALEXANDROS

"Sorry? You almost get yourself killed. You distract my boys from the most important night of the year, and all you have to say for yourself is *sorry*?"

Fortunately for Ophelia, my rage at her stupidity is drowned out by the intense relief that they did not hurt her. More importantly, no vampire bonded with her and realized what she is. That the two pledges were our own did not cross my mind for a second whilst I was tearing them limb from limb. Nor did the fact that they were probably going to use her as bait, and therefore were calculated and ruthless and exactly the kind of new recruits House Drakos values.

Her bottom lip trembles. "I d-don't know what else to say." Her voice is a mere whisper. She winces, pushing herself to a kneeling position and blinks up at me. Her blue eyes are wet with tears, and the sight of her on her knees looking at me like that is enough to shred my last sliver of control to pieces. Desire, powerful and intoxicating, snakes through every part of my body. She submits so willingly and easily that I could…

I close my eyes and focus on Xavier. *I have her. She is safe.*

Thank fuck! His relief punches me in the gut, but it is followed by a buzz of fear. *Is she okay?*

Yes. Now get back to work.

On it. But please tell Ophelia I'm going to spank her ass so hard when I'm done that she won't sit down comfortably for a month.

The hell I will tell her that. The words alone are enough to make my fangs and my cock ache. His relief at her being found is no longer enough to mask the desire coursing through him at the thought of what he is going to do when he gets his hands on her. So I block him out and hope that she will no longer be on her knees looking up at me with that expectant expression when I open my eyes.

Taking a deep breath, I force my eyelids to lift. Dammit. What kind of curse has been placed on me? She is still there, her vibrant eyes locked on my face like she is waiting for permission to move. Perhaps I should be the one to punish her for being so reckless. Right here in the darkness of these woods.

I could pull her across my lap and lift her tiny skirt. Tug down her panties and take all of my frustrations out on her creamy skin. Turn it blood-red. It would be no less than she deserves. And it would surely lead to one thing. My cock aches at the mere thought of it.

"I know sorry isn't enough, but I..." She shakes her head and tears leak from the corners of her eyes. "I can't explain it."

That is suspicious enough for reason to wrestle back control from my base desires. "What can you not explain?"

The soft curve of her throat works as she swallows, and her pulse flutters beneath her pale skin. "It was like I had to come here. Like I..." She screws her eyes closed. "I know it sounds ridiculous, but earlier tonight I had no intention of coming here. I mean, I wanted to, but I knew it would be dangerous, and as much as I wanted to know about the Hunt, I'm not an idiot. I don't want to die."

The hairs on the back of my neck stand on end. "So why did you come here?"

"I had this really overwhelming feeling that the boys were in trouble and they needed me here. I know that's stupid—what could I do to help? But..." Her eyes widen. "They are okay, aren't they?"

I nod.

She places her hand over her heart. "Oh, thank god."

My mind fills with questions. Did something or someone lure her here? Who is trying to hurt her? How do I protect her when I have no idea what she needs protection from? Why does—dammit. There is no time for this. Not now. "We need to leave."

She nods and plants her hands on the ground to push herself up. Her immediate compliance provides yet more fuel for the ache in my cock, but my attention is stolen by the stream of blood trickling from the cut in her knee. Unconsciously, I lick my lips and my fangs protract farther, painful in their throbbing need to take her.

"You're bleeding." The words unintentionally sound like an accusation, and a sweet blush creeps over her pale cheeks.

"Sorry." Did she just purr that word, or am I imagining things? My senses are clouded by the scent of her blood mingled with my sordid desire to throw her into the dirt and fuck her into her next life.

I tear off a strip of fabric from my shirt and hold it out to her, but she simply blinks at my outstretched hand, her pulse racing and her breathing growing harsher and heavier with each passing second.

I shove it at her, my sanity close to snapping. "To dress the wound. The last thing I need is for you to be bleeding all over these woods on the night of the Hunt."

Realization dawns on her face, and she reaches out to take the material from my hands. Her fingertips brush mine, and I don't miss the spike in her heart rate that mirrors my own. Nor can I ignore the scent of her growing arousal.

"Thank you, sir," she says in a sultry whisper.

Sweet demons of the netherworld. "Stop that, Ophelia."

"Stop what?" She wipes away the blood before tying the fabric around the wound on her knee.

I suck in a breath. Even the air is thick with her scent. The sound of branches breaking in the distance chases away an image of me simultaneously sinking my fangs and my cock inside her. "Can you run?"

She hobbles forward and winces. "Not fast."

With a muttered curse, I scoop her into my arms. Her breath hitches, and her body radiates heat. "You d-don't have to. I can run a little."

"The sooner we get you out of here, the better." I do not add that the pledges and hunters are the least of her worries and that she should be most afraid of me. That the resistance I have built over two thousand long years is currently hanging by the very finest of threads.

I take off running through the woods, and she is forced to wrap her arms around my neck. I ignore the way her skin on mine makes liquid heat sear through my veins. Ignore how the beast inside me roars and rattles the steel cage controlling him, ravenous with unparalleled hunger. I force myself not to focus on the delicate weight of her in my arms and how she will feel unbearably heavy the moment right before I set her down. For it will be in that singular moment in time when I will tell myself that I will never hold her again. I shove all of that aside and focus on finding the fastest route back to the house whilst avoiding coming into contact with any other beings along the way.

"I'm sorry I'm so heavy," she says.

"You weigh next to nothing."

"You're breathing kind of heavy."

That is because I am waging war against all my instincts. Every ounce of restraint I possess has been enlisted to prevent me from taking you right here. To sink inside you in all the ways there are and make you scream your proclamation to the entire world that you are mine. I keep all of that to myself, but I do give her another truth. "I am still working hard to suppress my anger at your stupidity, Ophelia."

She looks so sad that I almost regret telling her that. I blow out a heavy breath. "So you felt somehow compelled to come here?"

She blinks. "Yes. That's it. Like something was calling to me. Like I had no choice. Can that happen?"

Who could have done that? Of all the things that seem to happen in Ophelia's life that put her in harm's way...or my way—and right now that could be one and the same...

This is not the time for this. My sanity and control are too close to the breaking point. "It is more likely your connection to the boys brought you here." Hopefully my lie buys me time to figure out the answers to all her questions and mine.

"Oh, I see. Then they won't be too mad at me, right?"

We reach the house, and I stop running and set her down on shaky legs. I brush a lock of hair behind her ear, and she leans into my touch. She is looking up at me in that way again, full of trust and longing. Heat and desire and impotent rage burn inside me. I am not a man deserving of that look. Not even close. And that is why this thing that seems so inevitable between the two of us can never happen. "They are going to be incredibly mad, Ophelia."

"But will you tell them I was drawn to them by our bond?"

I shake my head. "You disobeyed them. You must suffer the consequences."

Her bottom lip juts out, and once again, all I can think of is delivering those consequences myself. I need to get far away from her—for both our sakes. "Go inside. And if you leave this house again tonight, I will deal with you myself. Understand?"

Sweet hell on earth, her pupils blow wide and she gasps in a raspy breath that lets me know she would enjoy that almost as much as I would.

"Ophelia. Now!"

She nods. "Yes, sir." She spins on her heel and runs into the house.

I blow out a long breath, hoping it might do something to ease the anguish and white-hot need that fester in every cell of my body.

It does not.

53

Xavier

Axl grins at me, and his fangs glisten in the moonlight. His shirt is soaked with blood, much like mine. The Hunt is over, but the spell blocking our bonds will remain in place until we leave the woods.

"Where is Malachi?"

"Here." He steps out from a thick crop of trees, shirtless and caked in mud and dried blood. His green eyes sparkle. Ordinarily I would share their post-Hunt high, but Ophelia is still on my mind. "How many of ours made it?"

"Just seven," Axl replies.

"Malone and Jensen made it, right?" Malachi asks.

Axl shakes his head. "Both dead."

Damn. They were by far our best candidates this year, and we were all sure they'd make it.

"You okay?" Malachi asks, likely sensing my somber mood. I jerk my head, signaling we should leave, and they follow me out of the woods and away from anyone who might overhear. "I hate to bring the party down, but I need to tell you both what happened during the Hunt." As I relay the events of the evening, their fear and helpless frustration and agitation perfectly mimic what I felt earlier. And by the time we get back to the house, they are every bit as eager to punish her as I am.

We get close enough to the house to see Alexandros sitting on the porch in the dark, alarmingly still.

"Is she inside? Is she okay?" Malachi asks, an edge of panic in his tone.

Axl must read something in Alexandros's expression that Kai and I can't see because he chuckles. "She's not gonna be for long."

The professor stares at us, a frown furrowing his brow. "I do not think she intended to disobey you."

I fold my arms over my chest. "What do you mean?"

He runs his fingertips through his beard. "I think something or someone compelled her to go to the woods tonight."

"With magic?" I ask. "Who is powerful enough to do that? Does it mean they can get inside her head and make her do stuff?"

"A number of witches can cast such a spell. But no, they cannot get inside her head. I would ordinarily be able to detect such a spell within these grounds, but I was not able to sense it with all the magic in the air this night."

"So we could all be compelled? In theory?" That would fucking suck.

He shakes his head. "Vampires and demons cannot be compelled, at least not by witches. And the magic draws on the subject's individual fears and desires. Ophelia was led to believe you were all in danger."

Malachi sighs and drops his head.

"The tiny pink-haired cupcake was coming to save us?" I shake my head in disbelief. Ophelia is going to be the death of my sanity. She's the most fearless person I've ever met in my long life, and that's what led me to fall in love with her to begin with, but it also makes me want to tie her to my bed and keep her safe. I'd happily tie her to my bed for other reasons too…

"Fuck!" Axl scrubs a hand over his face. "What was she thinking?"

"I think you all know that she was not thinking, only acting in a foolish desire to save you three," Alexandros says, his voice stuffier than usual, before standing and briskly straightening his clothes. "So do not force yourselves to endure unnecessary pain by being overly harsh on her. She has been through enough already this night."

My hands ball into fists. "Who had her? Did they hurt her?"

"Two of our own pledges. I believe they intended to use her as bait. But she was unharmed."

"You killed them?" I ask.

He scowls. "Of course."

"I bet it was Malone and Jensen," Malachi says.

Using a girl half their size as bait sure sounds like their deal. They would have been ideal candidates for turning. Still, the desire to tear them both limb from limb for laying a finger on my girl burns hot inside me. Lucky for them the professor beat me to it.

Alexandros makes his way down the porch steps and heads out across the lawn.

Where are you going? I ask.

Away from here is his only reply.

We stare after him until he disappears into the darkness.

...

Ophelia is sitting up in Malachi's bed when we find her, the covers pulled up to her chin.

"I'm sorry. I thought you were all in trouble," she blurts out as soon as we walk into the room.

Her eyes are red, and there are tear tracks streaked down her cheeks. Malachi crawls onto the bed and slowly pulls the comforter off her, revealing her body inch by delicious inch. She's wearing panties and a tank top, and dammit, my cock is already hard. Whatever punishment I had in mind is pushed out of my head by thoughts of covering her sexy little body in bites and kisses so that I can remind myself that she's mine.

He stops when he gets past her thighs and reveals a blood-stained strip of white fabric tied around her right knee. He presses a tender kiss on it, and she sucks in a deep breath that makes her juicy tits jiggle. I pull off my shirt.

"What happened, sweet girl?" he asks.

"I fell on a rock," she says, a distinct tremor in her voice.

Axl growls. "Did anyone hurt you, princess?"

She shakes her head. "The professor found me before they could."

I take off my jeans. "You know, Cupcake, we should put you on a leash after what happened tonight."

Her eyes go wide.

"It's the least we should do," Axl agrees, pulling off his clothes now too.

Malachi peels off her tank top, and I crawl onto the bed, spreading her legs wide and running my nose up the inside of her thigh. I snap my teeth, feral to taste her.

"I won't do it again," she whimpers.

Axl joins us now too, his hand snaking up our girl's thigh. "I was gonna take a shower, but I think we need to get Ophelia a little dirty first."

Malachi nuzzles her neck. "Yeah, who needs a party when we can have so much more fun here?"

"There's a party?"

Axl palms her pussy through her panties. "For all the pledges who made it."

I flick my tongue over her skin and brush my nose over Axl's hand. Ophelia's head tips back. "Can we go?" she asks.

"Nuh-uh. Naughty girls don't get to go to parties, princess."

I press my lips against her sweet skin and murmur my agreement. When Axl pulls her panties aside, the scent of her pussy has me growling with need. I watch him sink a finger inside her, stretching her tight wet heat around him.

"Does being a naughty cupcake make our girl wet?" I ask him.

He slides his finger out of her, and it's thick with her arousal. "What do you think, bro?" I suck his digit into my mouth and groan as her taste floods my senses.

Malachi sucks on one of her stiff nipples, and Ophelia looks down at the three of us, our hands and mouths all over her hot body. When I sink my fangs into the supple skin of her thigh, her eyes roll back in her head.

Axl tears her panties in half and laughs darkly when she whimpers a feeble protest. "Oh, princess, you're going to be fucked so hard you won't be capable of walking anywhere for the next week."

And for the next few blissful hours, we take turns eating and fucking our girl until she's begging us to let her come. When we finally take pity on her, she comes so hard I swear the earth shakes.

. . .

Alexandros stares at me over the rim of his coffee mug while I chug my protein shake. I place the glass on the counter when I'm done and smack my lips together.

A muscle in his jaw tics. "Now that the pledges are turned and under their sire's protection, what are your plans for the day?"

Not let Ophelia out of my sight. Fuck her as many times as possible. Give her a few more lessons in the art of sucking cock.

Not that she's not already good at it, but practice makes perfect, right? I think those things but don't dare say them aloud, and fortunately he's got better things to do with his mind than listen to what's in mine. Instead, I shrug.

"Maybe you should all start taking classes again," he suggests.

Was he listening to me after all? I frown. "Classes?"

He nods. "College classes. With Ophelia."

Nobody on campus asks questions about why the society commanders don't attend class. It's kind of an unwritten rule, and I can't recall the last time I actually went to one. Obviously I am not here for an education. But classes with my girl could be a ton of fun. "I'm down for that, but any particular reason why?"

"What happened at the Hunt was no accident. While Ophelia is curious, she is not inherently stupid. Something or someone compelled her to go there. Although I am confident nobody knows what she is, she is also growing closer to the witches, and that is a concern in and of itself. Her new friend Cadence comes from a powerful family, and now all of the other witches are paying more attention to her, probably picking up on her energy. Not to mention the vampires who will start sniffing around her soon enough."

I growl at the thought of anyone *sniffing* anywhere near her. She's mine.

He places a hand on the back of my neck, and I lean into his touch like a pet desperate to be stroked by his master. "Do you feel her powers growing?"

"Yes."

He stares into my eyes. "You will need to monitor her more closely. All of you. I fear we can only hide what she is for so long, but the longer we can do that, the safer it will be for all of us."

Anxiety balls in my throat like a wadded-up tissue. It's not a feeling I'm overly familiar with, and I don't fucking like it. "You truly think people would hurt her if they found out what she is?"

"I know that they would, Xavier."

His words cut through me like a knife. For a moment, his eyes soften and he looks at me the way I've wanted him to from the moment he turned me. Like he fucking cares. "I warned you not to bind yourself to her."

"I know." I clear my throat. "But I would still do it again a million times over."

He drops his hand from my neck and shakes his head. "Then you are a fool."

54

OPHELIA

"Come sit up here, Pyro." Axl grabs my hand and leads me to the back of the lecture hall. I don't miss the admiring glances he attracts from the students we pass.

I glance at my usual seat near the fire escape. "But I always sit near the front." Two rows from the front to be exact. Something about not being at the back, front, or in the middle is oddly comforting for me.

Malachi takes my other hand. "It's way more fun at the back, baby."

"Yeah, so much fun." Xavier laughs darkly

"Is she with all of them? Ugh," a girl mutters as we pass. A round of giggles follows. My cheeks flush with heat, and I pull on Axl's and Malachi's hands, trying to hurry to the back row, but Axl stops in his tracks. He turns to face the two giggling girls and flashes them his biggest panty-melting smile. Despite what they just said about me, they flutter their eyelashes at him.

Squeezing my hand tighter, he lifts it to his lips and presses a possessive kiss on my knuckles. "Yeah, she's with all of us, and we all know how badly you'd like that for yourselves, ladies."

Xavier wrinkles his nose. "Yeah. Can smell your pussies dripping at the thought of sucking all our cocks from here."

They both gasp, their pretty faces turning beet red. *Oh dear god! Please don't make a scene.*

Too late. Xavier walks along the row of seats and grabs hold of the girl who made the snarky comment by her jaw. He squeezes so hard that her eyes bug out. "If you ever even look at my girl wrong again, I will peel off your skin and make your friend here wear it as a coat. You catch my drift?"

She nods, all the blood draining out of her face as she blinks up at him.

He gives a satisfied grin and releases her with a push so her head snaps back. People are staring and some are muttering, but nobody dares challenge my boys. Even those who don't know what or who they're looking at are all too aware of the power they wield in this school. We make our way to the back row, which is currently occupied by some of the football players and their girlfriends.

"Leave!" Axl snaps his teeth, and they scramble out of the seats and move to another row.

"That was kind of rude," I whisper. "And there was room for all of us."

Xavier flashes me a wicked grin. "No, Cupcake. We're gonna need this row all to ourselves." The deviant look in his eyes has warmth pooling in my core, but I'm sure they're not going to try anything here. We're in class. And this is Professor Drakos's class!

As though I conjured him by thinking his name, Professor Drakos walks in. "Take your seats," he orders, before shrugging off his suit jacket and placing it on the chair beside the podium. He stretches his neck and flexes his muscles, and a round of dreamy sighs ripples through the lecture hall. Not that I blame any of them. He is absurdly hot, in a brooding, angry kind of way. If you like that kind of thing...which I definitely do. There's a reason Heathcliff was my first literary love.

"Sit, baby." Axl pulls me onto his lap while Xavier and Malachi take the seats on either side of him.

The professor is staring at us—scratch that, he's glaring, and my already warm cheeks are now on fire. "Can I have my own seat, please?" I ask quietly.

Axl sinks his teeth into my shoulder through my shirt. "No. Now stop wriggling, or I'll take out my cock and make you ride me."

I gasp louder than I intended, causing the people in the row in front of us to turn around. "You would not," I angry whisper.

Axl tucks my hair behind my ear. "Oh, you know that I would, Ophelia."

"Your attention. Now," the professor barks, clearly unamused at the distraction we're causing in his class. The students in front of us spin back around to face him while Axl bands his arms around me and Xavier lets out a quiet chuckle. Malachi offers me a wink before passing me my notebook and pen out of my backpack.

"Thank you," I murmur.

He rests his hand on my thigh and smirks.

The professor starts class, and I pay close attention to his lecture on Perseus and Medusa. I love history, especially mythology, and there's something about his passion for the subject that makes his features come alive. And makes heat coil deep in my belly.

I shift on Axl's lap, and he groans.

Xavier snorts like he's suppressing his laughter, and suddenly they're all having a conversation in my head.

Take off her panties, Xavier commands.

Yes, Malachi agrees.

No! I insist, and the professor shoots me a warning glare. I press my hand over my mouth. *Did I just say that out loud?*

No, baby. But he can hear us communicating with each other, Malachi explains.

Then can you please stop talking to each other about taking my panties off in his class!

Axl shifts me slightly, and I suppress a yelp. Then his hands are beneath my skirt and he's sliding my panties down my legs with his nimble fingers.

Stop! We can't do this in front of all these people.

Xavier snickers, but it's Axl's voice in my head. *I'm pretty sure we're behind them. And I only took off your panties, Pyro. Nothing is happening.*

Yet, Xavier adds.

Fuck me, you smell so good, baby. Malachi slides his hand up the inside of my thigh. I try to focus on making notes, but his fingers graze my bare pussy. My hand wobbles, making my pen skid across my paper. He leisurely rubs the pad of his thumb over my clit, then moves lower, circling my entrance.

I hiss out a breath. *Don't!*

Do, Xavier urges.

You mean don't do this? Malachi slides his finger inside me, and my back practically bows in half. *But you seem to enjoy it so much.*

"Stop!" I slap a hand over my mouth, but one of the girls in front of us turns around in her seat.

"Eyes up front, Miss Watson," the professor snaps.

She narrows her eyes on my face for a moment before turning back to face him. Meanwhile, Malachi starts slowly finger-fucking me. My notepad falls off my lap, and Xavier catches it before it hits the ground and places it on the seat beside him.

I need to take notes.

We've taken this class hundreds of times, princess. We have all the notes you need. Or you could always have a one-on-one with Alexandros. I bet he'd say yes if you asked him nicely.

A one-on-one with Professor Drakos sounds all kinds of hot, and I'm not sure if it's the thought of that or Malachi's skilled finger inching in and out of me that makes me whimper. But whatever it is, it causes Axl to growl like a dog. He shifts me again, angling my body so that I'm facing forward on his lap. The desk shields me from view as he spreads my legs wider, and I have to bite on my lip to stop myself from moaning out loud. He flicks up my miniskirt, revealing my bare pussy, and strums my clit while Malachi goes on fucking me.

You want a second one in there, baby? Malachi taunts, pulling his finger out.

Xavier answers for me. *Yeah she does.* His hand joins Malachi's, and they both slide a thick finger inside me. I drop my head back onto Axl's shoulder.

Good little Pyro, letting us finger-fuck you in class.

She's such a naughty little slut for us. Aren't you, Cupcake?

That feels so incredible, I moan inside my head. My orgasm builds quickly, swirling through my core and snaking up my thighs. But they know my body too well. Just as I'm about to fall over the edge, they switch things up so Malachi is rubbing my clit while Axl and Xavier move their fingers in unison. I try to clamp my thighs together to stop their teasing, but that only makes Axl spread my thighs even wider than before. Both Malachi and Xavier grip my thighs with their free hands and hold me open while Axl keeps one arm banded tightly around my waist.

I swallow a whimper. *Please let me come.*

But you look so pretty when you're on the edge, Cupcake. Squeezing my fingers with your tight little cunt.

Oh god!

And who does this tight little pussy belong to, princess? Axl drives in harder. *Tell us and we might let you come.*

You. All of you!

Xavier groans. *You're squeezing us so tight, Ophelia.*

Malachi chuckles. *Well, now I just feel left out, boys.*

My eyes shutter closed when Malachi's finger joins the other two. He goes on rubbing at the sensitive bundle of nerves with his thumb, that place where it feels like every nerve in my body ends.

I whimper, and Axl clamps a hand over my mouth, his palm flat against my lips. It's too much. They stretch me wide, and it burns and feels like heaven at the same time. I rock my hips, chasing the high they refuse to deliver. Axl presses his lips against my ear and whispers, "I really wish I could bite you right now, princess. That would tip you over that edge."

I mumble my agreement against his hand, my tongue darting out to taste his flesh. He growls, and I melt against him, my body no longer my own. I'm about to have the most intense orgasm of my entire life in a room full of people.

Xavier's animalistic grunts fill my head once more. *We're gonna have to let her come. She's so fucking wet. Someone's gonna hear us soon.*

Malachi groans. *But it's such a sweet fucking sound.*

And now I'm hyperaware of the noise of my wetness slicking their fingers. Shame floods me, battling for dominance against mind-numbing pleasure.

Axl's lips are still at my ear. "It's okay. We'll bite them all and make them forget if we have to."

"Hmmf!" I moan into his hand.

But we're gonna let you come now anyway, princess. You've been such a good girl for us. But I hope you know this is gonna keep happening if you insist on wearing these tiny little skirts to walk around campus in. Okay?

I nod, drawing in deep breaths through my nose. My body feels like it's about to burst into flames, and I can do nothing to stop it. Something unidentifiable lights up my veins. It's more than euphoria. I feel more alive than ever before.

Axl presses a tender kiss beneath my ear, and the three of them work in unison to drag out the longest and most explosive orgasm of my life. It feels like the very walls shake around us, but I hold it all in, swallowing down the guttural cries that try to tear themselves from my throat, letting them implode inside me instead.

My entire being shakes. I can barely see with my head spinning so fast. The only sound I hear is the blood rushing in my ears. I'm vaguely aware of their hands soothing me, rubbing out every last drop and allowing my climax to roll on in unending waves of pure bliss.

I bask in their tenderness and our deep connection that gives me a sense of belonging unlike anything I've experienced. Has anyone in the history of the world been this absurdly happy? I feel safe and protected in their arms, like nothing and nobody can get to me as long as I have them.

But then I open my eyes, and the first thing I see are the professor's eyes burning into mine with the heat of a thousand suns.

He knows what we just did, and he is pissed.

How does he know? I whisper, despite only talking in my head. *Is it because he can read your thoughts?*

Xavier snickers while Axl closes my thighs and wraps his both arms around me. *It seems like he can hear you in our heads now too, princess.*

Oh. My. God. The professor just heard me come?

He's talking to the class, explaining what to read for our next lesson, but his eyes remain locked on mine, his brow furrowed in a deep scowl. In my peripheral vision, I see his retractable pointing stick lying in two pieces on the ground.

Why is the pointy stick broken?

It snapped in half in his hand the moment you came, baby, Malachi tells me.

So he did hear me? He heard everything?

Axl sighs, his breath ruffling my hair and making me shiver. "He said to tell you yes."

Embarrassment curdles in my stomach. Malachi gives my hand a comforting squeeze, but I can't tear my eyes away from the murderous expression on Professor Drakos's face.

55

ALEXANDROS

She keeps her head bent low as she walks down the steps, her skin flushed pinker than her hair. Axl, Xavier, and Malachi walk behind her, protective and possessive. Her moans still ring in my ears, and I am this close to throwing her onto the floor and fucking her so hard that she screams my name all over this damn campus. My knuckles turn white with the strength of my grip on the podium. I could have easily chosen to block them all from my mind, but once I heard her soft moans, I was powerless to cut the connection.

I snarl. "What the hell do you three think you were doing up there?"

"I-I'm sorry, Professor," she says, obviously missing the fact that I place the blame squarely on the shoulders of my delinquent spawn.

I look past her at the grinning faces of Axl and Xavier. At least Malachi has the sense to appear contrite. "Do you think I enjoy teaching a class with a painful erection?"

Ophelia gasps, her pretty pink lips parted in a perfect O.

I clear my throat, aware that I have revealed far too much. "Listening to you coming for twenty solid minutes would be enough to make a eunuch hard, Ophelia."

She presses her lips together, and her shoulders bounce like she is stifling a laugh.

"We couldn't help it." Xavier shrugs. "It's the tiny skirt."

She is wearing her usual uniform—miniskirt and black lace-up biker boots—only today she has a white button-up shirt over her tank top. It is tied in a knot above her navel, the buttons straining against the weight of her perky breasts. She is way too distracting, and while I cannot blame them for being unable to keep their hands off her, it does not change the fact that their behavior was reckless. "Did you not feel the goddamn walls shake?"

"The ground always moves for me when Ophelia comes." Axl's lips twitch in a cocky grin.

"Just another earthquake," Malachi adds.

Are they really that clueless? The four of them stare at me blankly. I guess they are.

"Take a seat. All of you." I nod toward the seats at the front of the class.

"I, uh, have to get to English," Ophelia says, wincing.

"Yeah, and we have to—"

"Sit. Now!" I cut off whatever Axl was about to say, and the four of them do as they are told and take a seat.

I step out from behind the podium, my stiff cock finally softening. Not that I care about hiding it from any of them. Ophelia's eyes are immediately drawn to my groin area, and the flush on her cheeks deepens further.

"Eyes up here, Ophelia."

Her dark eyelashes flutter against her cheeks as she whispers an apology.

I ignore the effect that has on my raging libido and allow my eyes to dart between the four of them. "Do you not think it odd that we have been having so many tremors these past few weeks? How they almost always coincide with you walking hormone-buckets having sex?"

Malachi blinks. "Are you... You think Ophelia is causing them?"

"I am not," she says, her eyes wide with shock.

"Not purposely," I admit. "But yes, I suspect she is. And when you fuckwits behave like you just did out in the open, sooner or later somebody is going to connect those dots."

Ophelia's eyebrows pinch together. "I don't... What are you talking about? How the hell can I cause earthquakes?"

Malachi's Adam's apple bobs while Axl and Xavier exchange a look.

She scrunches up her nose, and it makes her pretty face look... I blow out a breath. My walls are never so close to breaking as when I am around her. I need to do better.

"Go. Leave her with me," I tell the boys, jerking my head toward the door.

She blinks in confusion. "Wait. Why?"

"Bye, Cupcake." Xavier gives her a gentle kiss on the head, and the others follow suit before leaving us alone.

I run my tongue over my teeth before sucking in a calming breath. It does not make me feel any less uneasy. Nor does it stop the torrent of guilt and bone-weary anguish from threatening to swallow me whole. She is still staring at me, her breath held in anticipation. Does she have any idea that I am about to irrevocably change the course of both our futures? It would be safer to speak through a bond, but I refuse to share one with her. That would put her at even greater risk. And the danger she already finds herself in all too often is why she needs to know who she is. It has become more perilous to leave her in the dark. But we cannot have that conversation here. We need a place we cannot be overheard by curious ears or magic.

"Come with me." Her scurrying footsteps follow me out the classroom door.

"Where are we going?"

"You will see."

She jogs to keep up with me as I leave the history building and stride across the quad. I hold open the door to Zeus Hall, then lead her down to the basement carved into the bedrock of the mountain. This part of the building is rarely used, especially at this time of the day. Still, I move swiftly. The fewer people who see us, the better. Whilst it is a rare occurrence, it is not the first time I have taken a student to the faculty library, and I already have an explanation about her keen interest in ancient Greek mythology ready if anyone should question me.

I come to a stop outside the twelve-foot solid bronze doors that were forged long before this college stood here.

Ophelia cranes her neck and studies the ornate images carved into the metal. "Wow! What is this place?"

I push open one of the doors, and cool air rushes out in a current. Her blue eyes widen with delight as the sight of the cavernous library unfolds before us. "Holy shit!" she breathes, then quickly covers her mouth and shoots me a worried glance, like I might scold her for cursing.

I usher her inside, and the door creaks to a close behind us, pulled back in place by its own weight.

"Is this like a secret library or something?" she whispers, her head swiveling left and right as she tries to take it all in.

I head for the far corner of the library and gesture for her to follow. "Not secret. Although it is the faculty library. Few students are aware of its existence."

"Is it just for—" She presses her lips together, her eyes darting around nervously. "You know, *special* people?"

I suppress my annoyance. "If by special, you mean nonhuman, then yes. All of our faculty and staff are nonhuman, Ophelia."

This time her gasp is followed by a sharp laugh. "No freaking way! Like...all of them?"

Without answering, I indicate for her to sit in one of the armchairs in the most secluded corner of the library—the theology section. The faculty and staff of Montridge University have little interest in and no use for human religion.

She perches on the edge of the leather cushion and tugs at the hem of her tiny plaid skirt. It fails to cover enough of her skin, and the scent of her arousal is a stark reminder of the pleasures lurking only a few feet away. And now the memory of her being brought to orgasm in my class a short time ago is sharper than a needle point. The way she moaned their names, how my boys were practically driven feral with the need to taste her... Sweet demons of the netherworld. She made my cock harder than stone.

"Can I take a look at some of these books? Could I—"

"Ophelia!"

She swallows, her huge blue eyes staring up at me, full of trust and innocence. Two attributes that are likely to get her killed one day.

"You are so much more than a witch, Ophelia." I drop into the chair directly opposite her, my eyes raking over her curves before they settle on her face once more. How can someone with so much power be so naive? It is almost like fate played a cruel trick on her.

She blinks, and I am blinded by a vision of her on her knees for me. My limbs burn with the force of holding myself back from taking her right here.

I clear my throat and glance around the room once more, ensuring there is nobody within earshot. "You know how it rains when you are sad? And how there are literal earthquakes when you come?"

Her cheeks turn bright pink, but she nods.

"That is because you are an elementai, Ophelia."

She leans forward in her chair. "A what?"

I can barely believe these words are about to leave my mouth. My knowledge of the elementai is greater than most. And it is entirely useless in the modern world. At least it was. "An elementai. They are infinitely more powerful than witches. A witch needs a spell to cast. They draw on the elements for magic. A witch who can channel water magic cannot do so if there is no water. But an elementai can create magic from nothing. They are some of the most powerful beings ever to have lived."

"That's...that's impossible." She shakes her head. "I don't have any magic. You know I don't."

I pinch the spot between my brows and take a deep breath. "The fire at your school. You never wondered how you created a fire from nothing?"

She shakes her head again, more vigorously this time. Tears stream down her cheeks. "I didn't start that fire."

"You did, Ophelia."

A sob catches in her throat, and her eyes implore me to tell her that I am making it all up. "You were not at fault. An elementai's power is finely tuned to their emotions. You had no idea you even had such abilities."

She balls her tiny hands into fists. "I don't have abilities," she insists.

I lean forward, my gaze fixed on hers. Staring into her eyes is akin to staring into a black hole. If I allow myself to be sucked in there with her, there will be no escaping the hold she will have over me. I suck in a breath and look away, breaking the connection before I speak again. "You do. That is why it rains when you are sad. Why the earth shakes when you are happy. And that is why your blood affected Axl the way it did. The destinies of both vampire and elementai are deeply intertwined." As for why... That is a conversation for another day.

She wipes the tears from her cheeks with the sleeve of her shirt. "I am not one of those creatures. I am weak and—"

That she even thinks that is an abomination. I grind my teeth and force myself not to roar my frustration. My calm, measured tone is a testament to the two millennia I spent learning such control. "No. You are not weak. Even without your powers." I stand and cup her chin, tilting her head so she is looking up into my face. Her vivid blue eyes, so innocent and trusting, pull at something deep inside me that I thought I had long since buried. "You are fearless in the face of certain danger. You are unwaveringly kind, in spite of how poorly you have been treated by the world. You, my little one, rank amongst the strongest creatures I have ever known."

Another fat tear rolls down her cheek. "I don't feel strong, sir."

Sweet demons of hell. That term on her lips makes my cock ache.

"If I have all these powers, why can't I use them?"

How do I tell her everything she is without baring my soul? I cannot answer her questions because I lack the answers she needs. The answers that I need. But the plea in her eyes pulls at something long forgotten, like a song that has gone centuries unheard but is so deeply embedded in the psyche that even a single note will bring the full composition rushing back. "I think somebody bound them when you were a child. Before you were old enough to remember."

"B-bound them? Like made me not be able to use them? But why?"

I drop my hand away from her face, but she continues staring up at me. "To protect you, perhaps. I do not know. It is an ancient practice that is rarely used, partly because it requires powerful magic that is uncommon in today's times."

Her expression lights with hope, no doubt elicited from finally learning a little about who she truly is. I try not to let myself wonder if it has anything to do with me. "Was it another elementai?" she asks.

"No." I shake my head. "That is impossible."

Her eyelashes flutter against her pink cheeks. "Why?"

I twist my neck from side to side and take a second to gather my thoughts. I cannot imagine how it would feel to be the only one of your kind. For a girl who has been alone her entire life, it is the cruelest of fates. Although perhaps that makes her better equipped to handle it than most. "As far as I am aware, you are the only elementai in existence."

Her mouth drops open, her beautiful pink lips glistening with her tears. I tip my face up to the ceiling and groan. This must be a test. A punishment for all the evil I have done in my life.

"The only one?" she whispers, drawing my gaze back to hers. "What happened to the others?"

Pain and regret crash over me, threatening to swallow me whole. Or drag me straight to the netherworld, where I belong. "They were all wiped out a long time ago."

"How? By who? Then how am I one of them? What—"

"Ophelia!" Her name leaves my mouth on a roar, but it is a plea. A plea for her to stop tearing at the tattered pieces of my soul.

"But I just want to..." Her bottom lip trembles.

I scrub a hand through my hair. "No more questions."

She jumps up, puffing her chest out and balling her hands into fists at her sides. "No!" she shouts. "You can't just drop that on me and then tell me no more questions. That's not fair."

My hand is around her throat before I can weigh the consequences. "Do not dare speak to me about fairness." Her throat works beneath my palm, her eyes wide and unblinking. "You need to learn to control your emotions, Ophelia. If you do not, there will be no hiding what or who you are when you tap into your power."

"Okay," she croaks, and the way she submits to me has me clinging to my sanity with failing restraint. I need to get away from her. Need to stop touching her. With a surge of herculean effort, I drop my hand to my side.

"You will tell nobody of what I have told you today. You cannot begin to understand the ramifications if anyone were to discover what you are."

She presses her lips together, and I can practically see a hundred more questions tumbling over each other inside her head. Thankfully, she only asks one for now. "Can I not even talk to the boys?"

"They are already a part of you, Ophelia. They know what you are. They are the only people you can ever trust not to hurt you. Do you understand me?"

"And you too, right?" she whispers, a desperate entreaty in her eyes.

I shake my head. "Not me."

Her bottom lip trembles, and I swallow down the urge to retract that statement.

I would die for her as surely as I would take my next breath, but she has no need for such knowledge.

56

OPHELIA

"I brought supplies." Cadence shakes a bag of Tate's chocolate chip cookies.

I pull two glass bottles of soda from my backpack and hold them in the air. "Me too."

Giggling, she drops into the chair beside me. "Girl, we make such a great team."

A smile lights up my face. Visiting the library has always been one of my favorite ways to pass an afternoon, but with Cadence, it's become a hundred times more fun. And after everything the professor told me yesterday, I could do with a distraction. There is no way on earth that I'm one of those elementai beings he spoke of. No way at all.

We're done with the pledges for today, baby. You need any company? Malachi's voice in my head fills my stomach with a warm flutter.

I've grown used to their presence in my mind—surprisingly fond of it too. They are never far from me, whether in thought or in physical form. *I'm okay. Cadence is here, and we're going to hit the books...and the cookies. Hard.*

He laughs. *Yeah, cookies are a good idea, you need to keep your energy levels up, baby.*

That annoying flush creeps over my cheeks. I dip my head so Cadence won't see and wonder why the hell I'm blushing simply sitting here in the library.

Stop it! I admonish.

He laughs again. *I'll come pick you up when you're ready to leave.*

I roll my eyes. *I can walk home alone. I'm super powerful, apparently.*

I don't doubt it for a second. You already have me and my brothers on our knees for you. But I'm still walking you home. Now, be good, and I'll see you later.

"Hey, did you hear that?" Cadence interrupts my conversation with Malachi. Did I say any of that aloud? Or even worse, can she read minds? She is a witch, and I still don't know what kind of powers witches have.

But she frowns and glances over her shoulder.

"No. What was it?"

"Like someone called out." She shakes her head and turns back to me. "I swear this place is haunted."

"You think ghosts really exist?" In all my conversations with the guys, I never thought to ask about the existence of ghosts.

"I think there are plenty of things in this world that can't be seen with our own eyes." She shrugs. "Doesn't mean they aren't real."

I nod my agreement. "I get exactly what you mean. Like sometimes you can feel something, even though nothing's there." I stop talking, afraid I'll reveal something I shouldn't. But long before I learned what I am—according to Professor Drakos, anyway—I always felt like something lurked nearby, mysterious and unseen.

Cadence leans closer and drops her voice to a whisper. "Have you ever made anything weird happen and couldn't explain why?"

My throat feels like it closes over. "Have you?" I croak.

She sucks in a breath. "Kind of. But then I'm…" She glances around us. "Can I trust you, Ophelia? Because my gut tells me I can, but I need to know that you won't tell just anyone about this."

I understand her dilemma because I don't know how to tell her that I share my headspace with three hot vampires without revealing too much about myself.

"Some people might freak out, is all," she adds.

I take a deep breath and go for it. "You mean nonmagical people?"

She smiles. "So you know about magical beings? I know you hang out with the Ruby commanders, but I wasn't totally sure if you knew…"

I nod. "I know about witches and vampires and werewolves and the like."

She grins. "Demons and warlocks too."

And elementai, I want to add but don't. "I won't tell anyone who might freak out. I promise."

"I'm a witch," she whispers.

"I knew it!" I mentally fist-pump the air.

"You did? How's that?"

I blink in confusion, but there's no hostility in her tone, simply curiosity. "I sensed something in you, I guess."

She arches an eyebrow. "Because maybe you're a witch too?"

"I don't have any powers, though. Why would you think that?"

She tosses her auburn hair over her shoulder. "Like you, I sense something. Some witch's powers are latent."

"Latent?"

"Uh-huh. Buried in generations of nonmagical beings. They may not manifest in each generation, but you, Ophelia Hart…" She sucks in air between her teeth. "I can feel your power buzzing just beneath the surface."

I force a laugh. "I wish I could feel it."

Cocking her head to the side, she scrutinizes me. "You will. We just need to figure out how to tap into it, is all."

"Maybe," I mumble.

She rests her hand on my arm. "Definitely."

"I guess it's hard to wrap my head around it when I know so little about the whole magic thing. Until recently, I didn't know anything like witches even existed, and then I came to Montridge and..." I blow out a breath.

She swivels my chair so I'm facing her. "Well, witches I can tell you about. What do you want to know?"

"I have no clue." I shrug. "It's hard to know what you don't know."

She arches an eyebrow. "How about I give you the CliffsNotes version?"

I nod eagerly, and over the next thirty minutes, Cadence gives me a brief history of witches. How some of the most powerful can channel magic to live for centuries; how they can only be born to other witches, but the gene can skip generations; and how the most powerful families' roots can be traced back several millennia.

"Wow!" I shake my head. "I can't believe I'm nineteen and had no idea that there was a whole other world literally existing alongside us. Magic is real, yet half the world's population doesn't have a clue."

"More like nine-tenths," Cadence says with a sad smile. "There are far fewer of us now than there were centuries ago. The human population has grown exponentially, but ours declines every generation. Not only witches but..." She snaps her mouth closed and grabs a cookie before biting off a huge chunk, like she's trying to stop herself from saying something she shouldn't. She points at her mouth. "These are sooo good."

"I know that vampires and witches and wolves have societies here."

Her hazel eyes sparkle. "You have been studying, Ophelia. So, you have to know there is something different about you too, don't you?"

I shake my head. "I don't know about that. I'm just fascinated by the whole idea, you know? Always have been, even before I learned any of it was true. While the other girls in my foster homes fantasized about being rescued from the dragon by a handsome prince, I dreamed of taming the dragon and becoming powerful enough to rescue myself."

Cadence leans forward and lowers her voice to a conspiratorial whisper. "Legend has it that dragons existed once too."

"No!" Surely that can't be true. I'm going to have to deal with the professor's annoyed grumbling about how I ask too many questions if I want to get the inside track on dragons, but it'll be worth it. "How fricking awesome is that."

"It would be if they were still around. But, assuming they did exist, they died out over a thousand years ago."

"Like the elementai died out?" The words come out of my mouth before I can stop them.

Cadence's eyes widen, and her mouth opens like she's about to speak when she's cut off by another voice that comes from directly behind us. "Hey, do either of you have a highlighter I could borrow? Mine died right in the middle of Hamlet."

I spin around to see we're no longer alone in our little corner of the library.

Cadence turns too, and upon seeing our new companion, a smile spreads across her face. "Oh, hey, Sienna."

Sienna tosses her long black braids over her shoulder and props her hand on her hip. "Hey girl. I didn't realize that was you." Her lips curve in a wide smile, and her dark eyes flash with flecks of amber. I stare into them for a few seconds, mesmerized by her. "How you been?" she adds.

She's one of the most beautiful people I've ever seen. Strong and athletic but with curves. Her flawless dark skin shimmers in the overhead lights, so tantalizing that I want to reach out and touch her. It's like she's covered in some kind of magical body glitter. I wonder where she got it, but that doesn't seem like an appropriate question to ask someone I just met.

"Same old. You know," Cadence replies with a self-deprecating laugh that serves to pull me out of my stupor.

Sienna's eyes flicker to me, and she smiles expectantly. However, I appear to have been rendered mute.

Thankfully, Cadence comes to my rescue. "This is my friend Ophelia. Ophelia, Sienna."

"Hi." Sienna offers me a small wave, then she runs her tongue over her bottom lip, and I'm almost certain that I hear a faint growl.

"Hi," I croak. "You're beautiful." Wow. I am such a moron.

Sienna's eyes sparkle with amusement. "Thank you. You're pretty cute yourself."

Why are you feeling all warm and fuzzy, Cupcake? Xavier asks.

I press my lips together and try to tune him out while Sienna rummages in her backpack for a highlighter.

Ophelia! Do I have to come over there and bite somebody? Xavier's warning growl has the hairs on the back of my neck standing on end.

No! I'm just talking to someone. Her name is Sienna. It's just that she's so…captivating.

That will be Sienna Brackenwolf, Malachi says. *Commander of the Amalthea Society.*

So she's a wolf. That makes sense.

Why? Axl joins the conversation now.

I think she growled at me.

All of their voices fill my head at once. *I will tear out her heart. You're ours, sweet girl. I'm coming over there.*

Relax! I admonish them. *It's nothing like that, you possessive Neanderthals. She's just... I don't know. I feel like I want to be her best friend.*

Never trust a wolf, baby, Malachi growls.

I resist the urge to roll my eyes. *Noted. Now please get out of my head or I'm going to start looking like a girl who has voices in her head.*

Xavier's laugh booms through my mind. *You are a girl who has voices in her head.* Then they all fall silent.

"So?" Sienna's voice cuts through the internal noise as she stares at me with curiosity.

I press my lips together and nod with no idea as to what she's asking me. A musical laugh falls from her lips before she speaks again. "A highlighter?"

"Oh, yeah. Of course." I spin around and blow out a breath before rifling through my pencil case and pulling out a bright yellow highlighter and handing it over.

"Ophelia, you are a lifesaver, girl. I'll hand it back as soon as I'm done."

I dismiss her suggestion with a wave of my hand. "You can keep it. I have plenty."

She tilts her head, her dark eyes raking over me. And I'm sure I hear that growl again, but Cadence doesn't seem to notice. "Thanks. Hopefully I'll be able to return the favor sometime." She winks at me, and I feel my cheeks heat with embarrassment. Or maybe it's happiness. At this point, I don't know what I'm feeling from one second to the next.

Sienna says goodbye to both of us and heads back through the shelves of books to the other side of the library.

Cadence nudges me in the arm. "Is that the first time you've met a werewolf?"

I shrug. "I dunno. I think so. Who knows at this school?"

That makes her laugh, and she bumps her shoulder against

mine. "She was right...you are cute." I shake my head dismissively. Her eyes narrow, homing in on mine. "Smart, too, if you know about elementai."

My mouth dries up like someone poured a cup of sand in there. "I think I read about them in a book." My heart is racing, but I force my voice to remain calm. "Are they legend too?"

She takes a few seconds to answer. "No, they were very real. Elementai were closely related to witches."

My curiosity is too strong now to let me stop asking questions. I will gladly risk the professor's wrath to know a little more about what I supposedly am. "What happened to them?"

Her eyes fill with sorrow. "They were wiped out."

I blink. "Wiped out?"

She nods sadly. "Hunted down and killed. Every single one of them tortured to death. From the oldest and most powerful elementai who had been alive for several millennia to the youngest babes." She shivers. "It was such a dark time in our history that nobody speaks of it."

"But why? And who hunted them down? Humans?"

She shakes her head. "Humans aren't powerful enough to overcome one elementai, and definitely not their entire species."

"Then who?"

"The vampires, of course. They hate the elementai. I guess they couldn't handle the fact that their species was so much more powerful, so they slaughtered them all. Misogyny at its finest, huh?"

My pulse spikes and my stomach rolls. I'm sure I must have misheard everything she just said. I swallow the thick knot of anxiety balling in my throat and force out my next words. "Vampires? Misogyny?"

"Elementai are female, and all bloodborne vampires are male. Some of them even turned on their own families. Their sisters, wives, daughters..." She shakes her head and swats a tear from her eye.

That can't be true. My racing heart goes into overdrive. "Vampires killed them?" I whisper.

"Yeah. I know they're super-hot and brooding and all—I enjoy some vampire company myself occasionally." She leans in and puts her hand on my arm. "But, girl, they can't be trusted."

My heart splinters into a million pieces, fracturing like tiny shards of glass that tear their way through my chest. Have I been fooled again? I allowed myself to be taken in by Axl, Xavier, and Malachi just because they make my body feel good. How could they not have told me? And the professor... After everything he said in the library about the power of the elementai and how special they were. Was he lying too? Anguish threatens to sweep me away.

I shake my head. No. No. No. I repeat the word over and over in my head. Cadence must have it wrong. It can't be true that vampires hate elementai. That they slaughtered thousands of innocents just because of their power. Because if that's true...

57

ALEXANDROS

Thunder rolls and lightning cracks the sky in two before the rain begins hammering on the glass with such force that the old frame rattles. Dark clouds roll in fast, obscuring the vibrant blue of the sky.

Something is happening to Ophelia.

I tune into Malachi and Xavier to figure out what is going on, and as soon as I do, her pain sears my chest as strongly as if it were my own, making me stumble back a step. Her bond with my boys grows stronger every day, and I can feel her more keenly through that than I have felt anyone else before, even those I actually bit.

Baby, what's happened? Malachi calls out to her. *Are you okay?*

She sobs her reply, and my own sorrow clouds my thoughts, obscuring the words. But I hear the words *elementai* and *did you know*, and my chest grows tight. She knows what happened to her kind. But how?

Come home, baby, Malachi says. *You're not supposed to be talking about that with anyone.*

I'm not. Not about me. I'm in the library with Cadence, and I asked if she knew about the elementai. She told me what happened, Malachi. How the vampires wiped them out. Did you know? Did any of you know?

Indescribable rage burns beneath my skin.

Xavier joins the conversation. *I'm coming to get you, Cupcake.*

No! I order him, aware that she will not be able to hear me. *I will get her.*

Don't be mad at her. She only wants to know where she came from. Malachi's plea echoes through my head. Mad is not a word I would use to describe the intense fury that boils inside me. I warned her not to speak about what she is. But his fear does not warrant a response. My focus is on getting to the library and putting a stop to the lies she is being subjected to. Damn witches.

It takes me less than a minute to get to the library, and her face is a mask of shock when she sees me approach.

"You are leaving."

She flinches but folds her arms across her chest and glares at me. "I am not."

My muscles vibrate with tension. At this moment, I possess neither the time nor the patience for her overt display of defiance. I grab Ophelia's arm, and her friend gapes at me, horror etched on her pale features. "Yes, you are." Without giving her another chance to argue, I drag her out of the library and down the short path to Zeus Hall. She finally stops resisting once we enter the building, but I maintain my grip as I lead her to the safety of my office. She keeps her lips pressed tightly together the entire time, her rage boiling inside her like a miniature inferno. Little does she know, her fury has nothing on mine.

I close my office door behind us and keep a tight grip on her arm. My fangs protract with a painful, burning hunger. "I warned you not to discuss what I told you."

Her brows pinch together in a scowl that does nothing to sate the desire coursing through me. "And I didn't. I only asked her if she knew about elementai. If you won't give me any answers, how else am I supposed to learn about them? How to control my powers?"

"I specifically told you—"

"I didn't tell her anything you told me." She tries to wrench her arm free of my grip, but I hold tight. Tears fill her eyes. "You said I have power, but I don't feel it. You said I have to learn to control it, but how do I do that if I don't even know what my powers are? What I am?" The last words come out on a sob that wrenches something deep inside my soul.

I growl in frustration and mutter a Greek curse.

She blinks and a tear rolls down her cheek.

"I will teach you." A sigh heaves out of my chest. "But you are not to discuss anything further with strangers. Do I make myself clear?"

"But Cadence is my friend."

I pull her closer. "Only because she does not know who—or what—you are."

She yanks her arm so forcefully that I release it for fear she will tear the limb from its socket. She folds her arms across her chest once more, her face flaming with fiery indignation. "Yeah, well, she had some very interesting things to say about the elementai and what happened to them."

Blinding rage courses through me, and I growl a warning. She ignores me and rubs the mark I left on her arm.

"What lies did she tell you, little one?"

She flicks her pink hair from her eyes with a toss of her head. Her pulse flutters in her throat, and the pounding of the blood in her veins calls to me like a siren's song. Her scent makes my mouth water, but it is the defiant tilt of her jaw that makes my cock ache. "How vampires wiped out the elementai. How they wouldn't stop killing and torturing until every last one was gone." The accusation in her tone snaps something in me, and I lose the control I have been holding onto since the moment I first sensed her in my house all those weeks ago.

My hand is wrapped around her throat before she can blink. Her blue eyes fill with fear and excitement, and I already know how this day will end. And to my eternal shame, I succumb to my baser instincts, allowing them to take the reins. I push her toward my desk, and the soles of her black boots squeak on the wooden floor as she stumbles backward.

"Shall I enlighten you as to what really happened to the elementai, Ophelia?"

"P-please," she rasps, her throat flexing under the pressure of my palm.

I drop into my chair and pull her onto my lap. Her plaid miniskirt rides up, exposing the creamy skin of her thighs, and the scent of her pussy clouds what is left of my faculties.

I loosen my grip on her throat, and she sucks in a ragged breath. "Please tell me, Professor." Her plea claws at the wounds etched deep into my soul.

I cannot tell her. Speaking about the horror of the elementai genocide is too raw, the pain too visceral, even after five long centuries. My free hand snakes up her thigh, and goose bumps break out along her supple flesh. My cock throbs, hardening further at the weight of her pressed against me. I shift my hips, causing my length to rub against her heat, and she whimpers, dropping her hips and seeking more friction.

"Tell me," she whispers.

"I cannot tell you, little one."

Her eyes swim with tears. "But you said…"

I press my forehead to hers. "I can only show you."

Her slender throat convulses beneath my hand, sending a current of electric fire down my forearm. Taking her will be brutal and cruel, but I am as incapable of stopping what is about to happen as I am of stopping the sun from rising tomorrow. It is the end of the world as I know it. An inescapable insanity and the beginning of the end. But it has been an inevitability from the moment I met her.

Her eyes seem to glow with hunger. My gaze trails across her face, over her cheekbones and along her jawline down to her neck. I move my thumb, exposing an expanse of skin at the base of her throat where her vein pulses thick with her blood. My fangs ache, and I flick my tongue over the tips, tasting my own blood when their sharpness pierces my skin.

I run my nose over her neck, inhaling her intoxicating scent, and a whimper tumbles from her lips. Her blood thunders beneath her skin, so tantalizingly close to my lips and my tongue that it hurts to stop myself from tasting her for a second longer. Without waiting for her consent, I sink my teeth into her flesh.

My fangs pierce her delicate skin. Her blood floods my mouth.

I am lost.

Her taste floods every part of me, tying me to her and this moment for all eternity. She permeates my heart, my soul, every cell of my body. I feast on her like a starving animal, a beast that has been caged for too long before finally being allowed to devour the object of its obsession. And *she* is my obsession.

Euphoric power lights me up from the inside out, sending me into a frenzy. I should force myself to stop before I drink her dry, but I cannot pull away. I want her. I *need* her.

She runs her fingers through my hair, tugging my head back and arching into my mouth at the same time. Then she moans my name, and the sound crashes over me, searing white-hot desire and the animalistic need to claim her into every cell of my body. I stop sucking and lick the trail of blood dripping down her collarbone. She grinds her pussy against me, and I mutter a curse and free my cock from my pants, basking in the sweet relief of allowing my aching shaft some room. Then I slip my hand between her thighs and tear her panties in half. She gasps, her eyes hooded with desire. And when I lift her to line the crown of my cock up with her entrance, she clings to me.

"You are soaked, little one."

She takes her bottom lip between her teeth and nods, and it is either an admission or her approval of what I am about to do, but I no longer care. I impale her on the full length of my cock, stretching her tight pussy so wide that she cries out. Her wet heat pulls me deeper, welcoming me as I sink far inside her. Endorphins flood my body, and the euphoria I felt a moment ago from sucking her blood ignites once more, only more dangerous and addictive.

I am going to fucking ruin her, going to take her to the depths of hell. And I cannot bring myself to care.

Her breath catches, and I rub my thumb over the pulse in her throat. Taking me by surprise, she rocks her hips, her tight cunt squeezing around my dick and making fire surge in my veins once more.

Show me! she pleads, her voice in my head stronger than my own thoughts.

I close my eyes and try to block her out, but she is already inside. And that should come as no surprise considering that she has already embedded herself in my heart and soul. Her power is astonishing, and we have barely begun to scratch the surface.

Please. Show me who I am, sir.

My fangs throb to take her once more, and I roll my neck to ease a little of the tension that has turned my muscles to stone. I release her throat and tug her tank top and bra down to expose one of her pebbled nipples. With my tongue, I flick the hard peak and skim it with my fangs, allowing a trickle of blood to coat my tongue.

My hands firmly grip her waist, and I rock up into her until her eyes roll back in her head. Then I trail my lips and tongue back up to her throat on the opposite side from where I bit her before, where the wound is already healing. Partly because of my saliva, but mostly because she is channeling some of her own healing energy now too. I feel it flowing through her as though it were my own.

Her scent overwhelms me once more, making my head spin. My own blood pounds a staccato beat in my ears.

"Alexandros," she moans. I reward her by sinking my teeth into her throat again and showing her the power of who she really is.

58

OPHELIA

"It's too much," I whimper. Children scream, torn from their mothers' arms. Fire and blood. So much blood. Her agony. His despair. A betrayal so deep and unnatural that it alters the fabric of a person's very being. Pain engulfs me, centuries of agony that he's kept buried deep in his heart. And I feel it all at once, the soul-eviscerating anguish that he carries with him every single second of every day.

Tears stream down my cheeks. My heart feels like it's being crushed in a vise. "It's too much," I say again.

You wanted to know the truth, Ophelia. This is it. His voice is as clear in my head as my own, and it's not unnerving at all. Not like when I first heard the boys. It's as though he belongs there. Like he's always been there and he always will be.

It hurts. A whimper is ripped from my throat.
I know.

As quickly as he let me in, he shuts me out again. At least he tries to lock down that part of his brain, but I'm already inside. The pain is overpowering. My lifeblood flows to where his mouth is attached to my neck. He pulls me down, sinking his thick length deeper inside me and rolling me over him so my clit rubs against him, creating delicious friction. The perfect harmony of pleasure and pain conducts a symphony of ecstasy within the deepest recesses of my body.

I have no idea what's happening to me, but my muscles vibrate with electricity, and I feel invincible. While I'm trying to understand the sensations hurtling through me, Alexandros dips his hand between my thighs and presses hard against my swollen clit. My core explodes into a billion fireworks, and I lose all control, all sense of time and space and reason.

I rock into him, chasing more of whatever it is he's giving me, because I feel like lightning in a bottle. And it's not only the spectacularly intense orgasm stoking this feeling; it's the power surging through my veins. Like wildfire laced with morphine. And it's not *his* power that I feel. Not like when the boys share their blood with me. This is like a rebirth.

My head falls back on a strangled cry, and his mouth is ripped from my flesh. Blood gushes from the wound, and he laps it up, coating my skin with his saliva to help it heal, but it's already closing over, being knitted back together by an ancient power that flows through me.

The room is on fire, agápi mou. His words are so clear in my head, like they're my own thoughts but in his voice. So deeply embedded in my consciousness that he's already become a part of my being. Sure enough, flames burn high and bright, growing closer with each second. But I feel only a gentle warmth from their lethal flame.

You may be immune to the flames, my little one, but I am most assuredly not. He suckles at my neck, much more gently than before. *Although I would be willing to burn before I would be willing to move.*

Panic grips my chest. The whole building is going to burn down and it will be my fault. Again. *How do I stop the fire?!*

You know how, Ophelia.

But I don't. I close my eyes and battle the raging emotions swirling through my body like a tornado. And like a tornado captures everything in its path, so does the tumultuous vortex inside me. Pain. Anger. Euphoria. Sadness. All of it rages within me, and the only thing anchoring me to reality is him. And if he wasn't inside me, with his arms around my waist, I feel like I might explode into stardust and disappear.

Focus! Find your light and focus. His voice is smooth and steady. Calming.

I have no idea why or how I understand what that means, but I concentrate on my solar plexus. In my mind's eye, I see a dazzling bright white orb. The swirling vortex immediately calms, allowing me to isolate each emotion. I focus on the heat prickling at my skin and picture the flames extinguishing around us while imagining all of the oxygen being sucked from the room.

A shiver runs down my spine.

Good girl.

I open my eyes. The flames are gone, but Alexandros's office is destroyed. The bookcases smolder as fragments of burned paper flutter to the floor like snowflakes made of ash. My heart aches for all the precious history within those pages that I annihilated. "I wrecked your office. Your books."

He stops feeding, and my head spins at the rush of blood flowing back to my heart. "You have wrecked much more than my office."

I'm not sure what that means, but I offer him a murmured apology anyway.

"You can burn down this entire world if you want to, little one. So long as you stay by my side while you do it." He bands his arms around my waist, and a wave of euphoria lights up my veins once more. "Or exactly like this. Whichever you prefer." He rocks his hips upward, sweeping the crown of his dick over a sensitive spot inside me.

"Yes, this please," I pant.

He licks the blood from my already healing neck and fucks me on his lap.

Please bite me again, I beg through our bond.

I have already taken enough tonight, little one.

I roll my hips over him, and he growls against my neck. *But it feels so good*, I whine.

I can make you feel good in so many other ways, Ophelia. He picks me up, wraps my legs around his waist, and lays me flat on his desk. My teeth clash together and stars pepper my vision when he drives into me.

He fucks me hard, and I feel his release building as keenly as I feel my own, and it's so overwhelming that I try to block it out, but I end up tapping back into his pain instead.

Not now, agápi mou.

My love?

Yes. His tone is so tender, so unlike anything I've heard him say before.

I can't not feel every part of him, and *this* part of him, it's his root, the center of his being. And his pain is partly my pain too. *But I can't…*

He thrusts harder, his fingers digging into my hips, and seals his lips over mine. My mouth instinctively opens, allowing him entry. The coppery tang of my blood fizzes on my tongue as he claims my mouth as easily as he's claimed the rest of me. His kiss is fierce and dominant, bruising and cutting my lips. But I'm lost in the taste of him and the punishing pace of his hips as he drives into me.

My focus narrows, homing in on the exquisite pleasure of our impending climaxes. I claw at his skin, pulling him deeper and closer as I try to take more. He growls, feral and unrestrained, and the sound makes my inner walls ripple around him.

For a few blissful moments, we forget the truth of what he just showed me and find oblivion in the beautiful and primal union of our bodies.

EPILOGUE

NAZEEL DANRAATH

Hidden among the trees surrounding Gaea's Green, I watch the room burn. I bound the child's powers a long time ago, and I would never disobey Kameen or dishonor the Order by breaking that spell. But they have no need to know that I suspected the girl was powerful enough to unleash her magic all on her own.

An elementai's powers are finely tuned to their emotions. It is both their strength and their weakness. The stronger the feelings, the more powerful the magic. And I have always known that to break a binding spell—particularly one cast by a Danraath witch of the Order of Azezal—would require a more intense emotion than Ophelia Hart was capable of feeling all on her own. At least at her tender age.

No, shattering a spell like that requires pain. Intense, soul-splintering pain. And so few carry a pain more profound than Alexandros Drakos.

Then they will awaken the protector of man,
And together they will rise to bring a balance that will reign for the ages.

A slow, unexpected smile spreads across my face. I have not interfered, per se. I merely ensured that two souls crossed paths in order to achieve their destinies. To restore balance to the world after five hundred years of chaos. Surely Kameen can forgive me for that.

Either way, my work here is done.

For now.

ACKNOWLEDGMENTS

As always I would love to thank all of my incredible readers, and especially the members of Sadie's Ladies and Sizzling Alphas. You are all superstars. To my amazing ARC team, the love you have for these books continues to amaze and inspire me. I am so grateful for all of you.

But to all of the readers who have bought any of my books, everything I write is for you and you all make my dreams come true.

An extra especially huge thank you to my editor, Jaime Watson. This book has been a true labor of love for both of us and I could not have done this without you. I appreciate and respect you more than you can ever know.

To my author friends who help make this journey all that more special.

To my lovely PAs, Katie, Kate and Andrea, for their support and everything they do to make my life easier.

And I can't forget my (not so) silent ninja, Bobby Kim. Thank you for continuing to push me to be better and for making each book release even better than the last.

To my incredible boys who inspire me to be better every single day. And last, but no means least, a huge thank you to Mr. Kincaid—all my book boyfriends rolled into one. I couldn't do this without you!

Doubling the Trees Behind Every Book You Buy.

Because books should leave the world better than they found it—not just in hearts and minds, but in forests and futures.

Through our Read More, Breathe Easier initiative, we're helping reforest the planet, restore ecosystems, and rethink what sustainable publishing can be.

Track the impact of your read at:

CONNECT WITH US ONLINE

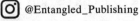 @Entangled_Publishing

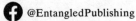 @EntangledPublishing

 @EntangledPub

Join the Entangled Insiders for early access to ARCs, exclusive content, and insider news! Scan the QR code to become part of the ultimate reader community.